To: BETH

HAPPY READING!

THANKS FOR BEING A
FRIEND TO SHELI

By Jenn 2/24/2008

Deathquest to Parallan

A Trilogy of the Land of Donothor: Part One

by
Benjamin Towe

Bloomington, IN Milton Keynes, UK

authorHOUSE

AuthorHouse™
1663 Liberty Drive, Suite 200
Bloomington, IN 47403
www.authorhouse.com
Phone: 1-800-839-8640

AuthorHouse™ UK Ltd.
500 Avebury Boulevard
Central Milton Keynes, MK9 2BE
www.authorhouse.co.uk
Phone: 08001974150

First published by AuthorHouse 3/29/2006

ISBN: 1-4208-9012-3 (sc)
ISBN: 1-4208-9011-5 (dj)

Library of Congress Control Number: 2005909143

Printed in the United States of America
Bloomington, Indiana

This book is printed on acid-free paper.

Table of Contents

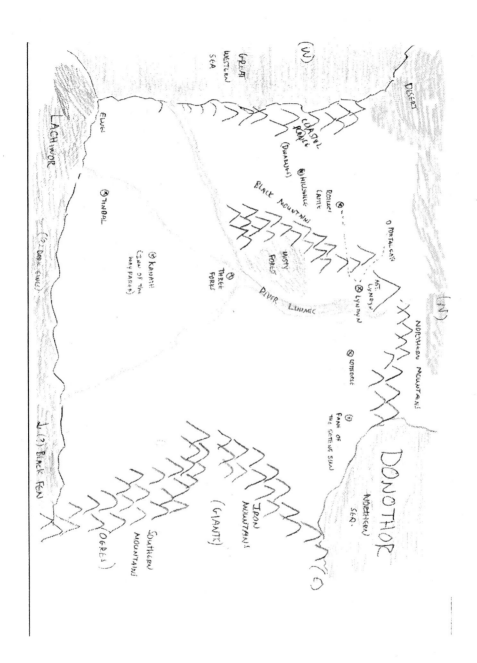

ix

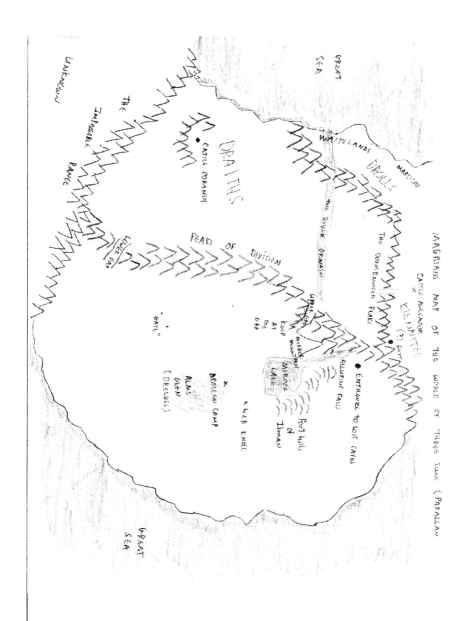

MAGRIANS MAP OF THE WORLD OF THREE SUNS (PARALLAN

Prologue

The two Spellweavers labored over the heat of the forge. Sweat fell profusely from their noble dark brows and the muscles of their forearms tensed with each strike of their hammers. Many beautiful gems were being forced into the shimmering elongated object that was slowly taking definition as a result of their physical and mental labors. The silence of the evening air was repeatedly broken by their voices, but the arcane phrases would have been understood by only a few.

The first muttered between incantations,"Why do we concern ourselves with the conflicts between Necromancers and Dwarves? These labors tire my spirit."

The second replied,"We have never been so encumbered by their conflict. You know the hold the wizard has over us. Do you want to remain obliged to do his will? Do you want Dwarven hordes traversing and foraging through our world?"

Disgruntled, the first continued his verbal protest by adding,"Do we want to empower the wizard more? Could he not challenge us more than an army of short-statured and ill-mannered brutes? They certainly lack the skills to reach our borders."

"Nothing is certain, my brother. The wizard managed to reach our domain," was the blunt reply.

"He is a wizard," the older replied.

They worked on into the amber evening bathed by the ever diminishing light of the three suns.

Incantation followed incantation and strike after strike of the hammers fell. Slowly the vorpal weapon was taking shape.

After a time of great effort, the second finally answered his complaining companion.

"I am instilling in the weapon the force of healing for its wielder just as he requested. But I also impart in the blade the inability to harm those of our ilk. It shall not spill the blood of the forest. He will have his power over the dwarves but he will not harm us with the blade. We can protect ourselves from the effect of his unrefined Magick. This Weapon will serve our people long after his time. He won't possess the blade for many time periods. There is little for us to fear," he finished definitively.

After hours of grimy work, the two stood over a shimmering blade adorned by many jewels. The elder painstakingly etched the runes and symbols into the hilt and the blood groove of the weapon. When the first raised the blade, the runes etched on the sword began to glow intensely, illuminating the area around them. He quickly placed the blade beneath his raimants to avoid exposing their work area to unwanted eyes that might be drawn to the bright light. He noted that several small scratches on his fatigued forearms had fully healed in the brief moment that he fanned the air with the blade.

The two marveled at their creation.

"How do you impart these qualities to the blade?" the younger added quizzically.

"Because I am taught well by the Teacher and I am the son of my mother. Look above you. The Gray Wanderer, the third sun Andreas, fills the sky. The Approximation occurs only once every several lifetimes. Do you not feel the waxing of the energies within you? It is youth that prevents you from feeling this. You will learn in time," his older brother replied. "Let us deliver our tithe so that we can be rid of our debt to this wizard and perhaps rid our world of him."

The two left the steamy forging area and entered onto the pathway leading to their prearranged meeting point. The brothers arrived first and waited impatiently. Their friend the forest was remarkably quiet as they continued to await the arrival of the magician. The elder brother thought that he had planned so well. But he could not have fully appreciated the treachery of the wizard. A soft swish filled the air as the younger noted with horror the Arrow of Clysis that tore through his brother's chest. The elder fell to the floor of his beloved forest without uttering a sound. The younger did not have time to incant or to draw the sword before the second arrow pierced him. The younger brother also dropped to the ground when the magical force of the arrow struck him. He could not find the strength to grasp the blade before the Magick of the unerring arrow ended his existence. The stillness of death matched that of the forest.

After determining that the brothers were alone, Morlecainen triumphantly moved to their bodies and retrieved the blade. The silence and invisibility spells had been negated when the released the first of the finely runed arrows, but the advantage that he had gained was insurmountable.

"Is this the best this world has to offer?" the wizard mused, managing a smile."And the fools thought that I would actually close the Portal Gate. I would not do that even if I had the knowledge to do so."

There were fine runes etched into the weapon. The blade shimmered in the amber darkness but the wizard was forced to use his Orb of Illumination to read them, as the light in the area was at its minimum as thought the ever approaching moon like object were choking out the rays of the other two suns. But a moon it was not. Moons did not radiate gray light. Thus the area was too dark to allow Morlecainen to study the runes without the aid of his own Magick.

Silence bathed the area as though the denizens of the forest were respecting the fallen. He found that he could interpret many of the elvish runes etched into the blade, but the forgers had included some arcane symbols that were foreign to the wizard.

The wizard incised his palm with the point of the blade. Brief lancinating pain came as he anticipated, but to his delight, the wound quickly healed as he gripped the blade. The evidence of the wound was manifested only by the few drops of his dark blood that had fallen to the ground near the slain elves.

Sheathing the blade within his robes, the wizard began the journey homeward. Even though the light was at its ebb, he could see well enough to traverse the path. He seemed to be getting accustomed to the strangeness of the fauna and flora.

He reached the portal gate. A brief incantation bathed him briefly in a mauve glow. He traversed the portal that had exacted so much of his energies to create; he was comforted somewhat by the return of the true darkness of night. Soon he reached the ridge upon which his modest castle rested; he could see in the distance the multitude of campfires of the dwarven army. At the foot of the ridge were the few fires of his own conscripts, mercenaries, and rogues, a paltry force gathered to defend this last bastion of the wizard's domain.

"Let them come now," he said smugly.

All his remaining personal guard had been dispatched to the force awaiting the dwarves certain attack. It only took a moment to disengage the Fireglyph from the castle doors, and only a second moment to reengage the magical lock. Morlecainen then entered his abode. He passed his lovely mate as she sat silently near the open fireplace where a warming flame flickered but there were no logs. She appeared to be knitting a garment for the girls. He stored the sleek bow and the realm's only known remaining Arrow of Clysis with his staff and secured the lock on the chest. The treasure had been well worth the cost of the other two arrows. He could only cause one inevitable death with each arrow, but the Magick Sword would empower him greatly in battle.

Another Fireglyph was activated by a single phrase. Morlecainen trusted no one, including his mate.

The wizard walked to the children's room and peered into it. The twins slept serenely as he watched. Morlecainen marveled at the precociousness and beauty of the girls. Would it be Chalar or Theandra to succeed their father when the time came?

But that is another story.

Many generations passed.

CHAPTER 1
Night Riders

The mission to Tindal had been much more arduous than the rangers had anticipated. More than five weeks had passed since the riders had left the citadel at Lyndyn, the largest city of the land of Donothor and the center of government of the kingdom. For within Lyndyn's fortified walls lay the palace of the ruling house of Aivendar. Prince Eomore, the eldest son of the beloved and just King Eraitmus and Queen Faerie, had led the party of ten of the elite rangers of Donothor from the walled city to the pastoral southern province of Tindal to investigate a disturbance at its border. The messenger from the farmers had arrived only a few hours before the King sent the party of rangers to answer the plea of his subjects for protection and justice. Such was the way of Eraitmus Aivendar, and this meant many cancelled plans for Eomore and his charges. Nontheless, the prince had always responded whenever duty had called. The messengers had said that a "few" goblins had been raiding the supply caravans to the outlying posts. Eomore had envisioned a brief foray into the dense forests to fulfill the mission.

In the usual manner the rangers had mustered about two dozen militiamen from the local folk, and with their rank so bolstered, pursued the marauding goblins across the border into the forests of Lachinor. Then the fun had begun - the goblin chieftain Gretch himself had come from the depths of the Black Fen of Boormork and was in command of the goblin forces. He had proven himself a very savage foe and the goblins, usually chaotic in their evil and mischief, had been quite organized in their efforts. However, the militiamen had fought well and eventually even the superior numbers of the goblins were overcome and the survivors fled into the depths of Lachinor licking their wounds. In the final battle Gretch himself had fallen before the blade of Prince Eomore. The victory had not come without loss. Several locals had fallen and the original party of ten now numbered eight.

Now the eight weary warriors began the long journey back to Lyndyn. The noble Loran, a veteran of eleven years on the force and a loyal servant to the King had fallen. He had been a dear friend of Prince Eomore as well. The novice Horrin had also been lost in the fray. Thus, the mood of the party of travelers was sullen, remorseful, and encumbered by grief. The knight riders were shrouded by silence as dark as the death cloaks which wrapped their fallen comrades. None of the riders made an effort to converse. No stories were being told of past exploits. Even the talkative little dwarf Deron had said little.

As they felt their way through the darkness, the shroud of silence enveloping them was broken only by the clanking of the hooves of the steeds striking the rocky road. The night air bit into them and each man must have in his own mind been thinking of home and its comforts. Certainly that's where Eomore Aivendar's thoughts were.

"A Teleportation Spell would sure be nice," the prince thought, "to be out of this miserable night - to be where one wanted to be infallibly in an instant- it would almost be worth putting up with the cantankerous mage Roscoe to have one."

But even if Roscoe were with them, the king deemed it proper and necessary that the royal family interact with and avail themselves to the citizenry of Donothor, particularly those such as the hearty and industrious folk of the southern provinces such as Tindal. Eomore knew that Teleportation Spells only worked on their caster and the prince was certainly no wizard.

Roscoe was the greatest mage in the land of Donothor if not in all the realms. He was as at times as reclusive and mysterious as he was powerful. He would have been a welcomed ally in this presently completed mission, because the goblin force had again been underestimated in its numbers and tenacity. Eraitmus was very tactful in dealing with the more powerful citizenry of Donothor and did not request their aid unless the situation was grave.

Roscoe's pompousness was balanced by the High Priestess Knarra who was a staunch ally of the king and who also had an intricate relationship with Roscoe. Her origins were also as mysterious as those of Roscoe, but the charismatic healer had given willfully and gratituitously to the populace of Donothor, and had asked little in return.

King Eraitmus had ascended to the throne, succeeding his father Oerl, some thirty years ago, just before the birth of Eomore. He was a fair and proud man who had ruled in the tradition of his forefathers in the house of Aivendar. Eraitmus had served as the Captain of the Donothorian Rangers, the elite guard of the kingdom and the right arm of the king. This role was traditionally held by the eldest son of the reigning monarch, or else the monarch's younger brother, which is why Eomore now held the position, succeeding his uncle Randyl upon attaining manhood. This was a prominent and a romanticized role, but it certainly held its disadvantages - specifically, extended forays to the fringes of civilization on the borders of Donothor to aid the local militiamen in the preservation of order. Donothor was, in general, a very safe and prosperous land. Monsters were rare in the central area of the kingdom. It had been years since a marauding dragon had invaded from the dismal reaches of Lachinor. However, the adventurous souls who inhabited the outer provinces were still subjected to such insults. The citizenry of the provinces provided many of the products which made life in the cities comfortable. These hearty souls were thought by the king to be the "backbone" of the kingdom. If they required support from the king, Eraitmus readily gave it to then.

Most of the time the support consisted of a small force of the rangers such as the present party, but occasionally a priest or a mage would represent the king through a quest in lieu of paying a monetary tithe. Once, even the irascible Roscoe had accompanied Eomore on a mission to the Mountains of Iron to give an ultimatum to a rampaging giant clan. Roscoe had gained his doorkeeper Braak in the deal. The giant submitted to the will of the wizard as an alternative to a good singeing. But the giant had over time supposedly become more of a friend to the wizard. Roscoe had been a burden to bear on the quest, but the wizard had certainly carried his own weight during the confrontation with the huge humanoids. Still, Eomore could only hope that adventuring with the old mage would not happen again soon!

But most of the time it was the sweat and sometimes the blood of the rangers who defended the people and the king's interests. Eomore knew that this was his "lot in life". It was his duty, his heritage, his fate, and sometimes his chagrin - there were times that the prince longed for the life of a commoner - a midnight scuffle with a rabid band of goblins was a far cry from a quiet evening with a woman, a joyous feast, or sharing ale with a friend.

"Oh, Loran, the times we had!" lamented Eomore as he rode along, thinking himself alone with hidden thoughts.

His mind had returned to his fallen friend. Loran had often been the first chosen by Eomore. Early in his career with the rangers, Eomore had often been accompanied by his dwarven friend Brenigen, knicknamed "Boomer" for his less than subtle volume of speaking. Few of the current rangers even knew Boomer's given name. Now Boomer was Eomore's second in command, and it was customary to leave the city under the auspices of either the Captain of the Guard or his second unless there was dire need. Thus, the two friends seldom journeyed together.

"Your loss grieves you, my prince?"- The words appeared in Eomore's mind yet the shroud of silence had not been broken by any spoken word! The Prince quickly became alert and was startled. Then he relaxed.

"Exeter!" he replied without speaking. "I have lost a true friend to the goblin's arrows. This accursed night lingers on forever. My heart aches more than my body."

"I'm sorry, my Lord"- the words again appeared in Eomore's mind.

"To answer your question, yes, his loss grieves me greatly, and I dread facing Imelda and the children to give them the news of Loran's bane. It won't really matter to them that he died valiantly in the service of the king." Eomore replied, again, thinking the words without saying them.

"There is no way to replace such a friend and ally - a just man and a loving father," the words of comfort again appeared in Eomore's mind, attempting to console him.

Eomore pondered: "I wonder if a Wish Spell or a resurrection balm exists at this time?"

"Those Magick are rare indeed, my Prince, and are as hazardous as they are rare. Folklore holds that reanimation is usually the realm of evil necromancers and usually results in simply the creation of automaton like zombies that serve their masters or else the production of ghastly creatures that might share a portion of their creator's powers. The soulless forces so created may again share an extent of the powers of their creator but their existances are solely for the service of their creator and are linked to that creator; thus the being will serve steadfastedly. Any being so created will share the demise of their creator. Let us concentrate our efforts on regaining the safety of Castle Lyndyn. We are thinking of legend and speculation and our thoughts are prejudiced by grief," responded the silent communicator.

Eomore had possessed the heirloom "Exeter" since attaining manhood. His Uncle Randyl had wielded the weapon with honor and dignity during his twenty-one year tenure with the Donothorian Rangers.

No one knew the origins of the great longsword, not even Exeter herself, but there were many legends.

The Magick empowering the Great Weapon remained a mystery even to the greatest mages of this and all ages.

The weapon had been in the possession of the Aivendar family for generations and she was borne by the Captain of the Ranger guard, as this was obviously the most important defensive position in the kingdom. Even though he had now carried her for nine years, the prince was still occasionally startled when the soothing female voice appeared in his mind. She possessed the ability to speak telepathically with her wielder. She was sympathetic and empathetic with the wielder as well, thus she seemed to actually feel the physical and mental wounds received by the person grasping her hilt.

No wielder of Exeter had fallen in battle since the artifact had come into the possession of the Aivendar clan those many generations ago. She was able to sense the presence of enemies as near as thirty paces and she had the uncanny sixth sense to realize which foe posed the greatest threat to her master.

Exeter appeared as a well made longsword, with a hilt formed of a reddish black material and a golden blade, which gave off a deep

5

red hue in the tide of battle. There were no runes upon the weapon and there were no gems adorning the hilt. Exeter's beauty was in her simplicity.

Likewise, the mages and even the greatest of the royal alchemists and the greatest of the dwarven amorers had been unable to determine the nature of the materials of which the weapon was made. No scratch could be made upon the material composing the blade. The special qualities of Exeter had saved Eomore many times, but she was just as valuable as a companion during times such as these - this dark, cold, lonely, and moonforsaken night!

Eomore was seldom without the vorpal weapon and likewise the royal chainmail armor that had been forged also many generations ago by the greatest of the dwarven armorers of Donothor. The armor he always wore under his flame red tunic which bore the royal crest of the Aivendars - the armor offered at least twice the protection of normal chainmail while weighing only half as much. The weapon and the armor were the greatest fighting treasures of his illustrious family, and on occasion Prince Eomore questioned his worthiness to carry them. The tunic bore the image of the Prismatic Dragon, an appropriate symbol for the family who had ruled Donothor with compassion, power, but also adaptability to the needs of their citizenry. The thoughts of doubt and the desires for the more mundane pleasures of life, which he felt often, left Eomore wondering if he could ever be the man and king his father was. Still Eomore had always taken up the crest of the Aivendars and gone off on every quest his father had asked of him. He had sometimes felt great resentment, and this is what troubled the Prince's mind.

"You need a "Mind Blank" spell tonight, my Lord," Exeter silently uttered. "The fatigue of the past five weeks is certainly taking its toll on you."

"Oh, probably not even that would help," Eomore answered with his own thoughts, "I feel that only the passage of this night and segment of our journey to the Hamlet Kanath and the waiting Inn of the Wayfarer where we can finally have some hot food and rest under blankets in a bed will restore any respectable reasoning to my mind."

Sometimes Eomore yearned for more privacy for his inner thoughts and that the vorpal weapon would not always be so tuned into his feelings, but usually she helped his reasoning. Certainly she would not "talk" to anyone else as long as he lived or else until he chose to surrender his duties to his own successor. That was a staggering thought, for it carried two connotations; first, that Eomore would marry and have a son to succeed him, and, secondly, that he would either be dead or ascending to the throne. Also, Exeter had never betrayed to him the secrets of earlier wielders even though the Prince had queried about his father and grandfather in efforts to learn of their reactions to sticky situations.

He couldn't decide which would be worse - his bachelorhood might be more valuable than the sword or the armor - but maybe the sword was the reason that the crown prince of the kingdom of Donothor had never been interested in marriage. Eomore swore that he heard a snicker appearing deep within his consciousness.

Eomore's wandering thoughts returned to the dismal night as the rain began to fall. It was a cold drizzle which seemed to coat them like acid then burn into their tired aching bodies. The sullen weary party rode onward into the silence of the night. Eight riders and ten steeds prodded on into the darkness. The middle steeds bore the corpses of the fallen Donothorians. Occasionally they began to pass a landmark that looked familiar to them in the dark night. A rare homestead appeared on the roadside. The riders were still on the fringes of civilization, and only the heartiest of the citizenry would inhabit these areas. Since night had fallen, the horsemen passed each dwelling unnoticed by the inhabitants. A quick inspection of the homes revealed that they looked more like small fortresses than homes -the windows were always shuttered and barred and wolvesbane and garlic were placed to fend off roaming creatures of the night, which Eomore himself felt were more fiction than fact. But legends made good fireside conversation and speculation for these strong border-folk who did not afford themselves many luxuries.

Even though these settlements were far from the mainstream of civilization, organized raids and uprisings such as the just squelched goblin troupe were uncommon, and the locals were accustomed to this secluded way of life and they were good, loyal subjects and were entitled to their beliefs, no matter how skewed they were.

But now, with the goblin insurgency crushed, all seemed secure, and the only sign of inhabitation of the dwellings were the wisps of smoke from the chimneys - that brought to mind a nursery song that Eomore had learned as a lad; how did it go? "Chim chiminy chim chim cheree," Eomore chuckled. But the only responses were a cough from one of the rear riders which had to be coincidental, the steady pitter patter of the rain, and a rather critical, "Oh, Brother!" from the sheath at the prince's side.

The elven cottages were always cheerier, as though they were reflecting their owners. There was always plentiful plant growth and greenery around the cottages even in the depths of the winter season. These elves were such a vibrant people and they seemed to have playful and beautiful Magick about then. Their proud faces and well-defined features made them particularly handsome in the eyes of Eomore. They were exemplary citizens and were welcomed to visit and settle within the borders of Donothor by the Aivendars. However, most of the elves chose to maintain their own civilization and lived in communities with strong family lines loosely allied for their common good.   The chaotic nature of the elves made then even more appealing to Eomore, who always walked "the straight and narrow" and did what was expected of a prince. Donothor was graced by a few of the fair people who chose to work alone or in small groups in these rural areas. They were not of great physical stature or constitutional makeup, but they compensated for these with great speed and their accuracy as bowmen was second to none. On rare occasions an elf had served with the rangers, and they were also expert trackers; however, Eomore had been denied the opportunity to work with them and he had never been able to number an elf among his personal friends. There were legends of great numbers of elves of different creeds living within the depths of the Lachinor. Some lore told of great magical abilities and great skills at creating weaponry. There were stories of questionable character among certain of the elven dwellers deep in the swamplands. These were stories for the campfire largely.

In these thick forests and cleared grain fields there were few of the dwarven people. In the more mountainous central provinces and even in the populated areas the little folk were numerous. They made up probably thirty per cent of the population of Lyndyn itself, and their numbers were well represented on the ranger force. They had been invaluable to the Aivendars in the construction of the royal palace and the battlements surrounding the capital city during the wilder uncivilized days. The dwarven kings and their armies had greatly benefited the land during the ancient wars. The dwarves had suffered great losses in those primordial battles.

In the present time, however, the dwarves were incorporated into the Donothorian society and served Eraitmus and not a separate king. The dwarves were organized and meticulous. The "stoutest of the stout" of the little people was, in Eomore's opinion, the second in command of the rangers and his true friend, Boomer the Brave. The little fellow had earned his title over and over again, and modesty was not Boomer's forte. Deron had accompanied the prince on this adventure, and the dwarf had fought well. His handaxe had cloven many hard goblin heads in the struggle deep within Lachinor.

"It will be good to see Boomer again. I hope Father does not have him off on a quest when we return. We could turn up a few tankards of ale." Eomore thought addressing his sharp companion.

But there was no answer. In many ways Exeter was quite like a woman. The rainfall became harder, and this brought Eomore back to his current situation and reality was not particularly nice right now. He bundled up in his tunic.

"Sure wish the armor was twice as resistant to rain," he muttered.

"Better be careful with those wishes," came her reply, "one might come true!"

They passed a small settlement - nothing more than a few houses, shops, and sawmill surrounded by a stockade. The riders came visible as they passed the gate and guard tower, for this village was fortunate - some time in the past they had been given an Orb of Light that illuminated the area near their gate and enabled the nightwatch to survey passersby with great scrutiny. The Permanence Spell cast upon the Orb would have required much time from the wizard that created it. Some citizen had paid dearly for this device but the scrutiny it provided was invaluable. Many a denizen of the wilds would be dissuaded from entering the area of light created by the Orb.

The flowing banners of the Aivendars were readily apparent to the night guard.

"Hail, Prince," came the greeting from the tower.

"Hail, citizen," the prince replied.

Returning the greeting of the woodsmen seemed a true privilege to Eomore, perhaps because the poor soul was forced to share the misery of this night by his own duty.

After another hour of riding and passing several more settlements, the party rounded a curve on a hillock and in the distance they could see a small cluster of lights - at last - the village of Kanath - the first appearance of civilization in nearly five weeks - there lay the promise of a warm meal, a dry bed, and perhaps even the glance and maybe conversation with a woman. Certainly there would be a tankard of ale, for a price of course, a dry mattress, and a loudmouthed innkeeper named Tarrance Frathingham - proprietor of the Inn of the Wayfarer. Frathingham had logged the visitors to his establishment over the years. The Frathingham study gave an estimate of the population of the area. The luscious meals of his kitchens had replenished the strength of many travelers.

There was a sudden feeling of great uneasiness - not really an immediate danger - anxiety. A free floating fear gripped Eomore.

"Exeter!" the prince queried, actually speaking the words.

"No, nothing, my Lord," came the reply.

"You don't feel anything," Eomore continued.

"No," repeated the blade, "I'm sure it's the fatigue, sire."

"Yes, I suppose, but I just don't feel….," Eomore began, and then his voice trailed off.

Eomore supposed that he was beginning to think about the reunion with his father. He knew that initially there would be words of welcome and greeting, but the conversation would eventually turn to the subject of marriage and an heir to the throne - it was a curse to be the eldest son of a monarch.

The horsemen entered the outskirts of the village of Kanath. The night watch greeted than with a robust welcome and they proceeded to the inn. Even though the hour was late, the place was buzzing with activity as it always was. Already they could hear the laughter from within.

People.

Mirth.

Laughter.

Insanity to restore sanity.

CHAPTER 2
The Inn of the Wayfarer

Dismounting was not a simple task, as the men felt glued to their saddles and their muscles ached. The inn's stable boys were already scurrying around preparing to lead the mounts to the cozy stables and a well-earned rub down and feeding. When Eomore reached the heavy oaken door, he reached out to turn the latch, and then reflexively jerked back his hand. Wooden doors might be trapped with poisoned needles in the latches or fireglyphs on the doorknobs. Then the weary prince remembered where he was. The only real danger here was the risk one's money belt took when he entered an establishment of Tarrance Frathingham. Still, it was hard to turn off the guard that one must exercise when adventuring in the name of the king. Eomore turned from the door and allowed his comrades to precede him into the inn. He watched as two stable boys led the horses bearing the bodies of the slain fighters to the small sanctuary across the square from the inn. One of the boys knocked at the door, and a man dressed in a simple black robe came out. He aided in taking the corpses from the horses to rest in the sanctuary. The curate wore the insignia of the Setting Sun on his robe. Clearly he was an underling of the great priestess Knarra, whose sanctuary was the Fane of the Setting Sun, the temple to Hiram and Lydia, the patron god and goddess to many of the people of Donothor. The cleric removed a vial from his belt and began a sprinkling motion over the bodies. Eomore was too far away to hear his words. If for no other reason, the now opened door allowed enough noise to escape the inn that a caterwaul would have easily been drowned out.

Eomore was suddenly aware of his name being spoken.

"Please enter my humble establishment for nutrition and a bit of repose," thundered the voice from within. "The prince of Donothor is forever welcome to share whatever we have to offer."

"Thank you, citizen Frathingham," answered Eomore as he closed the door. "A break from this night will certainly be welcome."

Tarrance Frathingham never gave anything away. But he always kept a clean and well run inn. The rotund cherub owned several inns throughout the land, but he had been born in Kanath, the son of poor timberjacks. Frugality had gotten him to his current position, a wealthy man for a commoner. The portly man was a good taxpayer and well respected by his neighbors. Eomore had seen him many times in Lyndyn seeking audience before the king. Eomore knew that the service would be good, the food would be hot and tasty, the ale would be fresh, and the rooms would be clean. Eomore knew the price would be steep. A Dakin didn't buy much these days.

The prince walked over and took the last of the eight chairs at the table chosen by his men. He nodded and motioned them to take their seats; as was their custom, even though tired enough to drop, they remained standing until he was seated. Eomore had tried to stop this little ritual, but it seemed important to the men to give him this treatment. They respected him and loved him, but he really could never be one of them. Rare were folk, such as the fallen Loran and the haughty Boomer, with whom Eomore felt like a man instead of a prince.

The room was boisterous. Frathingham had already called to the kitchen for a "bottomless" tankard of ale for them. The prince's eyes scanned the room. Obviously they had briefly become the center of attention when they had entered, but now the others were returning to their own conversations.

Most of the tables were occupied by Kanath's own folk, but there were some other travelers. Eomore's eyes were quickly captured by four of the fair people seated off in the western corner of the common room as far away from the light of the fire as they could conveniently get. It seemed that elves generally preferred the dark, as it seemed to be part of their reclusive nature. These were not ordinary elves - the cloaks were too fine, the longbows were too finely hewn, the facial features were too noble and pronounced- Eomore knew they were at least royal emissaries. He found his curiosity raging. His gaze then returned to the rest of the room. There were about twenty tables in this largest room of the inn, the drinking and dining area. Most of the tables were occupied even at this late hour. A great fire roared in the massive fireplace in the western end of the room. It kept two boys constantly running to keep it burning at such a roar. The bar was along the northern end of the room, and the proprietor had repositioned himself there and was doing a pretty good number on a large goblet of ale. It would seem that the fat man could drink up a lot of the profits, so to speak. There were several men seated at the bar, and Eomore couldn't help but notice that most seemed to pull up on their cloaks when the "law" had entered the room. He wondered how many might have a price on their heads, but his mind wasn't really on enforcement at this time. His mind briefly turned to his own pursuits of the rogue, Nigel Louffette, and how the rascal had always evaded him. He wondered again if Nigel could follow a trail as well as he could blaze one. If so, they should recruit him to join the rangers!

It seemed like an eternity before the large double door to the kitchen swung open and the servers came forward with the food for the weary travelers. There was a large roasted bird, an ample fruit and vegetable platter, and of course, more ale. The barmaid carrying the ale immediately caught Eomore's eye. She was elven - and exceptionally pretty. But then again it had been almost five weeks since the prince had really looked upon the fair sex. Still, her deep green eyes sparkled and reflected every candle in the dining hall. Her hair was long and flowing and was the same hue as a ripening field of grain. She exhibited the typical elven physique, and she moved with the gracefulness of the fair people. The simple brown serving dress revealed her alluring femininity.

The older matron referred to her as Cara, a lovely name to go with a lovely face, thought Eomore. This little country barmaid had completely captivated the crown prince of Donothor, yet she in her innocence probably didn't even know who he was. Maybe that's why Eomore felt such a stirring deep within him when their gazes met. Unfortunately, the prince knew the affair would end there, because the heir to the throne of Donothor should not be prone to one-night stands, either literally or figuratively.

"Cara," bellowed the ample proprietor, "more food for the travelers. We have a prince among us - royalty."

Eomore knew that the fat man was using this namedropping to boast his establishment. "Fit for a Prince" - he could almost hear the merchant bragging. Of course, the food and spirits were tasty, but they certainly could not compare in the least with the finer establishments in Lyndyn. The prince's eyes again scanned the room. He felt very self-conscious now that Frathingham continued to broadcast their presence. He noticed that the men at the bar seemed to shrink down even further onto their stools, and would have disappeared altogether if it had been possible.

The barmaid blushed, and then went on about her business. Eomore noticed that she glanced back at him as she moved so gracefully across the room. Her movement was so fluid; there was no wasted motion and her muscles created pleasing contours as she walked. She had to know that she was the center of attention. The noble elves had looked up from their table now and were looking toward Eomore and his charges. They had the same features as Cara. Their eyes seemed to look right into the essence of a man – to know his intentions even before he spoke or acted. This reminded Eomore of his first meeting with the High Priestess Knarra. The men went on with the meal. When they had finished they began to think of retiring. Many of the patrons had left the inn, but the elves lingered. Slowly one of their party rose and began to approach the royal table. Eomore and the elf made eye contact immediately and their gazes fixed one on the other. For an instant the prince wondered if he had been charmed, then realized that it had only again been a function of his fatigue.

"My Lord," the elf bowed deeply as he reached the table. "I know that you must be weary - too weary to listen to my sad tale this night, but I wonder if I may have audience with you in the morrow."

"I wonder if it is not I who should be bowing, traveler," responded Eomore. "Whom do I have the pleasure of addressing?"

"I am called Vannelei," the elf quickly answered. "I am an envoy of King Cyratiel of the realm of western elves of the Lachinor. I travel with this small party of our citizens. We have just failed on a quest that leaves our hearts heavy. The rest of my group intends to return to our homeland beginning the journey at once. I intend to proceed to Lyndyn to speak with your father but our fortuitous meeting here at Mr. Frathingham's fine eatery may be to my advantage."

"Friend, if you desire, we can talk now," Eomore answered.

He hoped the elf would decline the rash invitation.

15

"No," replied the elf, "you rust gather your hard earned rest."

With that the elven messenger bid them all goodnight and arranged to confer with Eomore at the morning repast. He returned to his small troop, and they silently exited the Wayfarer. Eomore looked around the room again. One by one his minions had excused themselves from the table and walked over to one of the three doors on the side of the room opposite the doors into the kitchen. The portals were labeled. Eomore sat too far away to read than, but he knew that the one on the right read "Private" and lead to the living quarters of the innkeeper and his family; the center one read "Spa" and led into an enclosed natural hot spring that Frathingham had used as the center upon which to construct the inn; the one on the left opened to a stairs which led upstairs where the rooms were. The prince was aroused (in more ways than one) by a flowing female voice.

"Would you have anything more, my Lord? "The girl innocently inquired.

Cara had returned to the table. Her light brown simple dress clung alluringly to her dark skin. Eomore doubted that there were any hidden innuendos in the girl's statement, but with the wily innkeeper anything was possible. He was uncomfortable with the very unkingly thoughts that he was having about the lovely commoner.

"No, thank you," he answered. "The meal was excellent, and so was your service."

He gave her a gratuity of five Dakin. The ways her eyes sparkled made him realize just how simple she was. It was probably the largest single tip she had ever received; the gratuity likely exceeded her usual weekly earnings. Perhaps the superficial quality was what appealed to him. Most of the women considered as appropriate mates for him were so complex that it was next to impossible to translate their words and deeds into what they actually meant or intended.

"Thank you, my Lord," she said as she bowed deeply.

She then turned away and returned to the bar area.

The room became filled with the melodious strumming of a stringed instrument, as an old blind bard began his nightly performance. The inn fell quiet except for the singer. This was the innkeeper's way of letting the guests know that closing was near and the sleeping guests needed peace and quiet. As he finished the last of his ale his mind returned to the elf - what could the traveler want?

Eomore had declined the innkeeper's offer of a private suite, electing instead to share a room with Deron the dwarf. He was so tired that he even bypassed the hot spring and went straight on up to bed.

"That was some rather unprincely thinking back there," Exeter admonished.

The criticism was bound to come.

"Why have you kept quiet about it for so long!" Eomore thought quickly. Perhaps the Sword could sense the annoyance in the prince's thoughts.

She reversed her psychology and planted this message into his fatigued mind. "We all need rest my prince. Perhaps tomorrow will bring the sun. We are, after all, only three days ride from Lyndyn. I hope you rest well."

When Eomore reached his room, the dwarf was already fast asleep. The little guy had taken the bed nearer the door and had left a candle burning for the prince. Eomore removed the cloak, the chainmail, and the sword's sheath, then fell onto the bed without even turning down the covers. Sleep was on its way.

Suddenly, the feeling of dread fell over him again. He sat up quickly. Nothing was there.

CHAPTER 3
The Story of Vannelei

The sword had been wrong. The morning had not brought the sun. When Eomore awakened, he realized that Deron had already arisen and had gone downstairs. The little guy was probably telling some slightly exaggerated story of his conquests in the battlefield or perhaps the bedroom, depending on the particular audience. Eomore chuckled. His diminutive companion had many of Boomer's qualities, including of course steadfast love and loyalty. Glancing around the small room, the prince noticed that the dwarf had remade his bed. It was difficult to see that anyone had occupied his half of the room. The dwarf people were a tidy lot who liked order and predictability. He stretched, and was amazed at the amount of soreness that remained in his well-conditioned body. Eomore stood well over six feet in height and weighed about two hundred pounds. He was quite handsome apparently, as he was very popular among the upper classed young ladies of Lyndyn; however, he felt most of them were more enamored with his station in life than Eomore himself. He glanced out the window. The rain had given way to a heavy overcast gray sky.

"The darn sun will surely be mildewed by now," he muttered under his breath.

"Good morning," Exeter said. The familiar voice appeared in his mind. "That is not a very royal greeting for a new day."

"It's the best I can do right now" the prince muttered.

He forgot that he did not have to say the words aloud. His thoughts returned to his encounter with the elves the night before. He first thought of the lovely maid and pondered whether she would be serving the morning meal. He wondered if she were wed. Then he felt the return of his memory to the noble Van- it was difficult to pronounce the elven names in the common dialect of Donothor.

The linguistics of the common tongue were just not adequate to give justice to the lyrical tones of the elven tongue. There was no adequate translation. Eomore spoke several dialects. He was even fairy proficient at goblin and hobgoblin- he supposed he had heard them curse him often and long enough that some of the language had to "rub off "on him. He was fluent in the Dwarven dialect thanks to his long association with Boomer. He finished dressing, slipped on the chainmail, sheath, and cloak of the Aivendar crest, and exited the room and went downstairs. Halfway down the stairs, he was met by the aromas and sounds of breakfast. When he entered the dining room he felt a sense of disappointment, because Cara was not there. True to form, Deron was seated at a table near the fire and was relating tall tales to the boys who should have been tending the blaze. As a result the embers were beginning to die down, a fact that would not set too well with Frathingham. A matronly woman, who might even be Mrs. Frathingham, was in charge, and servants were scurrying about bringing in trays of food. All of the rangers were in the room, having risen before their prince. In the far corner of the room, seated alone, was Vannelei. The elf's eyes beckoned to Eomore and the prince completed his descent of the stairs and went over to join the elf.

After he was seated the matron came over, took his request for the meal, and left the two men alone. They sat silently for a moment, and then Vannelei began to speak. The elf bypassed all the formalities of "good morning" and "how did you sleep" type small talk and went directly into his planned dialogue.

"I may have misled you when I introduced myself as an emissary of King Cyratiel. I am actually his son. That is the primary reason that I was chosen to lead this mission. I was chosen not only for my prowess as a hunter, tracker, and bowman, but also for my own vested interest in the dismal situation. Some forty years ago a young elven woman disappeared from her dwelling under the cover of darkness without leaving a trace. The only signs remaining were her crying infant son and the torn body of her guard dog when her husband returned from the hunt later that evening. The woman was called Mariniel, the most beautiful of her generation. Mariniel was endowed with great powers of Magick. She was the first wizardess that our people were graced with in many generations. Contrary to common belief, true wielders of great Magick powers are rare among the elves of the realms. The husband of the abducted wizardess was the then elven noble and now king, Cyratiel. Yes, the infant was I. Of course,

I have no memory of what happened. My father searched for years and grieved greatly for her. He left me to the care of relatives as he combed the lands for his lost mate. But never a trace was found. My mind's only picture of Mariniel, my mother, comes from the image that exists in the small portrait enclosed in the Luck Amulet that was blessed by the High Priestess Knarra and given to me by my father when I was but a nymph. Eventually the love and grief which drove him yielded to reason, and Cyratiel returned to his people. On the death of his father, he became the figurehead "ruler" of our people. Of course, Eomore, you are well aware that we consider individual freedoms paramount, and our council of elders with the "king" at its head only convenes when the community is threatened. I must admit that is rare, for we exist peacefully for the most part. "

Vannelei continued, "We do not hoard treasure, so the goblins have no real reason to attack us, and we remain geographically separated from our greatest racial enemies, the ogres, hobgoblins, the Dark Elves, and the many races of giants. However, we have again been struck by tragedy."

"On his return to his village, the bereaved Cyratiel was befriended by an elven woman named Corri, who had been widowed when her mate was slain by a nightmare, one of the demon horses that served the arch evil Uyrg, on a hunting trip deep into the Lachinor. Eventually the couple fell in love and married, and the union was consummated with the birth of a daughter eighteen years ago. Heather was a beautiful child and she brought great joy to her father. He felt so blessed that he named her for our most revered plant. She proved to be remarkably intelligent and was a ready student of the forest. Plants seemed to flourish whenever she walked by. It seemed that the Spirits of the forest had in some small way tried to repay the just Cyratiel for his years of grieving through this child. As she grew into womanhood, Heather became loved by all the peoples of our village and the surrounding communities. She accompanied her beaming father on many of his trips to the council meetings. There was hope that her skills of Magick would protect and nourish our people."

"Oh, but the cruel hand of misfortune has struck again. Some six weeks ago our Heather was taken from us. So many of the circumstances were like those of forty years ago, only this time there were unfortunately elven witnesses. On the dark starless night much like the one just past, Heather was staying the night with friends, when the unthinkable happened. The account is given by the only survivor of the tragedy, a thirteen year-old girl who saved herself through an invisibility potion. There was great mirth in the house as they celebrated the visit of the elven princess. From the outside, there was a growl from the faithful watchhound, then a painful yip, and silence. When the patron of the home opened the portal to investigate the noise, he was struck a single blow to the throat by a great dark hand and fell lifelessly back into the room.

"Through the door came a number of creatures who were as dark as the night and who moved as silently as wraiths. They systematically began to eliminate all the occupants of the room. The fallen man's eldest son managed to reach his short sword but the dark raiders merely turned back the blade as the young, but quite strong, elf struck. He then fell as his father from the crushing force of the blows of the great fist. There was one last hope. The matron managed to get an arrow into her husband's long bow, and the taut string hummed, but the perpetrator caught the missile in its flight and angrily snapped it in half. The killers then went into frenzy, and killed all within the dwelling except the survivor and the Princess. A great arm lifted up the princess in a single, effortless motion, and they then left as silently as they had arrived, bearing their quarry with them. Half in shock over witnessing the wanton slaughter of her family, the girl still managed to reach a neighbor's home to relate the grisly tale. Then she collapsed. The neighbors quickly ran to the site of the tragedy and unfortunately confirmed the story of the hysterical child. Eleven of our people lay crumpled on the floor," the elf said.

Vannelei began to weep.

Eomore sat silently as he waited for the elf to continue with the story. He thought of his own sister Trya, the light of King Eraitmus' eyes. Eomore loved her dearly. He began to feel great sorrow for the proud man seated before him. In his mind he could sense that Exeter sensed the sorrow as well and also that the great weapon thirsted for the foul ichor of the dark raiders.

Exeter was first of all a vessel of battle. Sometimes the cool and collected demeanor that she tried to project gave way to the zest for battle and berserk rage. This was one of the latter times.

After a few minutes Vannelei collected himself.

He continued. "In almost no time the news reached my father and he summoned me. We gathered our strongest and swiftest trackers and armed ourselves as heavily as we could. I carried my bow Truestrike as always and also took the Sword of Cyratiel, a vorpal blade given him during his meanderings. We almost never picked up their trail. We gave the raiders the name Death Wraiths, because of the description given us by the survivor. For beings of their reported size they left very little trail and we found that our progress was painfully slow. Our situation was complicated when we were ambushed by a large force of goblins two days west of here. Many of my men fell dead or wounded before we were able to drive than off. I think they became disinterested when we were noted to be traveling so lightly. At any rate, I sent most of my party home and tried to pursue onward with the men I was with last night. The rest of the party carried the dead and wounded back to our village. We picked up wisps of a trail as we crossed the border of Donothor, but the next day the lost time and the accursed rain led us to a complete impasse. We had no idea of where to go; no leads to follow. It was then that I decided that the four of us would come here to recuperate some of the strength that had left us; our spirits tired from weeks of continual exertion. I had chosen to proceed on to Lyndyn to discuss this affair with Eraitmus, as I am now at a loss as to what my next action might be.

"Donothor has so many resources. We are a proud people and disdain asking aid, but I grieve for my father. He is a kind elf who has suffered his share of heartache. Prince, I would give my dying breath to return Heather to him," Vannelei said. The elf began to weep again, and then he was silent.

Eomore found himself burning with emotions - hatred, pity, disgust, lust, anger, and frustration. The emotions overwhelmed him. He found that he could not speak, but his strong hand reached over to the noble Elf and clutched his shoulder. He then brushed away the amber tears that streamed down the noble face of the Gray Elf.

22

Vannelei then leaned into Eomore's wide chest and wept harder.

Eomore asked, "Has Magick been of any aid to you in your efforts to pursue the Death Wraiths?"

Vannelei tried to compose himself and answered,"We have not been blessed by one of great powers in Magick since the disappearance of my mother Mariniel. As a nymph, I had some abilities to enhance plants and to create light. Unfortunately I fell from a tree and remained unconscience for days. I only survived because of the great efforts of the healers of my people. When I awakened, I no longer possessed any abilities. The traits of the Magick are fickle. They are not passed from generation to generation as are physical and emotional traits. Many of our people have innate abilities to interact with natural forces and our senses are keen. We have great abilities to grow and nurture plants. But to create Magick as Mariniel- that is rare."

Eomore noted the elf's frustration.

"I have failed!" Vannelei cried.

"We all know that feeling, elven prince," Eomore answered.

He could certainly identify with failing in the eyes of one's father. But Eomore had never experienced the tragedy of these elves. Even his own losses seemed less, as he recalled the corpses lying in the sanctuary across the way.

As the elf had spoken, Eomore had noted a number of the things that he had said. When he spoke of his people, Vannelei had referred to than as "men, women, and children." He referred to himself as a "Nymph" when he was a child. Eomore surmised that the elf was trying to translate the elvish expressions into the common language of Donothor. Sometimes the lyrical terms of the elvish language were again difficult to translate.

The sadness of the noble elf was overwhelming. Eomore's fascination with the fair forest people was enhanced further as Vannelei spoke of the powers and natures of the forest peoples. The prince had learned more of the elves during the brief exchange with Vannelei than he had in all his formal studies at Lyndyn. His rudimentary knowledge of the elvish tongue helped the prince somewhat.

He pondered the nature of the creatures Vannelei had called Death Wraiths. Eomore knew of no such beasts in the facts or legends of his land. He wondered if they were the creation of a vengeful wizard, but he doubted that even a mage as great as Roscoe could create such a minion. Maybe they were liches, beings of great power thought to be spirits of evil wizards too powerful or too stubborn to yield to death. Liches were legendary. Knarra and Roscoe had spoken of liches after the Great War seeking the destruction of the Orb of Chalar. Eomore and many preceeding generations had been free of the fear of these undying menaces.

It was difficult to find the words to express everything that he was feeling now. It seemed most appropriate to welcome the elf to join them on their return to the capital. Eomore relished the possibility to have the company of the elf, as he felt he still really knew so little about the reclusive forest folk. This would give him the opportunity to learn more of them. He only wished the circumstances were better. But then, that was the way of fate and life. If these circumstances did not exist, Eomore would have never met Vannelei.

Finally he said: "Let's replenish our energies with a hearty meal. Then we will continue our journey to Lyndyn. My father is a fair and compassionate man. I'm sure he will make all the resources we have available to you."

Eomore felt a brief feeling of guilt when the thought crossed his mind that Eraitmus would have something to address besides the fact that his eldest son was twenty-eight years old and unmarried.

Cara appeared from the kitchen with a hot meal for them. For some reason, she appeared even more beautiful than she had the night before. Eloquently, she moved with elven grace across the wooden floor. Eomore gave her a pleasant greeting, and when she smiled her beauty seemed to have increased exponentially. Eomore felt warm and his face burned a bit. Eomore knew that she was a striking maiden. He had been away from Lyndyn for five weeks. He had not been away from the company of a woman long enough to confuse his judgment.

It may have only been only coincidental, but he saw her whisper to another of the barmaids and she moved herself to within ear range of the Prince's table.

She raised her voice just loud enough that he could hear her say, "I can't understand why Cara remains unmarried. She has such a way with the kitchen."

Eomore mused that this was a pretty good compliment for one maid to give another.

The group then went about the business of eating. Eomore settled the account with Frathingham, who wished than a safe return and a quick return to the Southland.

"My home is your home," the round one declared.

"Yes, for a price," Eomore muttered just under his breath.

The nine men exited the inn, and outside the stable boys were waiting with the ponies. The horses looked well groomed. Perhaps Frathingham was worth his prices. Eomore lurched backward as he saw the winged stallion.

"That is my steed," Vannelei stated. "He has lost the power of flight as have most of his kind - yet the wings remain - the ironies of nature are sometimes hard to understand."

The horse had vestigial wings - oh well, Eomore knew many men who had brains or strong backs, yet did not use than. It occurred to him that his men had puzzled looks on their faces, and then he realized that he had not introduced them to the elf.

"Fellow rangers of Donothor, this is Van, er, Vanni," the usually loquacious prince was again having trouble with the elven names translation into the common dialect.

"Just call me Vann, brave warriors," the elf smiled as he smoothed over Eomore's language dilemma. "That goes for you as well, my Prince."

"Thank you," answered Eomore.

Then silence settled over the men as they saw the curate of Knarra crossing the square with the two ponies bearing their fallen comrades. The curate had laboriously applied balms to preserve the dignity of the corpses. Eomore sensed the loss of his friend, but he also felt the groundwork for a lasting friendship had been laid for him and the elf. There was Cara, too. His mind's eye could return to the vision of her face if there were times such as the rainy night that he had just endured.

"Onward to Lyndyn, men," he said as he mounted his steed.

The chainmail glistened even though there was no sun.

Cara watched until they disappeared down the road leading out of the square.

25

CHAPTER 4
The Dream Chaser

The morning passed for Cara. The dark green elven eyes had watched intently as the riders disappeared down the main and only street of the township of Kanath. She knew, as she was preparing for the midday meal and trying her best to appear cheerful and gracious to the customers, the riders were probably reaching Threeforks, the town so named because of its location at the branching of the River Luumic into its three divisions along which followed the three main roads to Tindal and the southern provinces of Donothor. Three Forks was the largest community of the south, and was a major stepping-stone on the route to Lyndyn.

The inn was still rather quiet - there were only a few customers who were being entertained, more or less, by some wild stories from the rotund proprietor. Cara slowly turned and walked from the dining room into the kitchen. There the matron, Mrs. Frathingham, was supervising the preparations. Cara tried to lose herself in her tasks, but the dark elf found that she could not concentrate on the duties before her. Her heart was with the tall rider who had so abruptly entered and just as quickly left and had so greatly complicated her simple country life - her mind had accompanied her heart on the journey, so the lovely maiden had spent much of the morning staring into the soup bowls and wash basins. The dark green eyes retained the vision of her prince as he rode so majestically down the road toward another world at Castle Lyndyn. The observant eye of the matron had noticed that her usually most energetic, pleasant, and industrious server was in some other world.

Madam Frathingham knew the meaning of the expression on the face of the elven girl and the glow in those eyes.

She interrupted her own tasks and walked over to the girl, gently placing her caring hand on the diminutive shoulder of the maiden.

She said soothingly, "They ride into our lives, touch our hearts, then ride on - sometimes I wonder if their words and their eyes are not more deadly than the weapons they carry."

26

Cara reddened. The elf said, "Yes Ma'am, I'm sorry, I...I..."

The stout woman interrupted her. "It is certainly a young woman's privilege to dream of princes. We all do, or did, that. It's too bad that fate does smile more favorably on the less fortunate of us in regard to the worldly goods. Rare indeed is the opportunity to perhaps seize the substance of a dream and cause it to become reality. You see, my dear, I saw the same look in the young man's eyes last evening and this early morn as he watched you that I see in yours now. Perhaps you should pursue your prince, Cara."

"But madam, I am but a poor uncultured country girl and," Cara hesitated.

She was once again cut off by the matron.

Rebaccah said, "So you would have so little to lose - for most of us never meet the gaze of a prince, let alone a longing gaze. His eyes revealed more than the passing glance of a one-night journeyman. Years ago, I saw the same look in the eyes of a very successful young businessman whom I felt could never be interested in someone as simple as I. Yet, after feeling and conquering much personal doubt, I pursued my prince, and we have shared twenty-seven wonderful years together."

Of course Cara knew that she was speaking of Tarrance Frathingham, who must certainly be a prince in the eyes of his wife.

Cara answered the persistent encouragement of the matron with still more doubt.

She rambled, "But I would not know where to begin – I've never even been to Lyndyn - how would I act there - what of my work here - if I should lose this job!"

"I would suppose that being a barmaid might be above a princess, but I imagine that I might be able to convince the proprietor of this institution to allow you an indefinite leave of absence from your duties here. You have served us loyally now for three years. As to where to begin - it is always best to start at the beginning. I'm sure that your brother Cade could work a trip into Lyndyn into his schedule. He could accompany you on the journey. Of course you should be armed for you will have to traverse the Misty Forest to the north of Threeforks. Once in Lyndyn, it is said that the King's kitchens are always in need of good help. But since the manager of the castle kitchens is also the chief cook and also just happens to be my cousin Oren Bach, I don't think you will have much difficulty obtaining a position. I will send a letter of identification with you. "The matron said.

The matron seemed intent that this would not be an unrequited love.

She continued, "One must go to the den to catch the beast. There are not many princes to be found in Kanath. Child, chase this dream, this chance meeting, this rare opportunity to cheat fate of confining you to a life of poverty. I can sense good fortune for you in this. If you return to Kanath, I assure you that you will always have a position with us. I will handle things with the master."

Cara spoke again, but she could not believe it was her voice speaking the words. "By tomorrow, I could have preparations made for the journey. Cade I'm sure will ride with me. I have always wanted to visit the city. But I sure hate to leave you."

Tarrance Frathingham chuckled to himself as he listened at the kitchen door. He started to enter but instead returned to grace the beleaguered customers with more of his stories of conquest; he thought to himself as he sauntered across the floor that there was no doubt as to what his greatest treasure in life was - it was he who had married a princess. She was a "good old girl."

Cara gathered her wrap, and hurried out of the inn.

"Come by in the morning and I will have some nourishment for your journey along with some letters and good luck." the matron called to the girl.

The girl smiled, thanked her, and exited through the back door of the kitchen. She went to her small room in one of the boarding houses. It would not take her very much time to gather up what he had or needed. She carefully packed - the last things she placed upon the bed she first removed from a hiding place in the floor. There was a small crossbow with a quarrel of golden bolts - the handle of the bow and the bolts were laced with fine runes. There was an old Volume which was bound in leather which she took special care to conceal within her garments. She wrapped everything in her petite saddlebag, strategically placing the crossbow within easy reach. She sought out her brother and he was easy to find. Most folks thought of Cade as a ne'er-do-well, but Cara realized that the neighbors were not familiar with the slow maturity of the male elves.

Cade was merely seventeen and at this stage of his life he was too fascinated with the world around him to burden himself with things such as a job and wage earning. Cade readily accepted his sister's invitation and promised to protect her to the best of his abilities. He said this in very knightlike fashion and slapped the small scabbard which housed the short sword which the young elf treasured so greatly. He assisted her in making preparations for the trip.

The ride from Kanath began much as the night before had ended.

The deafening silence surrounded the riders; they were growing accustomed to this; there was a steady drizzle. The pace was quicker - each rider felt a sense of urgency about the journey. Of course, the greatest sensation of exigency was felt by Vannelei. They were still three days from Lyndyn, but another hot meal awaited then at Threeforks. Then there was more wilderness, as parts of the Misty Forest were as dismal as the lower Lachinor. However the laws of the Aivendar's and the frequent ranger patrols greatly cut down on the mischief that occurred there. However, the chance of encountering misfortune increased significantly if one ventured off the roads. The rangers discouraged the private citizens from doing this and warned the hunting parties to exercise caution.

Vannelei rode at the front of the small caravan of horsemen alongside Eomore. The Donothorian was amazed at how effortlessly the small winged horse kept pace with Eomore's well-trained animal.

Eomore had been disappointed by the lack of conversation, as he hungered for more knowledge of the elven folk. But he knew that the fellow traveler had much on his mind and had endured great tragedy. Somehow Eomore found his own thoughts returning to the captivating waitress at Frathingham's.

The sky began to break by midmorning and the horsemen could feel their spirits lifting with the appearance of the sun's long awaited rays. They reached Threeforks without incident and stopped as planned for a meal in one of the better taverns. The stop at the tavern rejuvenated the men, and they then proceeded onward, facing another three nights under the stars. The second night would unavoidably have to be spent within the Misty Forest, but the rangers knew several places of assured safety. During the morning ride, Exeter had talked almost ceaselessly - mostly about the pitfalls of one-night stands and the deviousness of women when it came to nabbing their "prey". Eomore usually had responded by nodding in his mind. After lunch however, he and Vannelei began to converse more. The elf told Eomore many things about the customs and histories of the elven people. For each question answered the prince had two more waiting. This did not seem to annoy the elf, as he seemed to enjoy taking his mind off his personal tragedies of recent times. They traveled well and reached their planned destination at the edge of the Misty Forest by nightfall. There was a meadow there which served as a stopping point for many travelers and the rangers shared the field with two other parties. Of course there would be guards posted, but this was a relatively secure area. As he reclined, Eomore found his thoughts returning to the small hamlet of Kanath to the south and to the pair of green eyes that so captivated him just one night earlier.

He again cursed the fate which made him a prince. He longed to see the woman again, but realistically, he doubted that fate would grant him another opportunity to glance upon her. Eomore did not realize that fate had a strong foe in the person of Rebaccah Frathingham.

CHAPTER 5
The Spawn Curse

Calaiz rose from another disturbed rest period. He stretched his enormous frame and walked over to the window which looked out from the royal tower of Castle Ooranth onto the city and the surrounding plain. The Peaks of Doom loomed ominously in the distance; the sky was filled with the reassuring amber glow produced by the conjoint efforts and lights from the three suns hovering over the land. In the other direction, north in the reference of the instruments taken from the other world, stood the Peaks of Division. There the Great Sea reflected Mirror Mountain, the greatest of the peaks and the lair area of his greatest enemies, the Kiennites. There would probably be no storms today and it would be a good day for the Draith Lord to show off his prowess to his people, the Masters of the Land, in the competitions in the royal arena.

For security reasons all windows in the royal tower were apparent only from the interior of the structure. From the outside, the tower appeared to be made of the solid black stone of which Castle Ooranth was built. The nature of the stone was unknown even to the builders of the fortress those centuries ago. The one-way windows enabled the leaders of the Masters of the World of Three Suns to observe the center of their domain in relative security. The race led by the immense Calaiz referred to themselves as the Masters; many others referred to them as the Draiths. Their silent movement mimicked that of wraiths of legend of the other world..

Calaiz was indeed a massive creature. He was humanoid - no, he was diabolic - but he was diabolically handsome. His skin was like polished brass, much more lustrious than that of the majority of the Draiths. His strong face had well defined lines that revealed every minor change in the affect of the powerful being. He stood over seven feet tall, and his mass was in excess of three hundred pounds, in the measurements of the peoples of the other world. Measurement in the domain of Calaiz was not based on mere numbers, but in deeds and power.

His hair was amber and flowing, and he gave the appearance of a demi-god. He was charismatic; he also gave the appearance of an invincible foe, and he might well be for any mortal being. But Calaiz was mortal. Though he was only in his early prime, currently only forty years old, in the quantums of time of the other world, the Draith Lord knew that the time had arrived for him to undertake the steps necessary to assure the continuation of his line. Now fully awake, the massive one found his mind returning to the problem facing him - a suitable mate; a consort who was worthy of carrying his heir.

For the Draiths, the reproduction of their race was not the simple matter that it was for other peoples. The Draiths had been taught a terrible lesson about underestimating the powers of their foes those generations ago when they were victimized by the "foaling curse" of the Kiennite Deathqueen, Anectrophenia. It was the time of the last war of the four powers. As usual, it had boiled down to the Draiths against the other three - the Kiennites of the north and east, the wandering dogfaced Drolls of the north and central and the Giants in the extreme northern mountains. In a World of Three Suns direction had long been one of instinct, but excursions into the other world had brought back many items including a device that pointed direction on its dial. The adaptable Draiths had chosen to incorporate this into their teachings and archives. The sun Meries seemed to influence the direction of the needle most, thus the directions based on the position of the sun Meries in the sky were noted and taught to the young.

After centuries of battles, the Draiths had never come so close to the total ultimate victory. The Giants had been decimated and their leaders slain, the race never again to be a power; since then the number of combatants in the wars and skirmishes was reduced to three. The army of Nargan the Red was perched at the very stronghold of the Kiennite Deathqueen; thrice the wicked wizardess threatened to ruin the race of the Draith King if the battle did not cease, but thrice Nargan crashed his forces against the walls of the castle. The walls were about to fall when history records that the king's ears could hear the wailing from the homeland those thousands of paces to the south and the tide sustaining the Draith onslaught ebbed. The land was filled with a chill and a brief blackness. As the light returned, Nargan knew that a baneful lesson was upon him.

There had been no final victory - through the ultimate limit of her povers, the Kiennite Deathqueen had caused the immediate death of every member of the female gender of the Draith race - Telepathically she had communicated to Nargan that the males would be next, and the Red King had no way of calling her bluff - she also assured the Draith King that the genetic curse applied to any females fathered by Draith males born to women of other races. Nargan could not know that the latter was true, but the threat to destroy the males had been no more than a bluff - the great draining of Magick had so weakened Anectrophinea that she sat helpless within her castle - the price of the Black Wish spell was that her full powers would never return. The Black Wish had cost the Deathqueen her ancient staff, a great source of her power. A Wish Spell cost the caster his item of greatest value. Those not versed in Magick lacked such knowledge.

Nargan could have walked through the weakened walls and could have slain all within. Calaiz knew this through his intimate knowledge gained from his life long study of Magick. The Magick held tight to their histories.

And of course only the passage of time had borne these things into fact. The Draiths had successfully crossbred, but every female child was strickened and died soon after birth - the full effect of the curse was that there were no full-blooded Draiths. They had been forced to a game of abduction by night to continue their kind. Of course this posed a special problem for the rulers and sages - only the finest of the "other" women would be acceptable. Through fate and conscripted service of captive sorcerers, the Masters had managed to find and traverse the portal to the other world and for many generations had been satisfying their needs through raids there. The origin of the portal was however not known and those who passed through it experienced pain; pain was not a deterrent to the Masters. The enslaved sorcerers were motivated by pain and had grudgingly forfeited the knowledge to Calaiz's forebears of the means to survive passage between the worlds. The Portal Gate was protected by powerful Magick, but Calaiz surmised the the Deathqueen herself may have been involved in its creation to fulfill her own needs, however arcane. In general the Masters felt they were weakened by each "thinning" of the blood - indeed, this had probably had been the goal of the Black Wish of the Deathqueen. She had hoped to not only defeat the Draiths in the last war, but also to assure the eventual domination of the Kiennites in the land. The Drolls and Giants, though savage and cunning, lacked the intelligence to really become dominant; the other peoples of the World of the Three Suns, such as the Drelves of the Central Forests were too reclusive to care or else were wanderers or just not numerous enough to pose a real threat.

But not even Anectrophinea could have anticipated the circumstances surrounding the conception of Calaiz, the Black Lord of the Draiths. Instead of being progressively weaker, he was without a doubt the most terrible liege in the history of the "Masters." No more powerful personality was to be found within the history books of the sages. In the past, Magick was always a tool of the enemies of the Draiths - only rarely had the black arts been in the corner of the dark people. Such an instance occurred when a Kiennite shaman had through torture and threat of genocide been compelled to assist in the opening of the portals to the other world. But now the black arts were at last in the hands of the Masters - in the person of Calaiz. He had been the spawn of Aixtin, who was the strongest physically of any recent lords - the old king had remained relatively successful in the combat games of the Draiths until well into his graying days, and a beautiful dark elven woman from the other world. The woman had great beauty and was versed in Magick. His birth had coincided with the Approximation of The Gray Wanderer, the sun Andreas. Rare were the times that the gray star came close to the World of the Three Suns, and on the occasion of the birth of Calaiz, the sun was closer than it had been since antiquity. He and the sages were loathe to admit it, but Calaiz derived most of his looks and great charismatic nature from his maternal blood - more importantly, in some way known only to the fates, he had gained abilities in the black arts - Magick had been so foreign, so alien, to the Draiths, that initially his father and his advisors on the council had been alarmed when the young prince began to reveal the amazing talents. The death of his mother at his birth had deprived Aixtin of the means to gain knowledge to channel the young Calaiz's energies. Even the pain of death had not secured adequate information from unfortunate captured Kiennites. A Drelve of abilities in the Magick had not been discovered for generations.

Perhaps it was the proximity of the gray sun and the passing of the spirit of his mother that had endowed the Draith Lord with his gift. This was the best theory that the advisors had come up with.

But the rulers eventually realized what a great boon this could be to the Draiths in gaining their vengeance and the domination in the land that they so desperately wanted to rule as Masters; a role that was so rightfully theirs. Still the powers of the new lord had been kept a closely guarded secret, less the enemies learn of him and attempt to strike him down.

Calaiz had matured now, and he was awesome - soon the armies would be strengthened to the point that the final conquest could occur. Under the leadership of the Black Lord, who united the powerful physical aspects of the Masters with the unfathomed strengths of Magick, the victory that had eluded them could be attained and the pangs of hatred and hunger for revenge could at last be satisfied.

Calaiz scanned the horizon. The sky was filled with the amber light, though blues and other hues peeked through. There were the three stars - each so different. Long had the Draiths studied the suns; as a race they had attempted to recreate in themselves the best qualities of the suns. Meries the fleet - a small brilliant sun which traversed the heavens in but sixteen of the time fragment known as hours in the other world, such that the land was never under the cover of total darkness; but instead the land was bathed with a waxing and waning cycle of light that occurred every eight of those hours, or twice for each cycle of Meries, which never left the horizon, only slinking down to the zenith at each cycle. Speed and brilliance, or a quick mind, were the attributes represented by this astral traveler. The scholars said that a thing called magnetism emanated from this sun and this lead to the direction definitions in the land; Orphos, a giant black star, a great distance from the land, which provided little light and warmth to the land, but which never left the skies; some scholars debated that Orphos was not a single sun but a combination of many, and derived its black color from the fact that it was too strong to allow even light to exist. It was like a great black hole in the sky yet which seemed to be a source of great power. Orphos seemed to control the movements of Meries. The Masters attributed that strength, dependability, and power were epitomized by

Orphos. The third sun, Andreas, the Gray, the mysterious wanderer, would disappear from the skies at seemingly random occurrences to reappear again on the horizon in between three to seven of the time periods, 24 to 56 of the "hours" units; Andreas, which emitted eerie gray light, was poorly understood, but many scholars felt the strengths of Magick waned when the gray star was not in the skies. Orphos did not exert any influence upon the wanderer. Again, on rare occasions the gray sun approached to the point of almost filling the sky and blocking out the light of Meries. No Draith king had ever led his force into battle when only the gray star and the Black Giant were in the horizon and when Meries was at its zenith. The light of Meries was essential.

Calaiz no longer was sure of this trusted wisdom. Magick was no longer just a threat and a tool of the enemies of the draiths. The Draith Lord felt comforted by the presence of the gray sun and welcomed it. He basked in ther gray light.

Orphos, for all his great size was also slow and rotated about the heavens every eight periods – but never leaving the sky- but his light was inconsequential at any rate. The Draiths and others of the Land of the Three Suns thus divided their time into periods based on the light and dark cycles of Meries. From the gray one, they tried to do the opposite that the star represented - order and predictability instead of randomness - and until this time shunning the black arts - it was rumored that the Kiennites and the Drelves worshipped Andreas or at least some manifestation of the sun. The legends of the forest peoples held that their greatest accomplishments had occurred during Approximations of the Gray Wanderer.

Calaiz was unusually contemplative as he viewed the stars. He thought of his mother who had died at the time of his birth. He had heard his father speak of her great beauty and wisdom. She was called a "Dark Elf" in the tongue of her homeland and had apparently come from excellent stock. She had never adjusted to her incarceration and had been unusually resistant to the indoctrination given to the "queens" brought in from the other world. Her will had been great, but eventually the conception had been successful, and she had birthed the Black Lord. She had shared none of her knowledge of the Magick with Aixtin and his advisors.

The great face briefly broke into a solemn expression before his subconscious had been able to halt the rapidly developing feeling of pity - emotion was not a virtue prized by the Draiths, but Calaiz was not typical for his race in so many ways. Calaiz knew that other peoples referred to his peoples as Draiths. He knew that the elders preferred tp retain the title of Masters, but Calaiz liked the connotations attributed to the name "Draiths" and the Black Lord actually thought of his people by this term in his private thoughts.

He was thinking of the pain felt by the family of his mother - but her sacrifice was necessary for the continuation of the line. He daily studied her portrait that hung in his chamber. Her pain grieved him. Calaiz ritually clutched the Amulet of the Green Stone that he knew was her prized possession. He cursed his own weakness in having these feelings. Often he would go to compete in the arena to try to relieve some of these frustrations.

He again returned from these feelings of near pity to the task facing him. The elven girl brought from the forests to him did not satisfactorily meet his standards. True, she was indeed beautiful and bright and would serve nicely as a nursemaid to the young, but she lacked the strength, constitution, and endurance to be the mother of his son.

Izitx and his scouts, which are how the Draiths referred to their most experienced warriors, had been trying very hard to succeed in the procurement of a suitable mate for Calaiz, but so far there had been no success. There was only one alternative - the Black Arts! Calaiz himself would have to determine who the "lucky" woman would be.

The Draith Lord moved methodically from the window to one of the large cabinets in his bedchamber. He uttered a command word which sounded as old as time itself, and the front of the cabinet moved aside, revealing its contents; a small spherical orb resting softly on a violet cushion. The great hands grasped the item and gently removed it from its resting place. He carried it over to the large table which dominated the center of the chamber. There he placed the orb on a carved device which accomodated it perfectly. Taking a flint, the great creature began to start a fire -the flame from the brazier began to fill the room with a dense green, then blue smoke. He began a

37

ritualistic, orderly sequence of lighting incense. Only the Draith Lord knew the significance of the order of his efforts.

Then he began to conjure. If anyone had been listening, regardless of race, he would have difficulty understanding the arcane phrases which emanated from the huge being. Long he uttered the incantation - at times the phrases were almost melodic - at times they would inspire fear in the bravest of men. As Calaiz went about the task, the milieu of the room changed many times; there seemed to be forces of immense power and spirits of forgotten and forbidden places filling the room, but then again it may have been the effects of the incense and the smokes. At last Calaiz wiped his profusely sweating brow and stopped the incantation.

He slowly peered into the orb. The small device which had been translucent filled with a blue haze; the haze initially seemed to hover, and then seemed to move as if blown by the seven winds as the sands of time itself. Then the device began to glow faintly, then gradually the glow enhanced to a brilliant violet and the entire chamber was filled with an aura. The haze began to clear; the orb began to reveal a place, clearly in the other world, for there was only one sun. There was a mountain covered with a dense forest; the area was cloaked with a thick veil of mist; there was a road leading northward to a great walled city; this was a place Calaiz recognized as a land called Donothor; there was a city called Lyndyn; there appeared a castle on a mountain within the city; he saw a bed chamber within the castle; he saw a beautiful woman; she as an exquisite creation. His dark eyes stared intently into the orb. The long tresses fell gently down her back, cascading over her ivory skin. The muscles were so well defined. Calaiz could almost hear the notes as the young beauty sang as she bathed, and he smiled. The orb and the Seeking Spell had not failed him, for this was the woman who must bear his heir. A woman named Trya - of the family of Aivendar - the daughter of a man named Eraitmus - the princess of Donothor.

The room cleared rapidly of its sights and smells. Calaiz returned the orb to its resting place and sealed the fireglyph with another command. He walked to the entry to his chamber. There again, he triggered the proper sequence of the six doorknobs and opened the great door. He instructed the guards that one of the three should summon Izitx. Shortly the older Draith appeared.

"My Lord "was the only statement he uttered.

"My faithful servant, I have found her! Come into my chamber," Calaiz hurriedly ushered the other into the royal chamber.

The advisor listened intently as Calaiz told him the specifics of the maiden's location.

He nodded silently and informed the King of the hazards involved in striking this particular city - he would certainly suffer losses.

"Take only your finest; we must move soon. The time is near - I feel war is only a few weeks away, and the indoctrination will take some time, particularly with such a strong willed woman," the Draith Lord instructed his most loyal minion.

"It will be done my Lord. We will begin preparations immediately but the abduction will require much thought on my part." answered the stone-faced amber creature.

He turned and went to the door.

"Wait, my loyal servant. Take this for your protection. The Magick are known to these people. Stealth and power may not be enough to sustain you," Calaiz said.

He gave a small amulet to the senior scout.

Izitx placed the amulet around his massive neck, where it appeared miniscule. He said nothing more and, knowing the combination to enter the chamber, Izitx let himself out.

Calaiz was again left alone. He again thought of the agony his necessity would cause an unwary family. He knew this would cost him some scouts, perhaps even Izitx. He thought again of his mother. Alone in the sanctuary of his chamber, the Draith Lord allowed himself the luxury of a single green tear. Calaiz had been given more than good looks and magical abilities by his mother - the Draith Lord was also the first of his kind to be burdened with a conscience.

It was at times a baneful thing.

CHAPTER 6

The Misty Forest

Lyndyn could be reached by circumventing the dense central forest by following the roads along the rivers and streams through the populated areas, but this prolonged the journey by at least three days. The road through the Misty Forest, as the central woodland was called, was patrolled intermittently by the rangers, but still the way was somewhat unpredictable. Most merchants sent their wares either upriver on barges or else over the heavily traveled and secure highways. But an armed party of Donothorian rangers should expect to meet no resistance to their progress through the forest. However, the way was rough, and the niceties of life were lacking. There was no steed alive which could traverse the expense of wood in less than two days, so the decision to go through the wood carried with it a decision to spend a night under the stars. The Misty Forest was much like the Lachinor - only much smaller; it was as though the two had been separated in some manner some years ago and the lower provinces had been stuffed between them. Of course Eomore knew that the geography of the region was the actual reason that the Misty Forest had been left unsettled. The great river separated above the forest into two branches and these circled the expanse of wilderness. There was a mountain range between the river's branches. The mountains for some reason remained much colder than one should imagine, and thus the thick expanse of trees remained almost continually enshrouded by a misty fog which rose up from the great rivers. This was how the forefathers had arrived at the name. The terrain was too rough for farming; there were too few raw materials to make mining profitable, and likewise the loggers could make a living in much simpler and safer environment.

Thus the area had remained a wilderness. It was a place where young men liked to prove their manhood and hunters considered it a paradise. But it contained many unexplored reaches and there were many legends about the place. There were many campfire stories of "those who did not return." Eomore knew that most of these were exaggerated and romanticized, but the prince still felt some apprehension each time he stood at the bridge crossing the river at the edge of wood. He always slept tentatively and lightly when reposing in the forest and was relieved whenever the trip was completed. The forest was really the last obstacle before the riders on their journey homeward. Lyndyn, the pinnacle of civilization, lay only another day's ride to the north once the bridge on the opposite side of the forest was crossed.

Eomore had slept soundly in the meadow. There was security. The prince had dreamed about the lovely elven maid. Even in his sleep she did not leave his mind's eye. "Just an infatuation" Exeter had muttered many times, but the prince could not understand this - never had he been so effected by a woman, and he had seen her for such a short while. He knew, however, that his responsibility lay to the north, in the city, and he was anxious to get on with the journey through the forest. He glanced over at the elf - Vannelei looked even more fatigued than he had the night before; it appeared as if the elf had not rested at all. The other members of the party were making small talk, and the dwarf Deron would occasionally make an attempt at humor. But these were invariably weak, because dwarves were not known for the appropriateness of the jest, and more often than not the jokes were simply bad.

There was again silence as the bodies were loaded gingerly onto the ponies and secured with rope. The small band then made their usual formation with Eomore and the elf in the front, and the lead ponies crossed the bridge.

Almost immediately, they entered the forest. The road was in fair repair, but there had been some washing from the recent rains. This slowed the horses as they had to carefully place each hoof to avoid a fall. They noticed a gentle grade to the road, and the cool mist began to surround than. The trees became thick on each side of the road and vision was reduced laterally to just a few feet to either side of the path. All had been here before, but each time in the Misty Forest was like a whole new experience. Their guard was up. At least one man kept a bow ready at all times and swords were drawn on an alternating basis. This was particularly advantageous for Eomore because when he held Exeter, the weapon could exercise her ability to warn of the approach of enemies. But not even Eomore could wield the sword at all times, so at times the riders were forced to rely on their own keen senses. Quietly they ascended the trail; it became more treacherous for the horses, and occasionally they were forced to dismount and lead the animals along the trail. Even though they felt constantly watched, the day passed uneventfully, and soon nightfall was upon them. They had not progressed as far as Eomore had hoped, but were forced to pause in their journey to move off the road and set up camp. The campsite was not ideal, but there was no ideal campsite to be found in the forest. There was a small clearing surrounded by a few tall oaks with many smaller shrubs around them.

The horses were tied and the group decided that they would post two guards; one with the animals and one within the camp itself. They gathered firewood and warmed their food. Then the air was filled with the aromas of the pipes of the dwarf and some of the others. They made no attempt to disguise their presence - the forest denizens knew well they were here.

The evening seemed unusually cool. Eomore had not rested well during his first rest period, and was already awake when Deron came to him to change the guard. He sat at the base of one of the large trees and watched the flickering embers of the fire. He scanned the edge of the forest - the darkness seemed to form demonic shapes which feigned advance then faded back into the reaches of his imagination from whence they had come. His thoughts returned to the coziness of the inn to the south - the girl was still fixed in his mind's eye. Remembering the depth of her eyes, he had felt as though he were drowning in them as she had gazed at him. He had never been subjected to a "charm" spell, but the sensation he had felt that night must have been similar. Eomore had certainly courted more lovely women, or had he? He could not understand shy she had affected him so. The prince spent the next segment of his watch exchanging riddles with the sword - he always lost. Fatigue continued to play its tricks on him - he could have sworn that a bush moved.

"Exeter?" he queried.

"I can sense life forces all around us, my Lord, but at this time nothing offensive." came the reply.

The companions returned to their small talk for awhile, and then he laid the weapon by his side and stretched. A few minutes passed, each seeming more like an hour. He squinted into the dim fire light.

More trickery and illusion were victimizing his tired eyes, no doubt. Then he focused again. The veteran Loran was standing about ten paces away from him outlined in the firelight. The tall man beckoned to the prince. Eomore stood, leaving the blade at his feet. It was so good to see his dead friend again. With a sudden wave of nausea, Eomore comprehended his thoughts - he reached down for the sword as Loran had taken two steps toward him.

"Shapechangers! "The sword urgently exclaimed. "I thought you would never ask! They are all around."

Eomore dove toward his friend and yelled at the top of his lungs. "To your arms! With haste!"

The sleepers began to arouse, and in an instant the bushes, rocks, birds, even the unburned firewood descended upon the awakening camp. The shapechangers were viscious and had the advantage of surprise. Eomore went straight for the brazen one that had impersonated his friend. The message of doom came quickly from Exeter, as the great blade sliced through the creature with ease. As the monster fell it returned to its own shapeless form. But quickly three others were upon the prince. As he fought he could see that the rest of his party was facing similar odds. Deron was doing well, although he gave way initially, and sustained a wound to his shield arm. The others too were embattled. With Exeter, the prince was too much for the vile creatures and they fell before him. He turned to the fray within the camp. The elf had been wounded by the razor like forearms of the shapechangers and his green tunic was stained that ominous deep red. One of the rangers had fallen and two of the beasts were upon him.

Eomore felt the desire to go to the elf in his heart; battle wisdom drove him to the fallen human. The great sword relieved the first creature of his head with a single stroke, and the second turned from his prey just in time to see his bane as the death stroke came. The tide was turning as more of the creatures were falling. Deron had joined the elf, and the proud Vannelei had proven himself by surviving with the odds against him and soon those enemies not slain were discouraged and fleeing into the woods. Eomore heard an elven slang expression that loosely translated as "illegitimates" and then the melodic twang of the elven bow - one of the fleeing foes was dropped in his tracks by the finely hewn arrow courtesy of "Truestrike".

Then there was silence. A quick head count revealed what Eomore had feared for he had not seen the other guard when the battle had begun. There were eight men but one of the rangers was at the edge of consciousness and the elf had a nasty wound to his shoulder. Eomore called Deron and another of the wounded and they ran over to the horses. There was a truly grisly site. The guard there had been unaware of the approach of the deceptive foes, and had been slain. The two other bodies were gone. The animals were unharmed; the horses were not spooked by the approach of the creatures because they also had the ability to mimic scents; no doubt the ponies had thought that more horses were approaching. They all felt a wave of nausea, then gathered the horses, increased the fire, and tended their wounds. The wounded ranger fell on into unconsciousness and became the second fatality of the treacherous attack. Eomore was angry - he had only lost two of his troop in the entire goblin venture, and now the losses had been duplicated only two days from home.

Exeter fumed. "I have failed you. But they can mimick shape and smell, and evidently disguide their intentions as well. I detected only neutrality even as they were engaged in the heat of battle."

Eomore answered, saying, "They were merely hungry denizens of the wilds, my ally. Basic survival instinct is not evil. You could not determine a cave bear or a mountain lioness to be evil. If they were hungry or guarding a young they would be a danger, but if merely present they would not pose a danger. "

He had heard of shapechangers, but none had ever been reported this far north. The seven men did not sleep any further that night, and with the first rays of light, they broke camp and proceeded through the forest as expeditiously as they could. Still the trip extended to nightfall of the following day. Then they reached the northern bridge and left the Misty Forest.

CHAPTER 7
Return to Lyndyn

After exiting the forest the riders quickly went into the nearest hamlet where the town healers attended their wounds. The men rested well in the secure confines of the small community. The next morning the men assembled, and being freshened, they continued on to the capital city. The landmarks were so familiar that all could have proceeded alone now. At last in the distance they could see the peak of Mt. Lyndyn with the castle spires high upon it and then the outer walls of the great city. There were now many people along the road and the group received many greetings and salutations. The main gates were open, as they usually were. The gate guards were maintained, but this was largely an honor duty, because there had not been a serious threat to the city in many years. The citizens were free to come and go into the city; this was the wish of Eraitmus Aivendar.

The party was escorted to the inner curtain surrounding the castle. Here security was tighter, and the gates were closed. For within were the main barracks of the officers of the ranger force and the seat of government and the private dwellings of the king and his family. Lyndyn was a bustling and prosperous place; the kingdom was flourishing under the wise rule of the Aivendars, and even though there was still wilderness such as the Misty Forest, the dwellers of the forests did not pose a threat to the average citizen of Donothor. The sites and sounds of the city were a relief to the men, and most were dismissed to go to their families. Eomore himself would notify the families of the fallen men before he rested. This was the custom, and the commanders of each quest had done this for years.

It meant that Eomore would have to delay his own resting for awhile, but this was something that he felt strongly about. Vannelei was taken to the royal infirmary where he would receive the attention of the personal physician of the king, Sedoar. He would be able to rest there and would go before the king when his strength had returned to him.

Eomore went about his task - the most difficult by far was the contact with the family of Loran - he finally returned to his quarters shortly after midnight. He indulged himself with a trip to one of the natural hot springs for a long awaited bath, and then went to his room. The prince insisted on living in the officers' quarters in lieu of the royal suite as was customary for those of his stature. This was poorly understood by the king as well as the other officers, but they accepted the wishes of the captain of the rangers.

Eomore entered his quarters at last. The torch on the wall was lit, filling the room with an amber glow. There was a dark form sitting in the large overstuffed chair in the comer of the room. Initially the prince was startled, but when the figure stood, Eomore recognized the body habitus in an instant.

"Boomer," he said.

"Eomore,"the dwarf answered. "I've heard your quest was fraught with misfortune. It is good to see you again, my friend. "

The dwarf extended his roughened hand toward the man towering over him.

"Likewise, it is good to be home. Yes, I've lost some good men; Gretch was a dastardly foe. I've never seen goblins fight so viciously. They were large too. But tragedy struck in the Misty Forest as well. We must either beef up our patrols or else close the road. How have you been, Boomer?" Eomore answered, firmly grasping the hardened hand.

"We have fared well... I went on a couple of short quests while you were away. Some renegade weremen were giving old Roscoe a fit and we had to go up and straighten things out, "the dwarf said.

Boomer had a sneer on his face as he answered. Eomore knew that the dwarf shared the contempt that most of his race felt for wizards - and Roscoe was a difficult man to deal with, even for a sorcerer.

"I should think that the mage would be able to handle a group of weremen without any trouble. The weremen, after all, are only normal men who worship wolves and convince themselves that they can become wolves when the moon is full," Eomore noted.

"Oh, I suppose that his mageship felt it beneath his dignity to deal with them. It wasn't really much of a quest. They ran for the hills when they heard us coming. But one of them bit Fetts," Boomer replied.

The dwarf chuckled when he recalled the dumbounded expression on the staunch veteran ranger's face when he looked down to see the man chewing on his leg.

Eomore joined the dwarf in his laughter. Even as tired as he was he could see the humor in the story.

"But you mentioned you had been on two quests. I suppose that Roscoe was chagrinned to again fall into my father's debt. I just hope that you get to accompany him on his repayment quest whenever the time cares, "Eomore answered.

"Oh, I was saving the best for last. I know that you are tired, my friend, so I will spare you many of the details until we are talking over a bottle of ale, but we finally caught "him"; greed proved to be the rascal's undoing. I designed a trap using the "Black Diamond legend" and the guile of a woman. He was victimized by the trap, "Boomer said proudly.

The dwarf beamed as he recounted the story.

Eomore felt a brief feeling of great jealousy, for he knew that his friend could only be speaking of the cutthroat and master thief Nigel Louffette. The prince gave praise, saying,"Amazing - you are to be commended, Boomer, and I heartily congratulate you."

Eomore knew that if Exeter were within the range of his voice, the sword could detect his resentment and disappointment. Eomore had always hoped that he would be the one to capture Nigel, the man who had eluded them for so long. But at least he was finally in the hands of the law. Nigel's reputation was doubtlessly exaggerated, but the prince was sure that there was some truth in the stories of how the tall thin man would mysteriously appear where a dispute existed and usually one of the contenders would manage to meet with a sudden demise. The thief would then vanish as rapidly and mysteriously as he had come.

"Know that you must rest. Tomorrow the king will want a full report. Just between the two of us, his majesty is very high on the daughter of a wealthy merchant visiting from the neighboring kingdom of Bamalla. He has been anxiously awaiting your return" completed the dwarf.

He then turned and began to walk toward the door, after slapping Eomore on the back.

"Thanks for the warning - I hope that we can seize some time tomorrow evening to visit the tavern by the central market and turn up a few mugs of ale, " Eomore said as he watched the stout figure go over to the door and exit the chamber after a nod of approval.

The prince slept soundly - he dreamed very little, but a face that was becoming more and more familiar in his dreams reappeared. It was pleasant; it warmed the prince.

The next morning Eomore felt naked when he dressed without donning the chainmail which was like an outer layer of skin these past few weeks. Eomore had been awakened by the king's messenger with a request that he join his father for breakfast. Eomore had hoped to dine with the rangers - there were so many friends that he had not seen these many weeks. Instead he had dressed in a fine silken cloak bearing the crest of the Aivendars which had been a gift from a grateful recipient of an earlier quest. The morning was bright and he received many greetings from the staff as he crossed the castle grounds and approached the living-quarters of the king. The guards were in their usual alert posture and snapped to attention when the prince passed between them. Eomore bid them a good day and went on into the mansion. The way to the dining hall was familiar and there was just as much bustle and activity as usual, as the staff went about the tasks of beginning another royal day. As he neared the great doors that opened into the chamber the prince thought that fighting goblins wasn't so bad after all.

The hall was more magnificent than he remembered. There were several unfamiliar faces. The king was sitting at the head of the table conversing with a well dressed man. Seated to the right of the man was a young woman who was adorned in all the finery available for money to buy. She raised her eyes to look at Eomore.

The prince walked over to the table, bowed deeply, and said, "My Lord, it pleases me to see you again. "

Eomore really did not care for the formality that his father insisted upon. He would have preferred to have run to the graying monarch, embraced him firmly, and said over and over again how greatly he loved and admired the man. But he had to do it the King's way.

"Welcome, my son; I have feared for your safety because of your delayed return. My table is graced by your presence, "the monarch said. "Allow me to..."

When the king began the introduction, Eomore found a smile come to his face that he saved for occasions such as this; his mind began to roam elsewhere. From time to time he returned to the room in mind as well as body to acknowledge a handshake and when the time was appropriate, he kissed the fair hand of the maiden. She was beautiful, more than most men could ever hope for, but for Eomore, the beauty seemed lost in the pigments that she wore; the hands were so soft; she would indeed be a good princess. But as a mate...

Eomore sat at the table and the food was delicious. He was courteous but no more, and he could sense the displeasure growing in the eyes and expressions of the king. The meal concluded, the guests excused themselves one by one, leaving the monarch and his son alone. King Eraitmus Aivendar was a dominating figure. He was handsome, eloquent, and in remarkable physical condition. He was in his early fifties and stood about two inches shorter than Eomore; his long gray hair flowed down his back and in his royal garb he was indeed impressive. He was a just and respected man - a large pair of shoes to fill. The two men stood and in the privacy of an empty hall; the embrace, which Eomore longed for, came about. The prince loved his father dearly, and would lay down his life many times over for him - actually, Eomore had risked his life many times already; but he would do it many times more. The differences between father and son were actually small to the eyes of an observer; the matter of settling down and betrothal came up again and again in their conversations, and it led to many quarrels between the men.

On matters of state there was no disagreement on the part of Eomore, but on matters involving his own private life, the prince readily expressed his opinions. The fundamental breakdown came in the king's feeling that a monarch really did not or could not have a private life.

"We exist for the people - it is our duty, our responsibility, and our bloodline's fate to serve them and protect them" Eomore had heard his father say many times.

The men retired to the chamber of audience where Eomore gave his father a detailed account of what had transpired in the southern province and also told him the story of the wounded elf. The wise eyes of the monarch saddened when he heard the tale, but as Eomore suspected the king could think of little to offer. Manpower at this time would be useless, for it had been a full week since the elves had lost the trail. The kings' troops did not include a tracker with the expertise of the elves, anyway. Not even the human bloodhound, as Nigel Louffette had sometimes been called, particularly by those who had known his victims, could pick up the trail now. The king was greatly disturbed by the description of these "Death Wraith" raiders - what could prevent them from invading Donothor itself and ravaging their own women and murdering their citizens.

"Eomore, I fear we will have little to offer these elves and this brave individual when he is strong enough to come before me. But I also feel that our own security may be at risk. We cannot protect our citizens if they venture into the Misty Forest or the Wastelands; we must protect them in their homes and villages.

I feel we must employ every means at our disposal to try to learn more about these night raiders, who murder and kidnap. I shall consult the sages but perhaps we need more. I feel I shall call on service from the wizard Roscoe to see if his sorcery can aid us. Also, I have need of council with the Priestess Knarra on this and other matters. I would like for you to gather an escort and proceed to the freehold of Knarra and ask the priestess if she will grace me with a visit to Lyndyn. I know that you are fatigued, my son, but it's two days there and two days back, and I feel a sense of urgency about this - I can't logically explain this. I shall send Boomer with a larger group to the castle of the mage Roscoe – he is again indebted to me and has forgotten to pay his tithe again; the wizard may be able to assist us a great deal in these matters, if he will. I know the man is unpredictable, but he is a good citizen and he will always come when I summon him. The way for Boomer will be more difficult because they will have to unavoidably cross the Wastelands. I'm sure Boomer will understand that I am not playing favorites; it's just that you've just returned." The king paused.

A look of great contemplation furrowed his brow.

Eomore answered, "Yes, my king, we will ride tomorrow."

He did not tell his father that he had felt waves of uncertainty and concern ever since he had reentered Donothor. This sixth sense he shared with the monarch; but it was not a quantitive thing, and it was not always accurate either. Eomore was not excited about so soon departing again, but at least the journey would be a fairly secure and comfortable one. And Knarra was a fascinating person.

Except for the elves, she was the most fascinating person he had known. Knarra had been the high priestess of the Fane of the Setting Sun for as long as anyone could recall. The Fane honored Hiram and Lydia the patron god and goddess of Donothor - many of the population worshipped these dieties, though many others were monotheistic or druidical. Knarra was just and good - she never turned away the needy from the doors of her temples and her curates were expected to infallibly follow her example. There were many legends about the high priestess and many also included the wizard Roscoe - there were stories that the two had adventured widely in their younger years. No one knew the actual age of the priestess. She seemed to be unaffected by the passage of time. She now appeared to be an attractive woman in her early thirties, but she had looked like this since Eomore had first seen her as a child. Again there were rumors that she and Roscoe had discovered the secrets of immortality, or at least powers of restoration and longevity. Some thought that powers beyond those of Magick kept the priestess from aging; at any rate she had not changed for many years in her physical appearance. Eomore would enjoy seeing the woman. Even if he did not share all of her beliefs, he respected her sincerity in them.

He turned to his father and excused himself. He had to seek out Boomer and relay the orders for the missions to him. Eomore found that he was relieved that the conversation had not turned to marriage. Even with the enigma facing them regarding the disappearance of the elven princess, he left this meeting with his father in good spirits.

He wanted to find the dwarf. There would be time for a few rounds of ale.

CHAPTER 8
The Dungeons of Castle Lyndyn

The entrance to the great dungeons was in the heavily fortified eastern end of the castle. These were an enduring reminder of the unparalleled abilities of the Dwarven craftsmen of Donothor.

The dungeons were guarded by a small force carefully selected from the ranger corps. A man had to serve loyally for a minimum of at least ten years, and even then potential guardsmen were subjected to the personal scrutiny of the High Priestess Knarra. She would scan each man in a way only that she could do for even a vestige of evil. The guards were treated well, and the positions carried a prestigious honor among the soldiers and the common citizenry as well.

At the base of the donjon, the easternmost and greatest tower of the citadel, a flight of stone stairs led downward for about a hundred paces. These ended in a great heavy oaken door. Beyond this door was the primary guard room. Here six of the elite force was on duty at all tines. The room was comfortably furnished with pleasant tapestries, a well-stocked library, each of the common board games, and quite ornate furniture. King Eraitmus realized the important role these men played in the schema of things in the castle and the king depended on these chosen vassals as a vital link in the defense of his subjects and his family. The walls of the room were solid stone, as it had been hewn from the solid rock of Mt. Lyndyn. There was a door on the far side of the room opposite the entrance. This was always kept locked. It was also a one-way door; that is it appeared as a solid wall from the opposite side. It could only be opened from the castle side. This was one of the crowning constructs of the originators of the dungeon catacombs.

The one-way door led to a smaller guard room. Here two guards were always stationed, on a rotating basis every eight hours as well. Not even these interior guards could open the secret door. This second room was lighted by an "orb of illumination" and contained the essentials for the guards. With the changing of each shift, the inner guards and the outer guards construed the code signal for the shift. A series of knocks from within the wall allowed the opening of the wall. The inner guards kept the key to the locked door leading from their chamber into the stairwells to the retention chambers. The stone stairs down were laced with pressure traps. If someone were not perfectly familiar with the passage downward, he was sure to trigger one of the devices. The Dwarves' architects who painstakingly constructed the dungeons had made the pressure traps undetectable to the naked eye and even the skill of loyal elves and dwarves at noting stone traps did not enable than to find the traps with any regularity. This was the stress test given the traps by the builders, and their creation passed with flying colors those many years ago. If an unwary foot landed in the wrong place, a stone dropped downward from the ceiling immediately, both twenty feet above and twenty feet below the site of the perpertration, completely sealing off the passageway, and at the same time the turning of the great wench at the head of the stairs alerted the inner guards that something was amiss. There the guards could ascertain exactly where the offenders were, and could trigger the release of a harmless but infallible sleep gas into the sealed portion of the stairwell.

All that would be left to do then would be to raise the blocking stones with the aid of the wench, and the guards could then return the slumbering would-be escapees to their cells below. These pressure points were placed randomly along the stair but occurred on an average of every fifty steps, and there were about five hundred steps in the total distance of the stairwell. As a precautionary measure, all prisoners were blindfolded and carried down the stairs to prevent any exceptionally cunning thief from somehow memorizing the proper sequence of steps. The dwarves were very complete in their efforts, and it was assumed that the stairs were infallible. But over the years the competency of the stairs had never been tested.

For the great five hundred steps led to a large cavern, which was partly natural and partly hewn from the stone by the little engineers. On the far side of this cavern was a locked door which led to the prison proper. Inside the cavern lived the ageless steadfast ally of the Aivendars who was the reason that the upper traps had never been challenged. Taekora, as she was called, had served the Aivendars for… a long time. Taekora, the ancient prismatic dragon, was devoted to the priestess Knarra. Knara and Taekora had spent years adventuring in the Iron Mountains and "in the east." Afterward Taekora had come to the first monarch of Lyndyn; a just man called Eigren, the patriarch of the Aivendar family. The dragoness offered her services. She remained loyal to succeeding generations, and willingly accepted the role as guardian of the people she loved against the escape of the lawless from their appointed prison. The dragoness was well treated by the princes of castle Lyndyn. The royal chefs, who were screened as scrutinously as the guards, always brought her ample food each day when they brought food to the prisoners. The prisoners never learned that the great beast was a vegetarian.

The key to the door opposite the entrance to her chamber was kept by Taekora in a locked chest. There were two keys to this chest; one was on a chain around the dragoness' neck, and the other was kept in the security of the palace vault. If the door were tampered with in any way other than with one of the aforementioned keys, the "fireglyph" placed by the high priest would be activated - this would surely be the bane of the violator.

When the prisoners reached the chamber of the great worm, their blinders were lifted, enabling them to clearly see the fully one hundred foot length of the monster. Her body was constantly changing it's hew - such was the nature of this species of dragon, accounting for the name. When the great beast engaged in combat, it would draw forth in its breath scintillating lights which temporarily blinded her opponents unless they managed to look away. When the unfortunates turned to face the dragoness, she had the ability to accentuate the prismatic scales covering her great length again effectively blinding them. Taekora also knew something of Magick, as did all dragons, but she had never been known to employ this. She had never tasted human flesh; she had been instructed to subdue and not kill any escapees. Of course, the prisoners were brought down without knowing this. The great worm would gingerly sniff each when he was brought down, acting as if he seemed a tasty morsel. After the ritual of meeting the mistress, the lawbreakers were then led to their waiting cells. There had never been an escape- from the dungeons of Castle Lyndyn - this was common knowledge amongst the riff -raff, and served as a deterrant to crime in the capital city.

The Aivendars were a just and kind people, and the dungeons were well kept and the prisoners were well treated. This was of little consolation to Nigel Louffette - he loved his freedom and the practice of his trade. The wiry thief had eluded the Donothorian Rangers for nearly a generation, but he had finally been "sniffed by the beast" - the most dreaded fate of the criminal. Nigel had tempted fate once too often, attempting to garnish the "Black Diamond," but it had only been a trap set by Boomer the Brave. Nigel cringed when he thought of the dwarf boisterously bragging about the capture of the master thief and rumored assassin who had evaded them so long. At least he had not been apprehended by Prince Eomore. That would be unbearable - as if this confinement were not so already. Nigel had his memories and enough successful adventures and forays across the line separating law and crime to occupy two lifetimes. But the criminal was no fool. He knew that he was saved from the noose only because many of his black deeds were not known to or else could not be proven by his captors. Eraitmus Aivendar would not allow an execution unless the crime was truly heinous and the evidence was unquestionably reliant. In his mind Nigel knew that he had been "heinous" on more than one occasion - it was just that the evidence had never been solid - that was of course due to his skill as an assassin. There had never been a better one. The, man was brilliant - unfortunately, for Nigel, that brilliant mind now could only reach the conclusion that he was here and here he would stay.

CHAPTER 9
Short Journeys

Cara and Cade began the journey north from Kanath the day following the departure of the rangers. The two elves were riding fine ponies and they were travelling light. Both were anxious to see the city of Lyndyn, but Cara's mind had visions of greater things. They went northward without any hindrance. They were frugal, and spent each night under the stars. They came to the crossroads and had to make the decision regarding the shortcut through the Misty Forest. They decided to heed the warning of the signs posted and elected to follow the main road, skirting the forest. Each minute seemed like an hour to Cara, but she passed the time riding lost in her thoughts about the tall rider. Cade talked incessantly and really required only minimal attention to keep the dialogue running. They were one day into the ride around the forest when Eomore and his party were reaching the gates of Lyndyn. They spent the night on the outskirts of a small trading town on the river, knowing that with good weather they were only three days from their destination.

Eomore had found Boomer in the barracks after he left his father. The dwarf was not exactly overjoyed about another quest through the "Wastelands" to summon the reclusive wizard.

"What kind of name is Roscoe, Eomore? I have never been told." The dwarf queried.

"Nor will you likely ever be, my friend. It is the name that his mageship has chosen to be called. Roscoe has dwelled in the land for many lifetimes of normal men. No one knows his origins, except for maybe Knarra the priestess. But neither of them has ever disclosed their secrets. There are many legends of the two leading adventures to make our lands safe in generations past, "Eomore answered.

Boomer was a dedicated servant of the king; he muttered a few less than complimentary phrases about Roscoe and suggested that they quaff a few and that they get a good night's rest before their respective journeys began. While they were socializing the two fighters were also deciding how to equip themselves and how many men each would have to take. Because Eomore's trip to Knarra's freehold would be brief and predictable, the prince had chosen to take only two other rangers and light weaponry.

Boomer on the other hand was facing a three-day trek across some of Donothor's wildest regions. Roscoe valued his privacy and he made it difficult for friend and foe alike to reach him - Boomer wondered if wizards had or even desired friends. They decided that the force should consist of six archers and six Swordsmen in addition to Boomer. The two friends drank until the early afternoon, and then parted company to make their preparations. Eomore returned to his room and enjoyed a brief conversation with Exeter - the sword was miffed about being left alone with no one to talk to, and she said she was anxious to get off on another quest, no matter how simple and mundane. It might get the prince back into a proper frame of mind. He slept well again that night, but his dreams moved from the "pleasantness" of the face of the elven girl, to the tragedy of his new found friend Vannelei, and finally to nightmares about the night raiders they knew only as Death Wraiths. He awakened in the morning with another feeling of dread - free floating fear – something was amiss - something was going to come to pass - he had begun to feel paranoid. The preparations for the journey were so routine that he had to think little about them. He had chosen Deron the dwarf and a man named Tjol Bergin to accompany him. Tjol was a hardened warrior with a mean streak that stemmed from his rough early years; he had been taken in as a waif by a ranger and had been raised as the man's son. Deron was gaining a reputation as one of the young lions of the ranger force. Eomore thought that traveling with the always composed and gentle Knarra might do both of these men good; some of their energies might be channeled in the direction of usefulness. Both were loyal, but both were rough around the edges.

When Eomore finished the morning meal with his unusually quiet father, he went to the stables, where he found the two groups gathering for the respective trips. Boomer was grumbling under his breath about the pomp that had to be afforded wizards and about his own luck - bad, of course. Nevertheless, the dwarf had his men getting ready in an orderly fashion. Deron and Tjol Bergin were there also.

They had three fresh horses and supplies for what should be a light journey to the freehold of Knarra. Eomore still took the precaution of wearing his chainmail and carrying Exeter. After a few words of mirth, the prince and his two companions mounted their horses and bid goodbye to the others. At least the weather was not an enemy this time. They were blessed with a lovely day. The mist-shrouded hills of the Misty Forest area were clearly visible to the south as the riders left the outer gates of Lyndyn. They passed the many small communities which existed for and in the shadow of the city, and stopped in the quaint taverns for excellent meals along the way. The first day was entirely uneventful and they rested in Cottsdale, a place many called the sister city of Lyndyn. They were travelling almost due east on this trek, and sat out again on the second leg of the trip the next morn. There were still few clouds, and then the three reached the Fane of the Setting Sun, the freehold of the priestess Knarra, the most powerful woman in all of Donothor.

The temple was well constructed. There was an outer battlement, made necessary by the warfare of earlier years, but the gate was never locked during the day. Knarra made all welcome. She was a renowned healer, and many physicians would travel with their ailing to seek her aid.

The outer curtain was made of stone and rose some forty feet; at intervals along its length turrets rose higher where at one time vigilant watch was kept. Now these were mainly ornamental bastions and added to the overall impressiveness of the sanctuary. The great stone gate was already open; the riders entered during the waning light of the afternoon sun. There was a hearty greeting from the gatesmen; once inside, the beauty of the grounds captivated the riders - nowhere in Donothor could there be found such floral beauty; even the royal horticulturists of Lyndyn were put to shame by the growing prowess of the priestess Knarra. Life seemed to flourish as well as be mended in the gentle hands of the woman. There were many citizens here worshipping or gladly giving of the earnings and labors - theoretically, there could be conflict between the king and the priestess, but the two were steadfastly loyal to each other - each seemed to recognize the role of the other and each was not threatened by the power and charisma of the other. There were the old barracks where many valiant sons of Donothor had rested in the wake of battle - now vacant these many years. The main temple building sat in the center of the stronghold at the highest point. From its pinnacle, an observer could scan the valley below. The temple had long been vital to the defense of the kingdom because of its strategic location on this high ground particularly those bygone times when the goblin hordes attacked from the east. The Aivendars had just ascended to power and united the plains peoples into the kingdom now known as Donothor. It was during these trying times that the alliance between the kings and the priests had been made strong.

But Eraitmus Aivendar and Knarra were far more than mere allies politically; the two were friends, having adventured together often in their young years there were even rumors of a near romance - but Eomore felt them unfounded. As he began to climb the steps to the sanctuary, the prince felt again inadequate; he was about to meet again one of the legends and beloved citizens of his land. He could feel his confidence ebb - if only the battlefield were the only place a prince had to prove himself. He had not seen Knarra for several years - they removed their headgear respectfully as they entered the sanctuary proper. The tall robed woman initially was turned away from them, bowing to abate the painful woulds of an injured child. Gracefully, she stood in a fluid motion and turned to face the three men. Her maroon robes flowed down her majestic body. Her face belied her age - the woman looked no more than thirty, but Eomore knew her to be many times that age. There were gentle curves outlined by the clinging robe, and Eomore hoped that his crass companions were not lusting after her, and then he wondered if he himself was. She was attractive in appearance, but when she spoke there was such a melodious quality to her voice that Eomore knew would calm the crying babe and soothe the savage beast. She placed several items into the aumbry, a recessed area in the wall. She faced the travelers.

The thin lips moved softly; she said, "Welcome, son of my dear friend. We are graced by your presence. I would hope that you are only here to visit and share the blessings that abound with us, but in your faces I read worry and consternation. What is your purpose?"

Eomore answered,"You are correct, my Lady. We are here at the request of my father Eraitmus to secure your aid and counsel."

"Let your companions refresh themselves while we talk, Eomore," Knarra replied.

Deron and Tjol left them and Eomore carefully spelled out the details of the recent events to the woman. He ended again with the request of his father for the priestess to accompany them to Lyndyn to discuss the worries on the mind of the king.

Knarra's kind face broke into feelings of pity when the prince was speaking. Her eyes were deep blue, and they seemed to look right into a man's heart and read his true meaning, bypassing the facades and charades created by reasoning and words. Her hair was blonde and flowed like a river down her back. Around her neck she wore a necklace of prayer beads and also a platinum holy symbol which seemed to illuminate her face, carefully outlining her features. No- her hair was blue Eomore noted as he told her more of Vannelei.

She spoke again, "I shall be honored to accompany you to the king. I've not seen him in so long. This story is indeed worrisome to me as well. We have enjoyed peace. We shall dine together and depart in the morning."

Eomore noticed the mangled little girl getting up and running to her father, with no obvious wounds. The prince went outside into the courtyard to seek out his companions.

Deron and Tjol had explored the freehold thoroughly while Eomore and Knarra were talking.

"I've never seen such a beautifully maintained area. There are plants here that I have never seen. There are libraries filled with priceless and rare volumes that stand open to anyone to enter." Tjol said, seeming awed by the Fane.

Deron chimed in,"Yes, there are treasures here that are unguarded that I would keep under double lock and key."

"Knarra feels that knowledge and beauty are things to be shared by all. Monetary value does not concern her," Eomore answered his comrades.

Tjol added,"There is but one little stone room with a simple oaken door that barred our entrance. I could see no opening mechanism; there was no doorknob or handle that we could find.. There were no windows. Etched over the door carved into the simple stone was a single word or phrase. I guess that it was in common tongue but I don't know what it means. "Lylysis" was the lettering. What does this mean, my Prince?"

Eomore shook his head negatively.

"Did you disturb the room?" he asked.

Eomore almost dreaded hearing the answer.

"I pushed on the door a little, but nothing happened," Tjol confessed.

"I might have struck it lightly with my ax," Deron confessed, blushing somewhat.

Eomore was upset that his men were so curious.

"I will apologize to our hostess for you," the Prince said.

Deron and Tjol felt as though they were early school students who had been chastised by their teacher.

Knarra only smiled when Eomore told her of his companions' audacious behavior; a wonderful dinner was prepared for them.

Eomore couldn't resist the temptation to ask,"What is the meaning of the word Lylysis, my Lady?"

"We must all have our secrets Eomore," the great healer replied coyly.

With that, Knarra suggested an early retirement so that they could get an early start toward Lyndyn.

"You may share the confines of my entire domain save two-"Lylysis" and my sleep chamber," the Priestess said, smiling wryly as she rose and left the table.

The rangers rose and bade their hostess goodnight. Eomore could swear that the color of the flowing tresses of the Priestess changed again as she changed her expression; the Prince assumed that the effects of fatigue and emotion were affecting his judgment and powers of observation.

Eomore simply said,"Behave yourselves."

Boomer watched his friends ride toward Knarra and wished that he were going with them. But the little man knew the meaning of duty and he went back to getting his own charges ready. They had a rougher journey than the prince, and there would be some hazard in crossing the fringes of the wastelands. They formed into a column of twos with Boomer in the front and rode briskly through the gates of the city, turning immediately to the west. After four hours of brisk riding, the terrain began to roughen and the settlements began to become sparser. In the distance the Black Mountains towered in the center of the

Wastelands; their snowcapped peaks were so alien to the usual temperant clime of Donothor. The party stopped and dined at one of the inns that had up a "last chance for good food "sign.

They continued to make good time as they rode on into the afternoon, but by dusk, the road was rockier and the forests were thicker, and their guard was forced up. They stopped in a camp area that was tried and true, and the night was interrupted only by a brief encounter with a wandering bear who decided he wasn't hungry enough to tangle with this honery bunch. There were the usual calls and screams and uncertainties that the darkness always brought, but this veteran group slept well except during their appointed turns at guard. The morning came quickly and they were off to an early start. Boomer wanted to cross as much of the Wastelands as they could by day. The Wastelands was not as foreboding as the Lachinor to the south, but it was wild, much like, but more so than, the Misty Forest. There were many places easier to get raw materials and necessity has not forced the development of these areas.

The trees and foliage often darkened the sky; the foliage grew over the passageway which was loosely referred to as a road. At times they had to get into single file. It was one such time that the first encounter came. The party was advancing along a rocky segment when the rear exploded into a deafening scream. Boomer quickly raised his hands to his ears and hoped enough of his men would as well. He felt ringing in his ears, but he had been in tine. The seconds the scream lasted seemed more like an eternity, but eventually the Wailer had to stop to breathe himself, and Boomer knew the great catlike beast could only muster the volumn every few hours. He turned to see eight of his men stunned by the great noise and falling from their horses.

"Only five of us!" the lieutenant moaned, as he saw the dark feline form bounding toward them from the wood. The beast was deep red with fiery eyes and snarled incessantly as it charged. The men dismounted, preparing to meet the beast.

Unfortunately three of the five were bowmen, and there had not been enough time to get off an arrow shot. Indeed the wailer seized the rearmost archer and ripped him apart as the others retreated behind the charging swordsmen. Boomer and the other veteran attacked the great cat with their own animal-like fury. Othan, the second man, and Boomer had been in many scrapes together, but never had the two of them faced a full-grown wailer. The other two men were retrieving swords from their stunned comrades, but at this moment Boomer and Othan had to keep the beast of the woods at bay or else it would feast on ranger for many days. The beast swiped at Boomer with a great paw with alarming agility, at the same time biting at Othan. Boomer managed to avoid the blow but in parrying lost most of his momentum on his sword stroke, with the result being only a minor wound to the paw. Othan was taken back by the gaping maw, escaped injury, but lost his swing. Just a little more time - Boomer reflexively plunged his weapon at the chest of the beast as it reared to attack again; Othan following his lead. This time the fighters scored, and the beast's maroon fur began to darken with its own dark blood. The animal howled, dropped back a few feet, and then poised to attack again. By this time the other two men were flanking it. The men swung the weapons, but the bowmen lacked authority, being less proficient in the use of the longsword. The animal won this round. It turned with astonishing speed and the bowman fell to the force of the paw blow. He rolled to the side of the pathway, but was still breathing, though unconscious. The beast righted itself again and came right at Boomer. The dwarf dropped to the ground, rolled to the side, and delivered a deep abdominal wound to the beast. A heavy hindpaw racked across his right leg and Boomer felt the initial numbness, then the searing pain where the talons opened his flesh - but the beast had felt the last wound.

It rolled in fury, and then turned to again charge the men, seemingly unaffected by the multiple wounds. The four fanned out, awaiting the charge. The wailer roared and headed straight toward Boomer, leaving him wondering what he had done to be so fortunate and thinking thoughts like "what's wrong with those guys". But he stood ready and lept aside just as the forepaw ripped the air where he had been standing. His sword missed its mark as well, but Othan was able to land a strong blow. The archers again demonstrated their incompetence with edged weapons. The great cat righted itself again but was laced by three blades before it could muster enough strength to charge. Its dark blood covered the ground and as it hesitated, all four struck again, with Othan driving his sword into the back of the creature to the hilt - with a heavy thud the wailer met the earth and thrashed in its death throes. The men were breathing heavily for the fight had been far too close for comfort. Boomer bound the bleeding wound on his leg and turned to face the losses. One man was dead, but there had been no other critical wounds. The four went about arousing their comrades, but the stunning effect lasted several more minutes before they awakened. The party then interred the slain ranger deeply into the ground off the road and marked the gravesite subtlely, hoping to avoid furnishing an easy repast for an intelligent monster. Boomer began to feel the aching in the wound that he knew was coming. He had cleaned it thoroughly and now the treatment was tincture of time.

They proceeded onward without further incident before dusk, though they could sense they were being watched by many hungry eyes. They found a reasonably secure campsite at the base of a cliff with a brief open area before it - they were exposed, but so was anything that hoped to attack them.

The second night of their journey passed with a more somber atmosphere than the first. Other than a few nuisance interruptions such as an easily discouraged cave tiger and a small pack of deranged weremen who stumbled onto the camp, the night passed uneventfully. Boomer thought of Eomore and Deron, who by now were probably feasting with the gracious Knarra, as he gnawed on his dried beef.

The next morning, the men elected to follow the cliffs. They would reach Roscoe's castle by sundown if they were lucky. The cliffs gave them a false sense of security, false because they had traveled no more than two hours when the loud harsh screeches let them know that someone else wanted to have them for dinner. The birdmen were rare now in Donothor; unknown to Boomer, this small group was nesting in the cliffs. Unfortunately, they were fond of human flesh and seemed ravenous. It was a peculiar species. The females were small fragile things that could not even fly and were cared for by their vicious mates. There were a lot of theories as to the origins of the strange creatures with wingspans greater than eight feet and strong barbed claws that could easily tear a man apart. The men dismounted, cursing their fate and this journey, and prepared to do battle once again. Here the archers proved their worth. As the dark forms dived upon the men, the bowstrings hummed, and five of the winged attackers fell to their deaths. Boomer found that the power of flight was a potent counter to an accomplished swordsman, and after two unsuccessful swings, he reached for his bow. Othan had been luckier - his strong right arm had brought down to one of the foul fowl that had been a bit too brazen. The archers reloaded and fired again as the creatures regrouped and dived again.

The winged creatures had accomplished nothing with their first attack, but this time they were angered by their losses and failures.

The bows fired.

Boomer missed and had to move strategically downward to the ground - that's how he would describe the battle if he ever got back to the bars. He saved himself by throwing down his bow and falling face first to the ground. The diving birdman, expecting contact, had too much momentum and could not pull up from its dive he crashed into the cliff wall and fell with his wings damaged. The dwarf gathered up his sword and gladly slew the beast. On the ground, Boomer was in his element and was too much for him. The other archers managed to drop three more of the flyers, but one unfortunate bowman felt the full force of the talons and fell limply to the ground. Othan was quickly to his aid and his great blade killed three of the beasts as they landed to gather their spoils. With their numbers rapidly dropping the birdmen screeched angrily and retreated. Quickly Boomer directed his men to gather themselves and get to the cover of the forest. The fallen archer would recover, but his wounds would force the others to aid him; he could not ride alone.

They remounted and rode on.

A sense of urgency fell over them and they pushed themselves. Exhausted, they reached the end of the cliffs and deep forests; the gloomy castle of the archmage rose in the distance. Not many monsters prowled the area near the castle. The wizard did not take kindly to it, and had singed many unwary beasts with his fire spells. The castle itself was tended by the macabre creations of the wizard plus a few persons and things loyal to him for whatever reasons. No one knew how old Roscoe was. The royal historians could only guess. He had clearly lived beyond the normal span, yet he appeared as a robust bearded man in his middle years. The mage was tall and rather thin, but his physical strength was exceptionable. The man was as mysterious as the arts he practiced.

The weary party of rangers closed the gap between themselves and the gray castle as the sun reached its ebbing stage. The castle moat teemed with various and sundry creatures and a rather ragged looking man stood on the far side of the moat - clearly the outer portcullis guard. There was a stone area before the castle proper and several large statues were located there. Some were chipped and weathered. The guard stood by the heavy portcullis that had been used to raise the bridge covering the moat. There was an open area in the castle wall but there was no door jam. He saw the approach of the men, but did not seem to recognize the banners of the house of Aivendar.

"Go away, "he uttered; the raspy voice managed enough intensity to span the moat.

"We must have audience with your master at once, "Boomer responded.

"The master wishes no disturbances - go away! "The voice was more emphatic.

Boomer was in no mood for this. The journey had cost him a man, and his own leg was aching from the wailer wound.

"You either drop this bridge or I'm going to jump over and..." Boomer was interrupted by the sudden loud grating sounds that signified the lowering of the heavy bridge.

A tall figure stood in the darkness of the aperture leading into the castle. He was flanked by two figures that dwarfed him. The man outside the castle bowed deeply when tall figure spoke.

"Your impatience does not surprise me, Boomer, but the man was only following his orders. Do you not expect the same of your men?" the man asked, with sarcasm dripping from every word.

"Roscoe, I am here at the request of my king, Eraitmus Aivendar, who asks..." again the dwarf was interrupted.

"I know why you are here. You have made your presence well known in the wilds. I do regret your misfortune. I yearn for the days of the shadows. I suppose the growth of civilization drove them away. I've yet to find servants as loyal. Enter now to rest your men. My servants will dress your wounds and feed you. "The mage said.

Roscoe turned and walked into the castle. The two huge figures motioned for the men to follow. A haggered giant and an immense golem pointed the way. The golem bore great resemblance to the statues in the castle foreground- he was moving.

Bizarre was not an adequate word to describe the enceinte, the quadrangle, of the gray castle. The tastes of a wizard left a bit to be desired. Roscoe's eccentricity was renowned. Overall, the place was rather austere, but there were areas of finery. The men passed several rooms filled with many volumes, and several other rooms with large tables covered with flagons of fluids, smoldering incenses, and unrolled scrolls. There were large collections of the things he needed to practice his trade. Boomer shuddered as he glanced into the different rooms. He didn't know the nature of the experiments and he didn't want to know either. He briefly remembered that Eomore and Knarra should have reached the sister city and were half way back to Lyndyn. The men separated with Roscoe and Boomer leaving the others to enter the main study of the mage. A black cat hissed at Boomer as he entered, then jumped upon the wizard's shoulder. Boomer looked at the man - the gray beard drooped down covering his neck, but the fineness of his facial features were still apparent. He would probably be considered handsome by many women's standards; his hair was a stately thick gray to match the beard; his deep green eyes favored those of a forest elf. He wore a loosely fitting robe with many arcane symbols upon it; there were many pockets.

"My dwarven friend, I sense more than a consultation is at hand. At any rate, it is better to be prepared. These Draiths sound tough, don't they?" the wizard spoke; he went about the various parts of the room.

Boomer muttered a reply, but continued to watch the tall man. He did not seem to waste a single motion. Everything he did seemed to have to be done in an exact way. Such was the way of magic users. Roscoe placed two leather bands around his wrists, and then placed several carefully wrapped items into the oversized pockets in his robe.

He opened the drawer in his great desk, after muttering a phrase in some forgotten tongue. He gingerly removed a large leather bound book and inserted it beneath his robe, binding it to his chest. He then took an ornate staff from aumbry in the corner, and motioned to the cat, which leaped into the largest pocket of the cloak. He picked up a container from the desk top, and then turned to the dwarf.

"I'm sorry to leave you, but I feel a sense of necessity about this and feel I should use my own mode of travel. You may rest here as long as you need. My servants have been told to make you comfortable and to tend your wounds. I shall go to the king," Roscoe said.

Roscoe then began to contort his face and to utter phrases that the weary dwarf could not begin to comprehend. The mage then threw some of the gray powder from one of his many vials into the air and began to gesture with his large hands. The room filled with a grayish mist; there was a deafening clap of thunder and a blinding flash of light. The mage was gone.

Boomer sank into the chair. His thick muscular leg ached and he was feeling all of the strain of the past three days. He had accomplished his mission with minimal losses. He thought of Eomore and Knarra again; how he would like to visit the fascinating kind woman again. He hoped these powerful citizens of his land would be able to help the noble elf and to discover a way to recover the princess of the elves. But he was merely a fighter and he had served the king as directed. He would allow his weary men some rest in the security of the castle of the wizard. They would return to Lyndyn in a few days. The giant came into the room and dressed his wound. Dwarves held a natural mistrust for the giants; the peoples had warred since… the peoples had always warred. Braak, as the giant was called, tried to make the visitors comfortable. The dwarf stretched himself and fell asleep in the armchair in the chamber of the archmage of Donothor.

CHAPTER 10
Night of Terror

Oren Bach was as rotund as any kitchen master had ever been. He was especially happy with the young lady that his cousin Rebaccah Frathingham had sent and recommended to him. He had taken her to the royal leisure chamber to introduce her to the monarchs, for the Queen wanted to personally screen all new kitchen servants. Oren Bach wasn't sure what to do with the young male elf. He supposed that he might work out as an errand boy.

Cara's stomach felt as though every butterfly in the kingdom was there and struggling to get out; she walked down the long corridors from the kitchen areas to the family room of the castle. She had freshened herself and bathed earlier and wore one of her native green dresses. Her eyes scanned the art works along the torchlit corridors as she walked along. Oren talked more than her brother Cade, if that were possible, so Cara did not have to keep up much of the conversation as they walked along. They came before the great doors and saw the ever present royal crest of the Aivendar family. Cara's heart raced as she remembered the first time she had seen that crest, on the vest cloak of the tall warrior called Eomore. She felt a sudden urge to turn and run as the chef turned the great levers and the massive doors opened inward into a brightly lit chamber. There were several people seated in the overstuffed chairs in the room. The walls were lined with tapestries that were finer than anything that she had ever seen. Most of them depicted scenes from life in the pastoral kingdom, but some depicted the past glories of the Aivendar men in battle. There was a large table in the center of the room. On it were silver and golden serving pieces and numerous trays of fresh fruits and vegetables. The chef announced their entrance; Cara felt the gazes of many pairs of eyes. Anxiously she scanned the room.

She saw an older man and woman seated near the large fireplace where the logs burned brightly. They were dressed in garb befitting a king and queen. Near the king sat a noble elf with his arm bandaged. She recognized him from the inn. He was called Vannelei and he possessed the saddest pair of eyes she had ever seen. There was a beautiful young woman combing her long tresses by the fire near the queen who smiled at them as they entered. Cara guessed that she was near her own age. There were several heavily armed guards standing about the room who were so motionless that they reminded her of the toy wooden soldiers that her brother played with as a child. The queen beckoned to them and they went over to the group. Cara realized that the prince was not among the party; she could feel her heart sink a little, but since she really didn't know what to do when she did see him again, she felt some relief at the same time. The introductions were formal, and Cara bowed deeply to each person and managed a smile. She sat down and they talked quite awhile.

There was a great flash of violet light followed by a deep green smoke. Everyone in the room was startled and the guards ran to the side of the king. When the smoke cleared, a tall man in a robe stood silently. There was a black cat sitting upon his shoulder. The men relaxed.

Roscoe had arrived.

The night air was unusually cool, and the sky was moonless and very dark. There was silence which seemed accentuated over the norm. Rayton had served the king as a ranger for more than twenty years but his hand was not as quick as before so he had served as a guard on the castle perimeter for the past three years. There was some prestige to this duty and Rayton knew that he had the confidence of the king. His family was well treated by the Aivendars. The duty was not strenuous and largely just a formality.

Rayton never saw or heard his attacker. A great dark hand came against his throat that shattered his spine and he fell silently and lifelessly to the ground.

The streets were not very busy and on this cold night the party of several dark robed characters did actually not look unusual at all. Their progress was unimpeded until they reached the shadows of castle Lyndyn.

Izitx had researched well and it was paying off. The soft conversation of the two men in front of the wrought iron gates was easily heard by the keen ears. With a great leap two dark figures flew into the night air, and the victims did not have time to react. There was a muffled moan, then only two dark forms towering over the crumpled bodies. The gate was opened and silently they ascended the stairs. Three more guards fell as they were unfortunately in their assigned locations. Izitx smiled at the predictability of the humans - it would be their undoing - and they fell so easily. They scaled the wall of the castle easily and one by one dropped through the window leading to the hallway that led to the bedroom of the quarry. Silently they proceeded to the door and and then leaped into the room. They were met with an empty chamber. Izitx frowned. For the first time his plans had gone astray. The others looked toward him. He thought deeply - the fallen guards would soon be discovered and in numbers these humans might be a problem, particularly if angered. His mind retraced what he knew of the castle and the habits of the humans. They would have finished their meal - of course, the family room as the humans called it. The smile returned to the evil hard face. He quickly instructed the others on the change of plans. The dark party then exited the room.

A woman came out of one of the adjacent rooms and met her death from a single blow from the nearest Draith. Izitx knew the exact route, and soon they stood outside the room they were seeking. The Draith scouts listened at the door. There was much conversation. Izitx bade his minions good hunting and threw open the doors. The nine Draiths entered the room. Izitx lingered at the entry to survey the room.

Shock fell over the royal family and their guests. The recent arrival of the magic user was still the topic of discussion and the king had just finished the introductions; Vannelei stood and drew the Sword of Cyratiel. Two guards stood before the king and queen. Oren Bach leaped under the table. Roscoe turned to face the door, and Cara stood near the king. The Dark Intruders moved with incredible speed. They did appear as the wraiths of legend.

The first guards fell before than, without really getting in an effective blow. Two Draiths began to move toward the king and the others fanned out into the room. Unfortunately there had only been six rangers in the room and two were already dead. But the Draiths were in for more of a fight than even Izitx had anticipated. For Karder

71

Lin the champion had drawn duty this fateful night. The champion responded to the attackers with tenacity and his long sword found the thorax of the first Draith to reach the king's area. The wounded raider had found the rangers platemail and the force of his blow was ineffective. In the far end of the room the two guards fell before the marauders leaving that area undefended and three Draiths began to flank the noble Karder and his remaining companion. However, Roscoe had not been idle. The mage began an incantation and leveled his long finger at the advancing Draiths; there appeared a glowing light of mauve color which began at the wavering digit then fanned out to encompass the three and the room filled with the odor of burning flesh.

Two of the three fell motionlessly and the third writhed in agony on the floor. By now Vannelei was standing by the side of Karder and the three stood ready to defend the monarchs. Eraitmus drew forth his ornamental septre and prepared to wield it as a heavy mace. Ignoring the pleas of Karder and Vannelei, the king stood beside the fighters before his terrified womenfolk.

From the door Izitx gave an angry snarl when the magical fire had slain the three Draith scouts, for the third had soon stopped his anguished throes. The remaining six scouts approached the four men attempting to separate them. Izitx drew forth a device from under his cowl and slinked into the room. The first Draith charged Vannelei. In his well state the elf may have had a chance, but the charging foe managed to avoid the thrust of the Sword of Cyratiel and the elf narrowly avoided a fatal neck wound. He still took the full force of the blow to his upper chest and the sickening snap of his collarbone could be heard around him. He fell from the force of the blow, at the mercy of his foe, and slipped into unconsciousness. The Draith raised his dark hand and prepared to deliver the death blow as he snapped the blade of the elven sword with his massive foot, when his own great body was lifted high into the air and fell with a crushing force against the far side of the room. Cara could see the hand of the mage directing the journey of the attacker through the air. Fortunately Roscoe had anticipated the vulnerability of the elven prince. The fallen Draith stood and attempted to reenter the fray. Simultaneously, the ranger to the right of Karder fell with a fatal wound to his chest, suffering a direct blow over his heart from the clutched fist of the tall opponent. Not even the platemail had protected him. Karder had once again at least broken even with his opponent slicing across the forearm of the Draith as the blow glanced off his breastplate.

The king relied on the savvy gained through years of campaigns. His septre parried the attack of the first opponent. But now, there were only two, and five Draiths surrounded them. The sixth, the one in the door, moved rapidly around the room. The king was unsuccessful in his second parry; the hand of his attacker glanced from the mace to his brow; he fell stunned to the floor. Karder felled the previously wounded Draith with a deep chest wound, but it was to be the last heroics of the great veteran, for the other three descended upon him and he fell to the blows.

Roscoe had been repositioning himself as he saw the ineffectiveness of the fighters stand. He attacked as the Draith prepared to finish the fallen king. A bolt of the electricity flew from the mage's hand and blasted the Draith into oblivion. The others turned to face the wizard. Roscoe did not like the odds - five of these birds in the various parts of the room; he could not watch them all. His eyes turned toward Izitx - he began an incantation and gestured in the direction of the Draith leader - the dark hands raised an orb and as the mage pronounced his spell the forces seemed to concentrate in the small orb and flew back toward the caster. Roscoe howled as his own spell struck him, and he fell stunned to the floor. The hideous Izitx barked commands to the others and moved toward the fallen mage, planning to exact his vengeance. The women were at the mercy of the marauders who seemed to have a definite plan; Izitx felt his anger grow as he closed upon his foe. He looked at the five bodies of his scouts. Only four remained and there would be other guards to fight. They had to complete the mission.

So far the screams of the women had not brought any other opponents into the room. He now stood over Roscoe, and the mage was just beginning to arouse.

"Wake up. Time to die, "Izitx muttered in the common tongue.

He did not know much of the human tongues, but these words seemed especially pertinent. He laughed hideously as he raised his massive forearm. Roscoe's eyes were foggy as he faced his doom when suddenly the Draith was struck by a blast of white-hot heat. Izitx howled in agony and rolled across the floor. Roscoe aroused enough to see the frail dark elven female beginning to gesture again. Izitx managed to reach his feet, barked to the others, and demanded a reply.

He screamed "Another day!"

He led the other four toward the door.

As consciousness left Roscoe he saw that the last two carried a blanket; he noted its occupant moved futilely within their grasp. The other two assisted their badly wounded leader. With haste, they exited the chamber.

Cara looked in terror around the room. Near Roscoe lay the fragments of the shattered orb, dropped by the leader when she had wounded him. Oren scurried out from under the table and ran to summon the royal physician. Cara ran to the mage; the Queen attended the king; Roscoe was already awakening when she reached him. He motioned to Vannelei.

Moments later the healer Sedoar entered with his assistants and quickly began his efforts. The king was aroused and did not seem to be seriously wounded. The elf was in a great deal of pain, but likewise would survive.

Roscoe stared inquisitively at the frail elven woman.

The queen emitted a horrified undecipherable scream.

Looking around the room for the first time, they noted that Princess Trya was missing.

CHAPTER 11
Aftermath

The room was quiet as the physician and his aides attended the wounded, and the victims of the sudden attack tried to regain some of their senses and composure. The king recovered quickly; though physically wobbly, he urged Sedoar to attend the others and managed to reach one of the overstuffed chairs by the table. By this time the commotion had brought several guardsmen to the sitting room; they were visibly dismayed by the scene. Eraitmus summoned one of these men to him and instructed him to bring the commander of the ranger force. In the absence of Eomore and Boomer, this duty fell upon the broad shoulders of a tall veteran warrior named Gosway.

Soon thereafter, the fully armored Gosway stood before the king. By this time Roscoe was straightening his garb and its myriad of contents. The mage picked up a dried spider which had fallen from one of the overstuffed pockets of the cloak, then began to study the fragments of the tiny orb which had so nearly been his bane.

Vannelei was in a great deal of pain, but his wounds were not critical. The physician's assistants tried to assist him to the infirmary, but the valiant elf directed them to help him to the side of the king; he struggled into an adjacent chair.

Cara continued to try to comfort the distraught queen; the young elf was shying away from the gazes of the perplexed wizard.

"I was already armed, my Lord, as that is my custom when I command, but I was inspecting the dungeons when this carnage occurred. I came to you as quickly as I could. I have heard from my men that we suffered heavy losses among the castle guards and perimeter guards as well. We were able to detect the direction of their escape; one of the tower guards saw the dark shapes fleeing toward the Wilderness Road and not in the direction of the Black Fen. My men have readied our fastest horses and I shall go now to bring justice upon them, or die trying," the big man said.

His voice cracked with emotion as he spoke to the king.

"My noble servant, your courage and loyalty do my saddened heart and aching bones uplift, but your plan is not the best," the king said, trying to speak resolutely, but all who listened could tell the he had to force almost every word. "The misfortune of our new friend Vannelei teaches us that these vile creatures are indeed difficult to track. If a trained party of elven hunters could not successfully follow them, I doubt that our horsemen would be able to do so at night."

"I fear the king is right, brave warrior," Vannelei followed. "Their trails are but wisps and are far too subtle for even the best of trackers. These foes are as wraiths. They rob us of life with their bare hands and destroy our finest weapons by merely the force of their weight. They seem more sinister than anything that has emerged from the great Black Fen of the south. Their trail moves away from the source of our most frequent enemies. We must have all our resources available to us before we begin the pursuit; I say this with a heavy heart for I know the anguish of losing one deeply loved. But a hasty chase would destroy all hope of regaining her."

"Gosway, I want you to send your fastest horse and most able rider directly to the east, toward the sister city. He should meet my son Eomore in the early hours. He should be traveling the main road with the priestess Knarra. We will need their strength and wisdom if we expect success." The monarch said.

The king placed his hand upon the shoulder of the warrior as he spoke. He could sense the frustration in the eyes of the man who had served him so loyally for so many years. Gosway was a man of action and delay frustrated him.

The king turned toward Roscoe as if to ask if the wizard approved his decision.

Roscoe stared back and nodded, saying, "I too think we should learn from what Vannelei has told us. I myself long to meet the dark commander again, but we should organize ourselves. Eomore and Knarra will be a great help. We will need the greatest trackers in the kingdom as well. If I knew exactly where they were and if I didn't feel I should stay to protect you, I'd teleport to the freehold." The mage spoke in an emotional voice.

Gosway turned, excused himself, and whirled out the room.

He said as he exited, "All men have been called to duty, my Lord. The security of the city must not again be breached."

Then he was gone.

Roscoe walked over to Cara.

"Who are you?" he asked.

The question was not asked in an entirely friendly tone, even though the elven girl had just recently saved his life.

"I am called Cara," she answered, not volunteering any more about herself.

"Why have I never heard of you? You are alarmingly familiar to me," the mage continued.

By now the others were in tuned to their conversation.

"I am from Kanath, sent here with the recommendation of Madam Frathingham to serve in the kitchens of the king," she replied, hoping this would satisfy the inquiring mind of the wizard; she was wrong.

Roscoe wanted to know everything about everybody and everything in the land.

He continued, "Before Kanath, maiden?"

Cara blushed and at the time wished to be anywhere else.

She struggled with the words, "My brother and I were orphaned as small children; I know little of my past. We were brought to Kanath years ago by one of the merchant caravans and have lived there since."

"How do you come by the Magick, my dear? I doubt you could have stumbled upon the powers. Tell me how you came to possess these powers?" he continued.

"I… I'm gifted. I… I don't really understand it myself. I've read the old book many times but it doesn't even explain. It merely…" she stopped.

Roscoe still as not totally persuaded that the whole story was being told; Cara, of course, knew that it was not; it ended there.

The king interrupted to say, "From what I've been told, we are greatly in your debt, Cara. I shall want you involved in the next day's discussion."

"But my Lord, I am but a simple servant girl – I just did what I could to help. I know nothing of strategies and tactics. I would be like a minotaur in a china shop on any quest," Cara answered.

"I conscript your powers, maiden. We all will have to contribute what we can. The tactics will be the responsibility of my son Eomore. The wisdom I'll entrust to Knarra. The trickery will fall to you, Roscoe," the king said, beginning to feel the agony of his wounds as he finished.

"Sire, you must accompany me to the hospital," pleaded the physician Sedoar; this time the king yielded to his persuasiveness.

Gosway shed many tears as he walked to complete the task placed before him by the king. He chose the three fastest horses and the three best riders that he had and gave them the instructions to journey to the east to find Eomore. He thought to himself that is would have been so much easier for the mage to teleport, but, as Roscoe had said, there was no way of knowing the exact location of the prince and his party. Roscoe might spend the entire night aimlessly looking for them; repeated teleportation spells would needlessly tire the magic user; they would be no better off. For, although the great wizard loathed admitting it, Roscoe's powers were not without limits. In addition to the many arcane incantations and obscure ingrediants, rest was a major requirement for the regeneration of those powers.

The king was right. They needed to speed up the arrival of the prince. What a baneful thing that Boomer and Eomore were away at the same time! But what a fortunate thing that Roscoe and the dark elf were in the party of the king at the time of the attack!

Gosway wished his horsemen success. With any luck, they should meet the prince on the main road and should be able to expedite their journey back to Lyndyn. The rangers had trailed the invaders a short distance along the Wilderness Road, but had returned without pursuing further; they were not strong enough or organized enough to successfully engage the awesome opponents. At least the guards knew the general direction of their flight; it was not the anticipated. The night raiders were headed away from the Lachinor. Their trail went northwest.

CHAPTER 12
Bad News on the Road to Lyndyn

Eomore and Knarra were enjoying their journey together. The prince was fascinated by the vivaciousness of the woman who was adored by so many Donothorians. They had rested well and joined their two companions for a hot meal before beginning the journey that would return them to the capital city of Lyndyn. Some of the difficulties of the past few weeks left Eomore's mind as they conversed. Of course Knarra could not converse with Exeter, but the sword also enjoyed the talks. Eomore was somewhat surprised that Exeter would admit that any other female personality would be worthwhile companionship, but the High Priestess Knarra emanated an aura of charisma and wisdom. She exhibited an outer beauty that was difficult to describe with words. Many defeated enemies had embellished Knarra's stature with assertions that she possessed and used a powerful charm spell. Legend were the stories of campaigns into the Black Fen led by Knarra and Roscoe in days past- generations of men of Donothor had passed since the campaigns to defeat the evil wizard Boormark. Eomore was not the best student of history. There were many stories of the adventures of the wizards.

Yet Knarra's appearance remained youthful.

The four began the trip uneventfully with well fed and fully rested horses. They had ridden for an hour, passing numerous citizens going about their day to day activities, when they saw several horsemen coming rapidly toward them. Eomore grasped the hilt of the sword but received only the message that these were the kings' men and not enemies. Gosway had chosen well as the riders had accomplished their assigned task.

"Hail, prince – I bring sad and woeful tidings," began the sergeant of the guards, "for the princess Trya is a victim of treachery. She is carried away in the night by the dark raiders. Many of our people are slain, with even the king and the mage Roscoe injured in the fray. The great warrior Karder Lin is slain, defending the King. His majesty asks that you ride with great haste to the palace."

Eomore felt the same apprehension that he had while riding on the road to the hamlet Kanath. Only now there was a reason for the feeling. He was feeling "fear" not "free-floating fear." The sensation was the same!

The lovely little princess, his sister Trya, kidnapped by these little known Draith creatures! His father wounded! Many friends slain! The sanctity of his home violated! He managed to ask about his father; the man replied that the king had been stunned but was now in the care of the physician and again with his senses. It was Knarra who asked about the mage; Exeter was the only one of the group to sense the great relief on the learned face of the priestess when she heard that the wizard was safe.

Eomore dismissed the men, directing them to an inn up the road. The four hastened their pace. There was not much conversation now; they realized the bleakness of the time. Eomore remembered that the elves had been unable to follow the trail of the creatures, and he knew the great skill the fair people possessed in this area.

He wished for a human bloodhound, but then remembered that these had been extinct for many generations. Most had been destroyed through the efforts of the organized thieves' guilds from the Black Fen and Lachinor's depths. The closest thing to one of the dog people in this tracking ability had to be the infamous Nigel Louffette, but Nigel used his abilities in other ways.

By early afternoon the towers of the city of Lyndyn loomed in the distance and the small group of riders moved swiftly toward them. The gates were heavily guarded and the large outer gates were drawn closed for the first time in Eomore's memory. The guards quickly identified the party members and the great chains in the inner portcullis strained to draw open the gate. Eomore pitied the laboring steeds; the prince would assure rewards for the loyal stallions.

The trip through the city was hastened by the guards, who were everywhere in the quadrangle and cleared the hysterical public from the paths of the prince and his party. Those who saw Eomore seemed to develop an expression of relief, and the prince immediately began to feel those old feelings of uncertainty in his role as the chief protector of the kingdom. Once they reached the palace, Eomore and Knarra were given escort to the main council chamber of the king.

Deron and Tjol were quickly assigned to other duties; Deron resumed the command of the perimeter guards.

The inner ward was also heavily guarded. Fear was a new emotion for this generation of Donothorians; the Aivendars had so dominated the evil forces from the Wilderness to the west, the Iron Mountains to the east, and the Black Fen and the Lachinor to the south. Trepidation was there now in the eyes of each servant that they met, and apprehension was evident even in the highly trained guards of the king. The prince and priestess reached the main chamber in the west wing of the castle and entered. There were four heavily armed guards at the door and also special defenses which were the work of Roscoe, no doubt; one of the guards whispered a phrase into the doorknob and the handle turned, allowing them to enter.

The room was filled with the most powerful citizens of the kingdom. King Eraitmus Aivendar sat silently at the table; his hands were folded in front of him on the great table; the monarch had a look upon his face that made him appear as though he were in another dimension. His wife sat by his side just as motionless. Roscoe sat alone in the far left of the room and appeared to be lost in leather-bound vellum, his brow wrought in concentration. Eomore recognized most of the king's trusted advisors seated in various places around the table. The elven prince was seated at the table with a large bandage covering the left side of his chest. There were also guards within the chamber. It was so foreign to see the castle so much like a fortress, though Eomore had heard many stories of similar situations from his grandfather those many years ago. Just as his ears became aware of the words of his father welcoming them home, his eyes met the haunting gaze of the dark elven female, who was seated on the hearth behind the table. Fate had in some way brought him back to these eyes that he had seen in his mind so many times since he left Kanath. Eomore briefly became oblivious to the rest of the room when the soothing voice of Knarra brought him back.

Knarra answered the king: "Eraitmus, my heart grieves that we must meet under such remorseful circumstances. I shall do any and all that I can to assist in this matter."

The priestess then turned toward Roscoe and their eyes met in an out of the ordinary manner. Not a phrase was uttered, yet it was certain to all that the two had exchanged something. It was as though each had quenched a lingering thirst.

Eomore said, "Oh, father, had I only been here in the hour of need. I did not know that one could feel such pain. What do we know?"

The king responded, "We know very little I fear. The battle was fierce indeed and we certainly can confirm the elves' opinion as to their ferocity as opponents. Even the powers of Roscoe were dulled by their devices, though he and the elven maid certainly saved our skins. They seemed to be motivated toward the capture of Trya. We hope this works in our favor and she remains unharmed. The advisors feel kidnapping is likely based on the fact that her room was invaded, and they repeated the pattern of stealing a young woman. As to their motives, we can only speculate. As you recall, the elves were unable to track them. In their haste, some of our perimeter guards tried to pursue them, but we only gained the general idea that they left toward the wilderness. Fortunately, there has been no rain, but we feel futility when we think about pursuit. A large force would risk what little chance there is of following the trail, and the opponents are so strong that a small force would risk destruction. Of course, they had the element of surprise when they attacked us but even our great mage was unable to ward them off. Roscoe, what are your thoughts?" Eraitmus said.

The king yielded the discussion to the magic user.

Roscoe broke off from his eye encounter with Knarra to say, "I think you may underestimate us somewhat, my king, for their losses were significant. I singed the dark devils fairly well. But I am of the opinion that a small well-equipped force would have a better chance for success. My greatest alarm is that we do not know where to find them. I want to meet the vile captain again. We all have our scores to settle with this bunch."

Vannelei said, "Time is the ally of the Death Wraiths. Draiths! We must move expeditiously if we are to have any hope of regaining our lost treasures – these two beautiful maidens are worth all the gold and power in the land. I offer my bow. I request the loan of a blade."

He grasped the string of Truestrike.

Eomore said nothing but extended to the elf the sword of the fallen ranger Karder Lin. Vannelei accepted the blade which was light for its size; it was made by the dwarves' forges of Castle Lyndyn.

Knarra spoke again, "Also the great blade, Exeter, was absent when the Draiths, as you call them, fortuitously attacked. The tide of battle may have swung if the sword and its wielder were here. Of course, Eomore must feel no guilt over his absence from the city at that time; he was in service of the king. I can sense his feelings now. Again, I offer my services in whatever way you feel that I can help, Eraitmus."

Eomore knew that they all were waiting for him to speak. Even though he had the audacity to be nearing thirty and unmarried, his father knew that Eomore was the greatest fighter in the kingdom. With Exeter by his side, there was no man in the kingdom that could stand even with the prince.

The seconds seemed like years; a soft familiar voice telepathically placed in his mind the question, "Who is the greatest tracker in the land?"

This jump-started the prince's analysis.

Eomore started, "Following their trail is the first obstacle. I feel there is but one within the confines of Castle Lyndyn with the skills necessary to even try to succeed where the elves have failed; we may not be in a very good bargaining position with him. Roscoe certainly with his powers can be invaluable to us as well as Knarra. I wish that Boomer were here to serve as my lieutenant, but in his absence I would choose the dwarf Deron and Gosway as my lieutenants. We will need several other members. Vann, if your wounds are healed sufficiently, your bow and skills could help as well. Sedoar, your healing abilities will help us if we become involved in a prolonged adventure. I am glad that you practice what you preach and keep yourself in excellent condition. I must tell you now that I am unsure why the elven maid is among us. Her beauty is beholding, but that would probably do little against the night raiders."

"She is the reason that I am here now," Roscoe reluctantly interjected. "I do not know of her origins, but I feel we can use all the friends that we can get. I have asked her to join us and she has agreed."

"I shall not question your judgment on the matter, Mage," the prince responded.

He did not object to having her near and was comforted by the thought.

Eomore walked over to his father.

To the king he said, "I ask for the power of 'Royal Clemency', father, for our dilemma forces me to take an action that I would have never anticipated that I would. I cannot promise success, but I feel as everyone does, that we must use everything and everyone at our disposal to find these raiders, recover Trya and the elf maiden, and put a stop to these encroachments against our people. I must now go to the dungeons if this meets your approval."

Eraitmus had a puzzled look on his face.

He answered, "My son, I entrust the command of this undertaking to you; I will not question your judgment. You have the decree."

Eomore then excused himself and turned away from the monarch; he risked one more glance toward the elf maiden. It was difficult to imagine such a frail appearing creature possessed the power witnessed by his associates; there was even more power and mystery in her longing green eyes. He felt that he lost something each time he glanced at her, but the feeling was not unpleasant. He managed to look away from her and briskly left the family and friends who were placing so much faith in him. When he left the room, there was the fleeting desire to run into the courtyard and hide among the trees of the orchard as he did as a boy to escape the pursuit of imaginary boy-eating dragons. But he was a man now and was actually beginning to feel like a leader of his people. But his mind kept wondering if his father or grandfather had ever felt the same feelings of inadequacy that kept popping into his own mind. He hastened his pace and walked on down the hall.

Back in the room, Knarra silently went over to Vannelei and gently removed the bandages from his shoulder. The noble elf tried to keep the pain that was coursing through his body from revealing itself on his face, but he was betrayed by a frown. The priestess gently placed her fine hands upon the discolored and swollen tissues on his chest. Reaching into the pockets of her raimants, she removed a small canister made of a shimmering material. She reached into the canister which had no obvious opening and brought out a thick mauve unguent. She applied this to the chest of the wounded elf. The room was completely silent as she began a slow quiet incantation. Her facial features hardened as she concentrated on her task. This went on for several minutes and no one spoke. Cara was fascinated by this strikingly attractive calm woman.

Only Roscoe and perhaps Knarra herself knew the full meaning in the eyes of the wizard as he watched the tall graceful woman. Vannelei initially did not know how to react to the woman; then he began to relax as he heard the gentle phrases of her incantation. The pain began to leave his body, and his mental anguish was also briefly relieved somewhat. Knarra raised her head and looked directly into the eyes of the elf; Vannelei felt fully at peace. She then lifted her hands from the elf's shoulder; to his amazement the pain left with the hands of the priestess. The talents of Sedoar the royal physician were unparalleled in the medical field, but the powers of Knarra dwarfed his abilities. The elf bowed deeply before her, but Knarra quickly gestured for him to rise.

"What I have done deserves no tithe or gratitude," she said in her normal calming voice, "repayment to me and my Source can be through an act on your part to help one who is in need. When our minds touched I could feel the full extent of your wounds, elven prince. Your physical wounds are certainly minor when compared to your mental anguish. My heart aches for you, your family, my dear friend Eraitmus, and the Aivendar family."

With that she left the elf and walked over to Roscoe. She extended her hand and grasped Roscoe's wrist. For a moment the two again did not speak, but it was as though they were deep in conversation for their facial expressions changed many times.

"It has been a long time since our eyes met and our hands touched, Roscoe," the priestess spoke finally breaking the silence.

"Yes – too long," responded Roscoe.

Those who thought they knew him were amazed to hear the wizard express any feeling of emotion. Nobody, except maybe Knarra, knew Roscoe; the tall robed man was obviously lost in the woman.

"Are your wounds of import?" she asked.

"My pride took the biggest lick. Fortunately, I had only cast a stun spell at the vile creature. I hoped that we could take him alive to gain information. I have heard legend lore of the existence of reflecting stones; I had never before encountered one. This is a disturbing type of Magick; one that I hoped was lost. I am concerned about these beings. Why have we never heard of them and how could they possess such power? My fire spells would incinerate fully a normal man and even most monsters, but one of them nearly crawled away from it. What concerns me most is that we may only be seeing the minions of an even greater power. And what are their origins?" Roscoe pondered.

Question followed question.

"It's true that we have many more questions than answers, but I have developed a great deal of confidence in the eldest son of our friend Eraitmus, though I'm not sure what he is doing now. We'll have to draw our strengths together, as we have before," she answered grasping his hand tightly. The two then embraced, forgetting for a moment the task before them and returning in their minds to an earlier time.

CHAPTER 13
Bartering

Eomore went to the dungeon area of the castle, passing the many heavily bolstered guardposts along the way. He had not been into the dungeons since his last inspection several months ago, although he was responsible for the security indirectly, as this fell among his duties as the captain of the ranger force. On the way, Exeter and Eomore had communicated a great deal, mostly about how the prince should approach the delicate matter he was about to undertake, but the sword managed to get in a few comments about the fickle nature of women and the virtues of bachelorhood. Eomore knew that this was a manifestation of the green-eyed monster of jealousy, said to be more dangerous than a dragon, for he knew Exeter could sense his magnetic attraction to the dark elven woman.

A man named Gice was the sergeant of the guard this day and he snapped to attention when the prince entered the area. Gice was stationed at the top of the stairs at the landing just in front of the outer guard room. He gave a cryptic knock at the door and a burly man unlocked and opened it. There were several more guards here than usual, part of the overall increased security instituted by the thorough Gosway. Gice walked over to the far wall, which looked only like a wall, but Eomore knew that it concealed the panel that opened the inner guardroom. Again, Gice methodically knocked on an area of the wall. After the panel slid open and revealed a smaller, inner guard room; the men inside snapped to attention when they saw the prince, but Eomore quickly told them to relax. He really thought that all this formality was unnecessary, but the men, or at least their sergeants, seemed to enjoy it and felt it was important; the prince again went along with the formality. Quickly, one of the inner guards went over to the heavy wrought iron barred gate and opened it with a huge key. In the darkness they could see the long expanse of stairs leading downward.

"Prince, I shall lead you downward," Gice uttered, "Please be careful to follow my exact steps or else we shall become victims of our own devices and we'll have a nice snooze."

The big man chuckled as he found some humor in his words that Eomore was unable to appreciate. There was little ground for lightheartedness. But the prince acknowledged the warning of Gice and concentrated on every step. They descended for what seemed like an eternity, before a dim light revealed the end of the stairs opening into the large foyer of the dungeons.

A voice boomed around the corner, "Identify or be forever silent!"

Quickly Gice gave a signal that ensured their safe entrance.

A great shape revealed itself as the men entered the chamber.

Exeter muttered, "That blowhard sure does like to be dramatic, doesn't she?"

Taekora the dragoness welcomed the son of Eraitmus and presented the key to the cell area. The heavy lock yielded to the key and Gice opened the gate.

Eomore hesitated for a moment before following the guard captain into the dungeon confinement area. He walked over and spoke briefly with the great beast.

"It is good to see you again, Taekora, but I wish that the circumstances were different. I'm sure that you know the tragedy that has befallen us," Eomore softly spoke, remembering the sensitive hearing of his huge listener.

"Yes, young liege, I only wish that I could exchange some of the wisdom of my years for some of the vigor of my youth, so that I might accompany you on this quest. We have never had the chance to adventure together, but I never went out with your father or grandfather either. I haven't adventured for a thousand years. I suppose that my place is here now," she said.

The prince could see large amber tears welling up in the eyes of the giant.

"You serve us in a way that no other can, and now with our strongest to be away and in jeopardy, your aid in defending the castle and my father will be greatly needed. I must ask that you allow one below safe passage through your chamber, if all goes as I hope. The 'Royal Clemency' is in effect," Eomore stated.

"As you wish, my prince," she did not fully understand this unusual request, but as always, Taekora followed the instructions of the Aivendars.

Eomore went over to the waiting Gice and the men began the walk down the dark corridors. Almost immediately Exeter began planting in the mind of the prince such warnings as "enemy to the left" or "enemy to the right" as they passed the cells. Eomore thought to the sword that the warnings were not necessary because the men were securely behind their bars, then he realized that he had been grasping the hilt of the sheathed weapon, more or less asking for the warnings. He relaxed his grip and she became silent. The walking pace was brisk as they all felt uncomfortable in the dungeons. They came upon a locked door, then another, each time the guard producing the proper key. They were finally in the maximum security area. There were a number of cells, but not many occupants. Murder was a rare crime in the kingdom, as were other violent crimes. There were no political prisoners. The Aivendars were so just in their dealings with the populace that there had been little social unrest in Donothor for several generations. But there was one noteworthy occupant.

"I haven't really asked your motives for coming here, my Lord," Gice pondered, "but now that we are here, my curiousity overcomes me."

"Take me to the cell of Nigel Louffette, Gice," Eomore calmly answered.

"But my Lord, he is not to be trusted even for a moment! He evaded capture for so long. I can't even risk the remote possibility that the rogue might overpower you or find some other way to exact his escape," the guard said with the utmost sincerity.

"I must speak with the man alone, Gice," Eomore answered. "He could be of great aid to us for I know of no other that possesses his talents."

"As you wish," Gice said but Eomore could easily detect the disapproval in his voice.

A short walk across the corridor led to a small locked cell. Eomore recognized the figure in the neatly orgranized cell. Nigel was not handsome by anybody's standards. He was a gaunt, tall, and thin man whose years of lawlessness had taken their toll on him. Eomore did not know how old he was, but he looked older than the prince expected; he had not seen the man for a few years. But the facial features; the black eyes with their cold stare; the dark, neatly trimmed beard; the large scar on the right cheek; the coal black hair which fell to shoulder length – these features were unmistakable.

"Eomore Aivendar, prince of Donothor. Why am I graced with this visit?" The dark figure spoke, lifting his eyes from the thick volume he had been reading to gaze through the bars at the prince.

The voice dripped with sarcasm.

Eomore felt a chill course through his body as the man looked at him. He imagined that the many alleged victims of the man's blade had felt the same feeling- which more often than not had been their last feeling- he surmised. Then again, most of the allegations against the man had not been proven.

He managed to say, "Nigel Louffette, I ask an audience with you. Will you talk with me?"

"That is a strange twist, Prince, for I have asked for an audience with your father many times to defend myself against the injustice brought upon me by the foul dwarf called Boomer – injustice that resulted in my confinement here. But the only response I get is trial from the royal judges whom I fear would find me guilty even if I were a saintly man. I am an unfortunate tradesman, Eomore, just a little down on my luck. I'm sure that a man as wise as you doesn't believe all the stories about me. But as you can see, my schedule is very full – this book is followed at once by another from the royal library. I should imagine that I will soon become the most widely-read man in the kingdom, don't you? What could you have to say to me that would interest me enough to tear me away from my arduous appointments?" Nigel answered with the facetiousness again dripping like acid from his words.

Eomore could sense the great resentment the man felt for his confinement.

"Let me begin by saying that a 'Royal Clemency' might be part of our discussion. Would that interest you?" the prince responded, trying not to sound too desperate.

Nigel tried just as hard not to reveal his desperation.

The alleged assassin said, "I suppose that Wilver Slarshire can wait a little while for it's true that I haven't had good or bad conversation recently."

He closed the book and stood. He was not as tall as the prince remembered, probably a full three inches shorter than Eomore. But a man's deeds and his legends always seem taller than the actual man. But perhaps the cell made the man seem smaller.

"Open the door and leave us," Eomore said to Gice.

The prince removed the sheath containing the great sword and handed it to one of the guards.

"No!" Exeter cried in vain, as the sword left his hand.

Gice seemed to briefly hesitate until he saw the scowl of the determined prince.

"Yes, my Lord," Gice answered sharply.

He instructed one of the guards to hold a weapon on Nigel and ordered Nigel back from the door. He waited for the prisoner to comply, and then inserted the key into the lock.

"Boo!" Nigel yelled, causing the man to drop the keys.

Nigel then began to laugh uncontrollably as the man hurriedly picked up the keyring. Gice glowered at the thief but responded to another request of the prince to open the door by turning the key, releasing the latch, and opening the heavy bars. The six guards stood ready with weapons drawn and Gice rapidly stepped back and assumed a similar position.

"Just one false move, Louffette, and you will feel my blade," Gice uttered.

"Eomore, is that any way for your servant to talk to your tea guest? I feel so unnerved," Nigel sarcastically responded.

"Leave us and return in thirty minutes," Eomore said.

Now he walked into the cell and closed the door; the lock clicked heavily. The men rapidly left the area and closed the intermediate door.

Eomore and Nigel studied each other; if anyone had observed the confrontation, he would have seen the intense concentration on each man's face. Nigel was trying to uncover the motives that brought the prince to him and Eomore was trying to figure our how to assure the cooperation of the thief.

"Sit down, Eomore. All the comforts of my home are at your disposal. What do you want from me?" Nigel said, thinking that speaking first would give him an advantage.

Actually Eomore was glad that the other man had broken the ice.

"Nigel Louffette, I am prepared to convey to you the 'Royal Clemency' with the approval of my father in return for your assistance with a quest that is not without hazard. You will be released to your own devices upon the completion of the quest with the options of receiving a homestead in the Wilderness fringes or leaving the kingdom. At any rate, you will be a free man with no further obligation to the crown or the citizenry, other than the common one of obeying the laws of the land."

Eomore then paused, but he was met only with silence as Nigel stared coldly at him. Obviously, the prisoner wanted to hear more. If Nigel were interested he was doing a very good job of keeping his enthusiasm hidden.

Eomore continued, "Of course you will be expected to follow through until the completion of the quest. You will be protected as much as possible and will be asked to take no more risk than I myself will take. I give you my word."

"Eomore, I find myself very comfortable feasting on the food and reading the literature of the king. It is ironic that I am supposed to have spent the better part of my life robbing and cutting throats to make myself confortable and now that I'm captured it's all given to me and I'm asked nothing in return. I've felt the warmth of a woman, too. Eomore, but the warmth is not sufficient to thaw the ice that the fairer sex carries in its heart. Perhaps I should not leave this security to risk the hazards that you so tactfully mentioned. But I respect your honesty with me. I'll in turn be honest with you. What possible assurance could you have that I would not bolt as soon as we clear the palace? I'm sure you've heard the stories of my prowess in such matters," Nigel said.

The thief spoke without ever breaking eye contact with Eomore.

The frankness of the man surprised Eomore a bit, but he should have expected this.

He answered, "I would value your word of honor, Nigel, but you must have realized by now that escape is impossible from the dungeons of Castle Lyndyn. You will never be given another chance to exonerate yourself. As to your following your word, you must remember that you have been 'sniffed by the beast' in the vernacular of the thieves' guilds. She has never been victimized by a successful escape so she has not left her lair here. But she is not confined and would gladly pursue you. A man can change so many things but one thing we cannot do is change our essence; essence is detected by the nares of dragonkind. If you are willing to listen further, I will detail the request that I will make of you in order for you to earn your freedom."

Eomore could not help but notice the embittered man's attitude toward women. In some ways, could he be similar to this reviled person?

Again Nigel Louffette did not speak, but he did nod his head in a weak affirmative.

Eomore went on.

"My family has become the victim of treachery that I feel even you will despise. Last evening the palace was violated and my sister, an innocent of eighteen, was taken away into the night to destinations unknown to us by vile creatures that we call Draiths. They killed many of our finest defenders, including the champion Karder Lin. They withstood the magic of the mage Roscoe and very nearly brought ruin upon the entire royal party. These beings also stole an elven princess and evaded the pursuits and tracking ability of the elven hunters. One of the elves came to us for assistance, Prince Vannelei by name; I was away escorting the priestess Knarra to Lyndyn to get her assistance in this matter when the raiders struck. Nigel, your woodsmanship and tracking ability are legend. I personally have lost your own trail many times. I know that you are as skilled a follower as you are a deceptive quarry. We need your skills. These beings are very powerful. I don't know if we can find and follow their trail to confront them. If we do meet them, we will all be in jeopardy. I could not ask you to join us without telling you this. We do not have the luxury of procrastination. I must have an answer from you before the men return. I honestly can't tell you anymore of the foe, but I will tell the rest of our planned party. I'll be willing to take suggestions from you of course and you will be given a voice as a man and member of the party. I will at all times be in command. I await your reply."

Nigel began to stroke his short, neatly trimmed beard and for awhile he said nothing. Eomore stood and walked over to the bars. Nigel remained seated on the cot.

After about three minutes he said, "You ask me to leave a certain meal and a dry bed to undertake a Deathquest and offer me a forsaken spot of land if I succeed. Who are the other fools who serve themselves as though they were lambs being led to slaughter?"

Eomore faced him.

"I will lead the party. The mage Roscoe will lend his great powers to our efforts. Knarra the high priestess will accompany. The elven prince Vannelei, Deron the dwarven swordsman, the physician Sedoar, an elven girl Cara, Tjol Bergin – a tried warrior, and several of my strongest and most skilled rangers will make up the group attempting to follow the raiders."

"A fickle magician, a holy head, two long-eared freaks, a sawbones, an idiot, and a prince – a motly crew to go on a Deathquest. Yet you must know that my greatest weakness is my love of my ability to go where I choose when I choose. I will say in advance that I will perform my 'duties' to the best of my abilities, because my own life will likely be in jeopardy. I will also say that from what you have told me, we are all fools and have little chance of success and better chance of death. Death, however, is the better alternative only when compared to two other things – marriage and imprisonment. I will not question your command unless you try to do my job and do it incorrectly. But don't expect any of this bowing and 'my Lord' stuff – that is not my ilk. I agree to your terms, Prince, and I know the strength of your word. I'm glad the tables aren't turned so that I don't have to trust myself. I'll need my cloak and its contents that the dwarf stole from me when I was incarcerated—I hope that nothing is disturbed. By the way, you did not mention the runt – has he run into misfortune? That would just break my heart," Nigel smirked as he spoke of the dwarf Boomer.

Eomore responded, "Boomer is my friend. He is away in service to the king and won't return for three or more days. We can't afford to wait. Gather what you want to take. I assure you that everything you had when you were captured will be secure in the prison vault."

With that Nigel began to move around the room and picked up a few things. Shortly the men returned and unlocked the door.

Gice brimmed with contempt and the thief seemed to relish it.

Gice spoke, "I'm going to take the precaution of blindfolding you, Louffette, just in case you should ever become our guest again. I warn you to talk the lawful path. Any treachery toward my prince and I'll personally pursue you to the ends of the world."

He then placed a thick black cloth over the eyes of the newest member of the '"team" and the group exited the dungeon.

They ascended the stairs carefully after bidding goodbye to Taekora. Eomore again strapped Exeter to his side. Once they were in the outer guardroom, the blindfold was removed from Nigel. He looked much more formidable outside the cell. One of the guards produced the former prisoner's belongings and Nigel spent a moment searching the cloak. He smiled and told Eomore he was ready.

Eomore grasped the hilt of Exeter and in his mind formed the thoughts, "Any threats or enemies?"

"None" was the reply.

CHAPTER 14
The Quest Begins

Vannelei stared in wonder at the dark elven woman. The elven prince knew little about his darker skinned cousins. The dark elves tended to be even more nomadic and chaotic than most of their peoples. Vannelei had never really numbered a close friend or confidant among them, though there had never been any malice either. He had heard stories of rare members of the dark elven tribes that possessed magical powers. However, he had always considered these to be rumors until he had met Cara. Something about her seemed unusual and yet familiar, but he could not put it together, perhaps because of his arduous trials these past few days. At any rate, the elven prince felt that there was more to her story than she had revealed to Roscoe, but was glad that she had intervened when she did. His thoughts returned to Eomore; he wondered what his new friend was trying to accomplish in the dungeons of Castle Lyndyn. Since the prince had left, the room had burst into acitivty as the servants were going about directed tasks to bring materials requested by the various members of the group. The physician Sedoar was busily arranging items in his large leather pack. Several other sturdy backpacks had been brought into the large chamber which had become the informal headquarters for their efforts. Under the instructions of Deron and Tjol Bergin, a number of other rangers and servants were systematically filling each pack with the essentials of wilderness travel. The rangers had done this so often that it was more or less automatic for them, although the packs for the women required some extra attention. Knarra and Roscoe were talking and helping each other to organize their own materials. Cara remained quiet. As Vannelei watched her, she gracefully went over to the king and excused herself from the chamber to go to her quarters. She seemed to glance back at Vannelei, with the deep green eyes flashing unspoken signals of resentment for the stares that she had been receiving. She left the room, but the overall activity was such that her departure did not seem to make any difference. Shortly thereafter, Eomore returned. There were many startled looks from those who knew the tall thin man accompanying him.

Returning to his father's side, he said, "Father, Nigel Louffette has agreed to assist us in any way that he can in return for Royal Clemency. I see that preparations are well underway. I think that we must be off immediately for we still have three hours before darkness. Any start we can get while the trail remains relatively fresh will help. Horses have been readied for the first part of the journey."

Eraitmus raised his brow, saying, "The freedom of this scoundrel is a high price to pay Eomore, but I am bereaved and I trust your judgment."

"Then the party will consist of myself, Roscoe, Knarra, Vannelei, Sedoar, the elf Cara, Deron, Tjol Bergin, Nigel, and the six men who are waiting with the mounts. Gosway, you will remain in command of the castle's defenses while I am away until the eventual return of Boomer. When he returns, if you have no word of us, give the dwarf this letter," Eomore spoke without changing his inflection at all.

He handed a folded parchment to the elderly guardsman who in turn nodded in understanding. The prince went over to his father and mother and gave them both a long embrace. At this time, Cara returned. Eomore could not help but notice how striking she looked in her dark green riding dress. It seemed to make her skin glow a faint color not unlike that of spring foliage in the thick of wilderness swamps. She had her small pack across her back with a light crossbow strapped such that it would be readily available at her hand. She smiled at the prince, acknowledging his gaze.

They then moved out of the greeting chamber and conference area and walked steadily into the brisk afternoon and on to the stables. There the mounts were ready, as well as the remaining supplies and rations. The fifteen riders mounted and rode off quickly, followed by three unarmored men whose task it was to return with the animals once their utility was finished.

The riders conversed little. Eomore and Nigel rode in the front, and the prince was a bit surprised at the horsemanship exhibited by his companion. Deron rode beside Tjol Bergin in the second file and neither took their eyes off the wily Nigel. They were racing the setting sun as they rode along the road nearing the wilderness. After about two hours ride, the ebbing rays of light began to cut down on their vision. But it was about the same time that they reached the point where the raiders had branched off the main road. They stopped and Nigel dismounted. The dark, cloaked figure looked much taller and much more prominent as darkness neared. Clearly night was the element of Nigel. The knave reached into an imperceptible opening in his cape and withdrew a tiny bit of an amber powder that fluoresced briefly as he scattered it into the air.

"Some value comes from the depths of the Lachinor," he mused.

After a few minutes of laboriously searching the ground and bushes at this point, he came over to Eomore and blankly said, "False lead. Nobody left the road here."

The thief remounted his steed and began to ride down the road. The others briefly hesitated and then followed Eomore's lead behind the thief. About three hundred yards further down the road, Nigel stopped again and dismounted. He walked over to a small thornbrush and bent down; he stood, producing a small fragment of a silken red garment. He walked forward a few paces again bent to the ground and sat there for awhile. He then returned to the others.

"This is our path to follow but the evening now becomes our enemy. Their tracks are faint and we must wait the morning light before we can pursue them."

"Time is of the essence," Eomore interrupted, "I feel we should press on tonight,"

"In the long run it will probably cost us time for we may lose the path of our quarry. I am rested. Last night I had the company of a good book and a dry bed, but I know that others of you are tired. The evening glow promises a clear night and I think we should stop, rest, and begin anew in the morning."

"His words are wise, Eomore," Knarra said in her usual reassuring voice.

It was hard to argue with Knarra.

"Alright," he conceded, "we'll camp here but restart with the earliest light." Eomore seemed resigned that the task involved finding the lair of the enemy, and that the battle would take place there. Likelihood of overtaking them on the road never seemed possible. His sister!

Silently they dismounted. Deron and Tjol assisted the other fighters in securing the animals which would be hopefully be returning to their comfortable stables the following day. The thoughts of the various members of the quest were on their own immediate futures. Each person went about organizing his equipment. All were familiar with this kind of venture. Eomore watched the elven girl intently as she prepared her pallet on the mossy ground. She went about the task in a very deliberate and organized fashion. She knew just where everything had to be. She glanced back at him and their eyes met, then locked together briefly. The prince walked toward her.

"Can I help you?" he asked.

Cara smiled. "No, I can manage, my Lord."

"Such chivalry – your ancestors would be proud that it hasn't died with them."

The female voice startled Eomore as it always did; then he remembered that others could not "hear" Exeter when she "spoke" to her master. He had such a habit of resting his hand on the hilt of the sword.

"She seems so small and frail," the prince thought back to Exeter. "Besides, as the leader of this expedition, it is my duty to get to know all the members well."

"Oh, brother!" Exeter responded.

The blade then skulked.

Eomore chuckled.

"Yes, my Lord?" Cara questioned.

"I… I was just thinking of my friend Boomer and how much he would enjoy this adventure. He is quite a funny guy," he answered, quickly regaining his composure.

"Then I should hope to meet him some day, my Lord," Cara answered, and resumed her preparations.

She blushed, and so did the prince.

The men gathered firewood, and soon a fire was blazing. Roscoe scoffed at the flints used by the rangers, but felt they would ask his assistance if they wanted it. The mage was glad that they had stopped; he was exhausted. The powerful Magick of the night before had taken a lot out of him and, as well, the stun spell had been reflected upon him. Roscoe was a powerful man, probably the single most

99

awesome figure in Donothor, but the more magic he expended, the more rest he required. This was the nature of Magick and not even Knarra's talents could reverse this. If Roscoe knew the reasons for the ebb and flow of the energies required for spell casting, the mage never shared the knowledge. There were legends of Roscoe's colossal battles with necromancers in antiquity. The mage dropped down on his blanket and stared into the growing fire. He mischieviously sprinkled a powder on the blaze causing it to roar briefly.

"We are at the fringes of the great wilderness. I think we will be relatively secure here, but still should take the precaution of keeping guards posted," Eomore said.

They finished their beddings and began to eat some of the rations packed for them by the kitchen staff. This was supplemented by berries gathered by the elves. Roscoe could swear that he regained a spark of energy when the frail fingers of the dark elven maid brushed against his brawny hand as she transferred the tiny fruits. A wry smile even traversed her face.

"I am not tired. I'll be glad to keep the first watch," Nigel volunteered.

Silence fell over the group as each awaited the other to speak first.

Eomore finally said, "Thank you, Nigel. The size of the camp and the area would make it advisable to keep a double guard, though."

"I'll stand the first watch," Knarra offered.

Nigel smiled. He knew that the idea was a good one so he did not debate, but he wondered if Eomore did it more for security or for watching his newly found guide and tracker.

Soon the others settled down. The priestess and the thief sat opposite each other on old stumps as their party fell asleep. Roscoe was asleep immediately. Most of the rangers were filled with an uneasiness centered on their cloaked comrade, but eventually even the most suspicious Deron wandered into his dreams. Fate, or perhaps good thinking, placed Eomore's pallet near Cara. He fell asleep; the last things his weary eyes beheld were the deep green eyes of the elf maiden gazing at him. There were nice things even in the wilderness.

Vannelei also quickly fell asleep. The noble elf had suffered two serious wounds recently and his weary mind took control of his body. He fell asleep wondering again about the mysterious dark elven female – why did she seem so familiar?

Time flowed slowly for the two guards. Nigel produced a large bladed knife from his back and began to whittle on a piece of wood. He looked over to Knarra.

He finally said, "I guess it must be pretty lonely at the top, huh?"

The comprehensive eyes of the priestess studied him. "What do you mean, Nigel?"

"You know, you have to spend all your time doing good deeds for low-lifes like us. You don't have time for yourself."

She replied, "No, I have many diversions, Nigel, and I don't grow weary of trying to help others. Is that what you mean?"

"Well, not exactly, I guess what I'm trying to ask is, don't you ever miss not having a man?" the thief smiled, thinking that he flustered the holy woman with that one.

"I have never taken a vow of celibacy, Nigel. There is a place in everyone's life for physical love as well as emotional love. I care about my people, but I have never ignored my own needs," she answered without ever taking her eyes off the man.

Nigel found himself without the words for one of the few times in his life.

Knarra again broke the silence by saying, "You lead a lonely life yourself from what I have gathered."

"I do okay," came the terse answer.

Knarra could sense that the thief had much on his mind, but she likewise could sense that he was reluctant to speak. They were quiet for the remainder of their shift and were relieved by Deron and Tjol. The night passed uneventfully and the first rays of the morning sun found them arousing and preparing to continue what Nigel called the Deathquest.

CHAPTER 15
Trails

They had at least been given a sunny day to begin their attempt to follow the trail of the Draiths. They were a day behind. The air was cool but refreshing; after a brief meal they were on their way. The horses were taken back toward Lyndyn and they proceeded the hard way. This area was familiar to several party members including Eomore, Deron, Tjol, and of course Nigel. Nigel gave tracking the appearance of one of the fine arts. The others found themselves becoming impatient and even at times thought him to be dawdling, but he thrice in the first four hundred yards determined that potential trails were false. Finally, he began to follow a meandering pathway through the forest, periodically stopping to observe a broken bough or literally sniff along the trail. He was occasionally aided by a fragment of the red silken fabric which fortunately for the trackers was not made for travel in the forest and frayed easily. He did not resort to the contents of his cape.

”How could we not discover his cache,” muttered Deron, frustrated that the thief's possessions had been in the vaults of trhe Castle Lyndyn dungeons.

They followed the trail for several hours, stopping only for food near midday. There were ample supplies of berries and other nourishments in the forest which helped to preserve their supplies and refresh them as well. Even Vannelei wondered at the skills of the tall thin human. He had thought that such abilities were restricted to the elven peoples and then only to select few. They were in deep forest for much of the morning but shortly after midday the trail opened out onto one of the savannahs bordering on the swamps of the western wilderness of Donothor. Desert lay beyond. Nigel hesitated before leaving the cover of the forest to cross the short grassed plain.

"It's hard to trust these birds," he said, seeming to talk more to himself than to the others.

He crouched for a moment studying the sands beneath his feet.

"It seems so unlike them to leave the cover of the forest and go into the plain. They have been next to impossible to trail and yet I can see sets of tracks across that grass that my blind grandmother could follow."

"Do you think it's a trap?" asked Eomore.

"The question is what kind of trap prince," Nigel responded. "I'm sure that they wanted us to follow these tracks. Unless they aren't very bright – which we all know is not the case."

"I wonder where in the Black Fen they are going. These meadows border the swamps. Certainly there could be no intelligent and civilized folk living there. We would have learned something of them before now," Deron interjected.

"From what I've heard these fellows are not exactly civilized, my short friend," Nigel reiterated.

The dwarf reddened with the reference to his short stature and the correction of his assessment. He started to become abusive himself when the strong hand of Eomore rested on his shoulder and he remembered why they were here. He would have to continue to suppress his own animosity toward Nigel for the good of the mission.

Nigel stood and stroked the short hairs of his beard. "Do you have any suggestions, elf?" he asked of Vannelei.

"I agree with your caution but I fail to see why they would go to all of this trouble when it would seem that speed would have been their sole concern," the elf answered.

Eomore stated then, "Their tactics seem a little skewed but do we have any choice but to take the bait?"

Nigel was scanning the surroundings all the while. He seemed to abruptly stop listening in the middle of the prince's statement and suddenly walked over to a point several yards to the side where the footprints entered the savannah. He had a quizzical expression on his face which seemed unusual on his features. Bending over to the ground he noticed the sand. He motioned to Vannelei and Eomore to come over.

"Look at this dirt!" he said seeming almost unable to control himself.

Eomore looked down at the smooth sand. "I don't see anything. It is only smooth sand, Nigel."

Vannelei likewise could not discern the reason for the excitement of the thief (in their minds they were beginning to think more of him as a guide than an adversary now).

He commented, "I fail to see the significance of this myself. The sands appear to be undisturbed."

Nigel continued. "That is just it – they are too smooth. It is as though the sand has been smoothed over. Go back to the others and take a break for awhile if you want. I'm going to follow this path for a ways."

"We'll wait for some time, Nigel, but we need to pursue the lead that we have into the clear area," Eomore stated firmly.

He and Vannelei walked back to the others.

Cara watched intently and wandered toward the general direction of Nigel. She told the others that she was not tired or hungry. She saw Nigel bending low to the ground, occasionally picking up pinches of sand and slowly moving along a narrow strand of sandy ground. The thin man continued for a short distance until he was just beyond visual contact with the main party. There was a shout from Eomore that Nigel promptly responded to by asking for a little more time. He followed the barely existent pathway, and then dropped to a crouch; a puzzled look came upon his face. He retraced his previous steps for a short distance then turned around and appeared in deep thought. Assuring that he had not been mistaken, Nigel returned to the point where the smooth sand ended. The area was about twenty feet squared; the area was covered by fairly low plant growth with no tall trees. The master tracker again bent down and studied the ground.

Silently two dark forms fell upon him from above. Only the fine tuned reflexes that came with a lifetime of thievery saved him from an immediate demise; the thief managed to roll aside just as the two Draiths landed upon the ground where he had been standing. He rolled to his left, simultaneously drawing forth a gleaming blade from within the folds of his cloak. He stood to face his assailants; it was rather uncomfortable to be cast as the underdog. The Draiths were about seven feet in height and their weaponless hands moved with incredible speed. These animals were quick! With a guttural voice, the left one made a brief statement, and the two moved toward their quarry. Nigel moved to his right as if to engage the creature on that side, then quickly wheeled and deftly hurled the throwing knife toward the other one, catching him somewhat by surprise; the Draith was unable to ward off the attack of the blade and screamed as it pierced his neck. The blade then performed its own form of Magick as it ripped through the dark flesh, springing out into three separate blades with the force of impact and the tall creature screamed no more. His throat had been ripped away as though he had been mauled by a devil dog.

"Way to go sweetheart," Nigel thought to himself, as that was his favorite name for the killing dagger.

But the thief could not relish the triumph for the second one was upon him and Nigel did not have any surprises for him. The Draith was angered by the demise of his companion and thrust his forehand toward the neck of his foe. Nigel managed to move aside just enough to prevent the landing of the full force of the blow; the blow did not crush his windpipe. There was enormous pain; the blow knocked him to the ground stunned him. The assailant leaped into the air and attempted to land with full weight upon his fallen opponent but Nigel recovered just enough to partially roll aside. Still there was the sickening crunching sound of his lateral ribs as the huge feet landed. The pain was so severe that he neared unconsciousness; survival instinct alone enabled the thief to get to his feet. He was swaying as he faced the attacker. Down the path he could hear the shouts of his party; they had obviously heard the sounds of battle. They were too far away. Nigel drew his dagger from his belt; he would at least make his killer feel a little pain for his efforts. Suddenly a stream of red fire flowed as a flaming fountain arching through the air and struck the second Draith. The big humanoid howled with pain as the flames burned his body. He turned to see the svelte form of Cara as she prepared to deliver another attack. Nigel tried to move forward to her aid as the creature charged her, but the pain dominated him and the thief fell to his knees and cursed his frailness. Cara stood her ground and delivered a second blast of heat; her power either weakened with the second spell or else she hurried her efforts and failed to complete the spell. She had managed to wound and slow the advance of the attacker; now he was only a few feet away; there was no time for another strike with her magic. She drew a small knife from her waist belt and prepared to face her opponent. She knew that her token resistance would likely be ineffective; this was not what she had in mind when she came north from Kanath those few days ago; she was resigned to make a good account for herself. The Draith smirked as he closed on the woman. The massive form glanced back at Nigel just long enough to assure him that the thief would not intervene and awaited his turn to die. But the tall creature found his plans for the orderly disposal of the two Donothorians were interrupted by the battle cry of their prince. Eomore could never remember moving so fast, but then again he had never entered a fray with as much vengeance in his heart. Seeing the frail elven woman standing firm against such a formidable foe spurred him onward. Exeter developed a dull red glow as the prince held the great longsword above and before him. The Draith turned and faced this new adversary; he left the elf for later. It did not seem to disturb the great creature that several other people were only a few paces behind the prince. The Draith had underestimated this foe; the prince was readily upon him with a shout. The longsword hummed and hewed into the flank of the dark creature, spoiling its first attack and producing a howl of anguish. But this was no easy conquest; the Draith spinned rapidly and attempted a blow to the right flank of the prince, but the chainmail effectively warded off the blow. If anything, the Draith injured his hand; the impassive face winced. Exeter, guided by the strong arm of her wielder, struck again; the blade sank into the thorax of the Draith; the huge being fell silently to the ground. The Draiths had felt the first of the revenge of the house of Aivendar.

Exeter seemed to pulsate as though she were satiated with the spirit of her victim. Eomore stared briefly at the fallen Draith, and then turned his attention to Nigel, quickly trying to ascertain the extent of his injuries. The tall gaunt man was in quite a bit of pain but was apparently not critically injured. Cara had gone over to Nigel as well. About this time the others began to arrive.

"Where did they come from, Nigel?" Eomore asked.

Sedoar and Knarra had reached the side of the thief and attended his wounds.

Nigel weakly pointed upward and said, "From above."

"He must be delirious, Eomore," Vannelei noted.

Their eyes began to scan the air above them. There were no trees in the immediate vicinity and even though the Draiths were impressive physical specimens, not even they could materialize from thin air; or, perhaps they could... at least they did not think this would be possible; they doubted that their opponent could leap such a distance as to leap upon the thief from the nearby trees. Knarra began an incantation that some of the party had heard before; Sedoar gave Nigel several small dried leaves from his leather pouch. Nigel relaxed when the pain which wracked his body was relieved.

Knarra continued her work.

Eomore turned to Cara.

"Are you hurt?" he asked.

He extended his large hand to her. Her small fingers intertwined with his; she fell into his arms and sobbed deeply. She lost control – but brushes with one's own mortality tended to do that.

"She saved my skin," Nigel stated matter-of-factly.

Knarra had finished her work.

Nigel smiled.

He continued, "Imagine. Saved by a couple of dames. If we make it through this Deathquest, I'll have to bribe everyone not to tell this tale. Thank you."

Nigel, forgetting his distrust for women, extended his hand first to Knarra, then to Cara, and finally to Eomore.

The party studied the fallen Draiths- muscular, fine featured, skin the color of unpolished brass. The creatures had moved with alarming rapidity; they had exceeded the party's expectations. The stories of the night of terror in Castle Lyndyn had not been exaggerated; Roscoe and the other survivors had not embellished the tale of the events of that evening.

Roscoe kicked the first Draith and muttered something. The mage then produced a bluish prism from one of the seemingly bottomless pockets on his large cloak. He uttered a few phrases, Cara understood the incantation, but she did nothing to steal his thunder. Raising the prismatic object before his eyes, the mage scanned the area around them. After turning a full 360 degrees he developed a quizzical expression; he tilted his head and looked upward through the scrying prism.

After a quarter turn of his head, the mage uttered, "Not possible."

Eomore queried, "What do you find?"

'What did you see?' did not seem an appropriate question.

Roscoe then frowned. Mages did not enjoy appearing foolish

He somberly replied, "There is a Gate."

"A what?" Nigel asked.

Roscoe continued, "A portal to another place; maybe another time; about six feet over your head, assassin, is a portal. I have read of them in the Old Volumes, but thought them legend. I doubt that it could have been detected without the aid of the scrying prism. Magick such as defending Glyphs are easily detected by a "Detection of Magick" spell. The power to create such a planar gate, or portal, is legend. The Gate Spell is lost to our world. The prism magnifies the aura of subtle Magick and detects the portal. I have used this prism for..."

Roscoe stopped before saying how many years.

He continued, "The portal explains how our 'friends' manage to appear and disappear with such rapidity. Only the fates will know what awaits us on the other side. Or even how we can proceed through it. Knarra and I can cast protective spells but I can't guarantee success. We risk a great deal by going on."

The mage was obviously concerned with this finding. It was unusual for him not to radiate confidence, if not cockiness.

"Then the path into the plain is a trap of some sort; it's at least a false lead," Eomore surmised.

Deron now said, "Should we return for reinforcements before proceeding?"

"No, I do not wish to risk many lives instead of a few. I feel that we are balanced, strong, and should be able to retreat if we have to. The Draiths are mortal as we are; I should imagine that if they are able to survive the transference from their world to ours, then we should be able to traverse the portal to their world. If they can breathe in our world, then we should be able to breathe in theirs. We should send three of our group back to the city to inform my father of the progress that we have made. Then they might lead a larger party back, perhaps even under the leadership of Boomer; I assume he has returned from Roscoe's, "Eomore said.

The prince spoke without hesitation.

"You are assuming a lot, my prince," Nigel retorted. "These guys are pretty tough. Old Roscoe nearly "bought it" by his own spell when he went up against them, I'm told. Doesn't that mean that these critters are resistant to Magick? How do we know this thing won't singe our hides? I can't see the thing when I'm looking right at it! How do we know it's a two way street?

"Watch the 'Old Roscoe' stuff. The Dark Warrior had a rare device that saved his skin. Trust Magick to me!" the sorcerer emphatically answered.

Eomore saw the wizard's hair stand on end.

He said, "Roscoe, I agree that you know more about this sort of thing than any of the rest of us. What do you suggest we do?"

Roscoe went over to Knarra; he motioned for Cara to join them. There was a lot of quiet discussion; Knarra seemed to be recalling an earlier successful collaboration. The three spell casters reached a decision. They approached the others.

"You will feel a tingling in your skin," Roscoe said. "We are casting a Protection from Magick Spell; its effects can be uncomfortable. "

The three then conjured; mysterious phrases filled the air; the arcane sounds mimicked a cappella singing; the lyrics unnerved even the prince.

Tjol Bergin commented, "All this mumbo-jumbo gives me the creeps. I would rather just find these guys, whip their tails, and rescue the princess. Ouch!"

He then rubbed what of his skin he could, though much was covered by the chainmail.

Roscoe bade farewell to his cat; he entrusted the 'familiar' to the messengers returning to Lyndyn.

He grasped his staff and threw a small feather into the air. He began to slowly rise from the ground. His dark cloak was flowing in the afternoon breezes as the mage rose above the group. He appeared weightless as he hovered; he was about six feet above the ground; he walked forward; he vanished.

The fighters noted that the women still concentrated heavily and were oblivious to the events in the air above them.

Then Cara spoke, "He is alright. He and Knarra have established an astral link. He has instructed us to come through as well."

"How?" Nigel interjected emphatically.

Eomore developed a baffled look on his face; it was an expression that all of them shared.

How?

The question was answered when a rope sinuated downward from site where Roscoe had vanished. The "rope "was a rainbow of fibers entwined; it had no appreciable weight; the cord dangled in the air. Its strength was unquestioned. Cara took the rope and it drew her upward.

Eomore dispatched three of the rangers to return to Castle Lyndyn. He gave the longest serving of the trio a parchment to carry to the king. The brief letter told of their progress.

The prince grasped the rope and it drew him upward as well. When the prince reached the top of this extraordinary ascension, he stood at the edge of a large grassy meadow; he was bathed with warm amber sunlight, no suns' light; a quick glance to the heavens revealed that they were three suns.

A small pale grayish sun rested near the horizon to their right; a bright yellow star was seen to their left; a huge, distant, distorted, celestial body dominated the center of the sky. The air was warm and sweet. Instinctively the prince grasped the hilt of his great weapon.

He was reassured by Exeter's calming response "None."

Exeter detected no enemies.

Cara was slowly scanning the horizon. Roscoe was virtually immobile; he peered through the small prism and guided the rope with his other hand. Eomore glanced into the prism; he was amazed to find that he was looking down upon his friends in Donothor; he saw the rope grasp and pull up Nigel, Sedoar, Deron, Vannelei, Tjol Bergin, and the three remaining rangers in turn. Only Knarra remained on the other side. They peered into the prism and watched her bend downward and etch a glyph on the ground. She incanted; the glyph rose out of the sand and became a small flaming stairwell. The stairwell reached the door of the gate; the woman walked up the "stairs" to the gate. The group saw the three "lucky" rangers turn toward home and rapidly depart. Knarra walked through the gate and stood by the others.

Most were experiencing pruritis and mild headaches, but none was worse for the wear.

Roscoe turned the prism to the side; with a wave of his hand the rope climbed back into his robe and the little prism vanished.

The portal was flush with the ground on this side and shimmered in the dull light. The shape was rectangular; the dimensions were four by eight feet in width and height.

Knarra etched another Glyph on the ground at the base of the portal and incanted. The Priestess touched the forehead of each of the twelve companions with her index finger; she uttered a short phrase and traced an identical pattern on each face.

Tjol again felt a brief burning at the site.

Knarra said, "This will protect you from the Magick of the Warding Glyph should you return here and I not."

Roscoe uttered a few phrases and the glyph faded from sight. The portal did not.

"None but our party shall use this exit. Mark well this site in your minds. Others cannot pass the Glyph safely. Even our countrymen, should they come to our aid, will feel the flames of the burning stair. If a creature dares the flaming stair, attempts to traverse the portal without Protection from Magick, and survives, that creature will be unable to return to Donothor without the Protection Glyph. Magick is not without limitations. My Familiar will relay this message to the King. That is why I sent Matilda back with the three." Roscoe said.

He added," Things are amiss in this land, but the forces of Magick seem to hold true. Red and orange trees and grasses seem the rule, but nature's forces also seem to have some order. The air is clear. The brook in the meadow is a deeper green than our waters but I sense that the fluid is potable."

He stopped talking and scanned the horizon. His brow furrowed and he appeared in great concentration.

He spoke again, "We will need to find our way back. And not even Boomer could miss the flaming stairs. We are here, wherever here is. I'll turn things back over to you now, Eomore. That was easier than I had feared. I didn't think we would make it," Roscoe stated

Roscoe massaged his temples; it was something that he did after exhausting spell casting.

The small group scanned the horizons of this new world. Nigel and Tjol returned from a short crawl to the brook with a volume of the liquid. Knarra removed a pinch of powder from one of the many recesses of her robe and sprinkled it into the liquid. She said a few phrases and pronounced that the fluid was as pure as any stream from Donothor. There were three suns in the sky which combined produce amber light. It was difficult to gauge direction, for even the astute Deron had to concentrate heavily. The smallest, most brilliant sun scurried across the sky while the largest hovered in midposition. The third produced an eerie gray aura.

Everyone seemed to be thinking "what now".

Eomore uncomfortably felt that all the eyes were turned to him. They seemed relatively secure here; certainly, no Draiths were in the immediate vicinity. He suggested that they move over to the cover of the trees at the edge of the great grassy field.

The plants seemed "normal" other than the dominantly red color. The flora lacked the familiar green of home. There were a myriad of small winged creatures and insects. So far no monsters had appeared.

They had started moving to the woods when an ominous humming sound brought a "Hit the deck" from Vannelei whose elven ears picked up the sound first.

They sprawled onto the ground; a dark arrow flew through the ai and struck the ground some twenty yards to their left. They could see what looked like a parchment attached to the shaft; the archer remained hidden.

CHAPTER 16
A Triumphant Return

Izitx awakened to the efforts of the "Menders" who were caring for the painful burns covering most of his massive frame. He again cursed the elven woman who had so deviously inflicted the wounds and cost him the joy of taking the life of the wretched magician. The pain of the wounds was easing because the Menders were so adept at their trade. These snow-skinned, pigmentless people were unique to the World of the Three Suns in this healing ability. No one, not even the Draith sages, understood the nature of this talent; the Menders had always been a sought-after commodity in all the camps of the various combatants during many conflicts in the troubled land. They were a reclusive sort who preferred to live alone in the great highlands; they were pacifistic and never offered resistance to capture. They were indiscriminate about their talents; that is, they would heal first one warrior then his enemy. Menders did not understand the concept of loyalty. Menders understood mending. They could be taught nothing else. For many generations the Menders had lived among the other peoples; the value of the Menders was appreciated even by the Draiths. They were spineless creatures in the eyes of one such as Izitx, but he was glad that they were here now that he had been the one in need of their talents. He then, with pride, remembered the expression on the face of his liege Calaiz when the party had returned with the woman. Granted, the prize had not been gathered without loss; some gallant scouts had fallen before the surprisingly stout resistance by the men of Lyndyn.

Performing the requests of his Lord Calaiz was the greatest ambition of Izitx; he sat back to bask in this feeling of satisfaction. Even though he had been seriously wounded and was near death, he had not relinquished command; he had given the prize over to the Black Lord before he had fallen in exhaustion. A time period had passed. (about eight hours). The rest had invigorated him. He did not want to die! He wanted vengeance! He wanted to slay the cowardly wizards who had taken his scouts' lives.

Izitx hated Magick!

The door of the advisor's chamber opened and the awesome figure approached.

"You have done very well, my servant," Calaiz said as he reached out to grasp the shoulder of the wounded advisor. "This one seems to have all the requirements necessary for the continuation of the line. I anxiously await the consummation. I only wish that the time moved more quickly; there will be certain pleasures about this task, I feel."

Izitx forced a smile. The one characteristic of Calaiz that disturbed him was the King's interest in physical pleasures. This could at times lead to inefficiency.

"My Lord, I am grateful to have had the opportunity to serve you again. The Menders are doing their tasks well and I should hope to return to my full duties after another rest period."

"How powerful was their Magick?" the Draith Lord asked.

"I am not attuned to the forces of the Magick as you are my liege. I know better the fist and the blade. My Lord, the fray cost us several good scouts. There was a male who cast powerful fires at us; my reflector turned his own spell against him. Your device was destroyed in the affair. Unfortunately, as I was preparing to finish him, I was attacked by a frail wench whom I thought was a serving girl. Her attack was somewhat less powerful but still very effective. I don't feel either was in the league with the Kiennites' Deathqueen, or perhaps even the highest of the Drelves' wizards of old. But we did catch them unprepared for battle. I regret the loss of your subjects and I should hope to be able to enact vengeance upon them at some other time."

"Do you think there is a chance of pursuit?" the king asked.

"No, I doubt that they wil be able to follow us. Even if they do, the trail meets a dead end. I have left guards to discourage them if they should manage to find the portal. I doubt that their constitutions would allow them to traverse the gate even if their Magick manage to detect it. They do not have you to protect them, my liege..."

"Then I shall continue my plans to mount an offensive against the Kiennites. I could think of no better consummation gift for myself that the head of the Kiennite Deathqueen," the Draith Lord uttered.

114

Calaiz smiled.

He could sense the powers of the northern peoples fading daily. The powers of Anectrophinea were fading like the ending rays of the sun of the parallel world.

The Kiennite Deathqueen!

"Heal swiftly, my friend. I have great need of your assistance in the days ahead," Calaiz said positively.

"Yes, gladly," Izitx said, confiming again his steadfast loyalty.

Calaiz turned and left the room, leaving the Menders to their appointed tasks. He left the healing chamber assured that his top advisor and friend would survive. Friendship, of course, was rather an unknown concept to many of the Draiths, indeed, to all when there were only purebloods. But the thinning of the blood had changed much. But there was more than loyalty, respect, and the classic Draith ideals between Calaiz and Izitx; though the emotional aspects lay entirely with the king.

The Draith leadership endeavored to maintain the ideals and purity of their race as best they could since the day of the Spawncurse. The Draith traits had remained dominant in all crossbreeding to this point. Genetics was a matter of concern to Izitx. Environmental conditioning could go a long way toward correcting the genetic losses from crossbreeding and the imperfections of the long arduous and frequently unsuccessfull and disastrous cloning process.

The "Teachers of the Creed," who were a society of staunch disciplinarians, were charged with the responsibility of teaching the youth in the arts and concepts of Draith society. The art of hand to hand combat, both offensive and defensive, was one of their most important teachings. Physical conditioning was begun in infancy and was stressed for every male; it always had been. When female children were captured, they were always subjected to physical and mental conditioning. The Draith alchemists, working alone or in conjunction with those who practiced Magick that had been allied or pressured into assistance by various means, had concocted over time many nectars and potions which enhanced the physical attributes and brought the nutritional status of the people to a level that no others could approach.

As a result, not even the huge Drolls were a physical match for the Draiths. Indeed their physical prowess rivaled even the rare giants of the far mountains.

But even the efforts of the wisest of the Draiths had been unable to circumvent the effects of the Spawncurse; even the female children of the mixed coupling failed to survive childhood. There were legends that Magick of the Deathqueen of the Kiennites would be broken with her own destruction; legends also said that she was immortal and an undying terror. Her origins were really unknown. There had never been a spell as powerful or encompassing as the Spawncurse in all the lands. Even with their greatest military successes, the Draith armies had never penetrated the fortress of the undying Shebeast. So no Draith had ever seen their greatest adversary, but they had captured scrolls that supposedly bore her likeness and had likewise found statues of a hideously gnarled being. As was well-known throughout the Land of the Three Suns, their closest brush with victory had been the baneful campaign of the Nargan the Red King which was ended by the Spawncurse.

As he walked along the corridors toward the meeting room where the Council of Elders awaited him, Calaiz remembered his own youth. He had been a star pupil even at an early age and had learned well. He was as physically powerful as any of his forebears, probably even inclusive of the ages of the purebloods; he had rewritten most of the athletic standards during his competitive time.

He again thought of the Spawncurse and its perpetrator – Anectrophinea. His hatred for her far exceeded any of his other ambitions. Except perhaps the 'heirquest' – of course the efforts of the noble Izitx had gone a long way toward solving the problem. Calaiz had only seen her through the one way mirrors looking into the chambers where she had been sleeping since her arrival at Castle Ooranth. But there were many preparations for the ceremony of consummation; there would hopefully be a campaign against the forces of the Drolls and Kiennites before the time of the consummation. Tradition held that this must occur during that period when the light from the suns was at its weakest – a time called the Amber Period. This occurred every forty dark periods, or some six weeks in the time quantums of the world of one sun. The Amber Period was a time of great import to all the people of Parallan- the World of the Three Suns- and was thought to be a time of special powers. There was time to get every thing done; the current Amber Period was near its end. The next would hold the ceremony of consummation.

There was time.

The Dark Lord was somewhat tentative about meeting her – an unusual feeling for him. He hoped secretly that there would be some chemistry between them and full indoctrination would not be necessary. He was doubly glad that his peers were not capable of mind-reading; stories were told that their foes the Kiennites were rarely capable of telepathy; Calaiz would never want his people to know that thoughts of doubt came to him. These feelings frustrated him greatly; all his training had ridiculed such things; he often wondered if others experienced the same feelings; feelings like the joy he felt on learning that Izitx would survive his wounds; feelings like the remorse he felt whenever he learned of another female child falling victim to the Spawncurse; feelings when he learned that a scout who had shared many conflicts with him had fallen in the field of combat. Why did these thoughts come into his mind when he knew that, as the lord of the Draith domain, strength and fortitude must dominate his thoughts? His decisions must be based entirely on logic and calculation!

Never on emotion!

Emotions – what a curse!

His mother had given him so much; but some of her "gifts" tormented the Dark Lord as he struggled within himself.

Calaiz proceeded toward the conference room. He always preferred to have Izitx with him for these meetings; the Elders were experienced and knowledgable. He had to be strong and unwavering in his dealings with them. Most of them were past their prime and beyond the age of campaigning; their advice was valued.

Calaiz was certainly smart enough to recognize the value of their contributions; he and Izitx shared the opinion that the Elders were too cautious. The topic of today's meeting was the recent reports of increased activity in the northern mountain regions between the Drolls of the Cu Mountains and the dreaded Kiennites of the northeastern plains. For years, these border areas had been scouted by Draith scouts and there had always been skirmishes whenever the different parties came across each other. In times past, the Drolls and the Kiennites had united against the Draiths; but usually, they were not overly fond of each other. The returning scouts had reported substantial troop movements between the two kingdoms; great numbers of Drolls had been crushed in the last conflict; they were now led by a young king whose name, in its native tongue, reminded Calaiz of a growling stomach that was in need of nourishment. The Kiennites were of course still led by the Deathqueen or at least by her memory or her pawns. Calaiz did not fear conflict with his old enemies – he only wanted time as his ally against them – he wanted the war to come when he was ready. He had hoped that the other two peoples would be unable to resolve their own differences and would not be able to unite against him.

The Drolls were large humanoid creatures – usually even taller than the Draiths- they were abominably ugly, probably even in the eyes of their own mothers. At least that was how a common Draith joke about them read. What they lacked in intelligence, they made up for in cunning and ferocity. They were dogfaced beings and seemed just as comfortable biting and clawing in a fight as with using weapons; they usually fought with heavy, well made swords and moved with surprising speed in combat. The Kiennites were less formidable physically but far more dangerous; certain ones of them were endowed with powers of the Magick; some had the terrible powers of mind control; for the draiths this was fortunately rare; it was difficult for even the strongwilled Draiths to resist. The Kiennites' physical appearance was similar to the gnarled goblins of the parallel world. But this outward appearance was gravely deceiving.

Calaiz loathed both, but certainly the Kiennites had been more baneful to his people.

The Draith Lord entered the circular council chamber; the quiet conversation stopped.

Every muscle in her body ached and cried for comfort.

Perhaps this is what awakened Trya Aivendar from the seemingly endless sleep; perhaps it was the perfumed warm compress that the elven girl was tenderly pressing against her forehead.

"Don't be startled," the soothing voice said, "My name is Heather. I think you are safe here."

Before answering, Trya looked around. She was lying on a large overstuffed sofa and sinking deeply into the cushions. The air was filled with a heavy floral scent. The chamber was rather plush and seemed to be sunken from the level of the large heavy door to her right. There were several women scurrying around the room; it was readily apparent that they were of diverse racial stock; though most were women; their ages varied. Some were matronly and much older but others seemed less than a generation older than Trya. The elven girl was very young; it was difficult to ascertain their age based on their personal appearance. Scanning the room further, Trya saw to her left there was a great glass window and sliding door which opened into a patio with dense foliage. There were several other women there tending the plants. The room and its contents were actually very lovely, and Trya was beginning to enjoy the beauty when she recalled that the last thing that she could remember was the attack upon her family at Castle Lyndyn. She did not even know if her parents and friends had survived the assault.

"Where are we? Who are you?" she asked.

Her mind filled with a thousand questions.

The elven girl had some insight into the dilemma. Indeed, she had arrived here under similar circumstances only a short time earlier.

She answered, "I'm not exactly sure. I've only been here a short time myself. It's hard to keep an exact track of time because the suns never completely set. I was taken from my people much the same as you probably were. But since I've been here I have been treated well. This is a great castle in a city which the inhabitants call Ooranth. But it is a kingdom I've never heard of, and probably in a different realm. The sky is filled with three suns of different color; the land is bathed with an amber glow and the sky is amber instead of blue. It's pretty, and quite different, but I much prefer our own land. The rulers here call themselves "The Masters," but others refer to them as Draiths. They are tall, muscular men, at least - I guess they are manlike, but the only women that I've seen are foreign such as we are. We are not locked in, but the Masters and the Matrons, which is what I guess that I am now, all say that we would not be safe outside the castle walls. According to the matrons, there are all matter of strange beasts and foliage in the forests, and since I lack a compass, direction would be almost impossible to maintain since there are three suns in the sky. I fear that I would not have the slightest idea on where to go first. I cling to the slight hope that help may come eventually, but the Matrons tell me that it never does."

"Why have they taken us?" Trya asked.

She feared that she already knew the answer to her question; she asked anyway.

"I can only speculate, but as I said, they apparently don't have any women. I fear that their intentions with us may not be entirely honorable. The Matrons say that you are special and are to be treated with utmost care. They keep mentioning 'the choice of the Great Lord,' but again, I'm not sure of the significance of all that I've heard. Again, I have been treated very well since I arrived here," Heather answered.

Trya sat up and retorted, "That sounds perfectly delightful, doesn't it? I can hardly wait to meet my benefactors. I can all too well remember what these Masters look like and their natures are far from benevolent."

She felt frightened and a wave of nausea came over her. She regained her composure and was comforted somewhat by the further words of the elven girl. One of the older women brought a platter of plush fruits and vegetables before her; Trya realized that the nausea had left and had been replaced by a ravenous hunger. It mattered little that she could not recognize any of the fruits. Still, the fruits were delicious, and she could feel the rejuvenation of her lost strength. After eating she was led to a private chamber where she bathed in a warm spring, was given a wardrobe, and draped with elaborate jewelry. Then she was led back to a smaller sleep chamber where she again collapsed. For the moment, fatigue still ruled; the elven girl was correct in that escape wasn't the proper avenue at this time. But the Masters had never tackled an Aivendar woman before.

Sleep fell upon Trya Aivendar.

CHAPTER 17
WHERE?

The arrow struck the ground some twenty paces from the nearest member of Eomore's party. Quickly, they scattered and dropped to the ground; each member scanned the forest edge; they squinted in the eerie amber light produced by the combined rays of the three suns. There was no movement immediately apparent to anyone. The amber sky required some visual adjustment, but the air was fresh and pure.

"What do they say about the frying pan into the fire?" lamented Nigel. "I can't detect any movement, but the angle of the missile would seem to indicate that it came from the dense brushes to our right."

Eomore was busily scanning for the unseen enemy as well.

The prince said, "Nor do I see movement. Is there not something attached to the arrow?"

"I think so," Deron added. "Should I try to retrieve it?"

"Not yet," Roscoe quickly interrupted the dwarf.

The mage then brought a small phial from the depths of his robe and began to utter several soft phrases as he sprinkled the violet dust from the container. He then closed his eyes tightly for a moment; he rolled over on the ground 360 degrees.

He said, "I can detect no invisible beings. I would suggest that the perpetraters are still hidden by the forest edge. Be wary as you stand."

Eomore removed the longbow from his back, which was no small task given their prone position. Suddenly he remembered Exeter. He grasped the hilt of the weapon.

He noted a somewhat sarcastic voice appeared in his thoughts, "I thought you would never ask! I detect no enemies within the distance of my power. But I feel strangely different, my Lord. Maybe stronger – maybe not."

The voice faded from his mind.

He replied to his own thoughts "I think all of us have to feel a certain strangeness about this place. At least we can breathe the air."

Deron then began to inch toward the arrow, for he was by fate the nearest to it. He was not attacked and reached it successfully. He pulled it from the ground without diffculty and returned to where Eomore and Nigel were lying. Roscoe had joined them. Knarra and Vannelei were flanking the physician Sedoar. Cara had drawn forth her crossbow and was lying hear the rear of the group flanked by the four remaining rangers. Eomore took the arrow from the dwarf and slipped the parchment from it. It was not unlike the scroll parchments that Eomore had seen before in the possession of Knarra. He unrolled the parchment and found long flowing runes stoked by a frail or small, fine intrument, perhaps using the juice of a red forest berry. The writing was however foreign to him.

"I cannot read this," he admitted.

"Definitely not anything that I've seen before," Nigel confided as he looked over the shoulder of the prince.

Roscoe slightly raised himself and peered at the runes.

"I think I know the language," he said. "This is similar to the characters of an ancient elven alphabet. It's similar to that in many of my ancient journals. I think this says, 'Do you serve darkness or do you serve the forest?'- But I'm not entirely certain. I don't know quite how we should respond to it."

"We were sitting ducks when the arrow was fired. He's either a terrible archer or else he tried to miss us. I think they could have fired upon us if they had desired to do so," Nigel added. "We need all the friends that we can get. At least these birds must be different from the dudes that we were pursuing; that has to be an improvement."

"I suppose that's true. I'm going to stand up without a weapon," Eomore said.

"Go ahead. We'll etch 'brave' on your tombstone," Nigel quipped.

"Any other suggestions?" the prince requested.

There was silence.

Eomore's words were convincing; his actions were slow and deliberate.

The prince stood at a snail's pace; he placed his bow on the ground in front of him. There was a whirring sound; he felt the urge to drop flat upon his face but remained standing; he saw a volley of arrows strike harmlessly some ten paces in front of him. There was again a parchment attached to one of the missiles. This time he did not hesitate; the prince walked straight up to the arrow and lifted it from the ground. When he unrolled the parchment, he found that there were the same archaic symbols. He turned and walked toward Roscoe.

"More fan mail?" the mage quipped.

Eomore gave the parchment to Roscoe. He studied the parchment. The group relaxed their guard ever so slightly. Knarra had joined Roscoe in looking at the epistle. Only the two elves and Nigel were unwilling to drop their guard.

"This is sort of a dinner invitation," Roscoe said. "It reads, 'sheath your weapons, stand in a tight group, and we'll come for you' as best I can tell."

"No way," Deron quickly interjected, "These guys aren't getting me without a fight. I'm not a sacrificial lamb."

Vannelei added, "I am a little uncomfortable with this arrangement myself. We could be wiped out with a single volley of arrows."

"It would seem that we have little choice," Knarra said, joining the debate. "We need some sort of direction in this strange land. I do not sense evil nearby; this whole land seems tormented. I fear we must trust that the arrows bring us closer to our goal and not to our doom. I fear that this land will have many more terrible surprises."

Slowly the group stood and reluctantly followed the example of their leader by sheathing their weapons. Nigel and Cara were reluctant. Both placed their bows on the ground. Both kept their concealed weapons. For a moment, there was silence; then they saw movement in several areas along the edge of the forest some fifty to one hundred paces to their right. To their left there was a great open expanse with intercrossing roads. There was a reddish-brown grass covering much of the area. Except for their color, the trees were fairly similar to those of their homeland in Donothor; some were quite unusual.

A slight figure slightly shorter than an elf emerged from behind a large ever-red tree. He carried a long bow with an arrow at ready. For a moment he stared at the group as though he were sizing them up and assuring himself that they were indeed not going to attack. Finally, Nigel lowered his bow; the figure stepped forward; at the same time several others of his ilk moved out of the forest; they had blended into the forest perfectly. The first figure moved toward them cautiously. As he approached, the resemblance that he bore to the elves of their own party became obvious; his skin had a definite greenish hue; the hue changed as he walked across the brownish ground. They noted that his coloration mimicked the grassy red fields upon which they were standing. Clearly, these creatures had some powers like the prismatic dragons of their world which some called a chameleon power. Or was he a changling? Could shape changers have followed them? In a short while there were some two dozen of the forest dwellers near them; they discovered an even more remarkable attribute of the foresters. Initially the apparent leader spoke; none could comprehend the meaning of his words.

Eomore spoke, "We can't understand."

He used the common dialect of Donothor.

The forest "elf" pondered for a moment.

He said, "That you speak this old dialect is heartening. It is not spoken in this world often now, but we are taught it as one of the old languages as saplings. We are glad that you do not number among our enemies. We certainly have enough of those as it is without more coming through the 'Otherworld Gate.' I am called Nibor. I am the sergeant of this guard. We are here at the request of our liege, the righteous Drolan, to observe the activities at the portal. My people always watch the 'Otherworld Gate.' We are servants of the forest and nature. What is your business in this land?"

Nibor spoke the dialect perfectly. The group was amazed that his speech and his color blended into his environment.

Eomore was perplexed by the forest creatures answering in the common tongue of Donothor.

Finally he asked, "Why would our language be taught here?"

Nibor did not have an answer.

He did retort," There are few languages in the known part of our world. Common tongues exist so different peoples can communicate. I am not a student of linguistics; I can simply understand your speech; like so many things, perhaps the words came through the ancient portal."

Roscoe eased the grip on his staff. He only had to touch it lightly to activate the languages function of his staff. The hard grip was needed to keep the fireball activated. The mage knew that the Protection Spells would still have protected the group. The fireball was his "ace in the hole." He had heard the expression being uttered in games of chance.

"We are from a land we call Donothor; we are here to set right several wrongs that have been maliciously and wantonly brought upon our lands. I am Eomore Aivendar, son of Eraitmus Aivendar, King of Donothor, and we are here at his request. We will be grateful for any direction that you can give us; for it is my beloved sister and the sister of my elven friend Vannelei that we seek. What is the name of this land and what do you call your race?"

Nibor answered, "There is no word that I know of in your tongue for the name that we call ourselves and our lands. You would not be able to express the name of the land and our people in our forest dialect,"

Nigel stated, "Then we will call you 'Drelves' and this parallel land we will call 'Parallan.' At least we have a name for the place where we will probably die."

Nibor did not change his color or demeanor.

He said, "We will lead you to a place of sanctuary, Alm's Glen; the Dark Period is well upon us, and the suns will desert us even further before full light returns to the land. You were certainly victims of malicious acts, but not wanton. Our enemies the Draiths, who call themselves Masters, do nothing without a purpose and they have long raided upon the womenfolk of your world and ours alike, for they have none of their own. That is a story, though, that I will defer to the elders of my people. Now we must move; the clearings are not secure. The Draiths use the portal. War parties are common. Follow me."

Their faces had expressions ranging from quizzical to hopeful to the distrustful scowl of Nigel Louffette. With a motion of his hand and a nod, Eomore indicated to the party and to Nibor that they would follow. The Drelves moved through the thick underbrush with ease. The journey was brief; they soon reached a clearing among the great ever-red trees. The yellow skies and the red-orange foliage were becoming familiar.

A very old Drelve emerged from the huge ever-red in the center of the clearing. He was followed by a matronly female. A number of other females emerged from the trees; they were quite fetching. All of the males found their eyes drawn toward them.

Cara flushed when she saw Eomore staring at the female nearest him. She moved closer to the prince, as if to protect her interest. Even the indomitable mage Roscoe was impressed by these nymphlike creatures. Knarra moved beside him and whispered something to the mage; he broke into a smile and gently reached out and took the hand of the priestess. Only Nigel noticed this. Perhaps the hardened heart of the thief prevented his taking any interest in beholding the simple beauty of the forest maidens; perhaps it was that he was not completely convinced that these new "friends" were all they purported to be. The older Drelve moved to the group.

Eomore had been reassured repeatedly by Exeter that enemies were not near. Eomore had tired of asking the blade about Nigel.

Nibor said, "I present these otherworlders, my King. They came through the portal this period and have been wronged by the dark ones. I present Prince Eomore of the land known as Donothor."

The Older One answered, "I am Drolan, the entrusted of my people, the servants of the forest, with their leadership. I welcome you to Alms Glen. This is our sanctuary. You will be safe here from the uncertainties and evils that ravage our land. I regret that the wise Magrian, our Teacher is away and securing the enhancing root which is so vital to us. But he should return after the next rest period. In the interim, we will endeavor to make you comfortable and try to replenish your strength. I am not sure what help we may be to you for many shadows darker than the waning rays of the dark period shadow our land. I understand that you have been touched by one of the greatest of these of shadows."

Eomore answered, "We are grateful for your hospitality. We fear that our mission will not be easy, indeed, will likely be hazardous. We know little of your land and even less of our foes. We appreciate any assistance that you can give us."

Drolan smiled and answered, "My people will escort you to guest 'trees' which will provide you room to refresh; we will prepare a feast of the wealth of the forest for you. Afterwards we can talk. I can tell you much, but the Teacher Magrian can relate so much more to you about the peoples and regions of our land. I want you to have a rest and await his return after the rest period."

"Thank you again," Eomore replied.

Several females approached and led Cara and Knarra away; males commanded by Nibor led Eomore, Nigel, Roscoe, Deron, Vannelei, Tjol Bergin, and the other three rangers to a welcomed bath in a bubbling stream. The waters were heated to a comfortable temperature by gray stones. In addition to Tjol, Eomore had chosen three other proven warriors for the task. He would have preferred to have the sword of Boomer at his side, but the dwarf was probably just now beginning the return trek from the castle of Roscoe. The three chosen men, though, had their own attributes. Banon Kessa was the perenniel archery champion of the King's tournament. Kryl Amme was an accomplished swordsman and a tenacious fighter. Cyrus Thorogood was a veteran of many campaigns and his bravery was renowned. He was an accomplished musician; his lute could be most soothing after a day of battle or travel.

Banon, Kryl, and Cyrus were steadfastly loyal to the Aivendars. The three rangers were Eomore's strongest opponents during competitions and tournaments. All had taken the trophy home.

CHAPTER 18
Captured

The amber period wasn't really dark in the sense of the blackness of one of the subterranean caves, but the receding suns bathed the land with only the faintest of rays. To a lesser degree this occurred each time the fleet star, Meries passed reached its zenith, and the peoples had different terms for this, most referring to it as the dark or rest period; the amber period was the time of greatest significance to the many peoples of the World of the Three Suns. Once every 6 weeks or so based on the time scales of the parallel world, there was an extended period of decreased light that lasted for about a week in those terms. Only during this time frame did Meries completely leave the skies. The "dark period" wasn't totally dark, but most of the light bathing the land came from the gray star.

The Forest Drelves considered the "dark period" a time of importance; and the Patriarch Magrian led the devout keepers of the arts into the forests in search of the enhancing plant which was necessary for their rituals. Magrian was very old and knowledgable of many things. The younger members of the party always benefited from these treks into the thick forests, for the old one always used the rest times to recount many of the legends of the land of the Three Suns. The Drelves were innocent bystanders to most of the wars in the land; but frequently their people were stolen away to perform the various demands of the warring parties.

The embers faded in the campfire as they gathered around the old one. The day had been successful for much of the enhancing root had been harvested to replenish the supplies of the community.

"For many generations our people have lived much as we do. While Draith, Kiennite, and Droll warred to gain dominance, our people strived to lead the peaceful life and assure the preservation of the forests. Like my fathers before me I am entrusted as the Spiritual Leader of the Drelves," the Teacher Magrian said.

The young Drelves were riveted to every word.

"I continue the teachings of our forefathers. Of many things you must be told." Magrian continued.

"Things were not always as they are now. At one time we were to be reckoned with in the affairs of the lands. These were the times of our greatest glory. Our borders were breached by powers from without and previously unknown. Our leaders endeavored to protect our people. That was in the time of the Four Spell Weavers and the appearance of the great blade. This was a weapon of great might which was forged from fires of Magick; a number of the Xennic Stones and a stone found in the seventh cave said to be a fragment of Andreas the Gray Wanderer were hammered into the hilt and blood groove of the blade. The Magick required to complete the blade incorporated the combined energies of the Spell Weavers at the precise moment of the closest Approximation of the Gray Wanderer, Andreas. We were never even in these strong days a warring people, but the others would allow us our domain without encroachments and harassments. The Great Blade was lost to us for a time. It was regained due to the efforts of the last Spell Weaver and a small band of Drelves. Its recovery cost the life of the last Spell Weaver. The enhancing root and the great blade together served to protect us. The weapon became to be known as the Draithsbane because of its particular powers against our most deadly enemies. With the passage of time our opponents grew stronger and more devious. Finally through acts of great treachery the Spell Weavers were gone; a disillusioned and power hungry young Drelve named Ramish compounded the treachery; the Draithsbane was lost to us. Ramish likewise vanished but the damage was done; the great weapon was lost; storied legends are all that remain. Our people were taken to the camps of the others and faced great persecution and trial. Eventually we made the forests our home where those like me have endeavored to preserve our heritage. But we continue to hope for the return of the Draithsbane and along with it some degree of security for our people. I have searched many lands for evidence of the artifact," the Old One continued.

The young Drelves saw the eyes of the aged Teacher mist over.

He said,"Its blade radiated the flames of its great creator, the Spell Weaver of Fire. The rituals using the enhancing root enable us to keep our heritage alive while we wait for the return of the blade. But we have waited long," the old man stopped.

"But there have been many dark periods since the last wars. In times such as these, we don't have to fear while in our homes, do we?" asked one of the young ones eagerly.

Another added, "The Traditional thinking was that the Draiths , who sometimes refer to themselves as the Masters, were so weakened by the curse of the Kiennite Deathqueen through the Black Wish that they would never rise again – this is how we were taught. The Deathqueen herself is said to weaken with the passage of time."

"Yes, that is the way things have been. But I feel a sense of darkness in the air that goes beyond that felt in the dark period. Both powers are waxing and not waning; another conflict is nigh. Aye, I fear the Draiths may be the nearest the total conquest than they have ever been," the old one added.

He then became silent and began to smoke the worn pipe that he always carried. The smoke was a wisp of violet against the amber air.

The camp became silent as they retired. The guards never saw the enemies until they were upon them; there was no warning call; the air did not hum with the finely tuned Drelves' bowstrings.

The battle did not last long.

The old one was rudely awakened by huge rough hands lifting him harshly. He was distressed by the cruel dogfaced creatures and their snarling. But years in these lands gave him enough understanding of the language.

He shuddered as he understood the commander's words: "Secure the old dog – kill the rest!"

His henchmen readily performed their ordered tasks; in their killing frenzy the Drolls failed to notice one blithe form roll from the clearing into the heavy brush.

The hunters then departed with their quarry.

CHAPTER 19
Needed Rest

The amber light waned a little further by the time the party gathered together under the greatest red elm tree. The Drelven females prepared an attractive feast for them consisting of various fruits of the forest. Drolan and Nibor were already seated at the large wooden table that had been brought out. They sat at the table. Cara looked very pretty in the forest garb that had been furnished her by the hosts. Eomore couldn't help but notice because she made a special effort to sit beside him at the table. Knarra still wore her deep red robe; the flowers given her by the Drelves were placed in her flowing tresses and her robe. Nigel thought the priestess's locks were redder in the waning light. She sat by Roscoe opposite the prince and the elf. With a gesture from Drolan, the meal began.

"Among us, only Magrian has seen your lands. Therefore, we know little more of your land than you do of ours, Prince of Donothor," Drolan began. "But at this time it's more important for you to learn of us. Still I hope to satisfy my curiosity in better times. Magrian is our greatest scholar but I shall try to begin your education. Enhanced by legends and lore, our archives tie our lands in some way to the Evilness that is the Kiennite Deathqueen. Magrian and a few other drelves were able to pass through the gate aided by the Magick of the Spell Weavers, which has been lost to us; traversing the portal was baneful; all met their doom except Magrian and one other, who managed to return with their lives but little else. Time clouds the clarity of the telling of the stories. Magick has given Magrian exceedingly long life; Magrian won't talk of this; he won't talk of his companion. He learned of the parallel world and returned to give us your concepts of time and direction. I do not know how the device works, but he used a small device to define directions which he calls north, south, east, and west; though in our land direction is somewhat relative; he teaches us you have but one sun; we have three. The teacher tells us that the giant Orphos is the determinate of direction here. Meries the fleet and Andreas the wanderer, the other two suns, are responsible for the light and the way of our land. The giants of the northern forests worship the suns with many ceremonies; these people have been decimated by the armies of the other three and now only exist in small clans."

Deron then spoke, "That sure is a lot to digest. This seems to be a complicated land. But these fruits are not hard to digest. I feel replenished of my strength."

A tankard of ale would have been welcomed by the dwarf and the others as well, but the foods were quite refreshing. The knowledge of the lands was invaluable and they relished the discussions.

Drolan the king then said, "Is your world not really just as complicated, noble elven prince? You are strengthened by our foods because you are so similar to us. I see a very diverse group before me. We know little of your combined powers. You undertake such a quest with these small numbers; you must be exceptional individuals. Is that safe to say? The Kiennite Deathqueen resides in an impregnable fortress. She is said to maintain perpetual youth and power. The Draiths grow stronger. No army has ever breached the black walls of Ooranth, the Draith stronghold."

Roscoe replied, "We have our individual talents, and Draiths have sampled some of them. I am not convinced that anything is impregnable and I'm not convinced that any man or woman is immortal. I should like to meet the 'Deathqueen' as you refer to her and see this impregnable fortress."

Drolan smiled, "This man is a bearer of Magick. I recognize the haughtiness. I hope your powers can substantiate the rashness of your words, my friend, for I would not even want to encounter Anectrophinea in my nightmares."

Roscoe skulked, and Knarra whispered to him. The two then stood; Knarra graciously excused them from the king's table. The two then walked over to the edge of the stream and began to talk.

Roscoe, in subdued tone, said,"The Magick required for the casting of a Wish Spell is rare in our world at this and any time. The Orb of Chalar is lost, thought destroyed with her. Legend talks of other powerful Magick, the Elixirs of Mastery of Magick. It is also thought that the effort of casting a Wish would exhaust, if not kill, the caster. And add to that Permanancy. You know the fatigue from casting a mere Warding Glyph, Knarra; this Kiennite Ruler is not someone that I feel we should encounter if we can avoid it. I am having diffiulty believing the stories of our newfound friends, though I see no reason that we should fear these forest people. They certainly could have raised more havoc for us at the portal had they desired. I can guess how the portal gate was created and who trespassed against these peoples if these legends are truthful. That was so long ago. There is an Essence..."

Knarra nodded, and then replied,"Things are not in this world as they are in ours. I'm sure you sense the increased turbulence in Magick as I do. There is power here that I have not felt in, well, a long time. Did you not sense a loss of strength with the setting of the Gray Star?"

Roscoe reluctantly acknowledged that he felt different; he could have simply been the sequalae of the energy he expended in helping the group traverse the portal. He noted that his learned companion avoided the subject of the number of years. In some ways, Knarra was simply a woman.

Nigel's eyes followed Roscoe and Knarra as they walked away. He wasn't sure why he was drawn to the priestess but assumed it was some subconscious feeling of indebtedness to her for healing his wounds. Why did he not feel the same when he looked at the elven girl who had so bravely come to his aid when he was attacked by the two Draiths? The feeling was uncomfortable to the thief; he had not experienced it for many years. The feelings of attachment to or need of his fellow beings were new sensations for the thief.

Cara heard little of the King's story. Her eyes remained fixed upon the warrior seated next to her. Eomore was aware of her gaze and occasionally risked a glance at her eyes; the prince felt that each time he looked into the misty dark green elven eyes, he risked falling in and came closer to drowning in her eyes. He too was experiencing new sensations.

He was just finishing one of the excursions into the maid's eyes when Exeter flashed a statement into his consciousness. "I want to hear more about the Draithsbane. Especially if the sustaining force of the blade is a male influence. I may as well get involved in this mating game."

Eomore had to fight to hold back the chuckle; sarcasm dripped like thick poison from the "words" of his weapon.

The prince of Donothor turned to Nibor. "What were the powers of the Draithsbane?"

Nibor answered, "She was the essence of the forest. She gave her wielder the reaction of the mongoose, the eye of the eagle, the smell of the Red Dragon, and the speed of the deer. He gained the advantage of anticipating the move of his enemy and gained the power of camouflage if within the forest, of falling from sight in the light of the suns. The weapon had other abilities that it imparted to only its wielder, including great longevity. The blade healed the wounds of its bearer. But she was tarnished by the foul hands of the traitor Ramish. The 'Locating Stones' that could define the location of the blade were stolen, probably by Ramish. The creators of the blade had never anticipated that one of our own would betray us. The creators had instilled protections for our people within the blade such that alien wielders would be limited in their abilities to turn the blade against us. She was called the Draithsbane because these foul beings were especially susceptible to her powers and her blade."

Exeter said, "I've suddenly lost interest."

Eomore had not. The prince was fascinated with weaponry. He had labored to understand his own sword and the thoughts of another great weapon also excited him. But particularly a weapon which was valuable against the Draiths!

He asked, "What did the blade look like?"

Drolan answered, "None of recent generations have ever looked upon her, but Magrian teaches us that she was a graceful longsword much like one that graces your own hilt. There were the runes of the ancient Drelven Spell Weavers placed upon her and these would appear only when she was in Drelven hands. Legend also holds that the blade's creators were the greatest of the Drelven Spell Weavers and were destroyed by treachery shortly after its creation. Legend again says the blade was a tithe to forestall the violation of our world by a powerful minion of the other world. The weapon was returned to us for a time. Then it was lost. We have long assumed that Ramish secured the Draithsbane in such a location that we would be fortunate to ever recover her. For he was not a wizard himself, but he was endowed with powers of illusion that were unrivaled even by the Kiennites. Perhaps his powers were not enough to satisfy him and this led to his seduction by evil. Time dulls the memory and fades the stories of legend."

"Are the Draiths capable of Magick?" Nigel asked.

"Only through the use of items," Drolan replied. "This has been a balancing force which has thus far prevented them from accomplishing the total conquest that they desire. They usurp the Magick of others, but it would be baneful indeed if the powers of the Magick came to them."

Nibor interrupted the conversation to say, "My friends, you must be weary. One thing that you must assure is that you get adequate rest. After the rest period, which is about eight of your hours, we anticipate the return of Magrian, who can satisfy your curiosities far better than we have been able to do. I have only provided the appetizer and he brings the meal. I suggest that you retire to the lodgings that we have prepared for you."

The luck of the draw placed Nigel and Deron, Sedoar and Roscoe, Vannelei and Eomore, Cyrus Thorogood and Banon Kessa, Kryl Amme and Thol Bergin, and of course Knarra and Cara. The lodgings were literally within the great trees and were quite comfortable in appearance. Nigel fumed about being stuck with a dwarf; Roscoe fumed about being stuck with a "sawbones;" the fuming was becoming more good natured as the members were beginning to develop more and more respect and trust for each other. Eomore found that he trusted his judgment and assumed the role of leader with more authority. He had found talking with the Drelven King enjoyable. The ties between their worlds fascinated the prince. He yearned for the return of the Teacher and more knowledge.

What lay before them?

What lessons could the Teacher give to aid their quest?

The knowledge of the light cycles was quite helpful. The great sword would be a boon but it seemed more the stuff of legend; possessing it was unlikely; maybe it was like the grapes that could not be reached by the winemaker.

"Probably sour anyway!"

They left the table and wandered off toward their lodgings, though their thoughts were certainly on the tasks before them.

Was this indeed a Deathquest?

Did they have any hope of success?

Would they recover their womenfolk?

Perhaps these questions had been the topic of discussion by Knarra and Roscoe; perhaps it had been something else altogether.

Eomore stretched. The Drelves had been right about fatigue. Eomore knew that it was perhaps a man's most deadly enemy. Even though his chainmail was amazingly lightweight for such armor, it grew heavy with time. He became aware of soft footsteps beside him.

Cara moved near him.

"Are you weary, my lord?" she asked. "It sounds scary, doesn't it? But I'm sure that you can lead us to success if anyone can."

Eomore suddenly felt some lifting of his fatigue. He looked at her. Her face seemed particularly radiant in the waning light of the great Orphos.

"Why don't you call me Eomore?" he replied.

"I am not sure if that would be proper – I am but a commoner. I would consider it an honor," Cara replied.

"I don't hold to the term commoner, my dear. I am honored that you take interest in me. I am grateful as my father was for your agreeing to accompany us on this journey into the unknown. Let's walk awhile."

"Watch yourself – a prince should not –"Exeter's warning was cut off when Eomore removed the sheath bearing the weapon and slipped the chainmail from his shoulders.

He reached over and took the small hand that anxiously awaited his; the prince and the beauty walked toward the babbling stream. Most of the Drelves seemed to be retiring as was most of their own party. Knarra and Roscoe shared the beauty of the brook and the mossy glen in the dull amber rays of the great orb which hovered above them. The Andreas, the gray sun, could barely be seen in the far horizon; the third; the little yellow sun which had been faintly evident when they first emerged from the portal into Parallan, was now completely gone from the sky. Their hosts had told them that this was the darkest time, the Dark Period; the third, the brightest of the three, would return to the sky in roughly seven days, spelling the end of another Dark Period. What was a day in the World of the Three Suns? Their internal clocks required adjustment.

"I know little of you, Cara," Eomore said inquiringly.

"There is not much to tell, Eomore. I was orphaned along with my brother Cade, who now serves Oren Bach, at an early age. I can barely remember my mother and have no recollection of my father. We were taken in by a kindly human couple who cared for us until we were old enough to move on. I had worked for Master Frathingham for two years and they treated me as a daughter. We came to Castle Lyndyn in an effort to improve ourselves," she answered.

Even in the dim light Eomore could detect a blushing of her exceptional facial features. She gripped his hand tighter.

He studied her. She was a full foot shorter than the prince and totally feminine. Yet there was an undeniable strength about her; he found his own strength bolstered when he was around her.

"How did you develop your talent?" he asked.

She answered, "I'm not sure 'developed' is the proper word. I've always had the spellbook and I remember my mother tutoring me even as a small child. But she was unable to save herself from the goblins. At least I was told that was how she was killed. She wasn't understood and was feared needlessly by those who did not understand the nature of Magick. The people who raised me often sheltered me from the local talk, but I've heard her referred to as the 'witch of the Lachinor.' I can't remember anything about her but kindness and that she constantly feared the 'return' of someone. I can tell you this so easily – yet, I've never been able to talk of this before. I feel like I can lose myself completely when I look at you, Eomore, and I can't put off telling you any longer. Back at the portal I feared that fate had taken away my chance to tell you this. I am devoted to you fully."

Cara gazed deeply into his eyes. Small rich tears welled up in her eyes and spilled out onto her cheeks. Small harmless sparks flew when one of the tears fell to the ground. Clearly she was pouring out her heart to this man who had so recently ridden into her life; a life which had been so uncomplicated.

137

Eomore bent over and kissed her lightly. He wiped the tears away. It seemed like the proper thing to do. They sat on a fallen log and for a long while said nothing.

Finally Cara asked, "Tell me about your sister. I had little chance to talk with her before the tragedy struck."

"Trya was a joy to us. Even as a child she and I had a special relationship and understanding. She seemed to understand better than anyone else the pressures of being heir apparent to the throne and how they weighed upon me. I've never been able to fully assume the role of royalty. But the last few days have taught me much about myself and I can see my father's viewpoints more clearly about the throne and many other things as well. We have grievous days ahead of us, my maid. I shall have difficult decisions to make. I will be strengthened by your presence," he confided.

"I shall be by your side with the best of my abilities. I am not sure what 'love' is, Eomore, but I think that is what I feel when I think of you," Cara replied, then they were again silent.

After a few minutes there was one more Orphos-light kiss. Eomore wished that it could have been a moonlight kiss; that would have meant they were 'home' in this special moment. They returned to their respective lodgings. Both were relieved that they had spoken the words that had been welling up inside them.

Knarra and Roscoe settled down near the brook. For the old friends there was much to talk about; the journey had denied them the opportunity until this time.

Knarra said, "It seems so natural to be trekking along on an adventure together. Was it only yesterday that we fought our first red dragon?"

The mage laughed. "Many yesterdays I fear, Knarra. But I still remember the first time the stench of the dragon fire met my nostrils like it was yesterday. Baylexa, she called herself, and she very nearly did us all in. Were it not for your heat resistance balm and incantation, we might still be residing in her stomach."

"As I recall, your spells went a long way toward bringing her down," the priestess replied.

"Have you ever thought how different things might have been if we had not had our callings; if we had been as the normal men and women of one of these worlds," she said with her voice trailing off.

"Often," he replied.

Their eyes met; Knarra's hair shimmered with all the colors of the rainbow.

They sat in silence in the amber glow, each reminiscing privately before they parted- they had parted one time too many in the past- and returned to their lodgings. Knarra could sense the radiance in the soft songs of the elven girl as she brushed her tresses. Could there have been a hint of envy in the kind heart of the priestess?

Roscoe joined the sawbones. The physician radiated nothing. He only snored.

CHAPTER 20
First Blood

The tranquility of the rest period was interrupted by shouts coming from the clearing in the middle of the great red oaks. Deron heard the noises and left his soft cozy bunk to investigate. He saw many Drelves gathered in the center of the area; they were very upset. The dwarf saw others of his party exiting their respective trees. Eomore and Vannelei joined the dwarf; they went to check out the commotion. King Drolan was distraught; he was kneeling over a badly wounded young Drelven male who tried to communicate but whose words were strained by his injuries. Knarra joined the gathering and ministered to the wounded Drelve.

King Drolan turned to Eomore and said tearfully, "Tragedy has befallen us. This is my son Vaylin. He accompanied the Teacher and the other keepers of the arts. A few hours ago they were attacked by a large Droll patrol. All were slain but Vaylin and Magrian. The Teacher was carried away by the foul beasts. He had warned us that dark times were ahead for us and that war would again ravage our lands. The Drolls would not take prisoners unless they had specific intent for him. Unfortunately they know much of our customs and beliefs; they know that the enhancing root can only be found in certain narrow ranges. No one else in the World of the Three Suns, Parallan, as you call our world knows the proper way of harvesting the plant; they may have been waiting to take him. My new friends, our tragedy and grief are great; your mission could have been aided by the knowledge of the Draiths and the lands possessed by Magrian. I can only speculate as to why they have taken him. I fear that we must now make an effort to retrieve him before this patrol returns to its base."

Knarra was bending over the frail body which weakened more by the minute. She began an incantation and rubbed a pungent polstice upon the nasty head wound of the Drelven warrior. Initially, the Drelven healers were somewhat reluctant to step aside for her, but her calming voice was hard to resist; it seemed impossible that this gentle person could harm anyone. All eyes were upon her as she worked, including Eomore's.

The prince spoke to the distraught Drolan, "We have felt and shared more that our share of grief, King. We are on a quest with little in our favor. The Teacher you call Magrian may well have been the first real aid to us. From our discussions at dinner last evening, I gather that the Draiths also place great significance in the Dark Period of your land. Either they have already violated our women, which you felt unlikely due to the short time they have been captive, or else they may await the next Dark Period. At any rate, we really don't have a starting point other than here. We shall give our assistance in trying to recover your beloved Teacher, not only to serve our own interests but also out of compassion for you."

"Prince Eomore of Donothor, you are indeed a noble man; I don't feel we can ask you or permit you to risk your lives on our account. The Drolls are fierce and heartless; we have little chance of defeating them even if we can catch them. Your direction is 90 degrees away toward Ooranth. The Drolls are our concern," the King answered.

"We have no information to benefit us in our quest, and I feel I must make every endeavor to help our chances. Our talents will help you as well in your upcoming battle," Eomore responded.

The prince found the decision easily made and realized that he had not sought counsel before making it.

Nibor then entered the conversation, saying "My King, I feel that the prince is correct in his assessment. We can and must help each other. I agree that the Draiths must have specific ideas in mind for your women, Eomore, and it grieves my hear to think about them in the company of the Masters of Evil, as Magrian has referred to them, but our immediate problem is the recovery of the one loved by us and the one who in all of Parallan can most help the other world party in their quest. Time is essential; without any guide to take us to the location of the attack, I can only guess as to where the attack occurred from what Vaylin told us before he slipped into unconsciousness. If the prince and his party assist us, I shall, if the fates allow and we return, aid them until their quest or my own life is ended."

All were startled as Vaylin sat up and said, "I make the same oath."

The head wound was healed; he looked remarkably well. Knarra's talents had again been a great boon; there was brief elation in the camp; one less had died. The celebration did not last long, for all knew that a moment's delay might make the difference between success and failure. Quickly the party members gathered their packs; numerous Drelves prepared to depart as well.

Nibor again talked with the prince about their foes.

He said, "We are no match for the Drolls in hand to hand combat. They will fall before our bows, as we are expert bowmen; their physical strength and ferocity in battle far exceeds our own. We must rely on speed and cunning against them. From what Vaylin has said, they probably are about a half-period- that's five of your hours- ahead of us. But we can travel much faster through these friendly forests and the Drolls must take at least brief respites in their trek; even they are vulnerable to fatigue. If fate smiles upon us, we may catch up to them while they are camped and our arrows may fell some of them to give us at least a chance in hand to hand battle. It is times like these that we miss the Draithsbane most."

Nigel listened intently as Nibor talked.

He said pensively, "Won't they just kill Magrian if we attack them?"

Nibor answered, "The nature of these people, and I use the word loosely, is to kill anything that is different or anything they don't understand. They make great sport of killing and if they were not on strict orders to bring him back alive they would have killed him earlier. The Drolls have a perverted sense of loyalty, but still it binds them to do what their superiors tell them to do, especially when they are in alliance with the Kiennites in times of war. For as much as they hate everything and everyone else, they hate Draiths more. You can bet that they have been told to return Magrian so that one of their superiors can try to extract what he knows of the Draiths from him. They will fight doggedly to perform their 'mission.'"

"Then they will have a good fight," Nigel quipped.

The others gathered around. There was a force of about a hundred Drelves armed with extremely well made longbows. Eomore's group was also ready.

King Drolen saw Cara and Knarra among them and said, "We cannot ask your women to fight for us. What if they should be captured? The Draiths at least have need of women which means that they are usually treated well as long as they do what they are told. The Drolls are savages and, well, I can't speak of the atrocities they might perform."

Knarra and Cara each expressed their feelings about the situation and the king accepted the decision of the women. Nibor was no happier about it than the king.

Nigel leaned over to him and whispered, "They are kind of handy to have around."

Nibor seemed irritated, and replied, "I'll not ask you to elaborate on that, sir; I can see you are no gentleman."

"You are right about that," Nigel dryly answered.

"But he does his job well and I'll vouch for him," Eomore said.

The prince realized that the Drelven leader was upset.

Vaylin joined the party in spite of the objections of his mother and father, and soon they were off. The Dark Period continued, but they could see the reappearance of the second sun on the horizon. Amber light continued to bathe the land; they were getting accustomed to it and there were able to make out more details of the landscape. The Drelves moved rapidly through the dense forests almost as though the trees pointed out the most expeditious routes to them. Nigel was at the front near the leader Nibor and at times he thought he heard the Drelves speaking to the plants along the way. Nigel was impressed with the speed of the forest dwellers for even he would have trouble keeping up with them and their trail would be extremely difficult to follow. In a little over an hour they had reached the site of the carnage, and the Drelves were grieving loudly at the site of their slain people. The trail of the Droll patrol was easily followed for subtlety was not a trait in these large creatures. They quickened the pace. Wildlife was bountiful, but most of the creatures were small woodland beings and even a large monster would not pose a threat to a party this size. There was surprisingly little noise as they moved along. Deron the dwarf found his curiosity almost as ravenous as his appetite; dwarves did not tolerate skipping breakfast that well. He asked the Drelves near him about the animals and monsters of the land and learned that they were bountiful, but more so in the mountainous and wilderness areas. Indeed, dragons were still numerous in Parallan, but the chances of encountering one in this area were remote. The Kiennite people often made pacts with the intelligent species; dragons would do their bidding in return for treasures and flesh. But the Draiths had little fear of dragons because dragonbreath had little effect against the masters of Parallan. No one knew why, but it was supposed that creatures resistant to Magick might also be resistant to creatures of Magick. To the fighters, it mattered little. They only hoped their blades could score some good blows in helping regain the princess. Deron particularly felt this. Magick was fine and had its place, and Deron did not share the contempt for wizards that Boomer the older dwarf and close friend of Eomore held; he knew that in most battles, the brunt fell upon those wearing the armor and wielding the weapon. Deron had never known a magician worth a lick in hand to hand combat.

The Drelves told the story of a legendary underground lair filled with dragons of all types and colors and ruled by a dragonqueen. Deron doubted this. Even though he had personally seen only the great guardian of the dungeons of Castle Lyndyn, Boomer had related that dragons were usually solitary creatures unless they were mating, and baby dragons were rarely seen. The dwarf's mind wandered here and there as they walked, or almost ran, through the woods. The Drelves remained alert for a sign that the quarry was near; everyone anticipated the fight sure to come. They pushed on about three hours beyond the ambush site, when Nibor stopped.

He turned to Nigel and said, "Have you noticed?"

Nigel responded, "Yes, there is not nearly as much animal or bird activity and these tracks seem very fresh. Caution is the word now. We must be careful not to become the hunted. Perhaps we should halt the main party here and scout on ahead. If I'm not deceived, I think I can smell the faint odor of a campfire."

"My thoughts exactly,"Nibor responded.

The two talked briefly to Eomore and then went on ahead as the word was passed along to the rest of the force.

Cara had not really had much of an opportunity to talk with Eomore. She could tell that he was preoccupied with the task before them. Still she had positioned herself in the marching file so that she wasn't far from him and they had communicated with their gazes whenever possible. The minutes seemed to drag by as they waited for the return of their scouts. There was time for nourishment; they tried to remain quiet.

Nibor and Nigel traveled quietly along the trail to a point where they were several hundred yards ahead of the rest of the group. Suddenly Nigel grasped the shoulder of the Drelve and pulled him down. Initially the Drelve was convinced that the human was going to do him in; then he saw the tall forms just ahead standing at the mouth of the trail and speaking in the lowpitched growls common for them. There were all of seven feet in height. They were very ugly, even in the eyes of Nigel, and had doglike faces. They would have been ugly in the eyes of their mothers. They wore crude chain armor and carried large broadswords. There were no others around; in the distance they could see wisps of smoke. They briefly debated whether to try to lower the odds by two but decided the best thing to do would be to try to find out the strength of the forces against them. Slowly, the two moved nearer the pair and endeavored to move past them. Each step seemed like a mile of marching but in a few minutes they were successfully out of the frying pan and into the fire. The good news was the Droll's camp was located in a fairly large open area which would be available and amenable to an arrow assault; the bad news was that there was more than a mere raiding party.

Nigel said facetiously, "That is a fairly small raiding party, isn't it? If this is what their raiding parties look like, I would surely hate to run into the whole army!"

Nibor began to understand the manners of his less than illustrious associate.

The Drelve retorted, "Good point, my friend. Seriously, this is at least a full phalanx, which is what the Drolls call their military units. I have never seen this many Drolls in the forest before. It is too near the border of Draith domain. They are so heavily armed and equipped. Could this be this first part of a major assault force?"

"I don't see one of your guys down there yet, but there must be at least five hundred of the dog faces. Wait a minute, there is a smaller one! Is that Magrian?" Nigel continued.

"No. He is armored. Woe! That is a Kiennite. Probably a magic-user, judging by the garb he is wearing," Nibor answered.

"That is just what we need, isn't it? I suppose that you and I have the option of going down there and whipping all those dog faces and magic users, don't we?" the thief stated.

Nibor didn't appreciate the sarcasm but he realized that was just Nigel's way of surmising the situation.

He said, "It concerns me that we can't see the Teacher. Perhaps he is in one of the tents, but they may have already sent him on. I wonder what they are up to. If only we could get closer."

"We can try," Nigel said matter of factly.

He inched forward in a low crawl, but soon returned. "I believe we've done everything that we can alone. I could take out the two guards, but it would alert the rest to our presence. Perhaps we should get back and discuss this with the others. I think we can kick these boys in the tail."

"I wish I shared your confidence, but I would not feel comfortable even if the odds were reversed," Nibor remarked with his gaze firmly set on the Drolls ahead. "You know, this looks more like an established camp. I think they shall be here awhile. Why don't you go back and bring the others forward, and let me scout on ahead to see if there are any other forces nearby. I'll meet you back where we first saw the two guards. If I'm not there in an hour, then I'm probably not coming."

'That is exactly what we should do," Nigel answered, "but I feel we should draw straws to see who gets the privilege of trying to get himself killed."

"No, that is my reward for knowing the area better. I have friends in the forest that might come to my aid, and we are able to blend into certain trees. The Drolls have an acute sense of smell that may be more attuned to your newness than to my own, since at least one of my kind has passed this way recently. Tell Vaylin about the Kiennite. They do not share the hardiness or constitution of the Drolls and if we can capture one of them, we can probably get out of him where they have taken the teacher and what they are up to."

With that he extended his hand; the two grasped firmly for a second; each wondered if the other would be successful.

Nigel's journey back to the group was fairly uneventful. They were less than overjoyed to learn of the odds before them. Vaylin spoke tactically for the Drelves in the absence of Nibor; there was much hurried discussion. Could they bypass this force and go on northward toward the Droll stronghold in pursuit of Magrian? No; they did not know if the Teacher was hidden in tents of the expeditionary force. Could they creep into the large camp and try to steal back the Drelven leader? No; the senses of the Drolls were too keen. Even with an invisibility spell, they would still not be silent and would still have scents. Even with a silence spell there would be problems; invisible and silent, they would be unable to coordinate their efforts.

A fight was in their immediate future. It was time to discuss tactics. The nature of the Drolls played to their advantage. They had chosen an open area to camp in. This was foolhardy. The attackers could get off a few volleys of arrows before things reverted to hand to hand. Roscoe had not been overjoyed with the mention of hand to hand combat; the wizard told the rest of the group to plan their strategy such that none of them would be immediately in front of him.

"I have a warm welcome in mind for them," the mage remarked.

Nigel then diagrammed the camp site. Eomore, Vaylin, Vannelei, and Tjol Bergin, who was a better than average tactician, began to plot strategy. They advanced to the planned meeting point; Nigel advanced a few yards to await the return of Nibor; the rest held back several yards and finalized plans. The Drelven force would divide and flank the enemy; the forces would position twenty paces beyond the bow range of their counterparts opposite them. The armored fighters would brace for a frontal assault, trying to prevent the enemy's getting behind them. Knarra and Sedoar would stay in the rear to tend to the wounded. Roscoe would begin the battle by attacking as large an area concentrated with enemy that he could. Cara would use her weapon to strike down enemy that might get too near the healers in the rear. Nigel's first task was to eliminate the guards; they could get closer to make the plans more operable. Hopefully, he would have the help of Nibor but so far the Drelve had not returned and his hour was almost up. Just when they were beginning to write him off as lost, he came scurrying up, almost out of breath.

He reported, "As near as I can tell, there is only one Kiennite; there may be more in the main tents. I could not see Magrian, though I heard some of the guards speak of him in cruel terms, saying they could not see what value 'She' could see in him. There are guardposts in the forests in various places but no others in the direction that we will be moving. There are no other major forces in the immediate vicinity, but they could be reinforced by a returning patrol. Our first estimate of five hundred is unfortunately accurate; they are well armed. We can expect them to ask no give quarter. We shall be victorious, or none of us will survive. Do you still wish to proceed?"

Roscoe said, "Not survive, indeed! They will regret the day their fathers met their mothers!"

"We are ready," Eomore quietly agreed.

Nigel then said, "I'll consider it a personal insult if you do not allow me and my sweetheart to take those two guards alone."

"I should help you," Nibor interrupted.

"To that, I must say thanks, my friend, but no thanks. You must stay to lead one of your forces while Vaylin leads the other. They will fall and they will fall silently," Nigel confidently stated.

With that the wiry thief brought the glittering throwing dagger from his robes and placed it between his teeth. At the same time he brought a garroting rope which was barbed and looked heinous. The tools of his trade made many of the others shiver; they were glad that he was on their side. The others moved into position. They assumed that the thief would be successful.

Cara moved over to Eomore and gently kissed him on the cheek.

"Good luck, my prince," she said, as her shyness seemed to leave her.

The points on the crossbow bolts contrasted with the tenderness in her eyes and the tear that trickled down her face. Eomore captured the tear in his gloved hand.

"Thank you," the prince answered.

Eomore briefly gripped her hand, and then grasped the hilt of his other maiden.

Exeter emanated a faint red glow; it may have been green- the green of jealousy.

"That is a magnificent blade," Vaylin said of Exeter. "I hope it serves us well."

"It shall," Eomore said.

Emotion left his face. He merged his essence with the blade to become the fighting machine that they were. There was time for a brief mental conversation between them as Nigel moved into position to perform his deed.

"It seems that we are violating a basic principle to slay the enemies of our enemies," Exeter lamented.

Eomore's response was "That is the way it must be."

Nigel was almost in position.

Suddenly Vaylin remembered an important point. "Roscoe, how will we know when to begin our assault? What will your signal be?"

The mage coldly replied, "You'll know."

Eomore and the Drelven commanders inched forward. The Drelves prophylactically trained their bows in the direction of the pair of unsuspecting guards.

They saw the dark form of Nigel carefully staying downwind from his quarry. He came to a kneeling position behind a great ever-red tree. He was scarcely more than five paces from them. He ascended the shaft of the tree like a great black spider- he was just as silent. In a moment he was perched on the first large limb over the dogfaced Drolls but still out of their range of vision. The Drelves marveled at his ability. With a single motion, he brought his sweetheart from his teeth to his hand and it sent 'her' through the air toward the great creature on the right. Before it struck its target, Nigel was airborne toward the one on the left with the garroting rope in his hand. Both targets were struck. The knife found the throat of its target and pierced the skin deeply; the blades sprang apart and ripped the throat of the beast; only a garbled groan was uttered. Less than a heartbeat later, the thief was upon the other; with blinding speed Nigel slipped the garroting device was around its neck.

Before he knew what was upon him, he was headless; the rope sliced through bone and flesh alike.

Both Drolls lay dead upon the ground; Nigel retrieved the knife-he was a killing machine.

"That makes up for them jumping me at the portal," Nigel muttered.

A woman had come to his aid!

Vaylin said with disbelief, "That did not seem fair."

The thief quickly searched the bodies and briefly scanned the area ahead to see if his grisly deed had been detected. When he determined that he had been successful, he motioned to the others to get into position.

They wished each other well. Knarra uttered a brief incantation. The game began. They hoped to gain advantage through surprise, throw the enemy into disarray, and mop them up. Eomore silently wished they were fighting goblins again. The Drelves got into position. Roscoe stepped up to the front, uttered an incantation, and sprinkled himself with a handful of sand- he slowly faded from sight.

He said, "I'll advance three paces into the clearing. You will know when to come forward."

With that his voice also faded; the men at arms moved forward. The clearing was several hundred feet wide; there were about two hundred Drolls in the western end enjoying a meal.

Eomore and his men heard a low pitched incantation; a great ray of fire emanated from the point of the voice. A hazy outline of the mage appeared as he began to speak loudly; they could see he was crumbling up a small piece of sulfur. Too late the Drolls sensed their bane- there was a great explosion of intense flame and heat which covered much of the western end of the clearing. The air filled with screams of agony as many of those in the impact area charred and died; those nearby suffered burns. The mage was now fully visible. None of the Drolls carried bows. The camp was in an uproar; they reached for weapons; some of the more observant ones charged toward Roscoe. But they needed time that they did not have- for first from the left, then from the right, volleys of Drelven arrows dug into them and many more fell. The camp fell into total chaos.

Then a huge dogface emerged from the central tent and began to make gutteral commands.

The Drolls responded to his commands, defended themselves with shields, and advanced on all three areas from which they had been attacked. The small Kiennite peeked out from the same large tent, and then quickly ducked back into it. A second volley of death rained upon them, and a third; but each time the shields became more effective and the losses were fewer. They rallied behind the apparent commander. They closed on Roscoe; the mage ignored the urging of Eomore and did not retreat. Instead the wizard began a second incantation as the Drolls drew near to him. It looked as though two Drolls might reach him before he completed the spell, but the first was dropped by a crossbow bolt through his heart, courtesy of Cara, and Sweetheart found the throat of the second, dropping him in his tracks. The mage completed the incantation, and pointed the index finger of his right hand at the heavily armored commander. An electrical charge emanated from the finger, unerringly struck the commander, and slew him. Roscoe then turned and moved back through the ranks of the fighters.

He said, "Good luck, boys; you all go on up there and kick their tails."

The Drelves continued to rain arrows upon the camp as long as they could; as more of the large enemy neared them they were forced to draw forth their short swords with which they were mush less proficient. Nigel quickly dashed forward and retrieved Sweetheart. He narrowly avoided the rapidly charging Drolls. All knew the easy part of the battle was over; they heard their screams of pain from wounds and they shared the burden of death with their enemies. Cara dropped two more as they charged, then she withdrew to aid Knarra and Sedoar. The air filled with the sounds of the clashing of metal upon metal. The Donothorian rangers fared well initially; their swordsmanship far exceeded that of the Drolls; the dogfaces made up for their lack of skill through numbers and tenacity. The Drelves were instantly at a disadvantage, and they began to fall in large numbers though they continued to inflict losses upon the enemy. Roscoe had anticipated this and had moved to a small bank. He bathed the Drolls to the rear on the right with flames of Magick; none survived. This turned the tide in favor of the Drelves and the Drolls began to fall back.

Unfortunately Roscoe attracted the attention of the Kiennite who had crawled into what he thought was an advantageous position. He prepared a nasty surprise for the mage but as he rose to deliver the spell, a dark cloaked form flew through the aired and he fell with a muffled sound. Nigel had incapacitated and quickly bound him. The thief's efforts did not go unnoticed; four Drolls were upon him. He drew his short sword, but the four were consumed by white hot heat which emanated from the delicate outstretched fingers of Cara. The Drelves under Nibor were in a lot of trouble; their numbers were quickly reduced; they were forced to retreat. The noble Nibor made his last stand a triumphant one as he felled three of the Drolls in a frenzied attack before they silenced his blade. This enabled what was left of Nibor's force to reach the safety of the forest.

Eomore did not see his friend fall; he was up to his neck in dogfaces. The casualties were mounting up; there were scarcely fifty of the Drolls remaining, but as Nibor had predicted, they fought to the death even though the odds were now against them. The forces of Vaylin came to the aid of Eomore's men, and they began to further split up their foes. They continued to mow down their opponents; Exeter scored repeatedly. But a Drollen blade struck down the shield of Cyrus Thorogood. The Ranger slew the wielder of that weapon, but a second struck at him as he killed the first Droll. The second pierced his chainmail and the valiant warrior fell wounded. That gave the others more lust; even though given the option of surrender, the Drolls fought until none of their number was standing.

It was over.

The air was as still as the death around them. Eomore and the others had finally found something in the land of Parallan that was identical to their own world.

Death was a common denominator.

Their losses were great. The hand to hand combat took its toll- fifty four Drelves were killed and several more were wounded beyond continuing. Nibor was slain. No other Donothorians were hurt, but all were concerned for Cyrus. Knarra and Sedoar were treating the wounded.

Nigel came forward with the squirming Kiennite.

"One present," he said, "and I will gladly kill him. The little weasel almost got the drop on you, Roscoe, and he's bitten me twice."

"Indeed," the mage answered. "Search the camp."

This they quickly did, but there was no sign of Magrian, only some of his belongings. A few Drolls returned from their guardposts, and they foolishly attacked, only to fall without inflicting more injury upon the group.

Interest turned to the prisoner.

Vaylin approached and asked, "What have you done with the Old One?"

The Kiennite only snarled and did not respond.

"Let me handle him, "Nigel requested. "I'll make him talk."

The thief went over to the captive and drew forth his dagger.

He grasped three fingers of the left hand of the small goblin-like creature and said, "You don't need all of these, do you?"

Knarra started to stop the thief. The threat made its mark.

"No, no, no! No pain. He was taken to the Kiennite castle by a teleport spell this morning. I'll serve. Don't hurt me. I beg you."

Nigel turned away with disgust. The thief muttered,"He is not worth dirtying my blade."

They spent some time aiding the wounded and giving their last regards to their dead.

After this was done they moved a short distance from the battle site and talked. There were many decisions to be made. The Deathquest had claimed its first victims, and they had yet to encounter the Draiths, the masters of Parallan.

If what the Kiennite had said were true, Magrian might now be beyond their reach.

CHAPTER 21
A Friend's Concern

Boomer had recovered from the leg wound he received courtesy of the wailer en route to Roscoe's castle. He had allowed his men ample time to rest and the servants at Roscoe's castle were most courteous though somewhat macabre. But eventually one could become accustomed to even a giant, a zombie, or even a flesh golem, if he were bringing one ale or food. Boomer had consumed quite a bit of Roscoe's ale before they left the castle in the Wilderness of Donothor. "Briar Garden" was the name that the mage had given the castle long ago. It was named for the red flowers that bloomed near the castle.

The trip back was not as urgent. Boomer was fretful to return to castle Lyndyn to find out what happened in the efforts to help the Elven Prince Vannelei. Still he felt he could not push his men. They had been given some "repellent" that the zombies stated would make them seem unappetizing to any carnivorous animals that they might meet in the forests. Some of the men were griping that the salve would also repel women for six months after they got back to Lyndyn. But they departed on the third day and made the trip back to Lyndyn uneventfully, aided by the repellent and tips on the best routes which had been given by denizen's of Roscoe's castle. Briar Garden wasn't a nice place to visit and Boomer did not want to live there either.

They became aware of some of the tragic recent events as soon as they encountered settlements; the stories ranged from near factual to very skewed to ludicrous; all were unnerving to Boomer; they hastened back to Donothor's capital at Lyndyn.

They were greeted courteously but there were no smiles. Boomer was told at the gate that the king requested an audience with him as soon as he returned. The dwarf left his steed with the gate guards. He couldn't help but notice that all the guardposts were at full strength, which seemed to confirm the worst. He quickly entered the inner ward and was taken before the king. The king and queen were seated in the family gathering room, the very site of the carnage.

The faces of the royal couple told the little warrior that the stories were true even before the king spoke.

Eraitmus Aivendar was a tired man; he did not project the usual dominating personality and high charisma so typical of him. Boomer saw eyes that were without sleep and fraught with worry. He called the dwarf 'his captain' and motioned for him to sit near him at the end of the long table where his daughter was seated the day the raid occurred. It seemed so long ago; it had only been a few days, but it seemed an epoch ago. With immaculate detail, Eraitmus told Boomer of the events befalling the kingdom these past few days. He included the message given by the rangers sent back by Eomore after the planar gate had been discovered. The gate had been watched since then. The rangers had been forced to excess duty but all had responded with unquestioned loyalty and under the astute leadership of Gosway, for the old veteran ranger had secured the castle and the city and there had been no further attacks. So far there had been no reports of any ruffians on the borders taking advantage of the situation and that was good news to Boomer since he was now the Captain in the absence of his friend Eomore. The news of Nigel's release was distressing to the dwarf but he knew that Eomore would make such a decision only if absolutely necessary. The dwarf's heart was not in the resumption of his duties of the defense of the kingdom. He yearned to be by the side of his friend and fight to regain the safety of the princess – to avenge Karder Lin and the others who had fallen before the Draith raiders. Othan had accompanied Boomer to the king's chamber and the eagerness to follow Eomore was present in his eyes also.

After the king had finished all the details of the grim battle and the information, Boomer spoke.

He said, "My Lord, I have seen the defenses that Gosway has arranged for the capital. There is no one better at commanding than he. I would like nothing more than to follow my friend and your son into the unknown and undertake the same quest that Nigel called the Deathquest. Othan and I would like to follow the others into the planar gate with your permission. We would like to take the same risks as our brethren. If we do not, we don't feel that we will be able to enjoy the taverns or other freedoms again."

"I would rather be with Eomore in the taverns tonight, but since we can't be there, I would like to join him, where ever he may be," the dwarf added.

Eraitmus pondered deeply.

Finally, he answered, "We risk so much – Knarra, Roscoe, Sedoar, the noble elves, good men – Boomer, can I gamble on losing you as well? We do not know what exists on the other side of that portal. We do not know whether you can traverse it safely without the protection of the High Priestess Knarra and the skills of the Mage Roscoe. I'm told these things by a cat! My mind is not strong. I am so weary. Yes, you want to go where your heart leads you. I am not too old to remember the loyalty of friendship. But you should meet with Gosway and discuss the situation with him. He has done so well, but the people need you here. Already I fear the loss of a son and a daughter." With that, he fell silent, and rested his head down on the table.

Boomer placed his strong worn hand on the shoulder of his beloved monarch. He would do as he asked.

The dwarf said, "We shall do our utmost to return the child and your son and my friend as well. Hope will return to our land."

Boomer and Othan left the monarch and found Gosway in the rangers' quarters busily working over the rosters. No man was a better organizer than Gosway. After a brief discussion, the men decided that Boomer and Othan would go to the gate with a squad of twenty volunteers among the rangers and take over the guard there. Gosway voiced a strong desire to go, but was ineligible because of his age and the fact that he was needed more to coordinate the defenses of the kingdom. The first twenty men that they asked volunteered. Such was their devotion to the Aivendars. The elf lad Cade offered his services; his skills as a rider enabled him to deliver messages. His pony was more agile and faster than the heavy warhorses. Cade called his proposition the "pony express." He wanted to serve as his sister had done, and the King granted his request.

They would ride in the morning. They needed rest; Boomer knew he could not rest until he again stood beside his friend. At the portal he would be as near his friend and prince as he could be in this world. Also, the portal was the only known conduit to the lands of Donothor for the perpetrators. By guarding the portal, Boomer felt he could best protect the king and citizenry that he loved so dearly. The dwarf hoped that the Draiths would be again so brazen to assault the land. His hard axe would be waiting. If the king wavered in his decision for Boomer to avoid crossing the gate, the dwarf would be in position to proceed. Boomer spent a fitful night- as much as he loathed users of the Magick, a Sleep Spell would have been nice.

CHAPTER 22
Ooranth

There was tension at Castle Ooranth.

The Draith scouts reported increased activity in the border areas and in the north between the Drolls and the Kiennites, the powers that historically united against them. Also the Dark Period was near an end; the skies brightened more with each passing heartbeat. The matrons and the indoctrinators knew that the Black Lord Calaiz had designated the end of the next Dark Period as the time of consummation; he had chosen the human woman called Trya as his mate. There was much to be done in preparation for this great ceremony; the prospect of war loomed greater with each report coming back from the fringes of their lands. Of course, war was not feared by the Draiths; war was a time to attain glory; the Draith people had waited long; hatred gnawed at their very souls; they longed for vengeance. Calaiz wanted the conflict, but he hoped for the proper timing for the struggle. They did not know the plans of the enemy. The Drolls were appearing audaciously confident.

Such was the situation as Calaiz sat in the Royal Chamber in the donjon, great central tower of Ooranth. He had awakened from another rest period which, as usual for the Draith Lord in these recent times, had been disturbed, and then he had conjured laboriously trying to learn more of the motives and strengths of his enemies. His scrying attempts were blocked by Magick of the Kiennites- probably spells of the Deathqueen. He expected this; this had always been present. As Calaiz had matured he could gauge his own strength relative to the Deathqueen through the amount of resistance he felt to his evocations and conjurations and through the profuse sweating that covered his hardened face. A broad smile developed as he felt stronger than ever this day. But he had sensed more during the long arduous session before his crystal. There were other powers present! Were these powers opposing the Magick of the Kiennites? These powers were significant. The smile melted into a frown – Calaiz did not understand this. He knew of no allies in this land yet the sensation he had felt was unmistakable – the Magick were like a great lake; any outpouring of powerful Magick created a wave upon the waters of this lake which could be sensed by other spell casters. This situation puzzled the Draith Lord and he knew enough about war to know that it was not a time for puzzlement. He would not turn away an ally in war; he would not divide the spoils. He was gradually regaining his vigor when he recognized the sound of the opening of the outermost portal to the royal chamber. That could mean only one thing and that was good news.

There was the familiar voice at the inner door saying, "May I disturb you, My Lord?"

Calaiz responded, "It pleases me greatly to talk with you."

Izitx entered the chamber. He was adorned in his yellow flowing robe that signified his role as the chief advisor to the king; he was the second most powerful in the hierarchy of Draith leadership.

Izitx simply stated, "I am recovered and wish to resume my duties. These are the most important of times to us. "He paused to study his king's face.

He continued, "I see that you are troubled, My Lord."

Calaiz answered, "Well, yes, in a way. I know that our fighting strength is at a peak and we couldn't be more prepared. Just now I could sense a further ebbing of the powers of the Deathqueen. Yet her resistance is great and I could learn little of their overall plans. I can confirm many of the troop movements that our scouts have reported. As we suspect, our enemies are not naïve; they prepare as we do; they hope to gain some advantage before War begins. But I sensed another presence in my efforts. There was a strong emanation of magic against the forces of the Kiennites. I cannot account for this though we should feel grateful for any assistance. If we have an ally, I would like to coordinate our efforts. Do you have any thoughts?"

"My most powerful Lord, Magick is alien to me. I understand of Magick only that which you have told me. I do not feel that our people will need any assistance; the Draith nation should never have to feel 'grateful' to any other; everything we have accomplished has always resulted from our efforts. Our strength is too much for them. They have nothing to match you, my king. Their trickery will not help them against us, for you can protect our forces with your powers;

you can do what the foul queen has done in the past. Victory will be ours," Izitx stated flatly and confidently.

"My confidence in our warriors is paramount, most loyal servant, but I dislike any uncertainty. Perhaps I over react. The forest Drelves can sometimes come up with a noteworthy strike against the Kiennites, but it's just that I've never sensed such power from them. They have not been a power of note since the falling of their wizards ages ago. We have to prepare for the consummation. I must soon approach the human. Again, I congratulate you! Your efforts will strengthen our people. Perhaps the next Dark Period will be the greatest in our history; we can celebrate the final victory in conjunction with my ceremony of consummation. Are preparations underway?"

"Yes, and all should go smoothly. We must soon join the forward ranks of our troops. I feel the first battles are nigh,"Izitx replied.

"Yes, I agree. We shall soon strike the first blow. I shall prepare for the day now if you will leave me. I shall meet the human today, and it shall be a great pleasure for her," he said, dismissing his servant and secretly wishing that his words were true.

Izitx bowed deeply and turned to exit the chamber. Calaiz heard the closing of the two chamber doors in order. He outwardly brimmed with confidence, but deep within he felt those nagging doubts! He paused for a refreshing hot bath and dressed in his formal robes. He took a short glance into the reflecting stone – he was an imposing figure.

Izitx left the royal tower and went to the lower chambers, following the meandering corridors until he reached the gardens. He strolled briefly through the gardens and he marveled at the plushness of the grounds. The air was invigorating. The matrons were going about the business of tending the plants. Izitx then reached the chambers of the maids and entered. There was a short walk to reach the chamber designated for the human woman who was the chosen of the king. He gave a courteous knock before entering; he knew that not even he could be brazen in his treatment of the queen-to-be; she was receiving the respect of her title even though she had yet to undergo the indoctrination. A matron momentarily opened the door. The room was bustling with activity; Trya Aivendar was seated in the center and the elven female was adjacent to her.

"I am Izitx, the servant of your Lord, Calaiz the Black," he said, introducing himself.

"I seem to recall that we've had the privilege of meeting before," the elf demurely responded.

Her haughtiness angered him.

"Wench, you live only because I decree it, so you will address me befitting my role. You are chosen as the lady in waiting to the queen and you will perform your duties to the best of your abilities, lest I determine other, less noble duty for you," the tall warrior stated.

It was apparent to the women that Izitx was not someone to anger and the room fell silent as all the older women bowed deeply. Heather and Trya followed their examples; this brought a smile to the hard face of the Draith. Trya studied him. He stood about seven feet tall and his body bristled with well-developed muscles. Izitx looked older than many of the males she had seen passing through the castle but his conditioning was unmatched. His skin was dark; there was a faint green tinge to it; she imagined that he would glow if he were in a totally dark room due to the luster of his skin. His eyes were a deep green and sparkled as he looked outward. His hair was white and dropped to just below his shoulders. His speech was clear and crisp. Trya wasn't quite sure how she could understand him and vice versa, but language had not been a problem since she had arrived here. It was as though all spoke the same common dialect, which was very close to that of Donothorian people.

The dark form spoke again, "Soon you will be graced by a visit from Calaiz; you will be courteous, appreciative of his time, and interested in his words; or else you will answer to me personally. Noble Calaiz has many things on his mind and all must go smoothly here."

There was no reply and he turned and left the room.

The maidens were left to their conversation and they discussed the confrontation fearfully. Moments later an older matron came into the room; she whispered to the other women; she came to Heather and Trya.

"All must leave now except the chosen," she said and took Heather's hand.

The elf first resisted, but the old woman was insistent.

She said, "You must leave. She will be fine. This is the way that it must be!"

The elf yielded and followed her out of the room.

Trya was alone, and the feeling was not a good one, but then again she had experienced few good feelings since she had been taken from castle Lyndyn. She again thought of her family; wondered of their well-being, and wondered if there was any chance of deliverance. Could she hope for rescue? Her thoughts snapped back to her present situation when she saw the door swing open.

She saw him standing there. His position was unmistakable. He was the most dominating figure of a man or at least a manlike being that Trya had ever looked upon. Unlike Izitx, this Draith had facial features that actually revealed some measure of feeling. His skin was more of ebony and the eyes seemed a warmer green. His hair was likewise darker than that of the other Draiths she had seen. His eyes and ears were unique to his type. They were almost elven in appearance; in fact that was what she had instantly noticed about his face. He stood even taller than his predecessor and was more muscular and youthful. As she looked at him, in addition to fear, she noted a more subtle thought had entered her mind; the thought that he was, in a very different way that she was accustomed to thinking, incredibly handsome. His eyes met hers, and she turned her head away. She heard the door close and there were heavy footsteps as the Draith Lord entered the room. He wore extremely ornate robes and carried a large scepter. His voice filled the room with a very soft melodious inflection. This differed from the booming words of Izitx.

"You are beautiful. Except for the paintings that I've seen of my mother, you are easily the loveliest woman that I've ever looked upon. I know that you are frightened, but I assure you that no harm will befall you. I shall attend to that. You shall be the first queen to rule over the whole realm the World of the Three Suns. I know, too, that you are confused and that thoughts of the past fill your mind with sadness; your life now is here with me. Memories of your past must fade; your destiny has brought you to me; I desire you greatly; the ceremony of consummation will unite us for the remainders of our lifetimes. You are beautiful past imagining and I want you more – more than anything. Just one smile from your face and I should gladly go off to war and even lay down my life. Such will be my devotion to you, but I'll need the same from you. Is there anything that you require? My people need you very much."

"Yes, I would require that I be returned to my own people. I am stolen away," she said before thinking of the possible consequences of confronting him.

"I would have anticipated that you should say that, for your spirit is as beautiful as your face, Trya Aivendar of Lyndyn. I know many things of you, and I know of no more suitable life-mate in your land or mine. Time and fate are my allies; I hope you will grow to love me," he answered.

"You seem to take what you want, so go ahead and take me; release me from this bondage; I prefer death to imprisonment," the woman said emphatically.

"That would not be right. My people and yours are very different, but we are not. I tell you that which I would be loathe saying to my peers. I am very lonely and it is no fault of my own that my blood makes me this way. I have needs that my kind never experienced before. What I seek is not lust. I have no hunger for that. I have strength, power, and the respect of my people; I am feared by my enemies and I am subservient to no being. I am master of the master people. But I need from you that which I cannot derive from other sources," Calaiz stated.

Trya noted his face was flowing with emotion as he talked.

"My fate is with my own people. You should have chosen of your own. I beseech you to release me. There may be reprisals that would be costly to both of us," Trya said, though less vehemently.

"That option has been taken from me, but I shall soon gain vengeance for that fact. I fear no reprisals from man or beast," Calaiz uttered.

Trya could sense the hardening of his word and face as he spoke.

He spoke a little while longer basically telling her that she had much to learn and that time would free her doubtful mind and melt her cold, cold heart. The Draith Lord then left the room and she was again alone. She should feel nothing but great hatred for this man; yes, he did seem more like a man, but there were more feelings that she could not understand as she sat there. In a few minutes, Heather returned and again the room was filled with activity.

CHAPTER 23
Aftermath

Their moods were still solemn and they could still see the smoke rising in the distance at the site of the battle. The land was now bathed with a more intense light and the sky was becoming a brilliant gold as Meries the fleet, the bright sun rose higher over the horizon of Parallan. A faint gray glimmer of the mysterious Andres appeared as a speck on the distant horizon now and the land was beautiful as it was bathed by the light. Unfortunately the small group of Donothorians and Drelves were not feeling the brightness of the day. The Deathquest had claimed its first victim. Cyrus Thorogood had succumbed to his wounds. They had lost a new friend and ally in the Drelve Nibor.

Nibor succumbed to his wounds in spite of the great efforts of the healers. Nibor was sorely missed by his people and the Donothorians. Noble Cyrus was not denied his Pyre. There was such clamor and flame on the field of battle that the Death Pyre was barely noticeable. Eomore retained the big man's ring in hopes of returning it to the widow Thorogood if he should return to Lyndyn. Tjol gave a brief eulogy. The lute was passed to Banon Kessa.

Two of the surviving Drelves had been dispatched to the Alms Glen to bring the baneful news that Magrian had not been found and that Nibor and so many others had fallen. They were to bring back help to retrieve the fallen comrades.

The victors were regrouping.

Nigel was first to speak.

In his usual eloquent manner he said, "We really kicked their tails, didn't we? It seems that is a rather hollow victory; for our goal was to get the old man back; instead we have this worthless knave that the boys call a Kiennite."

"We must plan," Eomore said. "We still need Magrian as much as the Drelves do. This gentleman may serve us better alive than dead, Nigel. The lack of a backbone can usually be worked to gain an advantage. If we encounter more of his kind, he could be used as barter."

"He is a snake in the grass, Eomore, and I would like to slay him now lest one of us wind up with a dagger in his back," Nigel replied bitterly.

"This Kiennite is one of their rare spellcasters. I warn you that their warriors are a different breed and are trained from birth to fight. If we encounter them, they will be far more likely to battle; though they are not as foolhardy as the Drolls and are far more intelligent. Their skills with weaponry are more advanced as well; but the magic-users are unusual and I'm sure they would like to regain this one. I think he said he was called—"Vaylin said.

The Drelve was interrupted by Nigel.

The thief interjected, "He isn't worthy of a name. He is to be called Weasel as far as I'm concerned."

The creature cringed. It did not know that Eomore would not allow torture. Its commander would have acquiesced to the thief's request.

"Keep him bound and silent. Weasel is a fine name," Eomore agreed. "Now we must determine what we should do next. It seems our path leads northward to the Kiennite domain."

"Assuming of course, that he told the truth," Roscoe said, "I seriously doubt that this one has the power to teleport another person. That is extremely difficult Magick and I think that he would have ushered himself out of here, were he capable. I suspect that he is little more than a trickster capable of minor Magick and I would venture to guess that the dogfaces carried the Old One along the way before we hit the camp."

"There may be some truth in what you say, but we have no other clues. Maybe they used a device," Vannelei said.

"Let's interrogate him more," Nigel added anxiously. "Let me cut off a couple of his fingers."

Tjol brought the squirming goblinlike creature forward and dropped him unceremoniously in front of the others. Nigel started to pull his dagger, but Eomore stopped him.

"Leave his fingers alone," Eomore admonished Nigel.

Cara walked over to Eomore.

The elf asked, "Could I try to persuade him to help us?"

Eomore returned a puzzled glance.

He said, "I'm open to suggestions because it seems the little vermin lied to us before."

The elf leaned down so that she was at eye level and stared at the creature.

"Look at me, little one," she said softly.

The beady eyes of the Kiennite drifted up and looked into her deep green eyes. She continued to speak to him in a soothing voice; he tried not to look into her eyes directly; she held his pointed chin gently in her left hand and turned his face. She uttered harmonious phrases they could not understand. Seven men, one dwarf, and fifty drelves would have walked off a cliff if Cara had asked.

As the others stood bewildered, Roscoe smiled and said, in a tone that was rather impressed, "Ingenious; the maiden is charming him. I would never have been able to get him to look into my face. A 'charm' spell is dependent upon some unwariness on the part of the victim and she was well into the spell before he realized that he was under attack."

Deron said, "It's a lot easier to look at Cara than it isto look at you."

The levity was appreciated.

Cara completed the incantation.

She commanded, "Your master is Prince Eomore of Donothor. You are not the master of your own fate. Who is your master?"

The Kiennite frowned, developed a trancelike appearance to his face, and uttered in quiet monotone, "My master is Prince Eomore of Donothor."

"Eomore, I think he will answer you truthfully now," Cara stated.

She tried to mask her satisfied grin as she strode over to the prince.

Eomore nodded to her in appreciation and faced the Kiennite.

"What was done with the old one called Magrian?" he asked the entranced figure before him.

"He was taken to the main force. He was taken on before you attacked," he stated in the same monotone.

"Where is the main force?"

"About three periods (one day) from here as you would measure time," the gnarly dude answered.

Eomore continued to ask the Kiennite questions. Roscoe had surmised the situation fairly well. The raiding party had turned the quarry over to fresh Drolls who had immediately skirted him off to join the major part of the Droll army to the north. He was indeed a novice who knew but a few spells and his purpose had been to give this forward unit of the forces some guidance. Their sole purpose in getting this far into the forest was to try to capture the teacher Magrian who was quite well known throughout the land as a scholar; they were specifically interested in what he might be able to tell them of the Draith stronghold and any weaknesses that might be apparent to the outsider. Basically, the Drolls and Kiennites sought from Magrian, ironically, the same information that the Donothorians did.

The effects of the charming did not persist very long, largely due to the creature's personal knowledge of similar spells; this facilitated his recovery. But the group had derived most of the information that they required of him.

Eomore went over to Cara and said, "Thank you. How do I know you did not do that to me?"

A smile betrayed his effort to sound serious.

"You don't," Cara replied demurely.

The party then rested a while and took some well-earned and needed nourishment. It was decided that the captured Kiennite would be taken back to the Drelve compound. They realized that they could not battle large forces. Numbers would never favor them. Thus, Vaylin dismissed many of the surviving Drelves, retaining only a dozen of the most vigorous. So it was not a formidable force that proceeded northward out of the protective womb of the Drelven Forest to continue their quest.

CHAPTER 24
Next?

A hurried march led the fatigued party to a knoll that was one of the higher points in the area surrounding the battle ground. The knoll was covered with fairly dense vegetation and several large trees from which the Drelves would be able to keep a constant vigil on the land below. Quickly the broadswords cleared enough area for them to find a place to repose and regroup. Security could not be complete, and Roscoe had felt less than comfortable and had begun an evocation as soon as all were within the chosen area. The mage pulled a small cluster of old spider webbings from one of those many pockets in his oversized robes – the others were forever amazed at how he seemed to always go right to the proper pocket for each component that he required for his Magick. He uttered several arcane phrases and threw the webbings into the air, with the final phrase resembling, "arachnidalis tohorribalis," but the exact language was indiscernible. Suddenly the knoll was covered by thick webs similar to those created by the great giant spiders that were still found rarely in the Donothorian wilderness near the mage's castle. The little knoll had been given the appearance of the lair of one of these great beasts. Once this was completed, Roscoe had found a particularly plush mossy site and had slumped down there. Magick was a great drain on spell casters, and Roscoe was no longer a prestidigitator; in other words, he was not as young as he once was, though no one would dare confront his ego with that statement. He was quickly into a deep sleep.

The others began to settle down, with Eomore and Vaylin designating guard shifts. Deron had volunteered for the first shift, stating that the morning's battle had keyed him up too much to rest anyway. The little dwarf didn't realize it, but all his compatriots felt the same way except Roscoe; the wizard could sleep only because of the mental fatigue that possessed him. Silently the guards assumed their positions; the Drelves climbed the trees. The Donothorians noticed that there was a symbiotic relationship between the plants and these forest elves; the trees derived something from the presence and touch of the Drelves; and the Drelves seemed to almost join with the trees when they interacted. Even if one knew that a Drelve were perched in a tree; and even more, if he knew where to look; it would be difficult to spot the quarry. Deron positioned himself in an advantageous spot where he could peer out between strands of the web and began his watch.

Eomore, Vannelei, and Vaylin were facing a dilemma; specifically, what to do next. The first item in the agenda was obviously rest; they knew that the Old One was getting further away from them with each passing minute; fatigue was their most immediate enemy. Time, or at least its measurement, was becoming very difficult for the Donothorians who were diurnal and were accustomed to dividing their activities along the orderly schedule of a day and a night. But, though they were learning to determine direction based on the great sun, the failure of nightfall to come was a big adjustment for them. Their very chemistries varied with the cycles of their sun and moon, and now there were three suns and apparently no moon. Eomore couldn't help but wonder what the long-term effects might be on them.

Cara had gone over to Eomore and spoken softly with him while Roscoe was conjuring. Both smiled; their hands gently touched. Then Cara also found a mossy spot and sat down. The perceptive eyes of Knarra could read the emotion written upon the fine lines of the fair elven face. The priestess walked over to her.

She placed an understanding hand on the slim shoulders, and said, "Are you troubled by the experience of battle, Cara?"

The elven girl sighed and replied, "Yes, I suppose – but my mind is filled with so many feelings. The wonderful warm feelings that I have when I think of Eomore, but as wonderful as those are, the taking of life by my own hand and powers – oh, it is a horrible new experience for me. For me, Magick had always been a plaything; it was something that might make others fear or misunderstand me; I think I know what my mother meant when she sang about the 'lost highway;' I think of my mother; I recall so little about her. I've never called upon the destructive force of Magick before the attack in the family room of castle Lyndyn. I've never turned my crossbow upon another living creature before today. Even though the dogfaces are scarcely more than animals by all they show us through their actions, I still am concerned that I found it so easy to slay them today when they were attacking Eomore and the others. It's this easiness that disturbs me most. Does the term 'today' even mean anything here? Am I wrong to feel so remorseful, or should I feel even more so?"

Knarra reached out and took her hand.

She answered, "I am not a judge of right and wrong, Cara. The feelings to which you confess are merely proof that you have a conscience. One of my teachers was fond of a quotation from antiquity that defined that moral person as one who was aware of what he was doing. I do not think that any of us would chose to be here in this place, doing these things, were our hands not forced. You responded to a drive to protect yourself and the one or ones that you cared for. Is that good or bad? I think it not a fair question. Perhaps the proper dichotomy would be necessity and wastefulness or wantonness. Yet, in some sense, killing is always a tragedy. Have you considered the possible thoughts of the Droll warriors as they attacked? From what I've understood from our Drelven friends, you and I would not have fared well at all had our men fallen and we ourselves had been captured. And what of the Princess Trya? What could these days be holding for her? Are we forced? Are we justified to kill? Were the Drolls justified in taking Magrian from those who loved him? Or the Draiths, in taking Trya? I suppose that some perverted logic could justify all this action by saying the end justifies the means employed to bring that end about. No, Cara, your feelings now, your feelings when you cast, your feelings when you fired your bow, and the questions you questions reflect conscience. Conscience – awareness of one's course of action and its implications to that around one – is a measure of strength, not weakness."

Cara studies the face of the woman.

Finally, she said, "What of Roscoe? His great power spelled the doom of more of the dogfaces that all of the rest of us combined. Yet he seemed unmoved. There seemed so much coldness upon his face. Can he no longer feel?"

Knarra answered, "Look at him now. It is more than fatigue that weighs on his mind. He cares and he feels. I've gone through many good and many bad times at his side. The coldness is a façade a good one to those who do not know him. You could not have a greater friend or a stronger ally than the archmage."

The priestess glanced over at the sleeping wizard – her eyes clouded a bit. Cara could see more than respect in her eyes.

The elf said, "Your words have helped. I cannot undo my deeds, but I can reflect upon them; I'm glad that I can do that. Words can soothe the mental wounds that balms do not reach. I shall continue to do my best to help recover the princess, though I'm sure it is now obvious to the rest of you that I cannot conceal what I feel for Eomore. Oh, Knarra, I hope that my feelings for him and his for me do not jeopardize the quest!"

The wetness in the eyes of the priestess became even greater as she responded, "Cara, I can tell you with certainty that many missions have been accomplished in spite of feelings. It seems that the necessity of the moment will override that which is inside us. Feelings can become misplaced and too late recovered, maiden. Do not deny your love for him. If you do, you may regret it greatly some day, when you look back on your life. It may be that true love is greater than any treasure in this, our, or any other world; while unrequited love might be even more baneful than the jaws of the dragon, the spells of the necromancer, or the sword of the champion."

With that, Cara reclined and curled up into a small ball on the moss; Knarra turned and walked away.

The thief's eyes rarely left Knarra except when he was charged with finding the proper path for the party. Nigel had never seen anyone like her. As awesome as Roscoe's powers were, Knarra was in subtle ways even more powerful. She could do with words and gentle touch alone more than most could accomplish with sword, spell and stealth. He was even more fascinated that the tall woman looked so young in face and body, yet so old and wise when one met her gaze. He had known many women, many beautiful women, yet he had never experienced the same admiration or whatever it was that he felt when he watched her. It was as though his own fatigue was lessened when he watched her. Maybe it was the fact that she had healed him after the Draith attack at the portal gate. Maybe it was an effect of the light of these three cursed suns. His mind went on a brief tangent as he realized how difficult it would be for one to engage in the thieving occupation in this bizarre place, because the dark of night was usually the thief's greatest ally. Then his thoughts were back to her. What did she think of him? He realized that she had to be appalled with the way he had dispatched of the enemies they had encountered, yet these were her enemies as well. Nigel Louffette had never cared what a woman might have thought of him or his actions. Still he would like to have this woman's approval. For one of the first times in his life, if not the first time, Nigel had failed to understand the ramblings of his own mind. Maybe he would have been better off to have stayed in the dungeons of Castle Lyndyn.

Deron suddenly stiffened at his guard post; the sound of rapidly approaching footsteps was unmistakable. Curse his lack of diligence; there would be no time to warn the others. He was relieved to see several Drelves who were being ushered into the camp by the guards who been just up the trail. The new arrivals were covered with sweat and looked greatly fatigued. One of the guards told him to relax; they were delivering important information for Vaylin and Eomore. It never occurred to the dwarf that they might be shape-changers or some other disguised monster, so he allowed them to pass. These Drelves had hurriedly traveled the forests at the request of King Drolan.

The first called to Vaylin, and the forest elf and Eomore beckoned to his call. "King Drolan sends these items from the personal chest of the Teacher Magrian to you, telling us to move with great haste for they might be of great value to you."

Vaylin extended his hand and received a rolled parchment protected by a leather sheet and a small leather pouch.

He then said, "I recognize these, though I haven't seen them in a long time. This device in the pouch is the 'direction namer' that the Old One salvaged from his brief excursion into your land nearly a generation ago. I believe he said your name for it was a 'compass.' One of the teacher's projects years ago was to use the device and try to create a mapping of our land. This parchment is the culmination of his efforts. As a sapling, I accompanied him to the great caves; it was a perilous trip indeed. We were almost eaten by a – that is a tangent. He traveled widely throughout the land in an attempt to complete this and he learned much of the land and its peoples. I suppose the teacher knew that the information that he held would make him a valuable asset to any of the warring parties should war again ravage our land."

He paused to unroll the parchment. Those who were listening to him found it interesting that he referred to himself as a youth with the same term that they used to describe a small tree.

He continued. "Yes, I was right. We must study this. Though it is incomplete and I myself do not understand all he has written here, it might be of great value to us. Our quest must take some direction. Again, Eomore, I am but the guide and interpreter of our land and you are the leader."

"I appreciate you allegience and confidence," the prince answered. "Where would the Drolls likely take the Old One?"

Nigel injected, "There are several sets of tracks leading northward from the battle area, which is the direction that our unwilling accomplice gave us. This route seems to lead toward the mountain range there in the distance."

"I would agree, "Vaylin nodded. "Those are the Peaks of Division and here they are labeled on the map. They divide our land thus their name. Some refer to them also as the Central Range, and the tallest of them is called the Mirror Mountain, for it casts its reflection into the great lake on the other side of us here, but still on this side of the range. As to answer your question, the patrol would be leading him to their superiors, whomever and wherever they might be. I suspect there exists again an alliance between the Droll and Kiennite nations, and that spells trouble. War must be imminent. As you recall, we were surprised to find such a large force of Drolls this far into the forests, but the Kiennite had told us their purpose was capturing the Teacher. I would doubt that they would have another substantial force here. The forest is foreign to them. Subtlety is their weakest link. The best bet would be that they are heading toward the northern gap that they control, and they will rejoin their forces there. But they may have many patrols between there and here. The Drolls swarm as though they were warrior ants in times of war; their numbers are incredible. They are the most prolific of all the peoples of Parallan."

Eomore and Vannelei remained engrossed in the words of the Drelven prince as he continued to study the map. Some plans had to be made; they knew brute force would not rescue the Old One. The route toward the Peaks of Division would be the likely course to find their quarry. The parchment was tattered and yellowed with age. The etchings were in the flowing runes that were very similar to the archaic elven writings of many generations ago. Vannelei remained mystified with the many physical and social resemblances that the Drelves bore to the forefathers that he had studied as a child. The elven prince felt more at ease in this strange land than the others because of this- but there was more – his mind sensed more of a link to this place – lately his thoughts returned to his mother and her disappearance those many years earlier. The circumstances of the disappearance of the two women whom they were trying to find with his mother's were so similar; this time they had a thread of hope; however, the probability of a successful quest was low.

The Drelves posted guards for all directions in the trees and along the paths. Deron rested now; he had been relieved by another of the forest Drelves. The leaders were still looking at the map when the dwarf walked by and collapsed near the huge figure of Tjol Bergin.

Vaylin continued his discourse on what he knew of the surrounding area.

"Once we leave the forest and its friendly confines, we will enter a far more hazardous milieu. There will be great open areas where cover will be difficult to find. We could be vulnerable to riders of winged or hooved steed. Often the Kiennites will ride firehorses or rarely even griffons. The Draiths have been known to employ more hideous beasts that darken the sky with their sheer size. Our feeling is that the highest nobles only will employ such beasts and only then if they must travel very rapidly, for the Draiths pride themselves on their own endurance. So even if we encounter steedless groups, the Drolls and Draiths are seemingly tireless when in pursuit of an enemy. We will have to be constantly on our guard, particularly once our efforts past this period are known. I fear the Kiennite Deathqueen in some way may already know of our presence – she is in many ways perhaps a more deadly foe than the Draiths themselves –so much of her power lies in our lack of specific knowledge of her

– legends tend to be magnified. But history has revealed that there exists a great force of Magick in the home realms of the Kiennites; whether or not this is one old woman, I cannot say. If Magrian is taken there, our task is magnified."

"It is painfully ironic that fate has decreed that we must oppose both enemy camps. It would be nice just to allow them to slug it out and destroy each other; time doesn't allow us that luxury," Eomore commented.

"True. Time is, of course, so relative. I fear your group will become increasingly more confused by the lack of the specific time increments that you refer to as days. We have no real equivalent here, though we do designate rest periods usually when the sun we call Menes the fleet, the brightest of the three, drops low into the horizon. Magrian tells me this occurs every 8 or so of your hours, but it is a variable interval. As you know we are never bathed in total darkness such as that which occurs in the subterranean caves." Vaylin then paused.

The sky developed a yellow-green appearance replacing the amber. The land was almost as bright as their homeland on a cloudy day.

Vaylin continued, "The darkness of the caves may have to be encountered. As you can see from the map, there are two easily traveled gaps through the Peaks of Division. If indeed war looms as we suppose, the southern of these will be heavily guarded by the Draiths and the northern by legions of the Drolls and Kiennites. The caves will be guarded only by the denizens who dwell there; I think I can remember how to navigate through them; it will be very hazardous. I doubt that any of you have ever had the misfortune of encountering anything as fierce as a cave dragon which feels its domain is threatened or else feels the pangs of hunger deep within its foul gut. The breath of such beasts chills to the bone much as the ice on the tallest peaks, so I'm told, and this cold slows the muscles, making it difficult to resist the advances of the monster. These caves were one of the explorations when I accompanied the teacher on his quest. He found many things unusual about them, suggesting that were not entirely a natural occurrence. We discovered some paths to navigate through them; this may help us now."

"Obviously the condition of our group is such that we must rest several of your hours. The forests will act as our ally in slowing the progress of the Droll patrol carrying the Teacher away from us. What they must use twenty time units to traverse, we can cover in five, even encumbered as we are with non-Drelven people. We must allow our bodies to recover their vigor. Some of these nourishing roots will refresh us; sleep will also be needed. We should easily pick up their trail with the information gathered from the Kiennite and our skill."

Vaylin then went to check with the guards to see if there had been any significant activity at the battle site. Eomore nodded his approval of his suggestions, and then looked around at his "army." It was not a warming though to think of thirteen Drelves and eleven Donothorians pursuing an unquantified foe across increasingly unfamiliar ground, wondering all the while when they would cease to be the hunters and instead become the prey. They might face whole armies. Obviously, Vaylin was right in saying that discretion and stealth would have to be their main weapons. There could be no more bold assaults such as the one this morning – egad! He again caught himself using the frame of time reference of his own land. The word morning meant nothing here, though the word mourning certainly bore significance. More importantly there were no romantic enchanted evenings where a prince might entertain a lovely elven girl and talk of love and times before them. Were there to be times before them? It was a fatigued mind that tried to sort out his feelings. He was a student of nature– could there be only one true sun here? Was the black sun the dominator or was it just a great hole in the sky? Were the other two were only moons? Was the land of Parallan a moon? Or was this world flat? If so, perhaps it did not rotate? Were there no changes of season? Where was his beloved 'green'? Was that the reason that night never came?   But then again, Parallan was so different that the laws of physics and chemistry might not apply. Then again, those laws did not apply to Magick; Magick was certainly real enough. There was so much that he did not understand. Was he even the same man that drank ale in the bar with Boomer the dwarf and belittled the fair sex? The beleaguered prince submitted to the tiredness that enveloped him and reclined upon the moss; sleep soon was upon him. However, even in his rest, the dreams betrayed him; he relived many of the horrors of the recent days. It seemed that in only minutes he was awakened by the anxious hand of Vaylin upon his broad shoulder.

"I'm apologetic that I had to awaken you, but time allows no further luxury of respite. Those bearing the Teacher are gaining ground upon us and the scouts are noticing increasing activity at the battle site," the Drelve said.

Eomore answered, "How long did I sleep?"

"About five of your hours," Vaylin replied.

The prince stood; his body told him that he needed more rest. The others were already gathering their packs, and the Drelves were bustling around. Cara had freshened using the dew from the plush mosses and looked strikingly beautiful in the ever brightening light of the three suns. The sky now had a near normal appearance; that is, in places it looked blue, and there were little puffs of clouds here and there. These were of various colors, but the most striking were the red ones. This land was quite lovely once one became accustomed to it, yet none of them wanted to be here a minute longer than necessary. Eomore could hear the grumblings of Roscoe as he stood and adjusted his robes. The mage rested against the great wooden staff that he always carried. Vaylin came over to the prince again.

"The tree posted guards have told me that several parties of Drolls have returned to the campsite that we destroyed. They were originally disorganized and befuddled; they gained confidence and direction; their numbers swelled. They are sending out search parties and some have come close to our refuge. The webs have deterred them so far, though the last group fired arrows into the webs and narrowly missed killing one of my men. There are maybe a hundred of them and they could be sending for more forces. Their sense of smell is keen, and they may detect us if we linger here. I'm not sure that the Drolls have sufficient fear of spiders to stay away from this knoll if they think that we are here. Perhaps we should start on, if indeed our minds are set in the direction of pursuing the party carrying the teacher," the forester said.

"Then it is travel we must," Eomore said. He tightened the chainmail around him and placed his helmet atop his head. He placed his red outer cloak with the crest of the family inside his leather pack and donned instead one of the less conspicuous garments furnished by the Drelves. Exeter was as always by his side. He grasped the hilt and was reassured that there were no enemies in the immediate vicinity. The group gathered and designated a marching order; the guards signaled the way was clear; they made their way through the web and cautiously proceeded along the path toward the battle site. Twice the Drolls patrols narrowly missed stumbling upon them as they proceeded along the paths, but Nigel and Vaylin were able to anticipate the encounters and got the group safely away from the path. They were an easy match for a single patrol, which usually numbered twenty or so, but they wanted to save their energies in particular those of the Magick users; Eomore had been surprised at how much the efforts had drained Roscoe and to a lesser extent Cara; she had not called upon her abilities as much as the Mage. All recognized that Roscoe was the major reason that they had been successful in the first battle with the Drolls, though all had contributed. Even the dwarf had been impressed with the power of the magician in smiting the enemies. But their task was just begun. Skirting the burned out camp was not difficult, because, unlike before, now there were only patchy defenses set up by the patrols. The trail of the patrol carrying the Old One was a little trickier to find, but after some searching, Vaylin found an unmistakable (to him) sign of his Teacher's passing – small bits of the enhancing root at twenty pace intervals initially – to the Drelves' keen eyes and senses, the root was readily apparent. Once Nigel was able to detect the tracks left by this particular party of Drolls and the small patterns left by the Teacher's feet, the thief was easily capable of following the trail. The Drolls lacked the finesse of the Draiths in covering their tracks; for someone as skilled as Nigel, tracking them was hardly a challenge. But the trees were appearing further apart as they traveled along toward the Peaks of Division, and the mountains loomed now in the distance. Cover was scarcer and that meant even more precaution. Vaylin and Nigel seemed up to the task. They had to watch the skies.

Several 'hours' passed uneventfully; then they encountered the first significant expanse of open terrain. The meadow was perhaps five hundred paces across, and there was the reassuring sign of cover across the way, but the guides were both nervous; now the advantage would lie with any creature spying from the edge of the forest on the other side of the glen. Nigel and Vaylin huddled together briefly and there was a lot of whispered conversation; then, it appeared a debate. Vaylin came to Eomore.

The Drelve said, "We feel that it may be risky to cross. The light is now bright, and the Drolls will almost certainly have placed a guardpost on the other side of this clearing. Circumventing it would mean several miles of extra walking. Nigel has convinced me to give him the privilege of finding out what is waiting for us on the other side."

Nigel added, "Yes, I need some action. These dogfaces don't supply much of a challenge as far as tracking goes. I'll crawl over. The grass may give me enough cover. If I'm attacked, I would advise that you not intervene, though I would prefer that you did. If I can take care of whatever guards the other side, I'll signal. If they are too numerous, I may try to create a diversion to enable you to get across."

The thief smiled wryly as the others seemed to like his plan. He looked to see if Knarra were watching him in this moment of bravery, but the priestess was talking with Roscoe, which she seemed to do a lot of the time.

Nigel moved over to the edge of forest, then placed Sweetheart between his teeth and disappeared into the grass, which was about a foot high in most places. The Drelves trained their bows on the area immediately in front of him, but when he disappeared, they relaxed. The others sat though rear and flank guards were posted. All they could do was to wait.

Nigel was silently cursing his newfound tendency toward self-sacrifice and chivalry. He wondered if he were possessed with some disease of the mind. The ground in Parallan was just as cold, damp, and dirty as that of the homeland. Nigel thought to that it was good to find some consistencies between the two places. He was trying to reach a point some twenty paces to the right of where the path they were following reappeared going into the forest. That low crawling was easy for him for there were few rocks and he was not bothered by pesky things – things such as earthmovers or giant ants. He wished that he hadn't thought of the latter, but he could see no mounds in the immediate area. He wondered why this area was so cleared but that mattered little now. He made the edge of the forest without being attacked. Then he slithered into the brush and used his heightened senses. Another wry smile came to his face. Conversation – or something close to it –it reminded him of the grunting customary to the speech of the Drolls. Slowly he inched forward. There were three of them, standing just a few feet into the forest and on the same side of the path as he was. He studied the area. A large cablevine tree was near the unsuspecting dogfaces. He made his way over to it without being detected. It would be risky, but he felt he could take them all. He removed a leather pouch from his outer cloak, and found there two daggers and the small metal sealed container. He painstakingly removed the cap, and inserted the blade of the first dagger into the unguent. Moving slightly to his right, he froze as one of the three suddenly raised his arms and began to sniff the air. The other two began to slap him upon that back and seemed to laugh uproariously. The sniffer frowned, and then resumed whatever they were discussing before. A fatal error – the blade glided from the throwing hand and deeply pierced the thick hide of the sniffer – certainly only a minor wound, but the afflicted Droll began to clutch his throat and dropped to his knees. The other two hurriedly scanned the area for some sign of the perpetrator, but Nigel used the moment they allowed themselves to observe the anguish of their stricken comrade to leap across the path and rest in the brush on the other side. Luckily, he was not seen. Slowly the two Drolls began to probe the brush with crude longswords and now were on their greatest guard. They began to howl! Enough of that – the thief hurled Sweetheart toward the nearer one and his throat was ripped out. The remaining Droll had caught a glimpse of Nigel as he threw, and charged the thief. Not the best way to fight, thought Nigel, but when you must, you must; he leaped to his feet and brandished his remaining dagger. He easily evaded the first charge of the Droll; Nigel was much faster; the thief stabbed effectively with the dagger and created a painful wound on the third Droll's shoulder. The Droll howled and tried again to impale Nigel; he almost scored; the thief was thinking too offensively, and he felt a pain in his left arm; he was positioned for a strike of his own and his skill with the dagger was deadly; he found the throat of his opponent. The big thing did not fall immediately, however, and lashed at Nigel again; the blow lacked full force. Full force would have meant his own death, but Nigel only suffered a flesh wound in his left side. He managed to ignore his own agony enough and ripped the dagger through the tough skin of the third Droll's neck. The huge dogface fell.

"Darned shabby fighting!" Nigel murmured.

He struggled to keep his balance and inspected the pathway. Fortunately there was nothing there. Fortune though was not a predictable ally; he realized that he had been lucky. All his life he had not depended upon luck and this time he had nearly fallen. The pain was great, and he was alarmed to see the amount of blood he was spilling from his side. He bound the wound as best he could and struggled to the edge of the clearing; he advanced into the open just enough that he knew the keen eyes of the Drelves could see him. He then fell.

Vaylin yelled, "Quickly!"

Several Drelves hurriedly approached the fallen thief. Within minutes the group was safely on the other side of the clearing. Knarra and Sedoar attended the wounds of the thief. Vannelei and Eomore searched the fallen Drolls and found a crude sketching of what might be a map on one of them. Nigel fought to maintain consciousness; the kind touch of Knarra's hand was strengthening in more ways than one. With the bleeding stopped and the healing evocations in progress, he would recover; he soon was standing again, even though all were advising against it.

He insisted, "I'm alright. Is the path secure? I almost blew it!"

None of the others fully understood his meaning, though Eomore had an idea.

Nigel was coerced to follow in the midst of the party near Knarra, and no one saw the reappearance of the wry smile on his face; and his thoughts were along the line that being wounded wasn't so bad after all. He managed a "Thank you" but said little else; he was embarrassed that he had been unable to eradicate the three Drolls without suffering wounds. The others, especially the slight Drelves, marveled at the feat. Knarra did not comment. Deron said he was glad Nigel was on their side. Roscoe harrumphed but said nothing. Sedoar and Vaylin almost spontaneously called him a fool – but Nigel took no offense – for the first time in his life someone appreciated his deeds and cared for his safety. Nigel liked the feeling, but did not understand why.

After a few minutes rest they resumed the trail.

CHAPTER 25
Nightmarish Steeds

The Drelves always carried animal scents that had been concocted by Magrian and his charges; such things were essential to forest dwellers. They used these scents to disguise Nigel's handiwork; it would appear that the Droll's guards had met their fate at the paws of a marauding beast.

Soon they were moving up the trail again. Vaylin and Vannelei were now in the front with Drelves flanking them and in the rear as well. They were traveling in a fairly tight formation. The Peaks of Division loomed in the distance; there was an ominous aura about them as the party drew nearer. The great Mirror Mountain dominated the horizon. The Donothorians had stopped trying to anticipate the light conditions; the small brightest sun was fickle; it jumped across the sky, briefly dropped behind the peaks, sometimes disappeared altogether, and varied the illumination that the land received.

After about an 'hour' of marching up the trail through fairly dense forest, the forward flank guards rushed up to Vaylin. The Drelven prince ushered the group several feet off the trail and asked them to remain as quiet as possible. Soon they heard what first seemed like thunder; the sound persisted and grew louder. They heard the cumulative sounds of many footsteps. Shortly thereafter a small number of Drolls moved past them at a rapid pace. Immediately behind the Drolls there were three riders on exceptional mounts. The hoof beats of the steeds were drowned out by the large force of Droll warriors behind the riders. The first rider was Kiennite and was adorned in lavish robes. He wore around his neck an amulet with a rose colored stone in its center. His firehorse trotted methodically and effortlessly down the path. The animal was gleaming red; little sprays of flame emanated from its three nostrils as it galloped along the trail. The horse would be a deadly opponent. The second rider was a huge Droll who wore platemail armor; the massive firehorse bearing him was snorting steam as he labored to carry his heavy burden. The third figure was new to the Donothorians; those near the Drelves could hear a gasp from their forest allies. This thin figure wore a dark cowl; it was terribly out of place in the sunlight hours – it would have been more suitable in one's worst nightmare. Within the dark cowl they could see no face, only two glowing deep red lights where there should be eyes. There were bony digits gripping the reins of the misty steed. The steed appeared as unreal as the rider he bore; the two appeared to glide along the road. The Droll force followed the riders. They marched fifteen across and there were over a hundred of orderly rows. It was an impressive force with a definite goal in mind. The little group to the side of the road didn't know the plans and destination of the assault force, but the large force was proceeding in the general direction of the earlier skirmish. The enemies were so intent on their forward progress they failed to notice the quarry just off the road. Perhaps they thought no group would be so foolish as to move this far into their newly controlled area.

A few minutes after the large force passed, Vaylin led the timid group back onto the road. They walked a short distance up the trail and found an area large enough to talk together but secure enough to allow them some time to hide again if necessary. Eomore was relieved the Drelves had made the guards slain by Nigel appear to be victims of a natural attack.

Vaylin began to speak. "I fear they have word of our earlier deeds – the Deathqueen, whoever or whatever she is, is said to have many ways of knowing her realms and her minions."

"Looks like they meant business. I guess they can't take a joke. What manner of creature was that guy up front? Looked like he had missed a few meals," Nigel added. The others noted that the thief was pretty much back to his charming self as he asked his choppy questions.

Vaylin still wasn't accustomed to Nigel's expressions and looked confused. He recognized the acceptance on the faces of the others.

He continued, "Yes. There were at least two phalanges strong; from the armament he was wearing, I would say the commander was at least a tribal chieftain, maybe even a lord. The Kiennite probably is also a much more substantial foe than the one we met earlier. But the third was the most baneful. The Deathqueen must be aware of the powers we displayed and must be threatened. The phantom warrior is a creation of the Deathqueen's magic. It is a transformation of a paramount living evil into an even greater evil after life. The Magick required are powerful; the number of these that can be created is small. It was thought by our teachers that all were destroyed in the last Great War. I don't know how to fight him. Legend says they are greatly resistant to the Magick that created them and can be harmed only by enchanted weapons – I've never before today beheld one; that must have been a phantom warrior."

Roscoe had remained silent; the mage had encountered liches. He knew now that their prognosis for success dimmed further. The Mage had sensed the power emanating from the creature. Roscoe had hoped that his own Aura was not detected.

Knarra said,"They did not pierce my Shield Spell. There is evil in this world. I'm not sure that I can be successful in concealing our presence to the probing of their Magick if their minds are focused."

The sheer numbers of the Droll warriors would have been enough to intimidate them and urge them up the road; the presence of three exceptional figures was icing on the indigestible cake. It was mindboggling to try to comprehend the total strength of the Droll and Kiennite forces if they could dispatch such a formidable force to investigate the earlier skirmish- if indeed that was their intent. Vaylin commented that the evil alliance may have thought the earlier attack been carried out by the Draiths who had occasionally been abetted by renegade sorcerers in the past. The Drelves knew of no sorcerers dwelling within the borders of Parallan at this time. Vaylin remained convinced that the entity he referred to as the Deathqueen in some way knew of their successes earlier and the loss of her minions. She sent these troops to investigate and mete out her "justice." Charging into strength and leaving this formidable force behind them seemed grievous tactical errors; they did hold some small advantage in that the armies obviously did not have a means of pinpointing them; the enemies had just strolled right past them. Knarra's Shield Spell was Magick to conceal the Auras of Spellcasters. The Drelves had expertise at fooling the noses of the dogfaced Drolls. None of them knew what powers of the cloaked figure. But they were a small enough number to effectively hide – at least now. What alternative did they have anyway?

They increased their pace, moved rapidly for three to four hours, and rested for a little while. After three such cycles, they were forced to make longer pauses. The forests were thinning; there were more of the open areas; they skirted these whenever possible. In the distance the mountains dominated the horizon, rising majestically. They entered rolling terrain, indicative of the foothills. Vaylin referred to the area as the Hills of Ilma. The scouts scurried up the trees intermittently to peer ahead of them. They crested one of the hillocks and caught a glimpse of the great lake lying to their left –the mountains were mirrored in the clear waters of the large body of water. There were many legends of the lake; travel along its shores would render them precariously exposed; it would be necessary to depart the main trails and to do some trailblazing in the forests that bordered the lake. Fortunately Vaylin had traveled the area in less hazardous times and knew their route for now. But he, as well as the other Drelves, was disconcerted regarding the wildlife of the area, or more specifically, the lack of it. They saw areas that had been burned out and an occasional carcass. Obviously the animals had to fill a role of feeding the armies and the results were not always good for the forests. These lands normally teemed with wildlife and its sounds, but the small creatures were scarce and the air was quiet – too quiet!

The Donothorians missed nightfall – the time in their own land which usually ushered in a rest period and a welcomed slowing of the activities of the day. They were forced to stay on their guard because they were encountering regularly spaced Droll guardposts, manned by a dozen or so of the dogfaces. These posts were neither difficult to spot nor bypass, but it was obvious that supply lines and communication lines were established by their enemies. This meant that they were not tailing a single patrol that was tiring as they were, but more likely one being freshened at each of these outposts. It made their chances of overtaking the teacher's abductors before they reached a place of sanctuary unlikely. Their pace was slowed by the frequent detours necessitated by encountering the guardposts.

Near the end of what would have been the first day after the left the web knoll (if days had existed), the old nemesis fatigue scored upon them and they were forced to take a prolonged rest. All bore the strain of their endeavors, and they talked little. The rest area they had chosen was one of the rare densely wooded areas where they would have ample cover and would be able to post guards. They took nourishment and rested. Though they talked less, all could sense a bond growing ever stronger between them; they were a diverse group; there was respect and camaraderie; each appreciated the skills and contributions of the others.

Teamwork was their only chance.

Vaylin was particularly grim as he chewed on the dried plants and roots that made up much of his diet. Perhaps it was his own predicament, or perhaps the Drelven Prince feared the possible reprisals that the expeditionary force might throw upon his people if they should blame the Drelves for the earlier defeat and the killing of the Drolls. Hopefully they would be unable to defeat the forest and find their way to Alms Glen. King Drolan was wise and experienced. But these enemies were not opposed to scorching the forest if it served their purpose. Eomore's mind turned to the question of what would they do when they found Magrian- if they were able to save him. Obviously, finding and saving Magrian was just the beginning for the Donothorians. Eomore hoped he was the only one burdened by that question, but it had occurred to all of them. He could only hope that the Teacher would be safe; that they could save him; and that he in turn would be able to give them the information they would need to make their quest a successful one. How would the Teacher be able to help them?

The Drelves lost their feelings of neutrality. The kidnapping of Magrian, the killings of their brothers, and the raping of the forests had brought hatred to their hearts. Whenever they encountered small numbers of Drolls, the party had to hold back the desires to destroy them. They had to conceal their location if they could. Knarra maintained the Shield Spell to 'hide'the Auras and Essences of the spell casters. She sensed multiple scrying attempts.

During the rest period Nigel talked with Vaylin; Knarra and Roscoe had quiet discussions; Cara and Eomore had shared a few moments together; all attempted a turn at sleeping. All too soon the time came to resume the journey.

After about half a period (four hours), they reached the borders of the lake. Judging time remained difficult. The numbers of the enemy were ever increasing, but there were no concentrations of forces as large as the rapidly moving one they had earlier encountered. The pathways soon began a gradual but persistent upgrade. Vaylin had told them that the entrance to the great underground catacombs was to their right and about three periods of marching distant.

Daringly one of the Drelves approached a guardpost to listen to the growls of the enemy; it had been well worth the risks, for they learned that the Teacher had been brought this way earlier and had been taken to what guards had called "The Keep." The bad news was that Vaylin had reached the extremes of his earlier explorations and was not familiar with the road ahead. They were near the Northern Gap which was in the control of the Drolls and Kiennites and was a place avoided by the Drelves even in times of relative peace. Drolls were always on the lookout for candidates to serve them as slaves, or worse, as menu items. Their route seemed toward the Northern Gap.

After climbing the gentle grade for an hour or so, they encountered the Drolls more frequently, but still had been able to avoid detection; occasionally the dogfaces would stop and sniff the air when they were near. They were blessed as the Drelves said, but cursed in the minds of the Donothorians, by a brief rain shower. The clouds appeared, the rains came, and the sky cleared again in a matter of minutes. The Drelves enjoyed the rain, but Roscoe in particular did not. The mage projected an uncharacteristic image as he stood beneath a large pumpkin tree with a small parasol, which he produced from another of the numerous pockets in his robes, over his head. When the rain cleared, it became readily apparent that they would need more reconnaissance. Nigel, Vaylin, and Vannelei were chosen to scout ahead and to ascertain the nature of and location of what the Droll guards had called "The Keep," if indeed this was where the teacher had been taken. The others were to wait in the relatively unexposed area beneath the great pumpkin tree. The tree would provide them a repast, for it bore many luscious red fruits that resembled the apples of their own land. But here they were called pumpkins, and after everything else they had encountered, it seemed a minor point. The fact that the fruits were violacious did not reduce their deliciousness and the energies gained from the fruits were appreciated by all.

Vaylin had introduced the group to the fruits by saying,"A pumpkin a day keeps the healer away."

The scouting party left their bulky items and set out –they disappeared into the wet underbrush – the last sounds heard were a grumble from the human thief about the wetness. Guardshifts were determined; Eomore advised the others to rest. Cara moved over and sat beside him. Their eyes briefly met and the same sensations entered the mind of the prince as in the inn back in Kanath – which seemed so long ago; but again like yesterday. When was "yesterday?" He remembered where they were.

The rain enhanced the beauty of the dark elf. The beads of moisture accentuated the natural luster of her light ebony skin, and the depth of her green eyes was fathomless when the raindrops rimmed them. There may have been a tear interwoven there, but he could not tell. The two shared the fruits of the tree; their spirits were heightened by this quiet time together. The rest spot was secure for the moment and sleep was a welcomed visitor.

The three scouts found the going a bit more treacherous, but all were expert trackers and knew the ways of the forest well. Though it was far from easy, they managed to avoid the ever increasing guards. After an hour's march which would have been easy on the cobblestoned road below them but was difficult in the underbrush above the road, they came to a point where they had a clear view of the great northern gap through the Peaks of Division. The peaks did not pose as much of an obstacle as most of the ranges of Donothor; the gap greatly facilitated travel across them. The northern gap looked like a great forefinger from a massive hand scooped out of the peaks and created it. Some referred to it as the "Fancy Gap," for that it was.

They saw the great stone fortress perched upon a craggy bluff above them to the left or opposite side of the road. This stronghold, created in antiquity by powers and engineers long lost to the land of Parallan, sat about halfway up the climb up the gap and was positioned in such a way to provide maximal defense with a minimal force – but there was not a minimal force; the three could see innumerable

Drolls milling around the vicinity of the fortress. The walls were a deep gray stone that glistened as though they were polished to prevent their being climbed by an adventurous thief. The walls were as tall as twenty tall men standing upon each other's shoulders. There were a series of towers, one in each quadrant of the fortress and a donjon, a taller, central tower. A drum tower surrounded the gate. Two bartizans, large overhanging battlements, occupied the midpoints of the two sides of the wall facing the gap. The bartizans and the drum tower provided a huge area for archers to rain death upon advancing forces. Torchlights flickered from within the towers; they strained to peer through the openings that looked like pinholes from the distance of their observations. There was only one approach to the citadel, and that was blocked by two great doors that barred the portal. The great doors were far too heavy to be opened by even a dozen men, and appeared to block the only entrance. The ground immediately before the doors teemed with the dogfaced guards. The three watched motionless from the high ground to the right of the road, probably about three hundred paces from the gates. After a short time, they witnessed the arrival of horseriders. They recognized these as hundred or so of the gnarled Kiennites. From the group emerged one a little taller who was adorned in many robes and jewels. The Drolls bowed deeply before him and a group of Drolls escorted the Kiennite to the portal. The substantial distance separating them from the fortress did not prevent their hearing the grinding of gears produced by the inner portcullis wenches as they strained to draw open the gates. The Kiennite entered the stronghold and the gates closed.

"We aren't even strong enough to open the gate," Nigel said dejectedly.

Vaylin echoed his feelings, saying, "The task is a formidable one. My feeling is that the Teacher is indeed within 'The Keep' for I'm sure from the descriptions that I've heard that we just observed the arrival of the Kiennite Master. I can think of no reason they would send such an important figure this far away from their strongholds except to interrogate an important prisoner or similarly important circumstances. But I'd never even heard of one of their Masters leaving the confines of Castle Aulgmour, which is, I believe, the name Magrian gave to their stronghold in the Staghorn Mountains far to the right of us and bordering on the Great Sea which surrounds our land. He was accompanied by such a small number of Kiennites, too. It doesn't make sense, unless…"

His voice trailed off.

The three quietly discussed the best approach to the Keep. Nigel really missed his old ally darkness now. He said to the others that he felt he could scale any wall, no matter how slickened, if he had the cover of darkness; that cloak was not available to him now. Six eyes surveyed the area. After a time, they decided they could get a better look at the Keep from higher up the mountains, even though this would be more treacherous to them. Still there were few choices. It took the better part of two hours for them to inch their way along the side of the road to reach the desired goal of the high ground above the stronghold. They still could not see into the castle itself – the original artisans were too careful for that; they could see that the original assumption that the gate was the only means of entry was correct. Indeed there were no other doors and sheer walls rimmed the castle on the other three sides with canyon drops of several hundred feet.

"I'm really glad we came up here to see what we already knew," Nigel said disgustedly.

"But it's better to be safe than sorry," Vannelei added.

"I'm sorry you said that," Nigel said. "It is safe to assume that you have other words of wisdom to fit this pathetic situation?"

The elven prince smiled. He was beginning to almost appreciate the sarcastic brand of humor the thief possessed. But they resumed their scouting. They could see some battlements atop the great outer towers. Each seemed to be armed with catapults and several oil vats. Clearly the towers had rained death upon many unsuccessful opponents in the past. The Keep was a formidable fortress. Did they have a chance of penetrating it? Nigel surmised he had about as much a chance of sleeping with the Deathqueen tonight. He again realized that there wouldn't be a "tonight" – what a cursed place!

Vaylin then mentioned returning to the rest of the group, but Nigel, noting that they were about an hour's march from the crest of the ridge and that there were fewer Drolls, suggested that they investigate further. They would satisfy their curiosities, but they

191

also would derive some potential tactical benefits. Soon they reached the summit; the trees were rather thick in this area; Vaylin and Nigel scampered up one of the sturdier ones. Vannelei, who was the least inclined of the three to climbing, stayed on the ground to guard. Once they reached the upper branches, Nigel and Vaylin beheld an awesome site. For one of the few times in his life, even Nigel was speechless. The thief thought that these "few times in his life" occurred more frequently since he embarked on this Deathquest.

Below them was a wide plain – an expanse of several miles or even leagues – bordered on the far side by a much more majestic chain of mountains, some bearing a cap of pinkish ice and snow. To the far right or north there were more peaks as the valley enclosed on this end and ran north to south ending with the horizon there. There were many streams crisscrossing the valley which gave it the appearance of a watercolor relief of Donothor. The sky overhead was a deep yellow now and was clear but for wispy clouds of red, green, orange, and violet. Again looking at the floor of the valley, they noted it was bisected by a large flowing river which was probably a hundred yards wide. To the left or the south there was only the expanse of plain, a great grassy area, but the right or northern side was a bustle of activity. There was a great force massing there; there must have been tens of thousands of warriors from the number of campfires that dotted the land much like the flameflies on a clear night in Donothor. The numbers were so great as to bring to mind the picture of the swarming war ants which were such a bane to the farmers of their own lands in years of their migrations. Now they understood that the force that had passed them in the woods was only a drop in the bucket when compared to the total army. The two were awestruck.

Finally, Vaylin said, "If there was any doubt of the imminence of war, it is dispelled now. We must be looking upon the Droll War Legions. They must be massing for an assault on the Draith kingdom to the south or the left if you prefer."

"I prefer to be elsewhere," Nigel said succinctly. "From where do they come? How could they generate such numbers?"

Vaylin said, "The Drolls' tribes are a fecund race. They propagate incessantly; Magrian has taught us that a Droll warrior is gauged by his number of sons second only to his skill in battle. The Drolls are a tribal people who inhabit the forest lands that lie in the west but I'm not sure exactly where; I've never been there. In times of war, they forget their tribal differences to unite under a "King" who is a figurehead. Though fierce fighters as you have seen, Drolls lack the tactical skills that the Kiennites furnish to the alliance. The Kiennites are a mountain folk who live in the northern ranges near the sea that surrounds our land."

The troop movements appeared as ink flowing on a scroll as they watched. After a time the two descended the tree and told Vannelei what they had witnessed. Faced with determining a course of action, they opted to return to the others with the information; they hoped the Old One would be able to withstand the inquisition that he was probably facing. At any rate there was nothing that the three of them could do. A rapid descent soon found them back with the others and quickly Vaylin recounted their information. There was no joy in the mudfilled little clearing where they had taken refuge. The simple numbers of their mighty foes seemed to destine them to failure. The three scouts were given rations and sat with the others. Eomore motioned all to join around him except the perimeter guards.

He said, "We need a plan – a good one."

Deron added, "We need a miracle."

Roscoe corrected him, saying, "I've been known to throw a few 'miracles' around. We need an army – a big one."

Then Knarra broke into the conversation, "No, we need some darkness and some diversion. Roscoe, do you recall our adventure against the wizardess Phaedra?"

The mage smiled.

"The numbers were against us then, too," he responded, "but you darkened their day then. Do you possess any of the penetrating balm?"

Knarra opened her leather pack and produced a gray phial. "I was hoping to save this until we were in a life or death situation but we are near that now. The ointment within this phial when applied to your eyes will make you immune to the darkness that will come."

The others were puzzled, but Cara wore a look of understanding and Nigel expressed an air of expectation. Cara whispered to Eomore that the priestess must be contemplating a darkness spell. Eomore thought to himself that this would certainly confound the denizens of

Parallan. Knarra explained that the spell could affect only a limited area and she suggested that the area just before the great gate would be the most advantageous to darken. The Drelves were to create the needed diversion by trying to draw as many as possible of the Keep's guards away from it. They would be assisted by Tjol Bergin, Deron, Banon, and Kryl. A longbow attack would give them some distance and allow them to lead the guards on a chase through the woods.

Then Vannelei remembered the great obstacle posed by the door.

Roscoe said bluntly, "I'll take care of the door."

Eomore then summarized their plan and all agreed to their roles and understood them. The three scouts were allowed a brief respite, but all felt an urgency to press forward, wondering if the old Drelve would be able to tolerate much torture. None of them admitted fearing that Magrian might not be within the Keep. All signs pointed to it. Soon they were ready to proceed. Nigel would lead the main group up to the Keep. Vannelei would lead a group of six Drelves, Deron and Tjol to one area below the fortress, while Vaylin would lead the remaining six Drelves, Banon, and Kryl to a point several paces below them. They would arch a volley of arrows into the guards and at that signal the others would move into action. Nigel described the route to the tree on the crest in detail and they planned to gather there after the foray. All were hopeful, but most, deep within themselves, were quite pessimistic about their chances.

Eomore, Knarra, Cara, Nigel, Roscoe, and Sedoar moved into position near the fortress without being discovered. There they waited for the coming assault. In a few moments from the east and south of them, nine arrows rained into the group of guards clustered a hundred paces below the fortress; seven guards fell. Immediately nine more arrows sliced into the ranks of another group of guards and five more fell; one unfortunate was struck by three of the missiles. There was immediately a bustle of activity in the area, quite disorganized at first. A third volley of arrows flew through the air and attacked two other groups of guards. The archers were purposefully attacking different groups in order to try to disguise their numbers and make the Drolls think they were facing an all out assault. The losses of the enemy were adding up, but were really inconsequential given their large numbers. Still they seemed unclear of the direction of the attack, for the archers were moving after each volley. A fourth, then a fifth volley brought down more of the Drolls; they were completely confused; the bowmen might be able to slay them all if they had an infinite supply of arrows. Then the Kiennites began to move down from their positions near the Keep; though about fifty remained near the gate. The Droll guards on the outside of the Keep accompanied them, and with shields over their heads they could block many of the arrows. They soon pinpointed the locations of the attackers and began uttering instructions to the Drolls who soon were spilling into the forests. The six noted that the volleys were stopped and knew their comrades were now in a desperate race through the woods for their very lives. Knarra placed a small amount of the unguent over the lids of her five comrades. The material was sticky and had the texture of tar and almost the same color. There was just enough of it for the five. Eomore expressed the obvious concern that the priestess had not treated herself, but Knarra quickly explained that she was immune to her own black Magick. The tall woman then stood, precariously near to detection by the fifty Kiennites remaining outside the Keep and producing a powder that looked like the ashes of a burned out fire; she began an incantation. Clouds – black clouds – began to appear in the area immediately before the Keep. The Kienites began to scatter to avoid the fumes and were shouting, but the billowing clouds of darkness were moving too rapidly and were outdistancing their steps. Indeed, the six could see them tripping over each other as they rushed about within the great black clouds. It was almost humorous, but then they remembered that the inside of the fortress would probably be no cakewalk.

When the darkness enveloped the area, they moved forward. The physician had armed himself with a Drelven shortsword and was determined to make his contribution; Sedoar refused to stay behind. Entering the clouds they were apprehensive, but as Knarra had promised, they found their vision was not obstructed. Soon they were encountering the Kiennites and the few Drolls that had remained in the area immediately before the Keep. Nigel's blade found the throat of the first they met and he fell. Eomore was not accustomed to fighting under such advantage, but Exeter urged him and three swishes of the blade spelled the doom for three of the gnarled, goblinlike critters. Even Sedoar found the range, though it was obvious fighting was foreign to him, he fought to serve his prince. Cara felled two with her crossbow; Knarra saw the pretty face filled with grim determination. The Kiennites had suffered more than half their number in casualties before they even began to ineffectually swing their own weapons. One stopped his eyerubbing and began to motion with his hands as if to spell, but he was dropped by Cara's bow. Then there came an unexpected attack, though a blind one. A vat of hot oil splashed among them, scalding three of the unfortunate Kiennites but missing the six. Eomore cursed. Fate was kind not to have them take losses for such a bold error as forgetting to think of attacks from the towers. Roscoe cursed too and leveled his staff toward the tower. A bolt of blue energy flashed from the staff and the tower top crumpled from the force of the lighting bolt. Several Drolls fell to their deaths, one narrowly missing Nigel. Soon all the Kiennites fell before them. Crossbow bolts from Cara had dropped the only two who had nearly reached the fringes of the deathcloud. The geography surrounding the Keep had failed its defenders, for just as there was only one approach to the fortress, there was only one retreat. They were forced to move past the advancing Donothorians. The Kiennites were not nearly the fighters that the Drolls were and fortunately most of the dogfaces had chased the archers. Now the door confronted them. They were careful to avoid standing beneath the other tower on this side of the fortress.

Roscoe again leveled his staff toward the door and uttered a single command. "Open now before me!"

Within less than a heartbeat, the heavy doors flew open, and as they expected, twenty or so door guards were waiting, but they had no more success seeing into the deathcloud than did the Kiennites. They stood in an area some forty paces square and paused for a fatal second; purple flames exploded from the end of Roscoe's staff and they were consumed. When the smoke cleared, they waited for a moment. Behind them, two Drolls ran foolheartedly into the cloud and were quickly dropped by two well-placed crossbow bolts. Cara's aim was uncanny, but she confessed that her bolt supply was running low. Nigel edged up to the door. Roscoe indicated to Cara that she should be ready to take the left side of the door and he would attack any defenders to the right of the door. Eomore and Sedoar stood ready. Nigel leaped into the open area on the other side of the doors and must have looked similar to a great black cat leaping out of the darkness toward an unsuspecting prey. The thief dropped into a roll and the others saw several spears land just behind him as he rolled across the ground and then righted himself. The others used this diversion to step through the opening created by the doors. Nigel scurried behind a stone ornamental well that was probably his goal all along, as several projectiles missed him from the other direction. Roscoe leveled his staff toward the wall-stairs leading up to the observation area of the left tower where some twenty Drolls were charging downward. At the same time Cara raised both her hands and white flames emanated from her outstretched digits striking the guards who were descending from the already damaged tower to the right. Ahead of them they could see Nigel perched behind the well and beyond him the donjon, the dark central tower of the fortress, loomed ominously. There was no time to study it; from the side of the fortress opposite the great doors a significant number of guards were charging across the quadrangle. Roscoe and Cara scored heavily. The red flames from the great staff scorched the wall-stairs; those who were not slain retreated back up the stairs. Cara's flames did just about as much harm; however, two hardy Drolls survived and closed on the elf. Eomore and Sedoar positioned between her and her attackers; the prince was painfully aware of the additional guards closing across the open area within the fortress. The prince was thinking that they were unfortunately one magic user short when suddenly the corner of his eyes caught the glimpse of a column of blue flame descending from the heavens as his ears heard soft incanting from the priestess. Eomore had forgotten that Knarra had incredibly destructive powers, but usually loathed using them. The Harming Spell came in handy. The flames engulfed the charging warriors and suddenly the odds were in their favor. Exeter hummed as the prince dispatched of the first foe and Sedoar continued to prove he was a more than adequate swordsman by hewing the second. The little group braced themselves; breathing heavily, they looked about the compound. A hundred guards had fallen before them. The outer ward, or quadrangle, of the Keep was a large open area. The well was apparently a source of water in times of need. The outer walls served as a shell-keep; were many small constructions hollowed into the wall that served as quarters and service areas; but the dominant features were the five towers and the two bartizans- one lay in ruin and the second was flaming. There was no activity apparent from the distal outer towers now; their eyes focused on the central tower. It was perhaps two hundred feet in diameter and was at least three hundred feet in height, towering far above the rest of the structures. There was a large wrought iron door which was some fifteen feet in height standing before them. Periodically there were small apertures along its height of the donjon. The wall-walks between the outer towers had a ten foot margin along which guards could stand, but now they could see none. They knew the deathcloud could not cover them indefinitely and action was necessary. They made the logical assumption that the dark central tower would house their quarry. Roscoe was beaded with sweat from the efforts of the fight but the mage gamely pointed the staff in the direction of the door and true to form it opened before him. The inner ward stood before them. Fear and rationality left them as they entered.

The dimensions were the same as the outer dimensions of the tower. A wrought iron spiral stair rose from the center of the room and disappeared above them. There were certain strange though uncomfortable appearing furnitures scattered about the circular room. Their ears perceived lowpitched growling sounds and their eyes followed the sounds to the stair. Two large furry legs appeared on the upper rungs as the two-headed giant descended to do battle against them. The monster was hideous. He (or it) stood twice the height of a normal man and two equally ugly heads rested atop the torso. The muscular arms were both bore weapons – a great club in the right hand and a mace in the left. The creature moved down the stair with a definite purpose in mind – their destruction. Roscoe remembered stories he had heard regarding the resistance of giants to Magick, and this one had two heads. If two heads were better than one they could be in trouble. The stone floor echoed the creature's heavy footsteps as he moved off the stair toward the small group. As soon as he cleared the stair, Roscoe attacked. The ray opened a small wound on the left chest of the monster, but did not slow him. Cara struck him with a precious crossbow bolt and it imbedded in the thick fur of his chest. Knarra positioned at the door and split her attention between the fight going on inside the room and the compound outside where she caught occasional glimpses of the few remaining guards as they tried to regroup for a counterassault.

Eomore, Nigel, and Sedoar braced for his assault.

Speed was on their side, though they quickly saw that the left head controlled the left arm and the right head controlled the right arm. This and the fact that he had four eyes and two necks made it rather difficult to sneak up on him. The three had to fight him straight up. The spellcasters were watching the outer area where there was little going on. Perhaps the defenders felt the two-headed ogre would make short work of the foes. The left arm swung the mace toward Sedoar, and the force of the blow, though it did not strike him directly, still upset his balance to the point that he was unable to make any effort to counterattack. Eomore avoided the club but likewise was ineffective with his thrust. Nigel darted into the fray, slashed the lower abdomen of the monster, and opened a wound; the wound was too superficial to slow the creature. The thief moved aside but underestimated the speed of the monster and took a glancing blow from the mace – not enough to injure him but enough to get his attention. The beast was so outraged that he took his attention from the other two opponents. Exeter glowed with the redness of battle, but the club parried the blow. Sedoar scored heavily though, and slashed the left leg. The ogre howled in pain and then noticeably limped after the blow. He drew back, as did the three; the opponents studied each other. The ogre made the first move lunging with both weapons toward the physician and knocked him from his feet. He managed to avoid a fatal blow but the great club scored on the man's left leg and there was the telltale crunching sounds of bones breaking. The ogre had lowered the odds to two to one, but he lost several digits and the club as Exeter found the mark, guided by Eomore's steady hand. Nigel threw Sweetheart and the dagger found the right throat of the beast ripping it open. The right head lay limply upon the shoulder as dark ichor spilled upon the ground. The beast turned and hurled the heavy mace toward Nigel, but the thief managed to dodge the missile by leaping to the ground. Eomore used this opportunity to drive Exeter deeply into the creature's chest, and the great beast recoiled with such force that the blade was torn from the hand of the prince. He roared, moved backward, and then fell to his knees. Nigel charged and drove his shortsword to the hilt into the hairy hide. The beast moaned and slumped to the ground. Eomore moved over and extricated Exeter from its victim. Knarra went over to Sedoar, who was losing consciousness from the great pain; there was deformity of the wounded leg. No defenders emerged from the stairwell; they were apprehensive of climbing the stairs. There had been no sign of the Kiennite who had earlier entered the fortress. Nigel, Eomore, and Cara cautiously approached the spiral stairwell. The spiral was exposed in this large room, but when it entered the ceiling some twenty five feet above their heads, they could see it became encased in a staircase and spiraled up as far as they could see, ending in darkness. Roscoe watched the outer ward but there was little activity in the quadrangle. Knarra tended the fallen physician who was suffering considerably. Even the conjurations of the priestess were not enough to completely relieve his great pain, and there was such deformity of the leg that his effectiveness would certainly be reduced.

Remembering that the stair had supported the ogre's great weight and seeing no other immediate threats, the three began their ascent. Nigel moved like a cat up the stair, carefully inspecting each rung but still moving at a considerable clip. Cara and Eomore followed. After they had climbed a hundred or so of the rungs, Nigel saw a doorless opening to his right. The stair continued on upward. He strained his ears to listen through the opening, but the stench informed him that this was likely the lair of the ogre- still where there was one there might be two. Once his comrades had joined him, he started to enter the room, but Eomore grasped his shoulder and stopped him. The prince moved to the front and extended Exeter before him. Soon he nodded his head and motioned the others to enter with him. Quickly they fanned out so they could survey the entire circular room. The room was massive with the same dimensions as the outer dimensions of the tower with the exception of the twenty foot diameter stairwell in its center. They could not comprehend how the ancients had constricted the tower, but they easily recognized the stench. The room was littered with debris, largely valueless junk, and there were some old and perhaps some not so old bones. They wondered why any even semi-intelligent creatures would enter into a relationship with such a vile creature, but the bones and trinkets seemed to indicate what the wages of the ogre had been. Their search was brief, for unless the bones indicated an unfortunate demise for him, Magrian was not here.

Quickly returning to the stairs, they remembered the deathcloud created by Knarra was not permanent and the bones renewed their feelings of urgency about finding the old man. Where was the Kiennite noble? Lacking this answer was disconcerting to each and every one. They ascended the stairs another hundred rungs and saw the stair continue upward. They were this time faced with a decision, for there were two doors, one opening on the right and one on the left. Both were the same heavy metal material as the staircase and both were closed. There was a moment of indecision, but Exeter informed Eomore that there were no enemies behind either. Eomore was only partially comforted, for he well knew that the weapon was only accurate within thirty paces. The cylinder housing the stair was in the center of the tower, so the outer fringes of the tower would be well beyond the range of detection. For no good reason, they chose to open the left door first. It revealed a room that appeared to be little used, for there was a lot of broken furniture and many cobwebs. Still they had to investigate, not wanting to leave any rock without looking under it. The room was empty but for the spiders. Crossing again they stood before the second door. Nigel listened carefully at the door but could hear nothing. Eomore grasped Exeter again, but again the weapon could not detect an enemy. Cara gripped her crossbow. The quiet revealed only their labored breathing. All were tired. Eomore looked at the elf. He was concerned by the copious perspiration and the firm lines on her usually soft face. The spell casting and the physical effort were taking their toll on her. Eomore realized that she was the only member of the party who had actively been doing both.

Nigel thrust open the iron door and the three rushed into the semicircular room. There were small apertures in the far wall which allowed the light of the outer world to enter. There was a torch also burning near a suit of plate armor which stood opposite the door and was positioned to hold a halberd. The room was disorganized. In the far corner were several pieces of broken furniture, as well as several intact pieces of dressers, chests, and freestanding wardrobes. There was a large table in the center of the room on which were a number of parchments and possibly maps. In the left end of the room, manacled to the wall was an elderly man – or elf. Could they have found the Old One unguarded?

The weary face looked up toward them, saying, "The keys to my manacles are within the helm of the armor."

He spoke the Drelven tongue and Cara was readily able to translate his words.

Nigel stroked his beard. "I don't like this. Too easy. Ask your friend if we are indeed clear."

Eomore did so, and informed the thief that no enemies were within the range of the power of the blade.

"I'll go get the key," Nigel said, and began to creep into the room.

Eomore said, "No, let me. You have taken more than your share of risks."

Nigel momentarily hesitated, and then replied, "No, I should do it. I probably would have the best chance of detecting a trap. And there has got to be a trap here somewhere. I hope that old buzzard is worth all of this."

Gingerly the thief approached the suit of armor, keeping his eyes trained on the wardrobes opposite the old Drelve. Cara and Eomore began to move toward the old man, but Nigel motioned them back again saying he was convinced that there was some kind of trap; they just had not yet managed to spring it. The prince and maid heeded his advice and waited near the door. Nigel reached the armor. Just as he was about to examine it, there was a loud swishing sound overhead and a black shape descended upon Eomore and Cara. The prince managed to avoid the huge batlike creature but the wings knocked Cara off balance and she dropped to the floor, stunned momentarily. Eomore braced for another dive and this time the bat lacked the advantage of surprise and Exeter found its soft underbelly. A squeal ensued and there was silence again. Cara stirred and whispered that she was not hurt. Nigel returned to the suit of armor and began to probe at the helm with his dagger. He leaped back just as the halberd slashed downward and then forward, narrowly missing relieving him of his head. The armored arms guided the weapon through the air, and with a creaking sound the entire suit began to move forward.

"There is no one in there!" Nigel yelled, dumbfounded.

Eomore hastened to his aid to do battle with whatever this was. Cara moved forward also, but Eomore told her to watch the stairwell and shout if there were any other signs of attack. The prince did not bother to take the time to ask Exeter if there were an enemy within the armor, but the sword told him anyway that he faced a Magick and not an animate enemy. He charged the dancing suit of armor and evaded the first thrust of the halberd. Several times he warded off the blows of the halberd and he and Nigel again ineffectuality clanged their weapons against the metal.

He turned to Nigel and said, "Go to the Old One. Perhaps I'll be able to keep this at bay so that you could escape."

"I do not have the key. It may take some time to free him. I'll have to pick the lock," Nigel answered, as he dodged another thrust of the halberd.

With that, he broke off from the melee and started toward the old Drelve. Cara inched forward to join Eomore but really was unable to get near the armor and had no weapon to be effective against it. For that matter, neither did Eomore. Exeter would scratch and dent the suit in each place he struck, but did not slow the opponent.

Suddenly there was a groan from the thief and they heard him say, "Deception – tricking weary minds – the worst kind of trap..."

His voice faded.

Cara turned to see Nigel sprawled on the floor, seemingly unable to move as the old Drelve who now resembled a richly adorned Kiennite, pointed a thin wand at him.

"Oh, Eomore, I fear that death is near," she wailed.

Eomore thought to himself that she was probably right as he narrowly avoided another halberd thrust.

"Go to Roscoe!" he said.

She hesitated, and then moved toward the door.

Frustrated and tiring, Eomore dropped Exeter into the sheath and ran to the broken furniture where he retrieved a table leg which he swung with all his might, striking the armor, splintering the wood. That was no good either. The halberd grazed his leg; were it not for his chainmail, the thick blade would have penetrated his abdomen. The pain coursed through him; he sensed his doom and in frustration threw himself headlong into the metal chest of his opponent, and the two of them crashed to the ground. There was the brief realization that he had failed when he realized that the suit was no longer moving. The fall to the ground had, like an overturned turtle, incapacitated the thing and taken away the force that sustained it. Eomore did not have time to relish his victory for he heard the sounds of the Kiennite as he began to spell. The finger pointed at him dug like a dagger and indeed opened a wound on his head. Stunned, the prince dropped to his knees and heard nothing but the heinous laughter. The Kiennite stood over Nigel and prepared to impale him with his own sword. Eomore tried to stand but the strength wasn't there. He failed to see the frail woman standing firmly inside the door, aiming the deadly crossbow at the laughing Kiennite. Too late the Kiennite Master realized that the elf had not fled as directed by Eomore; Cara had returned after starting her descent. There were no second thoughts in her mind about killing. She wanted the death of the Noble and the bolt coursed from her bow and pierced the left orbit of the foe, causing a great screech; he dropped lifelessly to the ground.

Cara ran to Eomore.

Though weak, the prince asked her to check Nigel; he feared the worst. Cara ran to the thief; she found he seemed paralyzed but unharmed. A few moments passed; the effects of the wand that now lay beside the fallen Kiennite were weakening; the thief began to move. Eomore managed to reach them and they sat together.

Still no Magrian.

But at least they were still alive and had the chance to look further. Cara picked up the wand from the side of the fallen foe and began to study it. The Kiennite had forgotten that the polymorph spell had led to his speaking in the tongue of the creature mimicked, and Cara had ascertained the phrase he had uttered as he attacked the thief with the wand; she now knew its secret. Nigel was beginning to recover but would need a little more time. Cara stood.

She started toward the door, and said, "I'm going on up."

"No!" Eomore objected, but the great effort from the last fight prevented him from mustering enough energy to impede her.

He remained by the side of Nigel.

Cara entered the stairwell again and peered upward at the dark stair rungs. She like all the others had become accustomed to the persistent light of Parallan, but her elven eyes readily adjusted to the dark and she began her ascent. She was nearly as adept as Nigel at moving silently and soon reached the acme of the stair, finding that it ended some hundred rungs above the last encounter where she had left Eomore and Nigel. There were no doors at the top, merely a metal cap which covered the staircase to keep out the elements. Even before she discovered this the elf had estimated that she should have reached the top of the central tower from the amount they had climbed and the height of the tower when they had gazed upon it before. She listened intently before raising the lid and confirming that she had reached the top of the tower. There was a stone rail some five feet high surrounding the deck; perched upon it were four stone hideous figures which looked like the mythical gargoyles that adorned the castles of many nobles of Donothor. Their ugliness brought a shutter to her frail bones as she scanned the top of the great tower. There were remnants of the weaponry of ages past, broken catapults and decaying oil vats. But in the right half of the circular area was a small prison unusual in that it appeared to be made of a transparent glass; within there was an elderly elf – it had to Magrian from what she had heard of him. There were no guards apparent. She stared intently at the statues, looking for even the hint of a movement. Clutching the small Kiennite wand in her left hand, Cara leapt from the stairwell, carefully throwing the cover to the side to avoid being injured by it as it landed. She stood on the stone floor with the odd Parallanean sky overhead. In the distance she could hear shouts and growls in the forests as the Drolls pursued her comrades and below she detected a brief flash of flame and then heard the anguished sounds of the Droll castle guards who had apparently crossed Roscoe. Then all was quiet as she began to move forward toward the old man within the glass house. Closer inspection revealed a small key ring to her discerning eyes and there was a transparent key upon it. The old man who had been sleeping then awakened and begin to motion avidly for her to retreat, but she moved forward still reaching the cage. She reached for the keyring but upon touching it she heard a grating sounds of stone on stone and turning she saw the great gargoyle to her right suddenly animate and spring into flight directly toward her. Without considering other alternatives- later she would realize there weren't really any others- she leveled the wand toward the charging creature and pronounced the phrase "Aulgmoor demands" which she had heard earlier. The gargoyle paused in mid-flight and fell to the ground, smashing into thousands of small stones. The creature to her left then rose but there was the same result as the wand again served its new master. Then the two remaining creatures rose and began to circle the elven maid nearing her; the wand abandoned her. Taloned forepaws neared her from left and right – she stood erect, then suddenly dropped to the ground. A loud crash above her informed her that she got what she wanted; the two beasts in their zealous frenzy to tear her apart failed to realize their paths were crossing at a very inopportune time; they smashed together, each the bane of the other. Cara felt the pain as their remnants fell upon her legs, cutting into the smooth flesh. But her injuries were small; she stared at the four piles of rubble. The old man stood silently and motionlessly now. There was a look of great fear upon his ancient face as she approached; when she saw this she wheeled around in a full circle; there were no opponents apparent. Undaunted she took the key; her fine digits found the location of the keyhole. She inserted the key; she hoped there were no fireglyphs; her intuition told her there were none; she turned they key to the right; the walls vanished; the old one stood; his features hardened and he began to shout.

He uttered, "I curse the day of my birth that I should meet my end at your hands; though I could withstand your minions I shant be able to resist you, vile one! The illusion of youth does not impart true beauty to you!"

"Are you insane, old man? Are you called Magrian?" Cara asked, though puzzled.

"You know well that I am he. Though I've not before looked upon your face, I know your symbols and the wand gives you away, Deathqueen. Your face must never change for you look exactly as the paintings my forefather stole from your palace those generations ago. You are epitome of the saying that 'beauty is only skin deep'. You may slay me now, for I'll never bow to the likes of you!" he continued.

"Old man, my name is Cara and I am here to save not slay you. Vaylin leads my party here. The wand was taken from the Kiennite noble who was slain below us. I haven't the time to convince you further now for my companions are in great jeopardy. Come with me!" she said, sternly taking his arm.

The wounds in her legs ached now and every muscle strained as she led him to the stairwell.

The Old One's words reinforced an uncomfortable and foreboding sensation; she had felt powerful when she empowered the wand. She inexplicably regained her strength as if she had rested for hours. She had felt too comfortable with the destruction of her foes! Why had the wand failed on the third attempt?

Magrian now was the one with the look of confusion on his face. He questioned no further and followed her. She descended rapidly, finding that Eomore and Nigel had just begun to follow her. Eomore's eyes brightened when he saw her safe and the four quickly descended. At the base of the stair they found Knarra still working with the physician who was still in great pain.

Roscoe grumbled something along the line of "You took your jolly good time." but he had done a yeoman's job of keeping the remaining defenders at bay.

Sedoar tried to stand, but to no avail. Eomore grasped the hilt of Exeter and prepared to sheath the great weapon when the familiar voice silently appeared in his mind.

"I know that you will doubt me on this, my Prince, but I sense the presence of an enemy when the maiden holds the wand," the voice stated.

Exeter's "words" drove deeply into his consciousness.

Eomore sheathed Exeter and boosted the physician onto his back. The prince cast a glance toward Cara. The elven maiden looked exhausted, not dangerous.

Cara placed the wand inside the small leather pouch upon her back and drew the sword she carried in her small sheath which was really little more than a dagger. If she detected the glance from Eomore, she did not react to it.

The small party peered out into the outer ward and saw none there to impede them; they sped for the cover of the darkness. Reaching the still opened great outer doors, they could see a few of the enemy straggling around occasionally tripping over a fallen comrade and slashing their swords through the darkness.

"Do not attack them," Eomore said. "We'll try to escape unnoticed and reach the cover of the woods."

"I'll buy that," Nigel said.

As they moved along they were easily able to avoid the attackers who were blinded by the darkness. Magrian blindly followed the thief, led by his hand, and remained silent. They could see more of the Drolls and a few Kiennites gathering in the area immediately outside the area of Darkness. The old Drelve did pretty well considering he was blinded, too- Knarra had no more of the unguent- he blindly trusted his rescuers, so to speak. As they neared the fringes they realized that another diversion would be necessary to cover their dash back into the brush across the clearing. Roscoe and Cara briefly looked at each other; Cara weakly shook her head negatively, the mage once again raised his staff and directed his Magick in a line across the clearing and a wall of blazing flames appeared there.

In so doing, he said, "Make haste, for it won't last long. My power is rapidly leaving me."

Eomore motioned them forward and the small party shielded by the leaping flames managed to safely negotiate the longest hundred yards they had ever faced and fled into the brush, quickly gaining its camouflage. A few stalwart Drolls tried to come through the flames, but they were consumed and there were too few defenders on the group's side of the flames to strike against them. They did not look back as they ascended the mountainside; the prince strained as he laboriously carted the maimed physician. Amazingly, none of them had perished in the assault of the tower, at least not yet, but they were drained. Now they would need a little good fortune and a little time to make their escape.

Magrian paused briefly and rapidly construed snares and traps from the vines and underbrush; Nigel quickly learned his technique.

Eomore moved onward with Roscoe and the women, not stopping with them as they prepared the snares which they hoped would impede the pursuit they felt was certain. They hoped that perhaps the enemy, not knowing their full strength and respecting their Magick, would spend some time regrouping.

The climb was tiring and all were approaching exhaustion when Vaylin appeared from behind, or within, a great red elm tree and led them to the remnants of his party.

"We were fairly successful in our maneuvers," he said.

Vaylin then embraced the old one as they stood together.

Magrian revealed little emotion, but said "You have learned your lessons well, student. The forest serves those who respect and honor her. We are fortunate to be alive, and I am grateful to you. I doubt I would have attacked with such a small force."

"Especially if one is a sawbones and two others are women," Nigel quipped in, "But those other guys just had to take their chances against this crew."

The thief smiled as he thought his humor would lighten the situation; no one shared his whimsical feeling.

Magrian looked quite puzzled by the remarks. Knarra was looking after Sedoar; the others strained to hear the sounds of pursuit but for now at least it was quiet. Cara had literally collapsed; her eyes stared blankly into the heavens – was it appropriate to use that word to describe the skies of Parallan? With the exception of the Drelves, they had encountered no other friendly or even sociable elements in this bizarre place. Roscoe had rested the staff beside him on the ground and its heat seared the grass immediately under it. The smoke was dispersed by a quick kick from Nigel's boot. The mage failed to notice as he too was so exhausted that he could only lie there. Nigel noted the blisters on Roscoe's palms from the great heat of the staff.

Vaylin reported to Eomore that only one of the Drelves from his party had fallen, but the other group had been fragmented and two other Drelves and the ranger Kryl were not accounted for and feared slain by the enemy. Over two thousand of the enemies were dead. The others waited at the appointed place on the crest of the ridge. Ambulation was impossible for the physician even though Knarra had worked diligently with him. His wound was a grievous one, and it posed a real problem for them in that they now needed to move fast. Without much conversation they forced themselves to get up from the too brief respite and began to climb. Sedoar managed to walk with the assistance of a stout makeshift walking stick, another gift from the forest. Luckily they managed to make the ascent without any interference from their foes. They had chosen an area on the crest of the ridge which bordered on an open field; which would at least give them some visual advantage from attack and would allow them to make optimal use of their guards for their ranks were thinning. One old sage was hardly the equivalent of three Drelven warriors and a fighting man of the caliber of Kryl. The Amme clan had made another sacrifice to the service of their king. From this vantage point, they could see the massive force on the valley floor. The troop movements brought to mind the undulation of a great snake from their vantage point.

Far to the south the great figure silently stared through the one way wall and if he heard the soft footsteps of his advisor, he did not react.

"My Lord, the time is nigh. The last reports say the enemy is massing a great force to the north of the River Ornash. Our destiny calls us to the field of battle on the great plain where our forefathers earned such accolades for their valor. But we shall succeed where they did not. The victory that escaped them will not escape us," Izitx said emphatically.

Calaiz nodded but the Draith lord was lost in the beauty of the woman Trya.

He said, "She is the most beautiful thing my eyes have ever beheld, my friend."

Izitx was not pleased to hear these words from his liege. A frown accentuated the cruelty that lived upon his face.

After a pause, he said, "It is the woman's privilege to be your chosen, my Lord. Are you ready?"

"When I conjured this morning I could again sense the scrying eyes of the Deathqueen, but there was again a great outpouring of Magick within the land and I cannot determine its source. It troubles me that this force exists with the time of war at hand. I wanted the timing perfect, but the best made plans of mice and Masters oft go astray. Are our forces on the march to the positions we planned?"

"Yes, the captain Krow leads them now into the southern fringes of the Ornash Valley, there to engage the enemy. Within a few hours the battle will commence," Izitx answered.

"Then I must let my eyes feast upon this beauty once more and make my preparations. Prepare the beasts," Calaiz looked upon Trya.

Izitx threw his cape emphatically and turned to walk away.

"I shall await you by the wyvern stall," Izitx said.

Calaiz could not account for the outpourings of Magick that were felt in the land. But this was not directed against him. Could he sense the presence of an ally? Who else had the Deathqueen offended?

CHAPTER 26

War

Eomore rested briefly and fitfully for the prince was concerned because of the weak condition of his companions. He had grasped Exeter's hilt several times and each time the weapon had communicated no threat. Even the stalwart Nigel and graceful Knarra were wearing the signs of fatigue on their faces. Roscoe and Cara were sleeping deeply, but the prince kept his eyes upon the play unfolding before them on the plain below, which Magrian had termed the Ornash Valley. It was named for the great river that bisected it. The living waves of Drolls and their allies remained to the north of the river, though they were continuing to move nearer it. The play was set except for the entry of the other actors in the diorama below them. There was no sign of a Draith army, although Magrian had assured him it would appear before the Drolls crossed the river.

After allowing the Old One a deserved rest, Eomore anxiously approached him to try to learn something – hopefully a chink in the seemingly impervious armor of the Draith castle called Ooranth. Vaylin and Vannelei joined them, but the others continued to rest or stand watch.

Vaylin began the conversation by saying, "At least we did not have to enter the bowels of the castle of the Kiennite Deathqueen to find you, Teacher. Aulgmoor is, from what you have taught us, a totally baneful place."

The Drelve prince informed the Teacher of recent events.

Magrian was the only Drelve they had seen who wore facial hair. He looked like a very old elf in all other respects, but a long white beard fell from his thin face almost halfway down his chest, bearing resemblance to a thin wide-eared dwarf. He stroked the beard as he talked and his words rang as clear as a sanctuary bell calling the faithful to a ceremony of devotion. The old Drelve pulled a tattered hand-drawn map from beneath his tunic and studied it briefly.

Magrian answered, "Yes, the daring rescue from the Keep was easier than getting into the dungeons of Aulgmoor. But our paths

212

may still lead us there if we are to fulfill the quest our new friends face."

The others remained silent, waiting for him to continue, which he did after drawing several deep puffs from his pipe. "The first thing the Baron that you disposed of asked me was interesting. 'What is the secret of the great sword, old fool?' I believe he said. He asked a number of other things, but I usually answered his questions with one of my own, which he apparently did not mind answering since he felt, I'm sure, that I was a doomed Drelve. I think that fate, or some force, has led them into possession of the Draithsbane. I further believe that it lies in the treasure coffers of the Deathqueen at Aulgmoor. Eomore, you have asked if there is a means to defeat the Draith Lord. Even the massive force you see before us here will likely fall before the powers of the Black Lord of Ooranth. I feel that he will destroy the Deathqueen herself unless she manages some of her trickery. They refer to him as the Black King – black is the color that represents absolute strength to this people; black is revered by them; and they have never referred to one of their kings in such a way. Thus this Draithlord must be fiercest of all, including the legendary Nargan the Red who came closest to total victory many periods ago. Unfortunately, I have little personal knowledge of him and I do not know how he is so powerful, but suffice it to say that all we have heard of him is likely true. I have been unfortunate enough to have seen the inner sanctuary of both Castle Ooranth and Castle Aulgmoor. They make your Misty Forest seem a cakewalk. Yes, I've been there too. I would not like to choose between them. But we are likely to see both if fate allows us to come near the completion of this quest. A practical person, I must say that we will likely perish, but I shall do so, as I owe you any life that I have remaining. I was to have provided the beast of the tower with his next meal."

"Couldn't you have used your powers to escape?" Eomore asked.

The Old One laughed, "My friend, I am no wizard. My powers are the experience of a long life and knowledge of the forests. The enhancing root is a symbolic means for us to reveal our appreciation to the forest for the life it gives to us. I'm afraid you have been misled if you think I can perform the works of your people. I even thought the elven girl was the Deathqueen coming for me. She must think of me as an ungrateful scoundrel, but she does bear such a resemblance to portraits I've seen of the monarch of the Kiennites in her youth."

"What do you know of her?" Eomore asked.

"Anectrophinea has survived many Dark Periods beyond most of her race. She has many powers and there are many more legends of her. The Draiths blame the genocide that plagues their females upon her and in some way she may well have been responsible. She is, or at least once was, mortal, though I have not looked upon her for a generation of Dark Periods. Some say she has died and rules from beyond the grave, while others say she merely has been replaced by others as powerful. Suffice it to say that the Draiths believe that she still leads their enemies, but that is what the Kiennites would want them to believe in any way. The Kiennite ruling fortress Aulgmoor will make the Keep you just conquered seem as though it were an anthill of the lowest proportions. Still, success there may be our only avenue toward the ultimate goal of recovering your womenfolk and avenging your dead. The fortunes of time smile upon us in that war is now soon upon the land. As a Drelvling, I saw some of the last great conflict but that was another day – never have I witnessed such as that in the Ornash Valley – the field of honor as the combatants call it – this has been the traditional site of the first battles, for each considers an advance across the river as a gesture of war."

"Two things seem awry," Nigel injected. "First, I see only one foe. Are the Drolls going to fight themselves? From what I've seen, they are almost that stupid. Second, even though they are a little slow, I see no way we could sneak by a force of such magnitude, especially since there is no cover of darkness in this wretched place and even Knarra's Darkness Spell would not cover such an expanse. The enemy would simply rain arrows and spears into our darkened area."

Magrian did not change the expression on his face; he still appeared quite somber and responded to the observations made by the thief.

"Be assured that the Draiths are aware of every movement the Droll army makes. Their forces usually muster far to the south. As to the Drolls – do not underestimate them, my friends. You must remember that you have had the advantage of being an unknown quantity to this point; surprise has been your ally. The Magick you possess is great from what I've seen and heard. But the Drolls learn from their mistakes and they will fight you better with each encounter. They will be reinforced by Kiennite Magicians and Illusionists. Our land is not a wretched place. There is much beauty here if one appreciates it. There are wretched inhabitants here; I have seen that there are some within your realms as well. Finally, you are correct that we would never be able to pass through the army below us. I believe that my pupil Vaylin may have spoken to you of the underground caverns. There you may experience the darkness that you long for, but often the visitor never returns to tell the tale. I have been there and being sane, I never planned to return," Magrian commented.

"From what Vaylin has told us, the caves may be worse than the Draiths and the Drolls. I don't relish being a meal for a cave dragon or some other denizen of the darkness," Vannelei said.

The elf then continued, "But I will take any risk needed to try to find my family's lost maiden and the princess of Donothor."

"What you speak of is a real possibility. I can see that you are a determined group and are seemingly fearless," Magrian answered.

"Don't go that far," Nigel quipped.

"Your own motivations puzzle me, my friend, but I feel that I should dismiss the gut feeling that I have to never turn my back on you and trust myself to you as the others have," Magrian said, staring directly at the thief.

Nigel returned the stare and for a moment it looked like things might get hot when they became aware of a change in the valley below them. The waves of the Droll army began to swell and approach the river steadily moving nearer. In several places, it looked like they were trying to bridge the river. The little group remained silent except for some members arousing those who were sleeping. Soon all were gathered upon the ridge looking down upon the wide valley, watching the multitudes of warriors making their way across the River Ornash. They were probably using the wood of a tree called a corker, which was very light and buoyant, yet strong enough to support great weights; Magrian had told them of this wood. Then in the south, they saw the Draith host coming for the challenge. Another great dark wave moved up the valley at an incredibly rapid rate to clash against the other swelling wave. The battle was too distant to be giving any clear sound, but the group on the hilltop could a hear a steady drone from the Drolls, who were beginning to cross the river and take the steps across to the southern bank, steps which Magrian termed steps of no return; they made war inevitable. The Draith armies moved closer and the first forces across the river braced to meet them. From the vantage point of the witnesses on the mountain top, the battle seemed to be commencing in slow motion, but to Eomore and the rangers who had experienced such conflict firsthand, though not in such magnitude, the development and deployment of the forces was very rapid. The Draith force began to spread outward and soon gave the appearance of a great pair of hands coming together to smash the expeditionary forces of the Drolls. Within moments, the forces met with a battle cry that swelled up over the ridges and reflected the tenacity of the battle. Initially it looked like a stalemate, with both sides standing their ground, but eventually the superior numbers of the Draiths began to wear down the Droll advance guard which seemed to be taking terrible losses. But the Drolls continued to pour across the Ornash, replacing their fallen with a tide of fresh warriors. There were occasional bursts of flame within the Draith ranks and some electrical bolts from the far side of the river, signifying the Kiennite contribution to the battle. Each of these would create brief weakenings in the forward wall on the assault force, but the Draiths quickly shored up these bulges; the Draiths lacked the means of attacking the positions from which the attacks of Magick emanated. The battle waged for several hours at which time the Donothorian fighters realized for the first time that these fighters would not have the advantage of nightfall curtailing the intensity of the fighting. Could they fight ceaselessly for days? The river darkened from the ichor and blood as the fallen Drolls were pushed back into it. It was further defiled when the Draiths broke through and tried to cross but their numbers were too small to afford any real chance of success and they were mowed down from the other side of the river by Droll and Kiennite archers and also bursts of fire which left the waters of the great river sizzling. Eventually the Drolls were able to more than replace their losses and appeared to be gaining ground. At several points they wedged through the ranks of the Draiths and came perilously close to cutting their forces in half, but the rear guard of the southerners managed to avert the disaster. Though the Draiths were supposedly much more powerful individuals, the greater numbers of the Drolls seemed to be prevailing.

Indeed it looked as though the war would be a brief one when two dots appeared in the sky to the south. These dots moved closer and soon it was apparent that there were great winged creatures bearing much the appearance of small dragons with barbed tails. One of the landed immediately behind the Draith rear; it was as though the army had received a shot in the arm, for immediately the advancing Drolls were beaten back.

The observers of course could not ascertain that mighty Izitx had joined his troops and entered the fray.

The second beast circled above the battle and flew toward the hilltop where Eomore and the others were seated, sending them scurrying for cover in the trees; the winged beast turned to enter the battle. They could only glimpse a great dark rider upon the beast; it never came closer than five hundred paces to them; they could not really get a good look at Calaiz. They failed to realize that he represented their most baneful foe; they were not alone in this; the Droll and Kiennite legions in the valley who thought they were near rapid victory in the first battle, were about to meet their most baneful foe.

This was what Izitx lived and trained for. The great warrior dismounted the wyvern and proceeded forward; he moved to the thinnest region of the Draith lines. He disdained armor and weapon. He pushed through his own ranks until the reached the snarling and frenzied Droll warriors. Two Drolls left their wounded Draith opponents and approached the large unarmored intended prey, thinking that they were given easy pickings. Izitx's black robes stood out amongst the more hued garbs and armory of the Draith multitudes. The unfortunate Drolls were only in mid-strike with their broadswords when their lives ended. Mighty blinding blows came from both of Izitx's huge hands and shattered the throats of the enemies. The Draith warriors were uplifted by the arrival of their captain; a roar swelled from their ranks as the great beast bearing their liege swooped overhead and bore down on the Kiennite positions from which the painful and lethal emanations of Magick had been thinning the Draith ranks. The multitude of fallen brethren beneath ther feet spurred them onward as they advanced into the ranks of the Drolls. Izitx created a wide path to follow as the Droll casualties mounted before him.

The wyvern dove bearing its rider into striking range and great waves of violet flame burst from his hands, decimating three of the positions on the northern side of the river from which Magick attacks on the Draiths had originated. These were snuffed out with only paltry counterattack, as thin wispy trails of fire rose toward the winged beast. The dark rider skillfully maneuvered the beast to avoid the counterattack and let his own fires blaze toward those foolish enough to try to attack the wyvernrider. The fire beams that reached Calaiz seemed to merely reflect from the rider. The great beast rose to the far side of the valley, only to again turn and dive toward the Kiennite positions. Again, the dark rider struck, only this time the rays from his hands were white and a great section of the Ornash was frozen immediately and mists rose into the air. Many of the enemy attempting to cross became entrapped and many of those caught in the direct effect were instantly slain. Thrice more he attacked – blue, maroon, and finally a gray mist emanated from his hands. Masses of the enemy fell motionlessly before this last and seemingly most deadly ray. Not even Roscoe could recall seeing such a potent Death Spell. Soon the tide had turned and the Drolls were falling back across the Ornash fleeing before their foe. The Draith legions wiped up the remaining foes trapped on the southern fringe of the river; the retreating Drolls were burning their bridges behind them. It looked for a moment like the Draiths might pursue; the second beast landed behind them and they stopped their advance allowing the enemy to withdraw in first a very disorganized fashion, then more orderly as they came further from the river. There was a roar from the Draith legions. The Donothorians wondered why they had violated a basic principle of warfare by not pursuing their enemies. They saw the large number of horsemen pouring out of the gap, some thousand paces to the north of the river and the many foot soldiers behind them. A large reinforcement for the retreating Drolls had arrived. Apparently the Draith tacticians did not want to duplicate the mistake of their enemies by crossing the river only to be attacked before they were prepared for an onslaught. Could the ghost horse and its rider have been at the head of the reinforcements? If so, that reinforced that the Draith leaders had made a rational decision. The armies moved respectively north and south of the river and camped. Only then were the losses apparent. The combatants must have been standing upon fallen comrades to continue the battle. The river darkened to a deep reddish-black from the ichors of the fallen. Great chunks of ice floated amongst the many carcasses in the waters.

Even though the Donothorians had tasted battle in the field and forest, none of the current generation of men and dwarves had been involved in the great wars of their own world. Only Knarra and Roscoe had witnessed the Iron Mountain Wars and the war against the necromancer of the Lachinor. To witness such a large scale battle as a play on a stage was awe inspiring to them. Even though they were witnessing the struggles of alien fighters they were nonetheless affected by the carnage before them and sensed something of how the loss of so many comrades must feel. The Donothorians could not comprehend the animalistic feelings of the Drolls and the emotionless affects of the Draith masses. Vannelei was young, but others of the elves had witnessed the struggles during the great wars of their world. Death was a recent but growing experience for the elven maiden Cara. She found it more disturbing with each escalation rather than less.

"Do you ever learn to understand this? I feel so repulsed!" she frailly uttered, fighting nausea.

Fortunately the sounds and smells of battle had been at a distance, but she had full vision of the battle.

Roscoe and Knarra had shared the experience firsthand. Maybe that was the reason that the Archmage and the Priestess were the quietest of the group. Although death was no stranger to Nigel, the experience of their own battles at the forest glen and the keep at the northern gap and the great battle just witnessed made all the assassin's prior experiences pale by comparison.

"Any doubt that I had before has been removed now that I've seen the power of the Draith Lord. We must proceed to Aulgmoor to try to gain the Draithsbane, assuming it is even there," Magrian said flatly.

The others nodded silently.

They felt like meager pawns on a great game board. Hopefully they would not be mere sacrificial gambit. The opening was behind them. Was this midgame or endgame?

CHAPTER 27
Boomer's Vigil

Boomer continued to keep his vigil at the portal. He was supported by well armed and dug in troops. The dwarf grudgingly obeyed the orders of his king by not entering the portal to who-knew-where, but his heart ached to join his friend. The flaming stairs did not radiate heat, but the singed carcasses of the forest fauna that had risked the stairs were a good dissuasion. Roscoe's familiar, the cat Matilda, was much more than a pet; she had warned them of the great Magick surrounding the portal and the certainty of harm if traversing the gate were risked. Matilda had only implied in her purrs that returning from the other side posed the greatest risk. Boomer had seen a small furried creature bolt up the flaming stair to escape a marauding fox. The animal disappeared at the height of the stair which was well above Boomer's head but near the height of a man. Moments later, the animal briefly reappeared at the top of the stair, screeched loudly, burst into flame, and fell dead to the ground.

As the days passed, the duty became more boring, but they had to assume that further invasion could come at any time. The security of the kingdom was now in the hands of Boomer as he was the acting Captain of the Rangers, which was an honor never before bestowed upon any of his race. The dwarf played games of chance with young Cade, who learned quickly, and the dwarf had to resort to cheating to win with any consistency. Youth are too trusting, the dwarf mused.

No other portals had been found by the Acolytes from Knarra's freehold, but their skills were limited. The dwarf feared the alliance with Nigel Louffette. He still had no trust in the thief, but Eomore had known the risk of taking him along. Word from castle Lyndyn held that the good king Eraitmus was becoming more bereaved with time, fearing that he had no hope of regaining his daughter the princess Trya and had lost his son and heir in the process. The elven boy Cade had become extremely useful as an envoy; he and Boomer had become close friends.

So far the kingdom had not been subjected to opportunistic attacks; apparently the lesson given the goblins in Tindal had been a deterrent. But there was no known wizard in the land and the absence of Knarra was disconcerting as well. Donothor was more vulnerable than she had been in many years; the kingdom was reaping the benefits of the solidifying rule of the House of Aivendar. There still remained the Beast of the Dungeons, Taekora, and almost the full strength of the corps of Rangers. For now, all Boomer could do was wait and hope. He longed for a command from the king to follow into the unknown realm beyond the gate.

At the Temple of Hiram and Lydia, Yennil, the acting High Priest, endeavored to keep the works of Knarra going as well. Though devout, he lacked the power of the Priestess and the love of the people as well. Knarra had taught her chief Acolyte well but he still had much to learn.

In the wilderness, the castle of Roscoe had little to fear for the mage had created too many defenses for even the shapechangers and weremen to pose a threat. But there vigil was being kept also.

On a mountaintop in Parallan, the members of the Deathquest were preparing to follow the Old One on the journey to what would likely be a conflict with the Deathqueen of the Kiennites.

Sedoar was too lame to continue.

The healer had fought well and made a good account of him. He had entrusted the remaining scarce poltices and other supplies to Faryn, one of the remaining drelves who had spent the greater amount of time assisting Sedoar in his healing efforts. Eomore had to give the healer an Imperial Directive Command before the healer would agree. Sedoar had asked to have Exeter relieve him of his lame leg such that he could use a strong bough and limp along with the party. Such was the loyalty and love of the subjects for the Aivendars. The decision had been made to have two Drelves escort him back to Alms Glen, the sanctuary of the forest dwellers. It would be a perilous journey but less so than the one facing the others. Eight Drelves remained. Eomore, Cara, Roscoe, Knarra, Deron, Vannelei, Nigel, Tjol Bergin, Vaylin, Banon Kessa the archer, and Magrian joined these eight to make the party number nineteen. Nineteen thousand seemed too few, but still they prepared to move up the ridge and descend at a point chosen by Magrian to bypass the armies by braving the Caves of Parallan. After witnessing the power of the black wyvernrider in the skies over the Valley Ornash, they felt as a group that obtaining the weapon known as the Draithsbane was their only hope. The war would certainly serve their purpose in some ways but in other ways it meant that the number of patrols would be increased; however, Magrian felt that the ridges and the eastern slopes of the Peaks of Division would be relatively safe for them to travel. The Drolls and Kiennites were occupied with the known enemies on the other side of the River Ornash to be wary of a small group of travelers. That was their hope. Hope was stretching thin. None wanted to consider odds of success.

Was the greatest task determining the lesser of the two evils with which one could cast his lot? Was there a lesser evil? It was the Draiths that had wronged them. Yet there was something that seemed more civilized about the large warriors.

The party had rested fairly well, with Cara and Roscoe requiring the most respite. Knarra had placed balms upon the blistered hands of the wizard, which had helped to relieve the pains he suffered from the burns he had received from his staff from the great outpouring of Magick during the fight at the Keep. The Drelves had scoured the forest for items requested by Roscoe and Knarra to replenish their supplies. Would spider's web from Parallan behave as spiders web from their own land when used in spell casting? Such questions were painful to consider.

They had bade Sedoar farewell and the noble physician, still clutching the sword that he had wielded so honorably, limped off with the two Drelves who were to escort him back to the relative sanctuary of the Drelven King Drolan. The others began to gather themselves and prepared to embark on the next segment of the quest, turning now toward Aulgmoor and the foul heart of the Kiennite Deathqueen's power. But certainly her, or its, attentions would be somewhat diverted toward the battle in progress. Magrian convinced them that the most expeditious route to Aulgmoor would be through the underground caverns which would avoid the many patrols on the surface. It was a matter of choosing the least risk and now it seemed that they were debating a risk benefit ratio with each step that they were taking. Magrian discussed the first part of their route with them and suggested they take nourishment and be on their way, lest they be stopped by one of the winged scouts of one of the warring parties.

Cara sat beside Eomore. She reached into her pack and removed the small wand. She entrusted it to Eomore.

"I do not like the way that I feel when I hold this. Why, I don't know. Why was the Old One so afraid of me? Am I evil in your eyes? Please ask Exeter to assess me?" she said tearfully.

Eomore felt great guilt and chastised himself silently for doing what she asked. The prince also asked Exeter to assess himself when he held the wand. The wand felt like a stick to Eomore; Exeter detected no mischief or danger when Cara was without the wand or when Eomore held it.

The girl looked refreshed; the beauty, that had never completely left her even in her greatest fatigue, was fully restored. If anything she seemed to be lovelier as she stayed longer in the forests. She was in her element.

Eomore wondered if his mind were fully objective, but really did not care. One of her small smiles did more to refresh him than all the food he took. The prince realized that he had been conversing less and less with his vorpal companion; the sword was quick to remind him of this each chance she had. But Exeter had ceased to say anything detrimental about the elf – perhaps the sword had been with enough of the princes of Donothor to know when they were lost to the fair sex; Exeter still resented it. She thought Eomore was committed to his bachelorhood; she thought that he would follow the course of the first Aivendar to wield her, the great Ordrych Aivendar; Eomore was until a fateful night in a bar in Kanath. Two elven eyes had captured his heart! The Deathquest prevented the full expression of their love.

Cara recalled the words she had earlier had with the priestess Knarra. Were the state of affairs she and Eomore faced experienced similarly by Knarra and Roscoe at a past time? Cara liked to romanticize; the supposition was so attractive. Was it true? Only Roscoe and Knarra knew the full story. Cara felt it best not to pry.

During the last difficult days – she knew not how many because of the lack of nightfall – she had thought of so many things to say to her prince when she got the chance, but now that they were sitting together it seemed that their eyes were doing most of the talking; they sat near each other silently.

Nigel watched them briefly but his own eyes returned again and again to Knarra who usually responded to him with a smile.

The priestess and the mage were drawing nearer with each rest period.

After taking nourishment, they rose and began to walk along the crest of the ridge. Below in the valley the two armies remained a respectable distance apart seeming poised for the next combat. Eomore wondered which would attempt to cross the river first and what tactics they would employ. Rarely winged creatures bearing riders would dot the skies over their heads sending them scurrying for cover, but their progress along the crest there was largely unimpeded. The Drelves surmised that the animals that they should be encountering were likely driven away or else gracing the tables of the great armies. All of the land of Parallan was entangled in the conflict in the Ornash Valley.

Roscoe briefly paused and slowly scanned the armies. "There are great forces of the Magick on both sides of the river. I sense a presence..." but his voice faded.

Knarra looked upon his face, and then said, reassuringly, "There is great evil on both sides. But you are wrong, my friend; that presence that you fear is long lost from ours and any other world."

"The Evil seems so familiar," the Mage continued his voice fading. Déjà vu all over again.

Soon they were deeper in the forests and were gradually descending the eastern side of the mountains. They had caught a glimpse of a greater range of mountains to the north that Magrian had termed the Doombringers because that was usually what they did to all who entered them. Therein lay the stronghold of Aulgmoor. The range they were traversing swung around to the east and did not connect with the Doombringers; there remained an expanse of the valley jutting there; the Old One said that the underground caverns would place them within the tall range itself if they were successful in negotiating the caverns. All realized that there was no chance of moving across the open valley without detection; surely the Drolls would kill first and ask questions later if they encountered them again. As they began the descent the sights and sounds of battle were no longer with them.

The trek was not really hazardous. The topography was such that the terrain was rolling and cliffs were few. Their greatest adversary was the thick undergrowth. Deron and Banon stayed in front and hacked through the briars and saplings with their hatchets. They took care not to dull the edges of their swords with such endeavors.

Nigel, Vaylin, and the Drelves were more adept at evading the snares and the barbs and paralleled the main party to try to warn them of danger. Deep within the forest they felt not that far from home until they came through a clearer area where their eyes would betray the illusion by revealing again the presence of three suns. As they neared the base of the mountains there was more animal life. A large red bearlike creature considered them briefly as a main course but he was deterred by Deron's blade and barely escaped with his thick hide. The Drelves seemed happier now that there were other forest dwellers.

A rushing sound of water was heard ahead of them. Magrian called them together and advised them that this was an unusual area and they were coming upon a waterfall. They would be crossing behind the waterfall and proceeding onward.

"Ignore what your mind says to you when you are behind the water," Magrian said without giving any real explanation.

Slowly they approached the waterfall and saw a small ledge behind the water. The narrow ledge forced a single file march.

Magrian assumed the lead and proceeded onward, walking gingerly along the ledge. The total length was about thirty paces. The Drelve negotiated the distance easily. Nigel cautiously entered the stone ledge; the water was surprisingly warm for a mountain stream as it misted back against him. The ledge was about two feet wide and algae made it a little slippery. The falls dropped a total of a hundred feet and ninety of that was encompassed as a drop directly before him, crashing the water upon a number of large stones below.

"Jump. It will be pleasant," a soothing voice appeared suddenly in his mind.

The thief thought in return, "Now that would be stupid."

He found his foot slipping toward the edge.

"You might fly. You will impress your friends. You will make new friends and gain influence," the voice recurred.

It now seemed like a chorus and was more alluring than before.

Nigel began to think about it. The others could see he was pausing and there was obvious alarm on Magrian's face as he watched. The old Drelve quickly ran back into the chasm behind the waterfall and grabbed the thief by the arm. Nigel looked mesmerized. The thief shook his head violently and resisted the tugging by Magrian.

"I've got to try it. I've got to try it!" he exclaimed.

Magrian slapped his face hard and the two of them came hazardously close to slipping, but the ploy seemed effective; Nigel again seemed coherent and beckoned to the pleas and motions of the others to return to the safety of the near side of the waterfall. The Drelve and Nigel made it back in one piece; no one was across and the rushing waters seemed to be laughing at them.

All were now feeling tentative.

Eomore said, "Couldn't we just go downstream?"

"The stream is deep, widens and there are rapids," Magrian answered. "Besides, the stone passage behind the fall is safe, as you witnessed by my own crossing. But the place is enchanted and I underestimated your susceptibility to the enchantment. There are many legends about the "Alluring Falls" as they are called. Some say that a young and beautiful witch, much like our dark elven friend, I presume, was thrown over the falls generations ago and she pronounced a curse on the area with her dying breaths. As Roscoe knows Magick pronounced in the death throes of a caster are particularly potent. But others say the spirits of all who perish here remain eternally and long for companionship – trying to entice each passerby to leap and join their eternal unrest. Others say it's merely the mischief of water sprites that don't comprehend the significance of death and therefore are not aware of the gravity of their deeds. And there are those who say it's only the mind playing tricks on the passerby for he is expecting something to happen. I cannot answer the riddle, but I was nearly claimed here once and Mr. Louffette almost leaped to his end. We must take precautions; the passageway should be made safe. I should have anticipated this difficulty but I did not wish to alarm you."

Nigel frowned. "Don't worry about alarming us, old man. I'm toying with the idea of kicking your butt for slapping my face. I'd rather be worried than surprised."

Magrian smiled weakly, and then said, "I'll be more straightforward whenever I can. I believe that we can negotiate the passage behind the falls, and once we are past this, it is but a short distance to the hidden entrance to the caverns."

"I'm open to suggestions," Nigel said, still indignant about losing control.

His face remained flushed.

"Would earplugs help?" Deron asked.

"That would all depend, my little friend, on what an earplug is," Magrian replied.

"They are small furry animals that could fit over the openings to our ears. That might serve to keep the suggestions away from our minds," the dwarf answered.

"Good thought, Deron, but I haven't seen any since we entered Parallan," Eomore answered.

"That is the answer though," Knarra injected, "We must screen our hearing. Singing should suffice nicely, and I've longed for a song for quite some time now myself."

Tjol Bergin began to boom out a nonsensical and old traditional song of Tindal.

The vocals promptly prodded Roscoe to say, "Let's cross quickly before he remembers the second verse. No ghost could stand to listen to that."

Soon all joined in the vocalizing, but they took the added precautions of bringing out lengths of rope and brought them around their waists. Nigel and Magrian moved across the precipice and reached the other side uneventfully. They secured the rope to strong saplings on the far side. Tjol and Eomore remained on the other side securing the rope there and one by one the others crossed. Finally the two strongmen wrapped the ends of the ropes around their own waists and crossed the passage. They sang as loud as they could yet each felt a tickling sensation at the base of their brains as they crossed. Soon the group gathered on the far side of the Alluring Falls and Tjol stopped singing. No one seemed to be disappointed with that.

Knarra smiled at the big man, saying, "A little cooperation goes a long way, doesn't it?"

Deron smiled and said, "Tjol probably did scare all the spooks away."

The big man smiled too, and the entire party enjoyed the lighter moment, but soon they were again on their way. They reached the base of the mountains and were proceeding along a forest trail. Cara seized the opportunity to walk beside Eomore when there enough room for them to walk abreast. Their visibility was improved but at the same time they were more vulnerable, so the pace was quickened. In the distance they could see a rock formation jutting out from the mountainside.

Magrian remarked, 'Therein lies the entrance to the caverns. We must be on our best guard for it is a baneful place."

They reached a particularly snug area of forest growth where a rest was taken and inventories were made.

"I would like to study the Kiennite wand," Roscoe said as he approached Cara.

The elf looked toward Eomore as if to ask the prince for counsel, but Eomore quickly reached into his pack and produced the device saying to Roscoe, "I was keeping it safe for her."

"I cannot read these runes," the mage quizzically added.

Knarra sprinkled a small quantity of purplish powder over the wand and uttered a few arcane phrases.

"I cannot define its nature," the priestess said flatly. "Guard this carefully but remain vigilant to its presence."

A brief rest was taken.

CHAPTER 28
The Caverns of Darkness

"We will be enveloped in total darkness. Torches will be required for the most part," Magrian said. Having gone so long without full darkness of night, the Donothorians were almost looking forward to some time in the caverns. Unfortunately, they did not know what outcome was awaiting them.

"I'll take care of that," Roscoe said flatly, producing a small wandlike device from another of the many pockets of his robe. "Give me the wand you hold, Eomore."

Eomore hesitated for a moment, though he really didn't understand why, and then extended the device to the wizard. His hesitation brought a frown to Roscoe's face but this soon changed to a look of intense concentration as he stared at the wands. He placed them on the ground in front of him and produced another phial from his pockets. He started a brief incantation and sprinkled a powder from the small phial onto the two devices, causing them to brightly glow, and then settle down to a less intense emanation of light.

He said, "The light spell is cast, but there is no on and off switch as there is with orbs of illumination. If darkness is desired, the wands will have to be shrouded."

"My weapon can also emit light if needed," Eomore said.

Nigel's thoughts returned to a pattern of earlier times and he thought that one would have to pack a picnic lunch if her were going to pick Roscoe's pockets. The robe seemed to have bottomless depths and it seemed that the wizard could produce something to help them in any given situation.

Roscoe then said, "Just in case any of our members get any ideas when we enter the Darkness let me demonstrate something. Deron, place your hand into my pocket."

The dwarf seemed puzzled, but obeyed the request.

When the thickened hand reached the garment, a shrill voice began to scream, "Alarm, alarm, alarm! Peter Piper is picking your pickled pepper!"

Nigel's dark eyes met Roscoe's and tension mounted.

The thief said, "Deron now stand beside me."

Nigel brought "Sweetheart" from his waist and held the dagger upright.

"Now shout as loud as you can, my friend," the thief said.

Deron was doubly puzzled, but opened his mouth and began to sing the song they had used before. Nigel gripped the hilt of the dagger and the dwarf was bathed in silence – total silence as dark as the dungeons of Castle Lyndyn.

The thief said, "I guess we just have to trust each other, don't we, mage?"

A staredown ensued, but Knarra walked over to the two men and called them to her side. She placed a gentle kiss first on the face of Roscoe, then Nigel.

She said, "Both of you serve us so well, so we must have friendship between you."

Too late they realized the Empathy spell was cast and they reached out their hands for a solid grip.

Both said, "Magick isn't necessary for us to come together."

They apologized to each other; Knarra explained that no Magick had been used.

With the showmanship ended, they advanced to the rock formation narrowly missing a pair of stone hens that were nesting near the rocks.

Magrian bent down and removed several of the ovoid eggs from the nest saying, "These make excellent sling bolts."

Tjol turned to Deron, asking "What's a henway?"

The dwarf replied, "Is that what you call the nest? I guess I don't know. What's a henway?"

"Three or four pounds," Tjol replied and burst into laughter.

A little further down the pathway, Tjol skewered a rock snake that was hissing menacingly at them.

It gave the big man another chance for a one-liner as he said, "I'm only afraid of four kinds of snakes – big ones, little ones, live ones, and dead ones."

This produced a groan from all who were close enough to hear, but his levity was appreciated by most of them in these dark days – no, dark times had to be the expression, for again they had almost lost the concept and day and night.

Soon they reached a vertical crevice between two of the rocks that was the portal to the expanse of underground caverns. The opening afforded just enough width to allow the passage of a single armored man.

Magrian spoke, "Every step we take might be our last, so each must be thought about carefully before it is taken. Darkness is not our element, so for the first time since our association began you will be more comfortable than we. I discovered that one will not become lost if his movement is always consistent; one must always take the left most passage; I found my way to the great underground river. Once the river is found, it can be followed to its source at the Doombringers where Aulgmoor also lies."

Nigel quipped, "Don't everybody go for the opening at once. I suppose I should lead since many of you have the misconception that Darkness is my element."

The thief moved toward the crevice and after listening intently for a few moments, he slipped inside. He reappeared and motioned for them to follow him into the darkness.

The wands of illumination were brought out and Exeter was unsheathed. The weapon began to emanate a glow. Once they entered, the opening widened to an expanse some ten feet wide and a similar height. The floor was clearly not a fully natural formation as steps had been hewn from the stone. There was a gradual decline that Deron was able to guess at fifteen degrees or so. Dwarves had an uncanny ability to detect grades and direction below ground which probably derived from their early heritage. But Nigel led the way with Eomore at his side. Exeter was showing the way and detecting no enemies, but the vorpal weapon had stressed to Eomore that everything in this world was not always clearly read and not all enemies might be apparent. The thief was carefully inspecting the walls and steps for traps or weak areas. Magrian was close behind them with Tjol Bergin at his side. Then came Knarra and the archer Banon, and the eight Drelves who were lightly armed and at a disadvantage due to the darkness. Roscoe was walking in their midst using them as a ring of protection and in turn providing them with light. In the rear were Vaylin, Vannelei, Cara, and Deron. The men were heavily armed and Vaylin carried the wand to show their way. Exeter was clutched by the prince and sought enemies at all times; Deron was watching their rear diligently. Soon they were enveloped with darkness; the wands and Exeter were the only specks of light; this created the appearance of three fire beetles on a moonless Donothorian night. Most welcomed the darkness; their bodies drank it as they would water to quench a great thirst. They startled and were startled themselves by a large group of cavebirds after they had descended some two hundred paces, but silence again surrounded them as soon as the beating of the wings was beyond their hearing. A large arachnid menacingly approached Nigel as he scanned the left wall but Eomore was soon by his side and the light and blade of Exeter discouraged it.

Nigel annoyingly said, "I thought you could sense enemies with that sword. I almost became dinner for that thing!"

Eomore replied, "Exeter's talent applies only to creatures with intelligence or motives other than hunger, I suppose. Things are not consistent in this world. 'Who is an enemy?' may be a difficult question to answer."

"Or else it's getting senile," the thief retorted.

Exeter fumed and burned Eomore's inner ears for the next several minutes, but soon they were again on their way. They did not explore the narrow side passages but the rear guards watched them closely after they passed.

Exeter thought to Eomore, "Uneasiness begins to touch me, my prince – a feeling as though we are being watched and that our every move is known. Yet I cannot pinpoint a direct danger to you. There are many life forces here and they surround us. It is difficult but I'll try to warn you."

The diligence of the rear guards paid off when Deron noted a pair of green eyes looking back at him when he inspected one of the narrow crevices. The dwarf nudged Vannelei and slipped aside into the next opening they passed hoping to surprise the green-eyed creature. Unfortunately, the best laid plans of mice and dwarves sometimes went astray too, and this was one of those times, for the opening was already occupied; the first blow of the attacker relieved the dwarf of his sword.

The others heard shuffling sounds.

Eomore asked the blade, "What foe attacks?"

The sword replied, "Oh, Nigel may be right about my becoming senile! No wonder the force was so dim. Zombies – all around, and I fear they are not friendly."

The warning was, of course, too late; it was apparent to all of them that they were receiving a less that friendly welcome. Deron of course was the first aware of this, but even though the dwarf had been disarmed by the zombie, the creature moved so slowly that the nimble dwarf was able to recover his blade and scurry back to the main group. The zombies circled the party, but Eomore and Tjol encouraged the spellcasters to refrain from their Magick for the moment. Deron, Eomore, Tjol, Vannelei, Vaylin, and Nigel using Sweetheart were able to hew the zombies as they approached in waves, taking advantage of their slow movement. Even though there were many of them, the battle was soon over and the party had sustained no injuries other than the slightly bruised pride of the dwarven fighter. The zombies were readily ripped asunder by the cold steel.

They were regaining their composure when Exeter said to prince, "Though they are destroyed, I still sense a foreboding force. I still can't pinpoint it. It's like interference or – I'm not sure."

Eomore thought enough of the sword's opinion to suggest they move onward. Their minds all asked the same questions. Why would there be zombies in such a remote place? As the battle had shown, zombies made terrible guards because they were so slow and they fought ineffectively. They resumed their marching order and moved away.

When they were around the next curve, two of the skewered zombies reformed into the Adjuster – the demonic face smiled at the success of his diversion.

His guttural voice spoke to the walls of the passage, "My queen, it is as you thought – but if there is a magician among them, he did not display his wares. Yes, I shall follow them, but their deaths will be saved for you. Unless, of course, they fall prey to the beasts of the caverns. Oh, that does meet your approval. Yes, you should concentrate on the battle – my eyes, all four of them, are yours."

With that the towering form became silent and transformed into a cave bird and flew after them.

Exeter continued to feel the uneasiness but they moved onward.

CHAPTER 29
Caves

The cavedivers were more of a nuisance than anything else but the chittering of the small batlike creatures when they were startled could warn a significant foe of their approach. Many of the intrepid little force were debating whether the decision to go underground through the mazes was actually superior to traversing the plain of the battle. Each step brought them closer to the realm of the Kiennite Deathqueen, if indeed the old Drelve's memory served him correctly.

The Old One continued to guide them through the dark passages, which occasionally narrowed to the width of a broad shouldered man, while at other times a sizable army could travel. Magrian theorized that the forces of nature had shaped the tunnels in such a way that the dreadful beasts such as cave dragons could not escape to ravage the countryside. Then the old forest dweller debated his own reasoning, stating that if the dragon did exist, a narrow passage would merely serve as a minor inconvenience.

Eomore guessed that there was as much conjecture as memory in the Old One's guidance, but he continued to follow the principle of staying with the far left passage. Roscoe at times wanted to follow the right wing, but the mage had always been on the conservative side. Soon they heard the rushing of water; the Drelve had led them successful to a tributary of the underground river. The current was swift and the river seemed the width of ten tall men, lying head to foot. There was a rocky ledge to each side.

"Now the task eases a bit," Magrian said, "For we must now only follow the current. The river will exit the caverns very near the Kiennite fortress at Aulgmoor. There our task will truly begin."

Slowly they began to move along the river. Caverns of varying sizes opened to both sides and an intricate maze of passages led out of them. They continued to march for what Eomore thought was eight hours, resting about four. The pace was telling on the mage as his face furrowed with effort and beads of his sweat dropped to the cavern floors, as he labored under his heavy robes. When he concentrated heavily, the beads of sweat would burst into an array of colors as they struck the stone. Nigel and Vannelei continued to bear the burden of the point, though they were occasionally spelled by Cara. – the dark elf cast Energy Spells; this drained her somewhat but greatly refreshed the point bearers. Eomore was always near the frail elf though all had learned by now that her outward appearance was certainly deceiving. After each spell casting, her frail hands reached into her raimants and retrieved several small dried berries. The berries restored her energies; after each munching her face seemed to enlighten.

A Cave Eel lurched from its lair toward Deron, but the Dwarf dodged the attack. The creature retreated when faced with the blades of the warriors.

Deron unceremoniously righted himself and adjusting his armor, gruffly said, "Would be better to be on the point than in the rear. I'll be something's lunch yet!"

The big man Tjol bellowed, "So might we all – but you would be a tough morsel, my friend. I should think that the beast would have readily spat you out!"

He then broke into laughter.

"Very funny," the dwarf uttered.

Soon they were inching forward, trying to use the rocky wall as a shelter. They were forced to rely on some light source, but Eomore asked Exeter to remain dim.

He asked the weapon, "Why did you not warn of the eel?"

To this she replied, "My lord, the beast did not seek to attack you and I sense so much unintelligible, animalistic thoughts in these caverns that I could not sort it out. I apologize for my fallability."

His thoughts returned the reply, "You serve so diligently that no apology is required. These caverns fool each of us. Maintain the dim glow, my friend."

The yellow glow seemed to blush red for an instant then they assumed their trek, moving around the next turn.

The Adjuster watched them around the bend, and then changed from the cavediver form to a bipedal shape to follow. The rock eel again sensed nourishment and the beast bolted its thirty-foot form toward the intended quarry, its maw gaping widely. The try was fatal as bony hands grasped the great jaws, halting their closure, and ripped them asunder, the crunching sound echoing across the chasm; the huge beast fell lifelessly to the floor.

Deron quickly turned.

"What was that?" he uttered with a cracking voice.

"You are getting jumpy now, my friend," Tjol said reassuringly.

"I thought I heard something also," Banon inserted.

Tjol glanced at the others moving on ahead and nervously said, "We should not tarry. Our path lies yonder."

He gestured his companions to move forward along the path.

The remainder of the travel period passed uneventfully. Though they tried to move forward as long as they could between rests, they found their bodies demanded longer and more frequent repose. Their internal clocks were by now far out of synch due to their sojourn in Parallan; the Drelves were being confused by the unfamiliar darkness of the caverns. Deron estimated they had been in the sunless world two Donothorian days. They continued on the left of the swiftly flowing river which was being fed by other streams. They had scarcely moved forward when Nigel and Vannelei scurried back to the body of the group.

"There is the flickering of a light ahead," Nigel confided. "We shall go forward to see what we can learn."

"Yes, I see too," Eomore said.

The two dark forms moved silently forward and the group squelched the light sources. A few moments that seemed an eternity passed and the two returned.

"Big time trouble," Nigel solemnly said. "But not all the news is bad. Ahead there is a wide passage that opens into a cavern. Our path will take us through the cavern, for I saw no other means to rejoin the river. There is a large pyre in the center of the cavern which I think must be fueled by volcanic heat. The cavern extends at least four hundred paces in its widest dimension. In the center there is a great winged beast, though the wings are dwarfed by the overall size of the beast; a stone gray creature scarcely apparent to even my keen eyes, noticed mainly by the gusts of foul smokes escaping from its nostrils as it breathes.

Eomore said, "I thought that you said that the news wasn't all bad. I must say that you have given us a fairly bleak report."

There was clearly a lack of enthusiasm in the prince's voice.

Nigel weakly sneered, "It appears to be asleep and there is a rather large mound of glinting objects near its head."

"Small consolation," Roscoe added, gripping his staff tensely.

"I'm sure it must be a dragon of some sort, though I've never seen one," Vannelei reported.

Nigel gazed directly at Eomore and said in a monotone, "I ain't seen one either, but I've been sniffed by one. You ought to be able to give us some guidance here, Eomore."

"I've never seen Taekora fight and I can only remember the stories of my grandfathers regarding the great beasts. Their numbers are few in the civilized lands. My grandfather told that the prismatic species to which our guardian belongs fought more with cunning than brute strength. I … I fear I know little…"

Roscoe interrupted the prince to say, "Knarra and I have engaged the great worms, in the dungeons and plains of a younger Donothor. They are unique, just as you and I are individuals. It would surely help to know a little of the specific nature of this beast."

"If you are asking for volunteers to go up and find out how it likes its meals prepared, count me out," Nigel insisted.

"That isn't exactly what I had in mind," the mage gruffly answered, annoyed by the cloaked companion's crassness.

Magrian sensed that they were depending on him to shed some light on this dubious subject and the old one spoke after a silence which seemed like an eternity to him.

"I must begin by saying that what I know of dragons comes from the legends of my people. I have no personal knowledge of the beasts. It is said that the Cavedragon is unique and that it is invincible, or nearly so. Death pours from its gullet in the form of its foul breath and the spectre also rides on its vicious talons and maw. It may well be quite resistant to Magick and it may be the creation of the Kiennite Deathqueen – or vice versa. Common sense tells me that it probably will not have keen vision, but I only guess…" His voice slowly trailed.

"Perhaps stealth and not force should be the rule here," Vaylin injected. "If it sleeps we might be able to pass on by unnoticed."

The priestess Knarra then entered the conversation to say, "True, but we must have a plan. Battles with dragons are always followed by heartache, for they are fierce and wanton. We found one's best chances are realized when as many of the beasts senses are taken from it early in the onslaught. Certain Magick may avail some protection to us. But a systematic approach is essential if we are to have any hope of success."

They began a hurried discussion as roles were delegated. As they prepared to cross the cavern of the beast, Knarra quietly conjured and after her incantation, motioned each of them to her. She touched each of them with both of her hands. Deron was the first, and the others watched as his stocky frame bathed by first blue, then white, then red, and finally violet colors. The dwarf sensed cold, then fasciculations, then heat, and finally a feeling of the security that brought to mind the loving embrace of a mother at the side of a warm hearth on a winter's day. Each in turn felt the same – only the mage refused the assistance offered by the woman, opting instead to clutch and "talk" with his staff.

From the rim of the smaller cavern where the group planned, the Adjuster watched the efforts of Knarra with great interest. It sensed that the Cavedragon was about to do most of its work. The black form relaxed, allowing its basic natural appearance to again take shape. The hideous face was dwarfed by the massive hulking frame which towered over the height of a man and a mass of at least three. The Adjuster was going to enjoy a ringside seat.

The Cavedragon could not recall how long it had ruled the caverns beneath Parallan.

Its consciousness encompassed so much time and its talons had been the bane of so many cavern travelers that they were as grains in the sands of time. It shared a position of symbiosis with Anactrophidea – each allowing the others evil to proceed uninhibited. Phanres, as it called itself, was over eighty feet in length, stood almost sixty feet in height when reared upon its hindlegs. On its back were small vestigial wings which served only to aid in warding off blows, for they would never hoist its bulk into the air. Where was there to fly in the caverns anyway? Phanres was not versed in Magick – it held great contempt for those who were. The great beast had long since abandoned the practice of going above ground for prey and treasures – the caverns supplied it with more than enough even for a dragon's standards. Its alliance or at least coexistence with the Kiennite stronghold at Aulgmoor provided the beast with both treasures and the flesh of Aulgmoor's enemies and cast-offs. Few defenders were required to guard Aulgmoor from any foe foolhardy enough to try to gain access to the stronghold through the caverns.

Eomore's group had no knowledge of this cooperative effort.

Phanres was barely discernible from the cave floor in the flickering volcanic light of the great cavern.

Nigel started to enter, but the Drelven prince Vaylin held him back, stating that it was the turn of another to take the lead. The frail form slithered into the cave soundlessly – well, maybe not – and advanced precariously near the sleeping – well, maybe not – hulking form. Vaylin could feel the moist heat from the flaring nostrils of the reptilian titan; he felt his heart pounding. The Drelve froze some twenty paces from the head of the beast and motioned for the group to follow.

Terror gripped him.

The left eye opened.

A deep gravelly voice echoed through the cavern, "You wouldn't be trying to steal old Phanres' treasure, would you?"

Vaylin could not move for an instant, seemingly frozen in a trance by the gaze of the dragon; the others quickly began plan B. Small figures dotted into the cave. Vaylin felt a sense of defeat followed by a surge of anger – the anger of a cornered prey –with a cry he rushed toward the underbelly of the best with his sword extended. The dragon began to move but the Drelve reached the abdomen first and plunged the sword forward with all his strength, penetrating the scales- actually doing little more damage than a bramble bush might do to a man. He did accomplish two ends – first, he brought out the wrath of the beast; Phanres roared loudly; a green nauseating cloud spewed forth from the maw of the beast; the Drelve was lost from sight- second, he bought a valuable few seconds for the others to better position themselves for the fight of their lives.

The dragon smelled, heard, felt, and saw his foes, but before it could strike again, an arrow streaked from the bow of Banon the champion archer and struck the right eye of the beast. At the same time, Roscoe released a bolt of energy from the pinnacle of his staff that struck the left eye; the beast reeled from the force of the spell. Cara raised her hands and purple vapors emanated toward the head of the dragon; the cavern filled with the aroma of a field of violets. Knarra struck the stone floor with her small hand and the sound rocked the cavern. Roscoe's energy bolt gave Eomore, Tjol, Deron, Vannelei, and Nigel the opportunity to charge the monster with swords held high. Phanres was bathed by odors, deafened by sounds, blinded by his eyes' injuries, and felt excruciating pain coursing through its body from the multiple wounds. Infuriated, it belched forth another cloud of vapors, uncannily zeroing in on Roscoe, but the mage uttered a cryptic phrase and a breeze left his staff and sent the fumes back toward their source. This gave the swordsmen a chance to draw blood. Their blows struck the forelegs and the underbelly. Exeter glowed red with the lust for battle, but Eomore found that his swing narrowly missed the underbelly. After swinging, the prince had to rely on his quick feet to avoid becoming part of the next smorgasbord. Deron did not even attempt to land an abdominal blow, lunging instead at the hindpaw and scoring; the dwarf realized that a thousand such blows could not slay the beast; the blow could attract its attention. The dwarf scurried and narrowly avoided being crushed by the extremity that he had just wounded. Nigel hurled his Sweetheart into the underbelly; the blade penetrated the tissue between the scales; the spring action that could rip out the throat of a man-sized opponent only managed to open a six inch wound between the scales. The foul ichor flowed forth; the dragon felt the wound; the blade remained lodged between the scales. By hurling the knife, the thief was not in immediate jeopardy of being crushed; this gave him time to reach his bow. Banon unleashed a second arrow but it scarcely penetrated the scales of the creature's neck. Vannelei scored little more than the dwarf, but Tjol's height served him well and he drove his weapon deeply into the underbelly. The beast lurched backward taking the sword from his hand and the big man fell and rolled to avoid the recoiling tail. Cara spread her hands and white flames came forth tearing into the neck of the beast, opening yet another wound. Roscoe had been busy forestalling the dragon's breath and was unable to mount anything offensive. Knarra searched for Vaylin fearing the worst.

The dragon was sensory deprived, but it could tell where its pain was originating; the great talons racked at the points where Tjol and Deron had struck moments before. With lightning speed, the neck brought the maw forward and by a hairsbreadth missed the thief. Nigel was knocked to the ground; he fell upon his bow and smashed it. Tjol stood and searched for a weapon. Deron, Vannelei, and Eomore were avoiding the talons. The beast's actions gave Roscoe an opening; red flame streaked from the staff and burned deeply into the already wounded neck area, rocking the creature. Phanres wheeled and closed toward the mage, guided only by instinct and pain. Banon and two Drevles launched arrows, but again there was little damage done.

Tjol rushed to recover his longsword that dropped from the underbelly as Phanres charged toward Roscoe. As the dragon rushed by, Eomore slashed Exeter at the tail in frustration and severed the final two feet. Nigel commented under his breath that Eomore was almost always at the tail end of things, but the humor was lost in the furor.

Phanres felt searing pains in its abdomen but more from the eye wounds. The great beast strained to locate its attackers. Though the arrow pierced its left eye, the beast noted vague shapes of several figures. With as much force as it could muster the dragon opened its maw and sent a torrent of sulfurous flame and debris toward the figures. The cave filled with anguished screams as the flames enveloped the target; the screams did not long endure. Phanres squinted to see the several forms as lifeless as the stone collapsed floor of the caverns. Its own pain seemed abated by knowing it had lessened the odds against it and the dragon scarcely felt the blows of Eomore, Deron, and Tjol. With horror, Cara first noted that the beast had managed to pinpoint the location of the archers; the four Drelves lay upon the floor of the cave. Banon had scurried out of harm's way just in time; the bowman quickly fired three arrows into the beast and again struck the afflicted eye; Phanres saw only darkness.

During the last foray Roscoe had managed to scurry upon a ledge to gain a better vantage point for his attack and the mage again leveled his staff toward the dragon. A ray of amber left the staff and opened a wound in the neck of the beast. Cara had been unable to act; the elf was appalled by their losses; Knarra tried to move toward the fallen. The three swordsmen jockeyed for a more favorable position for their next attack. This enabled Phanres to turn and face the source of its most recent wound. The flowing robes of the wizard were unseen due to it weakened vision, and the last attack had for the moment exhausted the ability to breathe, but the formidable weapons of the bite and talons remained; the dragon lunged with lightning speed instinctively toward the ledge where Roscoe was standing. The mage reacted and just avoided being swallowed, but he took a solid blow from the left paw of the beast and was sent sprawling downward to the floor of the cave where he lay motionless; the staff fell several paces away. The dragon roared, reared, and turned its head to try to locate the others. Knarra witnessed the fall of Roscoe; Cara, who was standing near the priestess, noted the kind brow furrowed with anger; the usually peaceful eyes developed an angry red glow; the tresses became fiery red; the woman uttered a harsh incantation. The priestess then pointed her hands toward the ceiling of the cavern and a great bolt of violet flame funneled downward from the dome of the cavern and struck the dragon squarely upon the head. The force of the firestrike drove the head of the beast toward the cavern floor and the waiting blade of Tjol Bergin. The big man mustered all his strength, raised the sword above his head, and brought the longsword down in a great arc upon the neck of the dragon, opening a great wound. The beast lunged weakly and tried to raise itself, but Tjol, strengthened by the knowledge that Roscoe had fallen; quickly struck a second time and the force of the second blow severed the head of the beast. The hulking body thundered to the floor of the cavern.

For a moment the cavern was quiet except heavy breathing.

Tjol stood over the fallen serpent as though he expected it to rise again somehow. Vannelei, Deron, and Eomore stood nearby, also clutching their weapons. Cara, who was nearest Roscoe when he fell, began to move toward him, and Knarra returned to the fallen archers. Magrian and the four other Drelves who had not entered the cave slowly crept inside, while Nigel went about the grisly task of retrieving the throwing knife from the dragon's abdomen. The cave was filled with a myriad of smells and sights, most which were not pleasant in any sense of the word. As Cara approached Roscoe, she could see him beginning to move.

She heard the sound of the beating of the great wings over her head. The Adjuster had chosen this time to move into action. The great dark form flowed into the cave; dropped down; grasped the fallen Roscoe in its forelegs; swept out of the cavern; and followed the course of the river. No one had time to act. Vannelei had not found the broken body of Vaylin, but they could number four of their party lost to the Cavedragon – the four Drelven archers. Vaylin and Roscoe's fates were a matter of conjecture.

Transporting the unconscious Vaylin and the staffless and stunned Roscoe was an easy task for the Adjuster. One filled was grasped by each talon. If more talons were needed, the Adjuster had no problem creating another appendage. The Deathqueen would be pleased with the prizes.

Unlocking the secret to victory was at hand.

CHAPTER 30
War Rages

The battle on the great plain above the caverns waged incessantly, with no regard to the little party of Donothorians. There were many losses on both sides, though the wizardry of the Draith Lord Calaiz had certainly turned the tide in favor of the Draiths. Only the massive absolute numbers of the ranks of the united Droll and Kiennite legions kept them in the foray and kept the Draiths from successfully crossing the natural barrier of the river. The few giants aided as well, hurling stones and great spears across the breadth of the river into the Draith lines on the other side.

But on the ninth period, (the third day) the Dark Legions made a new assault on the river. Calaiz rode high into the air upon his winged steed and blistered the defensive positions on the far side of the river with his Fire Spells. The Kiennites tried to answer him, but he had protected himself and the steed with defensive spells and also had the natural resistance to Magick common to his peoples. The defenders were forced to draw back, suffering heavy losses before they did so. Izitx coordinated a ground assault with the barrage of the Draith Lord; several large wooden bridging sections were brought forward, carried by hundreds of the scouts. These were quickly placed in order across the river and served as a conduit for the Draiths. They were able to pour across the bridge forty across and soon gained a bloody foothold on the far side of the river. There was a constant battle for an entire time period, with the Drolls crashing again and again against the attacking Draiths. Losses were enormous, and eventually the Draiths were shielded from the arrows of the Droll and Kiennite archers by the fallen bodies of the enemies. After hours of battle, it was obvious that the Draiths had won the first phase of the conflict and had established a foothold of the enemies' side of the river. Grudgingly, the Allies withdrew to more defensive positions several thousand paces to the north. There they dug in and prepared for an attack they knew was coming. The Kiennites ordered the large Droll infantry to establish the first tiers while the archers and finally the few remaining spellcasters brought up the rear. The morale was boosted somewhat by the arrival of some reinforcements from the south and northwest, including two phantom warriors each mounted upon a fire stallion. These were directly dispatched by the Deathqueen and quickly assumed the command of the operation. There would be what they hoped would be a successful stand here, but if they failed, the next defense relied on the alliance of the mountain pass which led to Castle Aulgmoor.

In the Draith, camps there were many feelings of accomplishment. Calaiz sat with Izitx and the war council after the battle. The Draith Lord seemed fatigued, for the expenditure of the energies of Magick had taken their toll. Even the prideful Izitx realized that Calaiz had been the reason for their success. Otherwise, they would still be dug in on the near side of the river. Calaiz reclined on bedding of trampled grasses and bunched his robes beneath his head.

He turned to Izitx and said, "This is a good beginning for us, but I rest uneasy, my friend. For I sense there is still great outflow of Magick, and it is not from the foul Aulgmoor. It seems almost beneath us. With our being on the verge of great victory, I want no one or nothing to come as a surprise."

Izitx gnawed on a twig and replied, "My Lord, I know only, again, of the Magick the little you have chosen to tell me, so I do not question your feelings. Still, I see little reason to feel insecure based on what I have witnessed. The Kiennites fall like saplings before you. If they have a strong ally, then why do they retreat and cower as dogs waiting for us?"

"What you say seems reasonable. But we cannot underestimate the Deathqueen's powers. I feel sure that the evil sorceress would save her greatest strengths to provide her own defense. We have many more rivers to cross, so to speak."

"Now you must rest, for we cannot tarry here. We must strike again before they get too dug in," Izitx spoke assuredly.

In the Kiennite camp, the phantom warriors called the Drollen generals and the Kiennite commanders together. Their strategy evolved in neutralizing the new-found Magick powers of the Draiths. Their role was to destroy the magician while the others were to dispatch with the remainder of the Draith force.

The first hissed, "Surely, these vile beings will be crushed when they find their leader fallen. This becomes only a minor setback for us. Entrenched here we will inflict more losses on them and they cannot continue to match our superior numbers. The taking of Ooranth will be all the more easily accomplished. We shall act during the heat of the next battle when they are least expecting a rear attack, or else after the fray when they are feeding. I doubt he will be able to anticipate our invisibility for even a magician must be concentrating to detect an invisible foe."

With that, the leaders assumed their positions, leaving their secret weapons to plan by the campfire.

It was about this time that the Adjuster arrived at Castle Aulgmoor with its prizes.

CHAPTER 31
Another Aftermath

The Donothorians stood in the great cavern of the slain Cavedragon. Eomore, Vannelei, Tjol, Banon, Deron, Cara, Knarra, Nigel, the old Magrian, and three young Drelves were all that remained. A tired and dirty dozen. Alms were given for the four fallen Drelves. No trace could be found of Vaylin. Cara had retrieved the staff of Roscoe as the others had gathered their fallen together at the instruction of Knarra.

"They will not be carrion for the scum of the caves," the priestess solemnly declared.

She called forth flames from the heavens which consumed the bodies.

Tjol Bergin forced back tears to say, "It was the most glorious of deaths – the way Vaylin charged the maw of the dragon and the way the little guys were consumed by the dragon fires. But an expensive victory!"

"I'm worried of the fights to come," Nigel said succinctly as he scanned the cavern. "I don't suppose that any of you might know the nature of the creature that carried off Roscoe or where it may have been headed."

"A Demon… yes, a Demon of sorts," Magrian stuttered as he answered. "Doubtless a minion of the evil queen. Doubtless it carries Roscoe to Aulgmoor. Though we are weakened as we are, I urge that we use whatever we have to heal our wounds and follow to the castle of the queen. She may not expect us, if we rally."

Nigel had moved to the dragon's cache.

The thief spoke, "Big wealth, but not much to help us – a few swords, arrows, and a fairly nice throwing knife. There are many jewels and coins, but I have no desire to burden myself with them."

The others agreed. Knarra led a brief ceremony honoring the gallant fallen ones, and then produced whatever she could to help bind the wounds of the living. Banon retrieved what remained of the Drelvan arrows and one sleek bow from which to launch them.

Nigel watched Cara as the dark elf had been gingerly caressing the long oaken staff which had been dropped by the wizard during the melee with the dragon. She seemed to be studying the intricate carvings on the device but had a puzzled look upon her pretty face. Cara looked on edge holding the staff.

The thief asked, "I don't suppose that you can figure out how that thing works, can you?"

Cara did not answer immediately, so he repeated the question with a bit more intensity.

"I'm sorry. I didn't mean to ignore you. The runes on the staff are mostly far beyond my comprehension. My Magick is not well refined. I've never really studied the art very much. It has been more of a sixth sense to me. I fear that I shall only learn from the staff that which it wants me to learn. Perhaps Knarra should look at it?" Cara ended with her own question.

Knarra was visibly upset. The others had never seen the priestess so shaken. The woman had to force out her answer to the elf's question.

Knarra aid, "I'm sure that Roscoe has cast many protective Magick upon the staff. Yet he also has placed some of his own essence there. He always 'talked' with the device – perhaps the instrument may sense its owner's peril. It may be of more value to us than we realize. But these Magick are foreign even to me. Cara, there is no doubt in my mind that you are the one to wield it."

The elf bowed and replied, "I shall try, my lady."

Eomore placed his big hand on her frail shoulder and said, "That is all we can ask of you and ourselves as well. Already this quest has cost us dearly. Magrian, I know you must grieve for your prince Vaylin; the little Drelve may have saved us all. I share Magrian's sense of urgency. Knarra, your Magick has aided us again in recovering the strength that had left us, and now we must push onward- if only our legs would bear us as fast as the demon's wings."

They gathered their packs and resumed the pace. The weary legs moved rapidly and they hurried along the riverbank in the dark, damp underground caverns of Parallan. They marched for what seemed like endless hours, twice stopped to rest, and took what nourishment they could from the dwindling supplies of their packs.

Knarra was able to purify the waters of the river for their drinking so there was no problem there. Finally, their eyes strained through the darkness and saw a glimmer of light in the distance. As they trekked forward, they saw the light at the end of the caverns; the underground journey was ending. This segment of their journey had been costly; each wondered whether the light of the three suns would favor or hinder them. Magrian had said that the river exited the caverns on the far side of the central plain, where the great battle had been ensuing, and at the base of the mountain range housing the Kiennite stronghold Aulgmoor. Could that have been the destination of the winged creature which had borne away the mage Roscoe? Was a confrontation with the Deathqueen, a being more powerful than even the great dragon, inevitable? Would they even be able to get near the castle before being detected by the minions of the queen and destroyed? Did the Deathqueen even exist? If so, what matter of creature was it? Was the Demon merely a denizen of the caverns that had taken the magician only to quinch its appetite? These were among the many questions filling their cumulative minds as they neared the exit from the caverns.

Magrian had told them that they would have to cross the river to get to Aulgmoor. This became apparent as they neared the opening.

"Down!" was the hushed command from Nigel Louffette, who was in front of the small tattered procession.

Quickly they obeyed and soon the reason for his concern was apparent. On both sides of the riverbank, postioned upon the rocky ledges above it, were a substantial number of the large dogfaced creatures they had come to know as Drolls. The vile, vaguely Goblinesque features of the Kiennite commanders were apparent as well. The creatures had projectile weapons at ready and were obviously watching the cavern's exit.

"Somehow they knew of our coming," Nigel whispered.

"Well, there exists a state of war. They may be posted here at all times as guards," Vannelei added.

"No, the Draiths hate the darkness of the caverns. I shan't imagine that they would ever consider an attack through them. The Drolls are not bright, but the Kiennites are, and centuries of warfare teach us the habits of our enemies. I believe that they are expecting us," Magrian added.

"Then there is some hope that the creature that rook Roscoe did so out of purpose and not hunger," Knarra said with a ring of encouragement in her voice. "If they await us here they must have been warned by the creature as it exited."

"Unless the Kiennite master has a scrying device within the caves," Cara added.

"What is that?" Nigel asked.

"It is like a gem of seeing, or a crystal ball in legends," the elf answered

Her reply did not satisfy the curiosity of the thief.

Knarra was clearly trying to lead an air of optimism and added, "Those devices are quite unusual. I've only encountered one gem of seeing and it was only accurate over a very short distance. I still feel the beast alerted them. The Queen must know of us."

"Then that is baneful," Magrian glumly said.

"It seems our present problem is that we have at least two dozen of these guys waiting to try to do us in," Nigel commented. "Without old Roscoe's tricks we don't have good odds. I'll try to sneak ahead and..."

"You have my bow," Banon interjected readying to fire.

"Wait, I can help you," Cara said, stopping the archer in his tracks.

The elf began a quiet incantation and touched Nigel's shoulder and after a brief period, the thief became insubstantial, vanishing from sight.

"Where were you all my life, kid? We could have made a great team," Nigel chuckled.

Then they heard the quiet shuffle of his footsteps as he moved ahead.

Eomore felt his cheeks flush when Cara touched Nigel; it was a very new feeling for the prince.

Exeter chose this quiet moment to try him, communicating silent as always, "Now you know how I feel."

The thought waves were not well understood by the prince. Eomore had realized that he had been spending very little time "talking" with the companion that had been so loyal to him.

Just as he was beginning to feel really guilty, he heard Vannelei ask Cara, who now sat next to the prince, "Why don't you just make all of us invisible and we can just sneak by them?"

The elf started to answer, but Knarra beat her to it.

"Because they can still smell and hear. Also, it would be very chaotic for us in trying to communicate among ourselves. Mass invisibility is sometimes as much a curse as a help," the priestess counseled.

"Yes and the spell is difficult," Cara blurted.

She blushed and added, "I'm not always successful with the invisibility spell, either; it's difficult to cast the same Magick repetitively. My mother once..."

The elven maiden became quiet..

Vannelei stared quizzically at her as she inched closer to Eomore and placed her head upon his broad shoulder. The prince tugged on his outer raiments and attempted to adjust the chainmail beneath so she would be comfortable.

"I thought you knew little of your mother?" The elven prince asked her.

"I do," was the simple reply.

They were bathed in silence as black as the darkness of the deeper caves while they waited for Nigel to return. It seemed like an age before they heard the soft voice.

"These critters had a rather nasty surprise cooked up for us. There is a narrow stone pathway on both sides of the river where it exits the caverns, scarcely wide enough for two men abreast. They have archers posted at strategic positions above these keen ledges and then several of the big dogfaces, who are heavily armored, await anyone who might get through the arrows. I would estimate that there are about twenty of the enemy on either side and some two hundred paces ahead there is a heavy bridge constructed across the river. It is a fascinating construction. In most times, the span is across the river, but they have the capability of raising the bridge through the sweat of two dragon-sized beasts that are yoked to the bridge. I doubt that the beasts pose any threat themselves unless they stepped on someone. Thus, Deron will have to be helped there. There is no other means available to cross that I can see," the thief said. He smirked as he scored on the dwarf and could sense blush on anger even in the dark.

"If I could see you, your tail would be mine!" Deron growled, but Eomore urged his charges to save their anger for the enemies.

"We certainly don't have any problem finding trouble in this land, do we?" Cara commented.

"Yeah, and we cannot rely on the cover of Darkness. I would surmise that the suns are near their lowest points however; I couldn't see the little bright one. Only the big dark one and the odd gray one are there. As a good time as any to attack," Nigel added.

By now the Donothorians had become aware of the cycles of the "day" in Parallan. There were roughly three equal periods each lasting some eight hours – the first was as a cloudy day in their land; the second a bright cycle; and the third a slightly darker cycle than the first that was still brighter than the twilight they were accustomed to in Donothor. In addition, every six weeks or so, there was a "Dark Period" that lasted one week, in which the only light came from the huge dark sun that sat just on the horizon and the gray wanderer. This was the time of great significance to all the people of this world and apparently each hoped to win their current war before the next "Dark Period." Also, Magrian had guessed that the forthcoming period would be the time of Princess Trya's conjugation – conjugation being the term used by the Draiths for the consummation of a man and a woman in physical relationship.

Eomore disdained the fact that there would be no cover of darkness. How ironic, he thought, that he would feel so. So many times he had cursed the dark, noting the advantages that it had afforded his foes such as the goblins and even lawbreakers like Louffette. Now, here was the prince of Donothor wishing for darkness. Darkness, where there was no place for bravery. But what price bravery demanded, the prince recalled as he thought of his fallen comrades. Exeter used this moment to stop the prince in this line of thought and his mind returned to the problem at hand. He found his arm tightening around the soft shoulders of the elven girl and she seemed to soften more in his grasp.

Tjol Bergin was the next to speak; "Now I am glad we have the bow of Banon. I'm sure he could lay them out."

But Vannelei answered, "True, even though we can cast arrows with fair accuracy, their superior numbers and more importantly superior position would lead to our falling."

"It would sure be nice to have that bearded blowhard here," Nigel said, referring to the lost magician.

Knarra then said, "We must make do with what we have. Cara and I shall have to create as many problems as we can for them to enable our swordsmen to close ranks. We have proven before that we are superior there. If there are magicians present on their side, the battle may well be brief."

Cara nodded and stood.

"I shall cast a shielding spell before us, Knarra, and perhaps a fire spell on either side of the cavern's opening would equalize things a bit. I'll take the left. Nigel is invisible and I can do the same for one more," the elf said.

Her voice was cold, confident, and firm.

After a quick discussion, all decided that the old Drelven Magrian would best be served by the invisibility spell; he was told to stay well behind the party. Cara and Knarra conjured; they were ready. The women took the lead, walking boldly in the front with the shimmering defensive spell advancing before them. They reached the opening of the caverns and abruptly advanced through the cavern mouth and stood beside the river. Both females immediately began to cast their spells. The Kiennites unleashed the first volley of arrows but not before Magick had been cast. Cara pointed to the left; a great red sulfurous cloud appeared and preceded the explosion at the position of the Kiennite archers. Their small bodies were sent flying through the air. Knarra had pointed to the right and had unleashed forces to bring the flames down from the odd heavens of Parallan, but as she concentrated she was struck by a well-aimed arrow in the thigh. The pain of the wound affected the accuracy of the spell and as a result the flames struck only part of the planned area; three of the bowmen survived and readied a second shot.

Nigel cursed, "I thought the shield spell would protect them!"

Eomore answered, "It only serves as an absolute protection against the missiles of Magick. It only reduces the accuracy of a true bow."

The priestess yielded to the pain and dropped to one knee. Cara saw her plight and realized that there was not time for a second spell.

The elf pointed the long staff in the direction of the Kiennites and commanded, "Serve your master through the powers of your fires!"

A great fiery bolt emanated from the tip of the staff and the flames struck the archers. All were slain.

Cara then brought Knarra back into the wider open area inside the cavern and allowed the men to pass. They rushed up the narrow passage with Eomore and Tjol in the lead. Ahead they heard the growls of the advancing Drolls and soon they met still on the narrow ledge. It was two on two so at any given moment the odds were good, but defeating one opponent only meant that he would be replaced with a fresh foe. The initial forays were easy for the men; usually only two or three blows were struck before Exeter or Tjol's blade dealt a killing blow and the river was splashed with a Droll body. Soon the slow advance up the pathway took its toll and each ensuing battle was more intense. Tjol took a right shoulder wound and though he was able to slay the opponent, the big man was obviously near exhaustion. Eomore was still engaged in combat and a large Droll was upon Tjol. The air whizzed with the sound of the throwing knife as Nigel came to the big man's aid; the blade ripped through the Droll's flesh, felling him in his tracks. It availed enough time to Deron to allow the dwarf to rush past his friend and take up the battle. Eomore continued to battle by his side and soon they reached the widened area of the passage where the first archers had been. Vannelei and Nigel joined the melee and soon the enemies were slain. There was no time to rejoice, for the Drolls that had been on the opposite side had crossed the bridge and were advancing toward them. From nowhere, Cara appeared and leveled the staff at the advancing dogfaces. Uttering an arcane phrase she called forth the powers of the staff and again blazing rays of flame shot forthward and enveloped the enemies. Then there was silence as all looked around for new foes. They heard a voice from the rear.

"We cannot tarry now, for our approach is surely known. We must move," Knarra's voice was again firm.

The tall woman knelt by Tjol and applied some of the gummy material she carried in her pack to the nasty wound on the big man's shoulder; the bleeding stopped and the pain eased a bit. Banon relieved the big man of some of his gear.

Eomore studied the skies. The dark giant Orphos hovered just over the horizon like a huge fruit waiting for some giant picker. The star always seemed to be there, only minimally changing its position. It seemed to hold fast the land upon which they had been traveling. The sky was now amber in its hue and the prince could see the small brilliant red sun Meries appearing over the craggy peaks in the distance. By now the Donothorians had learned that the intensity of the "sunlight" here was directly related to the height of the little star. The mysterious gray sun Andreas was there again – the star that Magrian called "the Wanderer" and spoke reverently. Cara felt strangely stronger as she glanced at the Gray Wanderer. Roscoe's staff now felt comfortable in her hand. The runes on the staff, originally fuzzy, were becoming clearer to her eyes. She realized that many new incantations were appearing in her mind!

The effect of the three suns increased the light; in two or three 'hours' the peak intensity would be reached. Looking into the skies in the directions of Parallan's suns did not produce the discomfort or risk injury to one's eyes as did doing so in their own world.

They longed for more rest, but where was there a safe place for respite? At any rate, they could not afford procrastination and had to move onward. Exeter had not detected enemies in the immediate area, but the preceeding fight had resulted in both great visual and auditory effects. It would have been seen and heard for a good distance.

The prince again felt those old nagging feelings that ate at him internally, thoughts like "Am I really good enough to lead?"

Since he had met Cara, he had noted that these were fewer and he supposed that the fatigue factor was playing a major role now. Eomore looked at his party. They were positioned now at the site chosen by the Kiennite archers. Nigel was nervously crouched at the edge of this open area in the rocks. They were about a hundred feet above the river, which was torrential and rough on the rocks below. The angry waters had rapidly swept under the unfortunates that had fallen before the blades of the fighters a short time earlier. The thief was watching the drawbridge which could now be seen clearly crossing the expanse of the river joining the two rocky edges. Immediately ahead of Nigel the pathway narrowed again, but from his vantage point he had a clear view of the area ahead. On their side of the bridge, there was a rough road snaking its way toward the base of the mountains. Magrian had told them that their underground travels had placed them now above the Droll legions.

A warrior at heart, Tjol wondered how the battle progressed. He talked with Banon at length. On the opposite side, the great hairy beasts stood motionless still yoked by heavy chains to the great logs of which the bridge was constructed. There was a large flat area on the opposite side and beyond this they could see a rocky path leading upward to the slopes of the mountains. It did not require intuition to realize that this led to Castle Aulgmoor, the stronghold of the Kiennite Deathqueen. The prince again glanced back at the others. Vannelei and Deron were near Nigel, poised and weapon ready. Both were nervously anticipating their next conflict. The big man Tjol was now sitting, rubbing his wounded shoulder gingerly, but his brawny color had returned and he looked much better. Knarra's work had again aided them. The priestess had insisted that she was feeling well, but Cara's keen brown eyes had detected the limp and the wincing of the deep blue eyes when she walked; the elf passed this along to Eomore. For the first time Cara realized that the tint of Knarra's eyes were ever changing, particularly during casting times. The prince knew that the woman had given more attention to Tjol than herself. Lastly, the three Drelves clutched short bows and watched the caverns opening behind and below them. Faryn had used the poltices given him by Sedoar to help Knarra, applying some unguent to the wounded thigh of the Priestess. The vision of Knarra's exposed thigh was not wasted on Nigel. The thief continued to marvel at the strengths of the two females.

At first, it alarmed Eomore that he could not see the old Drelve Magrian, but he belatedly remembered that the nature of the invisibility Magick was such that the recipient of such a spell was rendered invisible until he used the Magick to his advantage in combat as Nigel had done or until the individual casting the spell willed it stopped. For now the old one was better off heard and not seen. The prince's wandering mind was brought back into order when he heard a hushed warning from Nigel.

The thief was motioning toward the bridge. Eomore strained his weary eyes to see the frail form of a Kiennite moving between the two titanic oxen. There soon followed a grinding sound as the efforts of the beasts began to raise the structure.

Vannelei quickly began to rush up the path and drew forth his elven longbow as he ran. Several yards up the path, the elf stopped, took aim, and fired an arrow from his quiver. But the shot was a long range and the intended target had the advantage of quickness and ample cover so it was a difficult mark for even an elven archer. The first arrow struck the back of one of the great beasts of burden; the animal ignored it. Undaunted, the archer tried again, but again the arrow fell short of its target.

Cara noted the difficulty he was having with the range and she took the small crossbow from her back and placed a bolt within it. Then, she grasped the great staff of Roscoe and uttered a phrase. After a moment of hesitation, the intricate runes on the staff began to glow and the elf was whisked up unto the air and deposited on the far edge of the bridge some fifty paces beyond the location of the Kiennite. It saw her land, drew a shortsword, and charged toward her. But Cara had planned this short journey well; her aim with the crossbow was deadly; she dropped the ugly little creature in its tracks still some twenty paces from her. She then reloaded and turned to face the mountain road above her. She expected the worst from the big animals, but they stood motionless.

They had raised the bridge only three or four feet.

With a shout, Eomore rushed past Nigel and ran up the rocky path as fast as he could. He wished that he could run even faster to reach her. He knew how tired she had been and he had witnessed what a draining of energies that occurred with casting Magick. The others followed; soon the prince had negotiated the hundred paces to the bridge. A quick glance revealed that there was none of the enemy behind or ahead of them. The elven girl was still alone on the other side. Eomore sheathed Exeter, ascended the slightly raised bridge without difficulty, fought back the urge to run to Cara, and helped the others hurry across the bridge. They passed between the great animals. Magrian had assured as they were running that the titanosteers would not harm them.

"I thought you didn't understand the working of the staff, yet it has served you well twice now," Vannelei asked as they reached the girl.

Eomore took her hand; she grasped his forearm tightly. He was amazed by how energetic and refreshed the she appeared.

Cara answered the elven prince, "I don't fully understand. I was not altogether sure what would happen when I commanded it to carry me over. I hoped for positive results. I am refreshed in my powers. I'm not tired,"

Her words reassured Eomore as she touched the prince's shoulders.

The party moved up the rocky road a few paces and stopped for a moment; Nigel and Vannelei moved ahead and scouted. They returned in a little while and told the others the way was clear for at least a little while.

"We'll never be able to get into it," Nigel flatly said.

"What do you mean?" Eomore queried.

"Let's walk up the road a short distance and you will get the idea," the thief replied.

They saw Castle Aulgmoor for the first time when they moved up the pathway. The only access was a narrow rock causeway, scarcely wide enough for a well-armored man. There were drop-offs of at least a thousand paces on either side of the passageway. The castle itself sat upon what seemed to be a flat-topped mountain in the center of a group of higher peaks. It was not a large castle but was clearly more accessible to flight than to foot travel. There appeared only to be the opening the stone causeway ended. With no darkness to hide them, there would certainly be no chance of surprise. Eomore could see why the Queen's enemies had never been successful at storming the castle; a force of a dozen men with bows and oil could keep an entire army at bay. The walls were of a mauve stone and they shimmered in the changing light of the suns. The rays of the "Wanderer" focused upon the spire of the donjon, the highest tower; each observer felt this was only a trick before his eyes; none asked the others to confirm this. There were five towers. Four were symmetric ant the four corners of the fortress and likely battlements; the fifth was against the far side of the castle and rose far above the others.

"You may be right," Eomore said to Nigel.

Then all of them stood in silence.

They could not see the resumption of the battle of the battle of the Plain of the River Ornash from this point, being well beyond and beneath the vantage point of the ridge from which they had watched the carnage before.

CHAPTER 32
War Wages On

The Droll and Kiennite forces had been digging in for the assault that they knew was coming. Position was certainly their ally, and the commanders, the dreaded phantom warriors, had organized the defenses well. The heralding of the new attack came with the spotting of the two black spots against the amber sky. As the spots drew nearer, the outlines of the wyverns became apparent and again the beleaguered Drolls were belted with Magick from the Black Lord Calaiz. Izitx rode along with his liege, mainly to survey the enemy positions so he could organize his ground assault. Vainly, the Kiennite spellcasters tried to attack the great flying creatures and their riders, but their efforts were as futile as those of the archers and spearmen whose shots fell far short of their intended marks. Finally, Yol, as it was called, rose above the Kiennite ranks and hovered above them motionless, drawing spellfire from the Draithlord. Calaiz experienced failure for the first time as Magick rolled off the phantom warrior much as grime off a goblin's back; it aimed a bony spear at the wyvern which bore Calaiz. The throw was uncanny in its accuracy over the great range and it struck the beast in the thorax. The loyal monster tried to continue to fly, but its death caused beast and rider to plummet toward the land. Calaiz landed upon the body of his steed about a hundred paces from the Droll hordes. But Izitx responded; the Draith lieutenant commanded the beast that bore him to dive; Calaiz was saved by the valor of his lieutenant. Yol sensed pleasure in its near success and returned to the cheers of the ground forces that rallied in spite of the fact that there were at least two thousand new dead due to Magick attacks upon the concentrated troops. They bolstered their ranks and awaited the enemy. They wyvern landed; Izitx escorted Calaiz who walked with a pronounced limp, to the rear and poured refreshment for his king.

"Now it is the turn of your people to take the fray upon them, my Lord," he said. "You shall be proud of our efforts. I have battled her phantoms before. Being of Magick, they do not fear spells. Like golems they are extensions of her evil and essence. They feel the blows of hardened fists and cold steel."

Izitx bent over and wiped the profusely perspiring brow of Calaiz and encouraged the leader to rest. He left to ready for an assault.

Calaiz found his weary mind returning to Castle Ooranth and the beauty of the human maiden there. His head ached and his great muscles twitched from his efforts. He was glad that only the noble Izitx had witnessed his physical weakness. Calaiz could battle incessantly in the arena, but Magick took their toll on Him. The gentle touch of the maiden's hand would remedy his aching brow. Surely his great victories would sway her opinion to favor him. He wished that his father and mother could witness the triumphs of their son on the field of battle. While he relished his successes, he found himself exceedingly unnerved by his brush with death. Only the efforts of Izitx had saved him. He had used so much of his energies in casting destructive Magick against the Drolls and Kiennites that he had been unable to muster any defensive spell to thwart his fall. He regretted the loss of the wyvern, for such well-trained beasts were rare indeed. Calaiz was uncomfortable that he could not suppress the feeling knotting up in his stomach. It was in times of fatigue that the Draith Lord's unfamiliar feelings found their mark. He received so much from his mother, but at what cost? No Draith leader had before borne these burdens.

Conscience.

It was not a trait that the Draiths would think highly of – so unkingly, so squeamish – he felt shame; but more than that, he felt fatigue and sleep overcome him.

Izitx was a fair tactician. He knew that the Drolls would be buoyed by the death of the wyvern and the fall of his king from the skies. So, in lieu of immediately attacking, he fed his men again, knowing that the Drolls were locked into their defensive positions and would be unable to relax.

He thought to himself, "I shall let the hunger in their bellies dim the enthusiasm in their hearts."

Calaiz rose to note the Meries disappearing and the sky approaching the darkest tones. He felt refreshed. He felt powerful again. He saw his men in files ready to move forward. The feelings of doubt left the Draith Lord as he surveyed the situation. He could sense the victory, the revenge that had so long been cheated from his people.

Castle Ooranth continued to bustle with activity, even though its lord was away at the wars with the bulk of the formidable armies. There remained the Elders and an elite castle guard as a defense against any improbable attack and there were the thought-to-be impregnable defenses of the castle.

Trya Aivendar remained a prisoner, or an honored guest as Izitx had said, and the hours, though difficult for her to measure, still dragged on quite slowly. She had become very friendly with the elven girl Heather and her treatment had been rather first rate, though her independent spirit still buckled against her confinement. The girls had often wondered if indeed she could exit the castle at will. The matrons had allowed her to tour much of the castle and she had seen the great outer door secured by the great wenches of the inner portcullis. There were always two Draith scouts there in full battle garb, but each time she approached, they would merely bow deeply and silently, then reassume their positions. These were a cold-seeming people. Trya and Heather had also been allowed access to what the Draiths called "The Room of Knowledge" which was an elaborate archive with many volumes. She supposed that the "Teacher" there, one of the group of older Draiths known as the Elders, had only allowed her to read books of his own choosing and careful screening. The written language was extremely complex and of many characters which were beyond her, even though she had had extensive schooling within the confines of her home at Castle Lyndyn. One book though, interestingly, had been translated into the elven tongue; unlike Eomore, Trya had studied and knew well the lyrical language. Trya was told that the translation was made by the Queen Mother, the mother of Calaiz, and had been rewritten by the Black Lord out of honor to his mother. It was difficult for the girl to imagine that a figure as imposing as her betrothed could write with such flair and feeling.

The volume itself dealt with the tragedy of the Draith race. It spoke of the glories of earlier generations and the powers of the

"Purebloods" before the time of the Spawncurse. It spoke of the coming of Anectrophinea and the evolution of the Kiennites from a cowering cave people to the most deadly foes of the Draiths. Then were details of the four great wars and the near total victory of the Red King in the fourth. Only the desperate curse of the Kiennite matron had prevented the conquest. There were chapters of the efforts to overcome the curse; all efforts of the alchemists had failed, as had other measures. Then there were stories of the finding of the "gates" connecting with other lands and the abductions that followed. Trya had first thought that this was likely propaganda, but her observations in the birthing chambers confirmed every female child of the union of the Draith males and the surrogates failed to survive the immediate neonatal period, even though the infants were normal in appearance. Trya could almost feel sympathy for the Elders as they watched this, but the only tears that fell for the babes came from her eyes- those of Calaiz had dried and were not detectable on the pages of the manuscript. These were an unfeeling people, but, she wondered, how much of this was due to this tragedy. The Elder professed that the Draiths were as they always had been. The 'days' dragged onward at Castle Ooranth – at least the time did. Trya too was losing her prior concepts of time as she remained here longer.

CHAPTER 33
Aulgmoor

They studied the task before them and Eomore felt that Nigel's initial assessment was likely true. Castle Aulgmoor was an imposing edifice. It sat perched upon the great conical peak surrounded by the circular gorge and only the splinter of the rocky path approached it, with at least a thousand foot drop on both sides. The narrow stoneway had an upslope of ten degrees. They were positioned at the point where the mountain trail ended and the thin conduit of a thousand paces began. The gorge surrounding the castle was in turn surrounded by the tallest peaks of the Doombringers. The edifice was hewn from the rock of the mountains. The glacis was a thousand feet of upsloping rubble. Clearly this was a fortress constructed through forces other than the sweat of many men.

Nigel had crept up the path a bit where his acute eyes had detected a device at the head of the trail leading up to the castle doors. It appeared to be a large ballista which aimed down the pathway. This was manned by three creatures that appeared to be Kiennites. The thief returned to the bulk of the little group to relay this information.

There was a good bit of hard breathing but they had pushed forward constantly watching their rears as they moved up the mountain passageway.

Nigel did not mind watching Knarra's rear; watching Deron's rear was another story!

No foes had come up behind them, as the Kiennite forces seemed occupied by the battles of the plain below. There was cover enough for them as they surveyed the edifice before them.

Nigel spoke. "I'm sure that I can take care of the ballista crew, but there may be more immediately behind the castle doors. I would imagine that there would be additional defenses here. Why have we seen so few defenders?"

Magrian entered the conversation, "True, but there has never been a successful assault this far forward. It would help to know how the battle below progressed. It may be that she is reduced to a minimal guard. If legends speak truly, Anectrophinea would not need much protection beyond her own terrible powers. The Cave Dragon certainly reduced attack from the caverns, and an army attacking frontally would be subject to easy destruction."

"I don't know if invisibility would be enough to get you close enough to attack, Nigel, for you might be betrayed by a falling pebble or a sound. I think it is safe to assume that they would reserve their best to make a last stand should that become necessary and these will likely be much more formidable than the Drolls who fall so quickly before our swords," Eomore said.

He continued, "Yet, if we attempt to approach directly, we are easy marks for missile fire from the device situated there. I, too, share Nigel's concern that reinforcements may be readily available. If we could... Cara, are you able to do a transformation spell?"

Cara shook her head saying,"No, I cannot."

Knarra added, "Only the most powerful of wizards are capable, and then there is considerable risk. We face a difficult task. A spell attack might be unsuccessful due to the distance, and it would certainly alert them to our presence, if they haven't already seen us. I feel..."

"I doubt they have, for none of them seems to have moved," Nigel added.

Cara then added, "And there are likely protective Magick here, though I detect very little without casting my own spells."

Knarra quickly added,"And I would not do that. Something is not right. I feel that Roscoe breathes within the citadel; why can't I ..."

Eomore recalled visits to Roscoe's castle and the complexities there and agreed.

Nigel then spoke up to say, "I could try to make my way up the pathway and skewer the guards, but I bet there is another way into this dump. They have to eat and they have to drink."

The thief tugged at the short hairs of his beard as he spoke.

"That is likely, but I do not see where it could be," Vannelei added.

"I think it might be there," Nigel answered. The thief pointed to the base of the conical peak far below them upon which the castle rested. A tiny rivulet coursed across the terrain at the base of the central cone. The water clearly exited from the base of the central conical peak.

Nigel continued, "But getting down there would be tricky. We would have some cover, though if we descended by the rocks to the left. The guards might not see us."

Deron, who shared the dislike of climbing with many of his people, then commented, "Yeah, they could wait to hear the screams as we fell. You aren't really suggesting that we go down into the gorge on some wild goose chase looking for a secret door that might not even exist. I would rather charge the ballista and trust my chances to the dwarf that constructed my mail."

"It would be a difficult descent," Eomore surmised. "But it might be worthwhile to try. Time is not our ally. We do not know what condition Roscoe is in."

Nigel then said, "If we had some way to get me down there ahead of the rest of you I could be looking around."

"But if there is no secret entrance, then we'll just have to climb back out and fight even more tired than we are now. I'd like to just go on up and kick as much tail as we can," Tjol injected.

"I appreciate the spirit that you show, my warriors, but strength is not our forte. We must gain whatever advantage we can. I agree with Nigel in that it would be worth our while to investigate other ways into the stronghold," Eomore said authoritatively.

(Exeter encouraged the prince after this by saying to him, "That is the way of the Aivendar.")

Eomore blushed; though the others noticed; they did not understand why; nor did they ask.

Cara said, "Combination of Magick is something that I've little experience with, but perhaps I can place a lightfall spell and invisibility upon you to enable you to reach the bottom. Maybe our foes won't be attuned to the casting of protective Magick."

Knarra reluctantly agreed.

The dark elf began to conjure and threw a small amount of sand over the thief; he again faded from sight.

Then she said a few more words and touched his shoulder. "Try a short jump first, Nigel, for it's not a spell that I've often used."

Cara was unnerved by a deep feeling of being scrutinized from without the group. Was her mind being probed? Was it just her uncertainty? She noted a slight headache after casting and relayed this to Knarra.

The others were busy checking their ropes and preparing for their own descent.

They heard Nigel's voice utter, "Give the sound of the Bob-black when you reach the bottom and I'll come to you if I'm able."

With that he uttered a "here goes," and there was a faint whistling sound and he was now gone from sound as well as sight. The call of the Bob-black was well known to all except the Drelves, and Vannelei quickly explained the nature of the little night bird to them.

The path of descent was not the most direct, but there was much foliage and a good bit of the grade was not severe. In contrast, the central conical peak upon which Aulgmoor reposed was bare of plant growth and was steep. Despite the grumblings of the dwarf, they were soon making their way down. Eomore insisted upon the lead, and he left Tjol in the rear to utilize the strength of the big man in stabilizing the ropes should they become necessary. Banon stayed at the rear as well, but with bow drawn and arrow at ready. The enemies on the footbridge were not moving. In fact they had stirred little since the group had first witnessed them. Vannelei and Cara watched the pathway. Magrian explained that the nature of the Draiths was such that they would consider anything but a frontal attack dishonorable and the Kiennites, knowing their enemies, would not likely show the same vigilance that they did at the exit from the caverns. That seemed more an ambush.

They began to move downward initially without incident. Then Banon slipped and a large stone broke loose and fell down the mountainside a few feet. All eyes went to the footbridge. Again there was no movement by the guards. Banon righted himself and blushed at his mishap.

The descent would be slow and laborious but at least they were not under attack and there seemed to be decent footing.

Nigel marveled at the ease of his own descent. How much easier things would have been for him in the past if such tricks had been available to him? But the situation at hand was a grim one. The thief now stood at the base of the central pinnacle that the castle stood upon. Circumferentially, the peaks encompassed him and above the narrow stone bridge appeared as a thread. He knew that it would take the better part of what used to be a half-day for the rest of his party to descend the cliff walls to get down to him; the base of the peak was huge; he hoped another entrance existed; he had much ground to search. He wondered at the location of the Kiennite stronghold and now how such a mountain formation could be created. Nature alone probably could not have formed it, though he had heard of burned out firepeaks, that some called volcanoes that had central depressions that were filled usually with water. This was like a great mountain that had its center cut out and replaced with a central peak. Nigel wondered again if Magick could be powerful enough to accomplish such a task. He had always been skeptical of Magick but his recent experiences had changed much of how he had previously felt about so many things. On with the task!

There was notably a lack of living things, both plant and animal, in the area at the base of the central pinnacle. The foliage extended to near the lowest portion of the wall, but it was as though and probably was intentional that the expanse at the base of the inner ring was barren. The soil was rocky and barren, which made him remember of the Iron Mountains of his land. He shuddered at the thought of that barren place, hoping that the inhabitants here were not as fond of human flesh as the dreaded Red Giants that inhabited the Iron Mountains. The thief studied the sides of the craggy peak. At the crest, he could barely see the towers of the castle bathed by wispy clouds and he wondered again if the mage were even within the walls at all and even if he were, the changes of his being in one piece seemed slim. His keen eyes then detected something – a rivulet of water moving slowly down the side of the mountain. The small stream trailed off and after reaching the base of the cliff, headed toward the opposite rocky wall where it disappeared. Worth investigating, he thought, and he moved away from the central peak following the stream some thousand paces to the point that it entered the cliff surrounding the central peak. There the water flowed into a small crevice and Nigel bent down and strained his eyes to peer into what should have been darkness but instead his eyes were met by a light as bright as a good torch, and he could see the water dropping down as a small fall and continuing across a small passage, which was some fifteen paces across and the height of two men. The passage extended in both the direction into the surrounding peaks and also curved backward unquestionably toward the central peak. The thief listened intently for a while but heard nothing but the gentle flow of the stream. He worked at the crevice with his dagger but the stone was hard. The stream had likely worked for countless generations to open its passage, but there was no means possible for his to squeeze through the small opening; not even one of the frail Drelves would be able to do that.

Nigel righted himself. It seemed that the central pinnacle would be the only access to the stronghold. Difficult but not impossible to ascend. For the first time he noted that the invisibility extended even to his shadow, for it was absent, even though the outer light was now substantial. There had to be a way – he decided to try the other approach and retraced his steps across the floor of the valley and began to climb upward toward the point the water exited from the side of the central pinnacle. This was not an easy task; he had to employ all of his tools and dexterity to climb up the side of the peak. After what must have been an hour's effort, he was successful and his efforts were rewarded; he noted that the water came through a small opening in the craggy peak. Nigel probed the opening with Sweetheart. There was no resistance to the blade. Illusion! Illusion tried to conceal an opening that could easily be entered by an armored man. A rounded opening carved to facilitate the egress of the waters and made to appear as solid stone. The illusion was betrayed only by the probing blade. Unfortunately, he had to become thoroughly wet in entering, but the rate of flow was slow and he had no trouble crawling into the opening. The floor was stone and underneath the water there was a growth of slime, but it seemed to be harmless, unlike some of the swamp slimes in Donothor. He continued to travel upstream, uttering unpleasantries at the dampness that enveloped him.

The passage seemed to zigzag endlessly but it was only 20 armlengths or so. The distance was exaggerated by the wetness. Nigel noted a steady upward grade. The wetness seemed to penetrate him more deeply as he inched along the cavernous passageway in the side of the central mountain. The water steadily poured from above but remained only a hand or so deep. The cavern dimensions remained rather constant, being about waist high and roughly the same width. Abruptly, the passage turned and in the darkness his keen eyes strained to detect that it became essentially vertical. Nigel found that he now had to strain even further as he began the ascent; the slime hindered him greatly. His persistence was rewarded, though, for the passage began to assume a more generous grade after twenty feet. His eyes noted a little flickering of light in the distance. The soft gurgling of the little stream obscured from his ears any noise that might be there to aid him; increasing his guard, he moved forward. Nigel estimated that he had been involved in the excursion about three hours, though time was difficult to guess, as always in this land. He wondered how his party was doing in their descent of the rocky wall outside. He hoped that he might be able to learn something from all of this crawling and wetness that might be of benefit to them. Certainly, most of them would be unable to follow his route up the passage. As he neared the light, he could now determine that there were voices there, indeed – multiple voices were apparent. The thief muttered as he wondered what surprised this cursed land held for him now. Remembering that he was still invisible, he approached the light source.

He found there a cavern some fifty paces wide. The near half was dominated by a pool of effervescing fluid that fed the small stream and in turn seemed to be fed by waters effervescing upward from beneath the mountain's core. The far end was bustling with activity. A passage some ten paces wide exited from both ends of the far side of the cavern, with one to his right seeming to go downward and the one to his left seeming to begin an upward grade, then ending at a door. The pool must serve as the source of water for the castle and its inhabitants, the thief surmised, as he watched as several small brutes looking very much like goblins were being ordered around by what looked like an ogre. Nigel had not seen an ogre for years; their fondness of human flesh made them less than exemplary citizens; they were not tolerated in Donothor or other civilized lands. It was rumored that there were large populations of them in the mountain ranges south of the Irom Mountains in the east and in the great swamp, the Lachinor. Nigel had not seen or heard of any of the inhabitants of Parallan speak of the large, hairy, humanoid creatures. Of course they had not heard of two-headed aberrations like the one that contested at the Keep of the Northern Gap until they had confronted the beast. This beast was not as imposing; yet it stood over eight feet tall, held a large club, and menacingly snarled at the goblinks – Nigel liked his new word – "Goblinks" seemed like the perfect name for the disgusting little creatures that groveled before the ogre.

Each of them carried two pails suspended from a thick stick; the pails were filled by others of their kind; they scurried off in both directions as he watched. There was almost constant activity, but the thief surmised that the passage to the north would be the ultimate goal of the party, and his own endeavor at present, to find them access, would best be successfully accomplished by seeking the passage to the right, which he seemed to instinctively label as south, though he really didn't know why. Clearly north and south were terms that had no real meaning in the land of Parallan.

He meant to ask Magrian if the 'compass' had worked!

When the activity waned, he cautiously crept through the opening into the cavern and righted himself, noting the relief expressed by his tightened muscles. The bucket fillers had seized the opportunity to flop down on the stone floor for a respite; the ogre maintained the scowl upon his fearsome face.

Suddenly the giant lurched forward and extended his thick neck and began to sniff and snort loudly, rapidly turning around the position he maintained near the edge of the pool. Nigel sensed his detection was imminent and began to move along the edge of the cavern. The ogre continued to strain its red eyes, even taking a torch from the wall and pointing it along the cavern, looking for the foe, or meal, that is could smell but not see. Nigel used every moment of the beast's indecision to make his way along the cavern and was near the passage opening, when he heard the shuffling of little furry feet as a party of goblinks entered the cavern from the outer passage. The thief realized that his greatest ally was the low intelligence of the ogre; it turned its short attention span to the task of getting the bucket fillers back to work. This gave Nigel the chance he needed; he bolted from the cavern. The angle of descent was steep and the passage wound several times. He stopped after several hundred paces to catch his breath. He realized that even he was not as young as he once was, but this was not the time to mourn over that. Suddenly he was aware of a sharp pain in his left leg and he glanced down to see a goblink gnawing on his invisible leg. A quick glance revealed that there were no others present and an even quicker thrust of his sweetheart interrupted the intended meal of the foul little creature. Fortunately there was a narrow ledge and Nigel lifted the frail form without much effort to the ledge to hide it from other passersby. Clearly he would have to be more careful for one could not relax for even a moment in this place. He did however disgusting it was to him, apply some of the creature's blood to his garments and rubbed his face with the brown tattered tunic that the beastie had worn, hopefully disguising his own odor. To his dismay, he was now visible, made so by his attack on the creature.

Soon he was moving again. He moved past two apparent outposts that were manned by a skeleton crew. The animated skeletons were armed with short swords, and there was one Kiennite at each location along with an ever-changing number of the goblinks.

Nigel then passed an area he recognized, relied on his ability to slink along the shadows. It was the rivulet of water entering from above where he had first peered into the passage. He knew now that the last segment of the passage he had just traversed was running between the central mountain and the peaks at the rim and directly above him was the base of the mountains surrounding the central pinnacle. Still, he had discovered no easy, or for that matter, even a difficult, access for the others. He began to wonder about another course of action but elected to move onward a short distance before turning back to again try to evade the ogre. Maybe the waterway would be their only chance afterall. Suddenly, he heard the clanking of armor coming from the "south" and he scurried up the wall of the passage, clinging precariously as two heavily armored and decorated Drolls accompanied by several guards and two elaborately robed Kiennites passed below him. They were moving at a fast pace themselves. He was not detected and dropped down to the floor after they had passed. His faith that there had to be another exit from these passages was renewed.

Another two hundred paces along the passage, he could see that the main passage curved back toward the general direction of the underground caverns from which the party had just exited, but there was a more narrow passage to his right leaving at about a thirty degree angle. Feeling a sense of urgency, Nigel turned to move up this side passage. Soon he had ascended to a small cave which was obviously on the side of the rim peaks. He noted that there were two Kiennites in the cave, each looking through the wall opposite the thief. Serendipity was an ally Nigel always welcomed and their attention was their downfall as they intently were observing some activity through peepholes in the wall of the cave. Swiftly the thief was upon them, throwing Sweetheart into the back of the left one and sliding the garroting rope around the neck of the second. Soon both had fallen silently before him. Nigel surmised that his must have been fairly important duty for he had seen so few of the Kiennites here and two were placed here. Curiously, he bent forward to look through the openings which were much like the murder holes that were used by the archers in the defense of castles. He then found that, as he suspected, that these were guards to spy on the floor of the canyon. He shuddered to think that he would in all likelihood be an ogre meal were it not for Cara's trickery. This cave was certainly not natural. Looking through the opening he could see that it availed a very good perspective upon this side of the canyon surrounding the central peak. The spies would easily have been able to see the party when they reached the floor. In fact, as Nigel scanned the rocks to his left, he thought he could detect some movement in the area where he had anticipated that they would arrive if they had continued along the most expedient route downward. He estimated again that it had been about six hours altogether since he had left them, so they should be near the floor of the canyon. An old pick was resting against the near wall of the little cave and it gave him an idea. He moved over to the passage and listened for a moment, and, hearing nothing, he moved over to the opening. He struck the stone with the pick and was relieved to note that a sizable chunk of stone broke away from the wall and secondly the pick sustained the force of the blow without shattering. He struck again and again, slowly enlarging the opening. Every ten or so strokes, so stopped his efforts, muttered about being reduced to manual labor and listened for intruders. About the fifth time, he did hear shuffling sounds and prepared himself for the worst, but instead, only two of the goblinks came through the passageway carrying what would have been a repast for the two slain guards. There really wasn't much of a contest, as Nigel quickly disposed of them. He stopped long enough to drink the water but he did not trust the appearance of the meat that the creatures had brought. He returned to his mining and briefly may have appreciated the efforts that had been required of the dwarven miners in his own lands, but he could not help but wonder why anyone would do it unless they were in a situation as he was and had no choice. His work was being rewarded; he had opened enough of the hole that he could press his thin frame through and look better at the mountainside. The results could not have been better. There was a gentle slop to the cliff that even the old Drelve would be able to manage; the climb would take literally only minutes. He moved onto the outer side of the cavern and welcomed the light of the three suns; he would welcome anything that would dry his clothing; he was thoroughly drenched with water, sweat, and even blood – both his and his enemies.

Nigel struck with new fervor as he enlarged the opening. He then reentered the cave, and noted that the front of the castle would have some view in this area; he pushed the fallen foes into a seated position; he then placed a loose stone after him to simulate the wall of the cave was intact. It was a chancy ruse, but he thought it might fool a quick glancer into thinking that the guards were at their post. He hoped that he could bring his party to the cave before his handiwork was discovered.

Nigel hurried across the floor of the canyon. As he neared the wall diagonally across from the cave, he found that his acute distal vision had been correct and indeed the movement he had detected had been his comrades, who were reaching the floor of the canyon just as he arrived at their intended point of descent. They were all safe – weary, tattered a bit more by the ten hour descent that Nigel had made in seconds thanks to Magick. Nigel quickly told them of the opening above and they mustered enough energy to rush across the thousand paces of the circular canyon and follow his lead up glacis to the small opening. Eomore was forced to remove some of his bulkier armor as was Tjol, and they passed it through the opening to the others, who went before them. Soon all were in the cave in the side of the central mountain. The torches still burned and the contents seemed unchanged. Nigel felt that they were lucky and it seemed that the guards' deaths had not been discovered. They pushed the carrion through the enlarged opening and took a much-needed rest, taking more of their precious rations. The guards posted easily detected the approach of the relief of the dead guards and disposed of them easily.

The real fight was nigh, but why were there no more defenders? How could they be undetected? Were they undetected? Why they were not attacked when they traversed the expanse of the floor of the circular canyon surrounding the central cone upon which rested Castle Aulgmoor?

Exeter was having difficulty identifying enemies.

Exeter fumed, "Who is an enemy in this place? Are we not attempting to destroy the greatest adversary of our intended foe?"

Cara and Knarra were reluctant to expend Magick. Knarra kept sensing a general familiar evil about the place and they still had no clue as to Roscoe's fate.

Eomore drew the small wand from the pack on his back.

"I could swear that I detected a buzzing sound from this device." The prince added.

The wand was noted to have a faint glow of greenish hue and there was indeed a low pitched hum from the device.

"I do not know how to approach this," Knarra added.

Cara interjected, "I felt a foreboding sense when I used the wand in battle."

Nigel said, "I would be glad to try the wand."

A chorus of "No's" answered the thief.

It was decided to wrap the device in a thick hide and return it to the pack of one of the fighters, Deron being the choice. The low-pitched hum disappeared when the wand came into the possession of the dwarf.

CHAPTER 34

Aulgmoor: More Trials

Vannelei assumed the guard and Eomore called everyone together in the flickering torchlight of the small cave.

"Nigel's efforts and his reports, though not encouraging, are nonetheless invaluable to us and I personally appreciate the great risk that he has taken. We seem to have some good fortune in that the numbers of defenders have been reduced by the war," Eomore began.

Magrian said, "That would seem to be the case. I would imagine that the important appearing individuals that Nigel saw were major leaders who were brought here for strategy and to report on the conflict. Scrying devices can only do so much. Even the Deathqueen must benefit from eyewitness accounts. The wyvern-borne wizard who fought for the Draiths has likely created many problems for them. We are unfortunately now in a place unknown to us except for those areas bravely scouted by Nigel, but I think it is a safe assumption that they have some idea of our location. We must proceed if we are to have any chance of finding Roscoe and the Draithsbane which we shall need if we do survive to approach the Draith stronghold."

Knarra said flatly,"I feel like a pawn in a boardgame. I feel our every movement is known. Maybe we are serving a purpose not known to us. There is only a token defense. How could we have not been seen coming across the floor of the circular gorge? And struggling up the side of the pinnacle? I realize that we were not in sight of the guards on the entrance bridge and Nigel slew those peering through the murder holes here."

Banon had been silent for a long while, perhaps reflecting on his close call with the cavedragon.

He muttered, "We always talk of a final conflict with the Draiths. Are we assuming that they will be the victors in this fray? I am only a man of arms and I'll serve my prince to my best in any battle, but perhaps these vermin will do most of our work for us."

Magrian turned to the burly man and answered, "To your query, I reply based on my knowledge of the history of our lands. In the earlier wars, twice the Droll hordes reached the plain of Ooranth, the expanse before the great stronghold of the Draith lords. Both times they were turned back. Many are the defenses there, mostly natural, but the cunning of the Draiths is surpassed only by their steadfast loyalty to their belief that they are superior. The Draiths must feel confident of victory. They are driven by the hatred spawned by genocide. Yes, my burly friend, I do speculate, but I know that we will have our final battle at Castle Ooranth if we are to retrieve the princess; the great sword will be of help to us even if we are to battle Drolls and Kiennites. But Ooranth is not our obstacle now. The pool Ogre will be perhaps the least of our problems."

Deron asked, "What about this passage? Do we not risk a surprise attack if large numbers of them return?"

Magrian's eyes glistened, "Yes."

Eomore said, "Now we must try to move forward. Perhaps fate will lend us another hand. We really must find out if Roscoe is here and then where he is."

Knarra spoke matter-of-factly, "He is here."

Just as the others were trying to understand her statement, Vannelei scurried up saying, "Company coming!"

Nigel said, "Nice to have you here."

Eomore and Tjol positioned themselves by either side of the opening to the chamber, and Nigel and Vannelei knelt before the peephole which they had quickly recreated with stone and assumed the position of the Kiennite guards. Soon three of the goblinks entered, but a single swing of each man's sword ended the life of one, and the third was knocked to the floor by the dwarf. Just as Deron was preparing to bring about its demise with his hammer, Vannelei grasped him arm.

"Wait! I have an idea," the elven prince said in an urgent tone. "Magrian, can you communicate with this?"

The old Drelve looked at the quivering hapless creature and said, "I'll try. This is a slave. The Kiennites enslave any weaker than them, and from its appearance, I would guess it is an underground dweller. Likely it serves out of fear and not loyalty."

Magrian then tried several garbled phrases more like animal gutteral sounds, but the creature did not respond, only continued to shake in the steady grasp of the dwarf.

Deron said, "It looks like an undernourished goblin. I can see why Nigel chose the name that he did for our weasel here. Too bad it can't speak goblin."

Vannelei added, "Maybe it can."

The elf then spoke in a soft tone; the tongue was all too familiar to the Donothorian rangers who had fought the goblins in the forests near the Lachinor. To everyone's surprise, the creature answered in the same cryptic tongue.

Vannelei then spent several minutes interrogating the prisoner, assisted at items by Cara who seemed to have good knowledge of goblinese as well.

Eomore turned to Magrian, "Your comprehension of our tongue was almost instant. Why is it difficult to communicate with this dismal creature?"

"Language comprehension is one of our abilities as it is of all the higher races of Parallan, but I really can't fully explain to you how we do it. I cannot read your thoughts but my mind tells me what you say. Your old dialect is taught to our saplings. The ability dates to the forefathers, the forgers of the Draithsbane –the lost Drelven Wizards- it is said that they imparted the ability to the weapon itself. Indeed, it is their essence. But I can't tell you how Cara can create the Magick that she does either. My friend, there is much, I fear, that we don't and will never know. Perhaps the thought processes of the creature are so primitive that I cannot establish a mindwave with it. The answer I give is inferior and I must apologize for it," the Old One said.

Deron quipped, "Its mind is probably a microwave, anyway."

Vannelei stood, "Roscoe is here. The demon brought him directly here. He lies in the dungeons, which are ironically above us. This one carries water to the prisoners there and he remembers one of Roscoe's descriptions spitting the water back at him."

"That has got to be him," Nigel said. The thief was somewhat sarcastic but also somewhat relieved.

Eomore stood and stretched his aching muscles. The weight of the chainmail seemed to grow with each passing moment and the prince was showing the strain of leadership.

He spoke, "We must proceed. There is nothing to be gained by waiting, even though our fatigue would try to convince us otherwise. It seems that this little one is our best bet for finding Roscoe."

The others stood and prepared to leave the uneasy sanctuary of the lookout cave. Looking back into the room all could see the unnaturalness of the chamber which had obviously been hewn in some way from the rock of the mountain. The chamber was probably created by enlarging the natural outlet of the small stream.

Eomore was particularly concerned by the fatigue evident on the faces of Knarra and Cara. For the first time, there seemed a limit to the youthfulness in the girl and the enduring youthfulness of the noble priestess was challenged. The long descent had been mentally and physically draining. The prince was sure that much of what disturbed Knarra was the missing mage. The prince realized how important the wizard was to realizing their ultimate goal of finding the women, Trya and Heather. But the eyes of the priestess spoke of a greater feeling.

Knarra longed for more than the wizard's powers.

CHAPTER 35

Inner Mazes

Quickly they assumed an order and moved forward. As usual, Nigel was in the lead with Eomore behind him. Knarra and Cara followed; Cara was still clinging to the staff. Magrian with Vannelei at his side and the three Drelves, with young Faryn in the middle position, followed closely and Tjol and Deron were in the rear. Banon kept his bow at ready and walked just in front of Tjol. The goblink was kept between the fighters.

Nigel rapidly led them to the junction with the main passageway; he listened intently; he motioned the others into the hallway. The thief clutched Sweetheart as he squinted to see into the dim light of the passageway; the light was produced by the flickering torches along the passage walls. Eomore clutched the hilt of Exeter and at this time the weapon was the only lady in his thoughts as he tried to remain in constant communication with the sword's enemy seeking ability. Again, inexplicably the effectiveness of the artifact had been reduced since they had entered the nightless land they called Parallan. Eomore surmised that part of the problem might be that there was so much ill will in the place. Perhaps there was the matter that the weapon was so far removed from the forgotten forges that had created it; though the prince had heard that similar things occurred when enchanted items were near their place of origin in conversations with Roscoe. The Nature of Magick was evasive.

Tjol led the goblink which had become their unwilling accomplice. The big man passed the little creature up to Eomore and Nigel and the elven prince; Vannelei reminded the wretched urchin that it would be to his advantage to cooperate with them. Although terrified, the creature seemed to understand and pointed its crooked forefinger in the direction of the pool minded by the ogre.

Cautiously, Nigel entered the passage and inched forward along the wall. Vannelei communicated to the leaders that there would be rather frequent, small parties moving through the passage, but that their informant had said that there were not likely to be any groups of sizable strength. Nigel had said that he would take the information with a crumb of gingersalt.

The major passageway was some ten to fifteen feet wide throughout most of its length. The group clinged to the sidewall but moved as briskly as they could. The slight grade to the passage was detectable by even those normally not attuned to such things. Deron judged it was some five degrees for the most part. Steadily upward. To what?

Through the knowledge that Nigel had gained during his earlier sojourn and the assistance of the spineless goblink, the party soon reached the proximity of the great humanoid. There were many legends about ogres in combat known to the Donothorian fighting men, but this group did not number one among them that had ever actually engaged one of the beasts. Eomore had never seen an ogre, though Boomer had told stories of glimpses of the fierce humanoids during his youth in the eastern mountain ranges of Donothor. Since most of the stories had been told over a tankard of ale, the prince had always accepted them with some reservation. The great humanoids once were numerous there but the dwarven King Travan had defeated them in the War of Banishments centuries before any of the current group was born – except for perhaps Knarra; and maybe Roscoe; and maybe Magrian, and maybe... They had no first hand knowledge, but they approached the encounter with some apprehension. Soon they heard the gentle trickle of the stream as it exited from the pool. There was intensification of the light at the end of the passage as they neared the pool.

Nigel inched ahead cautiously and soon returned telling the others that a large number of the goblinks had just left the pool area, carrying pails of water; the ogre was alone. Eomore clutched Exeter wondering if this could be like a knock from the sprite Opportunity – the children's story held that this playful tree sprite knocked only once – giving only one chance for action.

The prince was comforted when his mind sensed the thoughts of Exeter, which said, "Surely those that slew the mighty dragon could easily take the measure of a mere ogre."

The prince returned the thoughts, "I fear more the reprisals after the encounter, for we may certainly be discovered and brought up against more deadly foes. But a heavy blow from his great axe very well could spell one's fall."

He then spoke aloud, saying, "We should move now against him, but caution and cunning will have to counteract his advantage in size."

Knarra spoke, "I fear there may be a scrying device of sorts present; we should probably not use spellcasting. I sense great evil and power here. We should not reveal all our strengths. This is a vulnerable area, but they may be relying on its concealment from the outside to protect them. The war on the plains below us certainly seems to be playing in our advantage, for there seems a paucity of guards in this central stronghold."

Exeter thought –linked to Eomore,"I do not sense the ogre as an enemy'

Eomore answered, "Perhaps it is too ignorant."

"I agree," Magrian interjected. "The fact that we have seen such few numbers here suggests that they are so concentrating on the events on the Plain of Ornash that they are not watching their own backyard. We may have a better chance of succeeding than an army of Draiths in rescuing Roscoe."

Nigel again briefly detailed the dimensions of the chamber. There was a rather steep ascent just before the entrance to the pool cave which would serve to their advantage in approaching the cavern. For reference in the area, Nigel referred to this as South. Magrian the Old One was etching on the small slate he carried in his pack, though the term south confused him. The compass didn't work that well! The entrance was in the southwestern corner of the cavern with the pool filling most of the northwestern quadrant and the stream exited to the west near the midpoint of the western wall. From the entrance, the cave extended a hundred feet to the east and then was fifty feet deep. The ogre was seated in a large chair by the edge of the pool with the great axe adjacent to him leaned against the wall. In the northeastern corner of the room, there was a large wooden door through which the goblinks had carried their water basins. There were torches along the walls and the cavern was stone. There was a fresh smell in the room, obviously due to the mineral content of the water which seemed to effervescently move up from the depths of the mountain. It certainly could not come from the ogre.

There was another brief discussion after Tjol suggested sending the goblink as a decoy, but Eomore ruled the the creature would of more value to them later. Banon offered his bow, but initially stealth seemed their best ally.

The prince found that such decision making was becoming easier for him as this journey progressed.

The prince turned to Vannelei and Banon then asked, "Do you really think you can get off an accurate arrow shot? It might give us time to close on him and prevent him from calling for help."

Vannelei nodded and sheathed his elven sword and drew forth the fine bow he wore across his back. The tip of the elven arrow glinted like the graphite ring of a matron as he readied. Banon's long bow dwarfed that of the elf but would likely fall short in accuracy. The four warriors then inched forward. At Eomore's signal, the elf stood and the twang of the finely strung bow reverberated from the walls of the cavern. At the same time, Eomore, Tjol, and Deron rushed into the cavern. A loud groan filled the cavern as the arrow found its mark, striking the left shoulder of the ogre and burying deeply. Banon fired as well and the arrow struck the beast in the right thigh, but it scarcely seemed to notice. Banon slung the bow across his back and drew his scimitar. But the agility of the beast was surprising and it ignored its pain and grasped its great axe with the uninjured right arm; the fighters noted the left hanged rather limply thanks to the marksmanship of the elf. The others inched forward to observe the fray and noted that the ogre was indeed a monster, standing the height of two elves, but having the mass of eight or ten. The beast's agility was again apparent as it dodged the first thrusts of the three opponents, while at the same time delivering a glancing blow to Eomore's shield which staggered the prince. The ogre snarled and raised the axe above its head as if inviting them to attack. The voice spoke a variant of Dwarven and vaguely thanked them for becoming its dinner. Eomore feigned an attack, hoping to gain the creature's attention, but the beast did not fall for the ruse; when Deron thrust from the opposite side, the great axe swang through a graceful arc and crashed resoundingly against the shield of the dwarf, sending it flying and the dwarf sprawling across the smooth stone floor of the water cavern. The ogre rushed toward the dwarf to try to finish him, but was deterred when Eomore used the opening to drive Exeter deeply into the side of the beast, bringing forth a foul, dark ichor. The ogre screamed in pain and swang wildly in the direction of Eomore, but the prince was easily able to evade the ill-timed blow. Tjol was able to use this opportunity to score also but the blade of his sword was not as finely hewn as Exeter's and the wound was not as serious. Frustrated, the ogre moved back against the wall of the cave to the north but Eomore blocked the direction of the door and escape. Deron used this time to manage to leave the fray. The dwarf felt like he had imbibed several tankards of the tavern ale with only the unwanted after-effects. Banon arrived in his stead. Eomore and Tjol then advanced toward the beast, but jumped back to avoid a wild swing of the axe. Raising his shield, the prince rushed forward, bracing for the deafening blow that he knew would come; he was not disappointed as the axe fell soundly against the shield and blistered the hand of the prince where he grasped it. But the prince managed to retain his grip on the shield but was unable to take any offensive action. Tjol had an opening; the big man gave a thunderous yell and raked his weapon lashing across the thick hide of the great beast, opening a wide wound and gaining its attention. Banon swung and hewed two gnarled digits from the right hand, leaving only four remaining. When the ogre turned, Eomore leaped forward, left the stone floor of the cavern, and drove Exeter into the flesh of the creature to the hilt. He almost lost his grip on the sword when the ogre lurched forward. Tjol braced for an attack that never came – for the ogre stood motionless for a moment and then fell to the floor with a resounding thud- slain when the blade pierced its black heart.

Eomore stood and with great effort pulled the weapon from the beast. He was joined by the others. Deron was regaining his senses; Knarra administered a small phial of amber fluid to the dwarf. Eomore cleaned Exeter, using one of the raiments of the beast he had killed. Quickly they moved toward the door; Nigel listened intently. The priestess checked for fireglyph etchings or other Magick traps; the door was opened when none were found. A short span of stairs ascended behind the door. There were again torches along the walls. The stairs ended in a passage which slightly narrowed and extended some fifty paces where it ended and branched right and left. Eomore instructed Vannelei and Banon to keep their bows armed; a bowshot might benefit them. They resumed an order with Nigel again in the lead with the elf to his right and just behind him. They noted no activity and proceeded quickly along the passage. At the intersection they found that the right passage opened to stairs leading upward; at least one side passage was noted before the torchlight failed them passage faded into darkness. The passage to the left extended thirty paces and ended in a heavy, barred door, similar to the entrance of the dungeons of Castle Lyndyn. There was a single Kiennite guard who fell quickly and silently to the deadly stroke of Sweetheart. Eomore motioned them to the left after the goblink grunted that the strong door obviously led to the dungeons.

"It is too easy! It is just too easy!" Nigel muttered.

He led them quickly to the closed door. Deron and Tjol watched the rear. The door was ajar, but not locked and suspicion was high; Knarra cautioned against the Magick Detection spell offered by Cara. Nigel checked for and found no traps; the thief threw open the door; they saw a twenty foot square room with another door in the opposite wall. Three Droll warriors leaped to their feet but quickly fell before the swords of Eomore, Deron, and Tjol. Nigel removed a crude key-ring from the apparent leader who wore crude chainmail armor. He briefly studied the lock on the door, took one of the keys, and opened the second door. The outer door was reclosed; Deron and one Drelve were left to watch the passage.

"These guys sure must have never had any dwarves work for them," Nigel uttered.

He started down the stairs on the opposite side of the locked door. He descended six steps and the passage flattened. These were well lit to facilitate the poor vision of the Drolls who were more unaccustomed to the dark.

They passed several cells with bars made of a metallic material, but the dungeon was not extensive. Magrian pointed out that the Drolls and Kiennites were not accustomed to taking prisoners. The party came to a large door made of hardwood with small bars. The thief edged up to the door, sneaked a peak, and then moved back toward the others.

"I just don't like it. There is a small torture chamber and a single Droll guards Roscoe, who is chained to the far wall and seems to be unconscious. The door is locked but this is obviously the correct key," Nigel said holding up a three-forked key.

"I don't like it either," Exeter flashed to Eomore's thoughts. "But I cannot seem to find a threat."

"But there is a Droll there!" Eomore exclaimed.

He saw the startled look of the others; he realized that he had spoken aloud.

"I cannot explain it," the sword replied in an unusually uncertain tone.

"Let's do it," the prince uttered.

Nigel inserted the key, quietly turned it, threw open the door, and Eomore rushed into the room. The Droll fell before it stood.

The others entered cautiously. They stared at the frail wizard chained to the far wall.

"What now? Can't you revive him, Knarra?" Nigel queried.

The priestess remained silent. Slowly, she moved further into the room. She stopped ten paces from Roscoe; the mage slowly looked up; Roscoe's face winced from pain; tears welled up in his dark eyes. They heard a quiet hum emanating from the staff that Cara held.

Cara raised the staff; the elf hesitated briefly; she extended the staff toward Roscoe. Cara's smooth fingers gripped the staff; she whispered a single word which none of the others could understand; the staff hummed again. Cara took two steps toward Roscoe. She raised her right hand, diredcted her extended digits toward Roscoe, and growled something that sounded like "ANTHAFAN"; a beam of flame left the digits and struck Roscoe! A loud thunderclap followed. The room filled with a bloodcurdling scream; briefly they saw the true form of the Adjuster before the foul figure vaporized.

A muffled sound came from the iron maiden in the left corner of the room. Knarra moved over to the iron maiden, opened the door, and removed the somnolent Roscoe. Knarra removed a small flask from her robes and administered a sip of the liquid to the wizard. Roscoe responded and took the flask and quaffed deeply. The mage aroused.

"That must be some potent healing potion!" Nigel exclaimed.

"That was port wine from Three Forks," Roscoe answered.

"I was saving it for the proper time," Knarra said, smiling.

Roscoe's brow furrowed and he gazed sternly at Cara.

"Bring me the staff," he requested.

Cara hesitated. She had never felt anything like the power of the staff.

"The staff, please," Roscoe repeated with an irritated tone.

Cara grudgingly complied after being nudged by Eomore. She placed the staff in the right hand of the mage. Roscoe stood on shaky limbs.

"We are in big trouble," he coldly stated. "We couldn't have dreamed of what we were up against. Lose the wand. It's a locator that pinpoints our location."

Deron removed the thin rod from his back, snapped it in half, and kicked the remnants across the floor. The halves of the broken wand sizzled briefly and haziness filled the room.

The haziness in the room cleared.

"I know," Knarra dejectedly said.

The eyes of the Priestess and the Mage met and transfixed for a moment. The others could only speculate on the nonverbal communication between them.

"Unfortunately, she must know we are here now," Cara dejectedly said, "but I felt there was no alternative to using the Disspelling Word. We are too weak to battle the demon."

"She has known all along. That's why the beast was following us in the caverns," the mage responded.

They were relieved that he was alive but all felt the concern in the eyes of their powerful companions.

CHAPTER 36
Fears and Legends

There was no time to rejoice that Roscoe was safely returned to them, and only Roscoe, Knarra, and perhaps Magrian knew just how terrible a foe the great demon would have been. Eomore could tell that Cara had drained much of her strength; she actually slumped against Eomore.

Knarra stood as near Roscoe as she could. The stature of the mage seemed greater when he was near the strong woman. Roscoe retrieved his raimants from the iron maiden, and was relieved his items were intact. The pockets of his robe resisted probing by grimy Droll fingers.

Nigel spoke next.

He said, "This is a dead end and a difficult place to make a stand. I suggest we get out of here."

Eomore answered, "I agree with you. We have to try to find a place where we can regroup and regain some of our strengths."

The prince was concerned by the furrowed brows of the magicians, but now was a time for action and not worries. Roscoe took the staff and they began to move out of the small prison area. Deron and the Drelve reported that the only activity noted was a group of goblinks who turned toward the ogre pool area.

Nigel spoke, "I still cannot believe that the defenses of this place are so reduced. Something just isn't right. Are you sure that this 'Draithsbane' is so important?"

Magrian icily replied, "Without its magic you will stand no chance of gaining entrance to Castle Ooranth and battling the Draith Lord. I sense an evil presence here."

Knarra confirmed the same feelings. The party quickened their pace, facilitated by the well-lit passageways. Soon they were at the junction of the passage to the Ogre Cave; their fatigued bones were relieved that there were no foes to fight at this time. Nigel paused to study the passage ahead. It was one of the few times that the thief seemed to lack the take-charge confidence that he usually exuded.

They proceeded down the passage to the first door, which was on their left. To the right there was a small slit in the stone, which was much like a murder hole, which revealed a small ray of amber sunlight. Inspection confirmed that they were indeed now within the cone of the mountain proper. The passage they were following seemed to wind up the mountain in a spiral fashion with the doors opening into chambers on the interior. The entire structure had indeed been a construction of a creature instead of the eternal forces of nature. Nigel carefully inspected the door, opened it easily and discovered a massive chamber containing thousands of beddings with raiments typical of the Kiennite warriors. The room was unguarded and quite uninhabited. Roscoe expended a charge from his staff to check for the crafty creatures that might be cloaked with invisibility. The mage explained that he required rest before he could undertake much in the line of conjuring and that he had lost some of his materials from the linings and secret pockets of his now tattered robe. The mage pushed for a rest period, but Nigel was uncomfortable with the area.

Magrian said, "These must be the quarters of the Royal Guard, the elite fighting force of the Deathqueen. The battle on the plain must indeed be reaching dire proportions if she has dispatched the guards, though it is likely that they may serve as guards of passages to Castle Aulgmoor through the mountains.

As they had earlier surmised, the spiral tightened and they passed several other smaller chambers, each more elaborate in its furnishings, obviously the chambers of a more important minion of the mistress of the mountain. All the while there was a sense of being observed that they could not shake. Nigel led them into a darkened chamber, which was silent and uninhabited as well; torchlight revealed that they were in a reading chamber. There were shelves lined with many volumes. Many of the texts were foreign, but, to the amazement of the Donothorians, there were many volumes among the library that were the classics of their own literature, most of which were in the elven language, but some were the common tongue as well. The room was inspected quickly by Nigel; next the thief and the elven Prince Vannelei minutely studied the walls and shelves; when they were satisfied that there were no secret passages the group entered and began to take a much needed rest. Roscoe was exhausted;

Knarra, for the first time on the journey, exhibited signs of severe physical and mental fatigue. Eomore was amazed at the resilience of Cara, who managed to be close to him whenever the opportunity presented itself, often slipping her small hand against his hand behind his shield. Deron, who possessed the endurance typical of dwarves, offered to take the first warch. Banon insisted on helping; the archer still felt that he had not contributed enough in the fight of the ogre.

Magrian said, "This seems to be a recreational library and there seems to be nothing tactical here. It may be a relatively safe place to repose. I have difficulty with many of these volumes, however."

Nigel scuffed, "Now, that is a switch, for even I can recognize some of this stuff. What is 'Gripps Scary Tales' doing in this forbidden place? I used to read this as a kid. Anyway, I think it's time we all knew what you and the wizard were talking about back in the dungeon, priestess."

Knarra seemed to want to hesitate, but after glancing over at Roscoe, she began after seeing a nod from the wizard.

"We feel we are facing an evil not native to Parallan, but one derived in some way from our own world. I felt the Presence from the moment we traversed the Portal Gate connecting our worlds. I have not felt this Presence since since a campaign long ago in the depths of the Lachinor. Anactrophinea, as she is called, probably was known as Theandra in the nightmares of your forefathers.

"Generations ago, there lived in the central regions of our world, far south of what is now Donothor, a necromancer of great power named Morlecainen. His power was surpassed only by his evil and he found ways to live far beyond the years of normal men. He was said to deal with powerful demons from all layers of the black Abyss and gave sacrifices to these powers in return for his own betterment or at least benefit. It's thought that much of Magick came into our world in this way. He lived in a palace called Ylysis in the Lachinor. Eventually, though, the evil and the years began to take their toll on the mortal body of Morlecainen, and he sought to further his evil through progeny. He made alliances and his minions brought to him a beautiful dark elf that who was impregnated with the vile wizard's seed. She was bore him twin daughters, Chalar and Theandra, both as beautiful as their mother and as wicked as their father. As

Morlecainen aged, the rivalry between the daughters increased with each seeking a means of bettering the other. Their abilities were so nearly identical that this was no easy task. Chalar came into possession of artifacts of great value and power and spent much energy enhancing the already mighty items. In some way Chalar began to sway the balance of power from Theandra. She attained devices of great power, including the most dreaded artifact of evil, the Orb of Chalar, as it came to be known in legend. Our searches for the Orb in effort to destroy it came at great costs in lives lost. Chalar managed to banish her sister from the site of greatest Magick of Ylysis. Theandra faced annihilation should she ever return to the room of Sorcery. Rumor stated that she was destroyed in this way. We could never prove nor disprove the rumor. Chalar ultimately destroyed her father with an Arrow of Clysis. We found the sorcerer lying slain in his castle. Chalar was destroyed after great loss of life. We thought the orb destroyed as well. Roscoe and I have felt the presence and evil of Chalar. We feel a similar evil here. We fear that Theandra and Anactrophinea may be one and the same. The passage of time dulls the senses, even those involving Magick but perhaps this could explain the emergence of the Kiennites as a power in this world." Knarra said.

The Priestess completed her story; perhaps the discovery of the potential identity of their foe unnerved Knarra to the point that she repeated herself during parts of the story.

The room filled with silence when she finished.

"We may as well rest awhile. We are not going to sneak up on anybody here. And I dare any creature to come in here in a form that can feel pain!"Roscoe said emphatically.

Knarra and Roscoe settled down together and spoke softly to remain out of earshot to the others.

"If our fears are correct, we face great power," Knarra added. "So much is to be explained. If I am correct, she may only be vulnerable to attack from outside the realm. Only I can accomplish this."

Roscoe did not hesitate to object to this, saying, "If she brings her power and evil into this world, she must have to project herself into it. Maybe she really never "died". You cannot be sure that the rules of our domain will apply here. You cannot be sure that the spells will cast true between worlds. You cannot be sure. You just cannot be sure. You risk your own destruction. "

Knarra countered,"I can rely on our own realm. If I will recall her there..." The voice trailed off.

"You cannot be sure of your own survival," the mage answered.

Knarra replied dryly,"I'm not harmed by my own Magick. If we are dealing with Theandra, or even Chalar, only the sanctity of my Room of Cleansing will destroy her. We thought that we destroyed the Orb of Chalar; we did find the Room of Wizardry of Castle Ylysis. It exists now as my Room of Cleansing. Boomer's companions almost stumbled into it when they came to recruit me for this quest. I will have to risk this if we are correct. You know, only the purest of will can exist in Lylysis. That's why I've never been able to take you there..."

The Priestess managed to smile wryly.

Roscoe remained unsettled and did not react to her subtle but good-natured slander of his character.

He then said, "Who is the enemy here anyway? Are we not destroying the Draith Lord's greatest adversary? I still would rather take our chances with Ooranth. I'm wonder if the old Drelve is right about the necessity of the Drelvan blade to our mission. I would rather trust this staff."

Roscoe clutched his staff.

"More questions than answers, my friend. If Theandra exists here or anywhere else we would best serve Existance by elminating the evil. I thought we had reckoned with this. But we are here and because we are here, we must deal with the cards that we are dealt." Knarra added.

Roscoe could never remember his companion ever participating in a game of chance. She had taken many personal chances to aid her fellows however, and this concerned him.

"There would be another alternative," Roscoe added.

Knarra frowned and her flowing tresses reddened.

"I know that you have the power of a Wish Spell. But you know the risk. You have never cast one in our own land, let alone in such a foreign place," the Priestess said with no inflection in her voice.

The Spellcasters then gently grasped their left hands together and stood in silence.

CHAPTER 37
The Deathqueen

Knowing that their strength was so reduced, Eomore suggested that they may as well rest a while; since there was only one entrance through which any corporeal foes might approach them, the library was as good a place to rest as any.

"Rest. One place is as good as another," the prince said trying to reassure the tired group.

Roscoe had assured that in this small area they could put up a defense. Although Eomore doubted it, he was not about to question the mage.

The priestess Knarra drew forth a fine amber powder and sprinkled it about the room then uttered an incantation which was followed by a brief red glow.

"Hopefully, we will be free of scrying long enough to rest," she said.

She collapsed by the mage and both were fast asleep.

Eomore sat quietly he was aware of the soft hand of Cara, which lightly caressed him. The prince was anxious about the delay, but obviously the defenses of Castle Aulgmoor were skeletal and the old Drelve's assumption of the great battle was probably correct. The warrior within the prince envisioned the great conflict and felt drawn toward it. At the same time, he felt strangely secure here in this sanctuary in this area of apparent great evil and was glad he was here for awhile at least to gaze upon the beauty of Cara.

Cara slept soon after closing her eyes, breathed deeply, and snuggled tightly against his muscular left arm. Cara was oblivious to the ever-present chainmail which had become a second skin to the prince. His shield was rested against the wall. He did not want to shield himself from the warmth of the elf. He marveled at the flowery sweetness of her exhaled breath. Eomore realized that his right hand still grasped Exeter. Knowing that Deron was on guard, the prince relaxed the grip on the hilt of the weapon and silently sheathed her.

The telepathic message went along the line of "Thanks – I needed that."

Even the consciousness of the great sword required occasional rest; the prince relaxed somewhat and was comforted by the warmth of the female near him. He remained also surprised by the pleasant smell of her long, dark tresses and the beauty in her eyes which did not seem to diminish with the fatigue, labor, and sweat of the adventure. He slept but not deeply.

Deron kept a sound vigil and after four hours or so he awakened Nigel and reported that he had heard only one set of footsteps pass during the interlude that he watched, and those were not accompanied by the sounds of armor. There was never any hesitation at the door of the reading room. They had been left alone for his entire shift.

Nigel muttered, "I suppose that fighters here differ not from our land in this regard – few would be interested in the culture of the books. We chose well a place to repose."

The dwarf nodded and took his turn to slumber.

Eomore felt the gentle warmth on his face and was aware of the soft lips pressed against his cheek.

"It is time to awaken, my prince," Cara gently whispered as she kissed him.

Eomore looked around the room. Nigel remained perched at the door. Tjol, Banon, and Deron were quietly talking nearby. Magrian and the three remaining young Drelves sat at one of the tables pouring over a volume from the shelves. Eomore realized and felt poorly of himself that he only knew the name of Faryn. The other two had served faithfully but he knew them only as drelves. A loyal ally deserved more. The prince went over to them but after briefly talking to them he realized that he would have difficulty in pronouncing their names. Names were such an issue.

Knarra and Roscoe seemed to be sorting their remaining "supplies" for many of their spells required some mundane component. Vannelei sat nearby with his eyes fixed on Cara, and the girl stared briefly back. Thirteen against the evil of this mountain – and this was but the first step toward the final struggle on the plain of Ooranth. The prince again found himself wondering if they would even reach that stage of their quest. Nigel's referring to the mission as a Deathquest flashed back into his mind.

Standing, he shook off as much of the doubt as he could and said to the magicians, "Are we ready to proceed?"

Roscoe answered, "As ready as we'll ever be. The pinnacle of this evil peak probably holds our fate. We should move on. We are being anticipated. No one bothers to attack us here. The mouse must go to the cat."

The analogy seemed appropriate.

Nigel reported that there had been on activity during his watch and that they had been in the reading room about eight hours as best as he could reckon, thought their estimation of time was skewed in the nightless land of Parallan.

They assumed an order and Nigel and Vannelei took the lead. The spiral tightened as they ascended and they found themselves circling the peak faster. Occasionally they would pass a one-way window- apparent as only stone from the outside. From one such vantage they could look down onto the castle front and the stone footridge. The Ballista was still there with its three guards.

Banon surmised, "Since they know we are here anyway, why should I not eliminate these opponents with my bow?"

Eomore countered, "They serve us also should other enemies arrive. Any clamor that they create would alert us. We are not engaging our primary foe. The fact that there are no more defenders here may represent the fact that all may not be going well on the plain of battle."

The rooms were more and more elaborate, but all were empty.

The thief shuddered, saying, "I feel like I'm under the watchmakers lens and my every move is observed."

The others shared this feeling. Finally the circular ascending passage leveled and ahead they could see a foyer of great size. Nigel stopped the others and silently crept ahead. He returned in a short time to describe a fifty by fifty pace area with a large stairwell in the area to the furthest right as he glanced into it. The area was well-lit by magical means of some sort and there stood a single guard at the foot of the stairs, a skeletal form of giant proportion dressed in gleaming golden platemail and armed with a massive two handed sword. The creature stood the height of three men; similar in dimension to the two-headed ogre they had fought earlier. He had been unable to get a good look at the stairs but could comment that they ascended a great height before ending in a heavy wooden door. The group briefly concerned itself with the nature of the guardian.

"I don't see any alternative to a straightforward attack," Tjol suggested, gripping his own sword.

"Have you encountered even the normal sized animated dead that were created by the necromancers of old in our own land?" Roscoe inquired. "Because of their magical nature, they are quite resistant to the Magick. Much like the automatons or golems that serve my palace. Skeletons and zombies have made formidable foes and we can only speculate the nature of this creature."

"Your points are well-taken as usual, Mage," Eomore interjected, quite diplomatically, "but this time I wonder if Tjol isn't right. Certainly we near our objective for whatever end, and any maneuvering will only arouse the inhabitants of the pinnacle. We should save all our Magick for that which awaits us there."

Knarra started to say something, but Tjol gave a yell and charged into the room, the gleam of battle in his eyes. The others moved forward. Tjol approached the great guard and the hallway filled with the sounds of the clanking of his mail as he ran. Banon launched an arrow then charged after his friend. Deron and Eomore followed the warriors at a few paces removed, but Tjol had the privilege of beginning the encounter.

The big man braced himself for a blow, but found that he was able to come into striking range and, giving a yell, he arched his sword with all his might, only to find the blow swing through the illusion and his momentum carried him forward and sprawling onto the stone floor. Of course, the others witnessed this and found themselves standing in the foyer alone with the warrior Tjol in the indignant position on the floor. As Deron went to his aid, they were able to see clearly now that the stairs ascended some hundred steps and the great door at the top of the stairwell silently swung open. They braced themselves, each assuming a defensive posture in his or her fashion.

At the foot of the stairs the wispy skiffs of lavender smoke changed to the wavy form of a striking woman..

An evil voice hissed, "Come. I await you."

A clap of thunder ensued and the wavy form disappeared.

The wisps of lavender smoke floated up the stairs and through the door.

A raspy almost tantalizing female voice said, "Come, fools, to your doom. You bring me the victory that has eluded me."

Eomore looked at Knarra, and then to Roscoe, who was clutching his great staff. Both nodded, and the prince motioned to Nigel and Vannelei to begin investigating the stairs. Cautiously, they started upward, testing each step. The stairs were some ten paces wide, but Eomore chose to have them go forward only two at a time. First, the thief and the elven prince, then Eomore and Tjol, then Roscoe and Knarra, then Deron and Cara, then the three Drelves, the younger following the Old one. Banon held the rear with scimitar ready. Vannelei carried his bow and Nigel clutched his Sweetheart. Soon they were climbing faster and after an eternity, they reached the top of the stairs.

Inside the door was a room of ultimate splendor. The dimensions were some fifty paces broad and one hundred paces deep. The walls were lined with many paintings and reliefs, many of a lewd or suggestive nature, many picturing deeds of import by the mistress of the mounts, with an overhead mural depicting the great "Spawn Curse" that had been placed upon the Draiths.

On the lateral wall to their right was a life-size portrait of Cara – well, the resemblance of the young woman in the portrait to the dark elf was astonishing.

The light source of the room was not apparent and there were no windows, but the lighting was intense and brief volcanic hazes filled the room. The furnishings were exquisite and treasures lay literally on top of each other throughout the room. They could have gazed indefinitely, but their attention was gathered onto the two inhabitants of the room. Sitting on a sofa in the far reaches was a woman of dark features vaguely elven, who was surrounded by a violet haze. Standing near her was the frail young Vaylin, whom they thought lost in the cavedragon battle. He looked prominent as he stood wearing gleaming mail and holding a long sword which seemed weightless in his hands. The weapon was surrounded by a reddish glow. Runes on the blade emanated great light.

The woman spoke and the words stabbed their spirits like icicles, leaving them all cold.

"You know who I am. Only now do I know the great power of the artifact. I owe you great thanks for bringing the key to unlock its secrets. I know now that the Black Lord of Ooranth will fall easily before me, and the outcome of the battle below is rather moot. But more importantly, perhaps, you may provide me means of regaining what is rightfully mine in the other world."

When she finished speaking, she extended a finger toward them and Magrian dropped his walking staff and started walk toward the female creature. They sensed that Magrian was lost to them. The mage beamed the staff toward her and barked a command, issuing blue flame from the staff. The room filled with heat but the violet haze around her seemed to hold back the rays. Vannelei arched an arrow toward her simultaneously, but shortly before reaching the perimeter of the violet haze, the arrow turned and returned to its source, striking the elven prince in the right leg, causing him to call out in pain and fall. Nigel had Sweetheart in a hurling position, but quickly recoiled, remembering the garroting function of the weapon. The thief shuddered to think that he almost slew himself. Cara put away her crossbow and began to utter coarse commands, gesturing with her delicate hands as Roscoe readied the staff again and Knarra went to the aid of the bleeding elf.

The cold voiced graveled, "Would you slay your own Bloodkin, girl?"

Cara stopped in the middle of her incantation.

The woman continued, "Don't make such a mistake. Come and rule with me. Both worlds will be ours."

Looks of confusion filled all faces except Roscoe, who was too intent on his plan, Knarra, and Vannelei.

"I've suspected all along," the elf whispered to Knarra as he anguished in his wounds, "that Cara might be the descendant of the dark witch of our nightmares."

"I've known since the reading room," the priestess confided. "We have to trust the fates and her love for Eomore."

Roscoe boomed a command and lightning flew from the staff. She raised her hand and sent the ray back toward the mage but the staff absorbed the force and the room resounded with the clap of thunder. A stalemate.

Cara resumed her incantation and short bursts of flame went forth from her hands to first the woman and then the ersatz warrior with the great sword, but the rays failed to penetrate the haze and the sword reflected all. Eomore motioned to Tjol and Deron and the three advanced forward as the others spread to the corners of the room. The Drelve advanced toward them as Roscoe and the Deathqueen again engaged each other.

Cara stood silently, with her hands at her side. Knarra had removed the prince's arrow from his leg, bandaged the wound upon his leg, and applied a healing balm.

She then removed a small pouch from her raiments and placed them in the hands of the drelve Faryn, saying, and "Use judiciously these healing balms."

Exeter communicated to Eomore, "We enter a fight we cannot win, for I fear we cannot wound the bearer of the blade in the usual manner. I shall try for you, my lord."

Then the room resounded with the clash of the blades. The Draithsbane glowed brightly in the hands of the ersatz warrior who had been known to them as Vaylin.

Exeter glowed brilliantly red with the ferocity of battle, but the Draithsbane withheld each blow, while managing to strike rapidly, slightly wounding the dwarf, a wound that grazed his neck and could easily have been fatal but for a narrow margin.

Tjol and Banon also stood against the frail opponent who had never before shown such swordsmanship and slowly the prince and the warriors began to tire. All the while, Roscoe and again Cara threw blast after blast toward the Sorceress, but to no avail. The mage showed a furrowed brow but continued to successfully resist the spells cast against him. There was certainly a stalemate of Magick, but the warriors were beginning to tire from parrying the blows from the Draithsbane. They seemed unable to wound the bearer of the blade. Wounds healed on Vaylin before their their eyes. He disdained a shield and ripped the air with the flaming blade.

Cara was not as fortunate as she fell victim to a stun spell and fell helpless to the floor. Knarra tried first to silence the area around the woman, but the spell was ineffective. It did reflect back toward Knarra, but did not affect the Priestess. Nigel was poised to enter the attack against the Drelve, but the opponent turned rapidly and struck a glancing blow, which Nigel survived only due to his catlike instincts, but in so doing, the thief lost his balance and fell, striking his head against a table corner and falling into unconsciousness. Deron made it back to Faryn who applied some of the precious balm to the wound, and the bleeding stopped, but the dwarf collapsed from the fatigue.

Eomore could barely hold his own, as he marveled at the dexterity imparted by the sword as well as the speed at which Vaylin moved. The frail drelve would have won any competition in the games of Donothor. But this was no game and fatigue was becoming their opponent.

The prince dreaded the realization that they had brought her the Drelve that she needed to activate the Magick of her sword, and the Drelven Teacher to fully explain its powers to her. Each wound lancing his flesh sapped his strength further and he realized that only the dwarven chainmail kept the blows from being lethal. Tjol and Banon stood tall and the three of them managed to deflect the blows from the Draithsbane. How long they could do this was a growing concern.

Knarra saw Magrian reach the side of the woman and stand motionless there. She saw the effortless manner in which she casted her attacks and she also saw the fatigue on the faces of Eomore and Roscoe. The priestess removed her raiment, exposing her long form.

She shouted to Roscoe, "If what we believe is true, there is but one way."

He returned. "No! You cannot be sure – you may not be oriented, please!"

He was silenced when he had to raise his staff to reflect a bolt of energy cast toward him by the sorceress.

Knarra clutched her symbol and Roscoe saw her form fade and she seemed as wispy as the violet haze that surrounded the Deathqueen. She moved across the room. Immediately, the woman turned all offensive power toward her and burst after burst passed through the form of the priestess. Just as Eomore dropped to one knee with fatigue, the Drelve broke off the attack and rushed toward the priestess but even the magical thrusts of the sword passed through the form. Vaylin swung again and again but he could not deter the priestess. The flamimg blade passed through Knarra.

When Knarra reached the perimeter of the purplish vapors surrounding the Deathqueen, Anectrophinea stood and conjured furiously, but Knarra approached still, and developed a flaming appearance as she approached the Deathqueen. Incessantly, she approached the sorceress and a frail hand extended toward her. Roscoe saw a look of sheer terror on the face of Anecttophinea as Knarra's wispy hand touched her. The room reverberated with a voice vaguely like Knarra's pronouncing a single word.

"Lylysis!" emanated from the lips of the wavy form of Knarra.

"No!" the mage exclaimed.

There was a tremendous clap of thunder and in an instant both women were gone. The haze dissipated. The Drelve they knew as Vaylin dropped the weapon and fell, laden by the weight of his armor. The room was quiet except for their heavy breathing.

Cara stood slowly. She rubbed her temples.

Nigel awakened and asked, "What happened?'

Magrian stood bewildered.

Faryn rushed to Eomore to attend the Prince's many lacerations from the battle. Fortunately, none seemed serious. Banon and Tjol likewise had escaped serious injury. The dwarf had beem very lucky. Faryn's growing skills had facilitated Deron's stability.

"I am thankful that I did not kill any of you. I did not have my own will," Vaylin uttered."Since a sapling, I have dreamed of wielding the great blade and now such circumstances as these."

Deron and Vannelei glanced to see the slain bodies of the two young drelves who had fallen from spells meant for Roscoe..

Roscoe did not seem physically injured. He was profusely sweating. He looked exhausted. He was crying.

Eomore, Cara, Roscoe, Magrian, Vannelei, Vaylin, Faryn, Banon, Tjol, Nigel, and Deron. Eleven remained.

Roscoe stood, "There is no longer evil here."

They felt a foreboding sadness.

The Draithsbane lay upon the floor.

It was no longer glowing.

CHAPTER 38
The Victory of Calaiz

The Draith Lord was led to a place of presumed security by Izitx. The arduous deeds of the past battle were furrowing his proud brow with fatigue. The Kiennites had been no match for his powers and clearly the tide of battle had been turned through his efforts. He was in great need of rest as the dark period approached but it would be only a matter of a few heartbeats until the time to struggle would begin again. Izitx left his master and returned to the lieutenants to plan for the certain counterattack from the Droll legions and their own probable offensive. The dogfaced Drolls still far outnumbered the Draiths but Calaiz had more than equaled the magical prowess of the Kiennite casters combined and indeed their numbers had been greatly reduced in the fray.

As he lay on the blanket given him by his minion, Calaiz found his mind going in many directions. First he returned to Castle Ooranth where the beautiful maiden that he hoped to soon make his mate and produce his heirs waited. Her beauty had entered his mind many times even during the fray. Trya's face had been embossed upon his mind and his large hands could still sense the softness of her gentle shoulders. These remembrances had held him up against the odds in the prior battle and had comforted him many times. Deep in his thoughts, there was a seed of hope that she might even willingly become his consort, and this was a new sensation for the Draith Lord. He mused that if Izitx even thought of this in the least that he would reinforce all the old arguments about the superiority of the Draiths and how fortunate the maiden was to have been scurried away from her home to become the bride of the Black Lord. Yet there were the stories told to him of his own mother weeping in the privacy of her chambers when she thought none was there and the birth she gave him even though she was also torn from her homeland. There was the inescapable comparison between the maiden Trya and the elf that had borne the Draith Lord and their beauty was only the beginning of this. Calaiz found he was angry with his inadequacies and frustrated with this weakness of his- in thinking of the woman's feelings- he was glad that his minions could not guess these inner feelings. It seemed that in times of greatest fatigue these thoughts occupied his mind; this was certainly one of those times. The last fight had extended through two dark periods as both sides had jockeyed for favorable position; it finally ended with the Drolls falling back to defensive positions. Indeed they had been pushed to the proximity of the pass leading to Castle Aulgmoor and the witch herself. The battle lines looked excellent for the Draiths and Calaiz felt good about that. Yet his mind again turned to the feeling of another presence in the realm and he could not define it. Even though he realized that there might be a new ally for the Deathqueen, he felt confident of victory. Finally the time of battle took its toll and he fell asleep.

Urr and Yol left the disconsolate camp of the remaining Drollen generals as they had planned. The phantom warriors had seen the progress of battle and knew that the tide certainly was turning away from the troops of Anectrophinea. Even their great steeds had been destroyed by the spells of the wyvern-rider. Firehorses felled by spells of cold.

They deemed that it was necessary to enact their plan to liquidate the Draith leader who had so clearly swayed the fortunes of the conflict. Their shadowy forms wafted silently across the camp and soon neared the periphery. Surely even the Droll guards felt the chill of their presence as they passed. Once they had left the camp and neared the lines of the enemy, Urr nodded and they assumed a gaseous form and moved into the air. The Firehorses were mainly for presentation anyway. Even though the Draith guards on the perimeter were most vigilant, they passed undetected. Silently, they scanned the Draith camp until they saw the gathering of the lieutenants headed by the masterful Izitx. They hovered briefly.

Izitx stood from the fire in the amber light of the dark period and tried to account for the unaccustomed chill on his back. He scanned the horizons and indeed excused himself from the meeting and went to check on the master, which ironically led them to their quarry. Seeing Calaiz fast asleep, Izitx returned, and Urr and Yol descended to accomplish their task. As advantageous as their gaseous form was, they lacked the ability to do harm; their razor-like talons could only damage in their corporeal state. Even the necromancer abilities of the Deathqueen who had conceived them were not all encompassing.

The two landed near the sleeping Draith and materialized. The coldness was only felt in a narrow area so none experienced it but Calaiz; the Draith Lord pulled his blanket over him; he slept soundly. He did not awaken until Urr latched onto his neck –his leather-like skin began to give way to the talons; Yol gripped into his chest. Calaiz quickly was at his guard and threw the form off his chest but Yol continued the attack, forcing the Draith Lord to literally rip the taloned arm from its socket, still attached to his chest. Bleeding profusely, Calaiz tried to utter a spell, but Urr was back upon him; though dismembered, the arm of Yol continued to attack as another replaced it. Calaiz realized that his shouts were not being transmitted as the creatures had silenced the area. He fought vigorously, but their wounds healed as rapidly as he opened them and the multiple wounds he had received had slowly drained his strength.

In a chamber nearby, the prince of Donothor was undergoing a similar frustration and facing death.

Calaiz sensed the end as he neared unconsciousness and his foes seemed to grow ever-stronger. Death was claiming him as a prize. He had failed his people. He would not know the warmth of the maiden Trya.

Suddenly their hideous faces became frozen with fear and in an instant they were gone. The air was warm again. Calaiz managed to scream and in an instant Izitx was there binding his wounds and replenishing him with healing elixirs of the Menders. As he regained his feet, Calaiz stood and faced the pass toward Aulgmoor.

Turning to Izitx, he said, "She is no more. By some means my life is spared but I'm robbed of my moment of glory. Arouse your troops and let us end this thing. We have an ally that I have not anticipated and that I don't fully understand. We need the security of our home. We need the comforts of Ooranth."

At first Izitx wondered if the attack had affected Calaiz mentally, but soon he realized that the Black Lord was fully rational and he aroused the legions. Izitx could not understand the concept of comforts. Good food and drink, the first lieutenant would indulge, but he had never shared one of the wenches brought to Ooranth for breeding. Izitx was steadfastly loyal to his lord, but at times Calaiz would utter some nuance completely alien to his hulking lieutenant. Calaiz was alive. He still had a chance for victory. He still had a chance to see the maiden Trya again.

Calaiz mounted the wyvern and ascended into the air to watch the final battle. He did not sense the necessity of casting spells. There was little resistance as the Drolls scattered before the onslaught and the Kiennites fell readily before the stronger Draiths. There were none of the floating warriors that had slain his favorite steed. No spells emanated from the thinning Kiennite ranks. There was no sense of Magick on the field of battle. But from Aulgmoor, there was…

He did not know. He sensed an absence and a new presence. He sensed a relief and a threat. What did it mean?

He dispatched Izitx to go forth to Aulgmoor to destroy any that lingered there, reassuring the lieutenant that he no longer felt the presence of the Deathqueen of the Kiennites. He returned to the ground to reward his troops with praise and to organize the return to Castle Ooranth. The victory was his, but he remained uncertain as to why the events had occurred. There was still a strong force present for which he could not account.

"I shall walk before my legions to Ooranth and consummate my mating." Calaiz uttered as Izitx left toward Castle Aulgmoor to "mop up".

CHAPTER 39
On to Ooranth

The little party clustered together. Vannelei judiciously applied the precious healing balms to their wounds and Eomore placed his hand on Roscoe's shoulder. The Mage looked much older now; he had the appearance of an old man as the tears trekked down his face.

Cara stood by Eomore and Vannelei gave a glance of uncertainty toward her. The longsword lay on the floor where Vaylin had relinquished it. Magrian studied the sword, first by gazing downward at the vorpal weapon, and then gingerly picked up the blade. There was tension throughout the room when the old Drelve raised the weapon. The runes etched into the blade began to faintly glow. The Old One's face was watched closely to assess any change in his demeanor, but the group only noted a wry smile on his face.

Cara's eyes were fixed on the life size portrait hanging on the wall. The resemblance of the maiden in the painting to the dark elf was incredible.

Cara said as she stared at the portrait in disbelief, "I feel as though I am peering into a mirror. Could what she said possibly be true? I would gladly relinquish any powers that I have if it could mean that any blood linkage to such evil be dissolved."

Eomore had subtly grasped the hilt of Exeter when Magrian lifted the sword, and was reassured when the weapon noted no enemies.

"None of us can control who their kin are," the Prince answered. "Even if what she said were true."

"Please ask Exeter to look upon me, Eomore," Cara pleaded.

Vannelei interjected,"That might not be a bad idea."

The prince realized that he had already done this, but he was really questioning the effect that the new found weapon might have exerted on the old Drelve.

Eomore stopped her and placed his arm around her, saying, "You need not say anything more. I do not doubt you. I will however try to gain some insight into the weapon you hold, Magrian. Why does it appear differently in your hand than it did in battle?"

Banon took the sword from the old Drelve. Initially Magrian seemed reluctant but he relinquished the blade.

Waving it awkwardly through the air Banon commented, "It feels like a poorly forged longsword. No respectable dwarf would claim to be the forger of this weapon."

The blade remained dark when the archer grasped the hilt.

Vannelei took the blade briefly. "You are wrong my friend. This is a fine blade. It feels exceptional in my hand."

The runes reappeared on the blade, glowing more brightly as the elven prince held the weapon. The blade slipped gracefully through the air when wielded by the elf.

Magrian looked at the dark elf quizzically.

But Vannelei was a prince of a people of the forest. A smile grew on the elf prince's face.

"I feel my full strength for the first time since the battle at Castle Lyndyn on the night Trya was taken," He said resolutely. "I have full use of my shoulder."

Eomore then heard the anticipated feminine voice in his inner mind and Exeter again reported that no enemies were noted in the group including Cara, Vannelei, and Vaylin. The voice briefly revealed that there had been some initial doubt surrounding Vannelei when he held the blade but it could have simply been the elven prince's doubting of Cara. The sword itself emanated nothing.

Roscoe peered at the blade through his tears.

"I sense no evil inherent to the blade. The young Drelve was possessed by the Deathqueen and not the blade," the mage concluded.

Vannelei placed the blade into his scabbard which seemed to adjust to facilitate the length of the blade.

Magrian then began a discourse that held all their attention. "Our legend holds that the blade can only be effectively wielded by one of royal Drelvan descent. This is the first time that I have seen the Draithsbane, but the way that Vaylin wielded it in battle would seem to confirm that its power is brought out when held in Drelvan hands. I can understand why Banon finds the blade awkward. I can't account why Vannelei handles it so well."

They were aware that runes on the blade began to glow as Vannelei held the blade.

Vannelei again said,"I feel fully refreshed. Even my scratches are healed."

Magrian continued,"I am perplexed. Perhaps if I study the glowing runes. But I think I know why the demon did not attack us in the caverns when it had many opportunities. Also, the Cavedragon could have easily killed Vaylin when he was detected. It was all a plan to draw a wielder to her. I can only speculate as to how she came into possession of the blade. Perhaps Ramish's treachery extended to this. At any rate, Ramish, by legend, could not have exacted the full potential of the sword, just as the runes are more pronounced when Vannelei holds the weapon compared to me. I am not of royal descent."

"I also was able to look into the depths of her consciousness when our minds linked as she cast the powerful Mind Control Spell upon me. I suppose the lock of my hair that she needed for the spell was obtained by the demon in the caverns. My role was to supply her with knowledge of the blade as Vaylin's role was to wield it. I am not of royal lineage. She knew that she required the Draithsbane in order to be able to vanquish her foe the Draith Lord. Her powers were indeed weakened by the Black Wish. Much of her evil was carried out by her minions, and much of her power was reduced to the ability to cast illusion. Thus, the giant skeletal warrior. However, she had not feared her own safety, thinking herself immune even to the newfound Magick power of the Draith Lord. My last thought shared with her was the terror that replaced the evil when she realized that Knarra had the power to end her reign of evil."

The old one paused briefly.

He continued, "She was indeed the existence of the black witch of your Lachinor. Theandra, as she was known to you, longed for vengeance that she could not attain. She had channeled that energy to becoming the master of this world. Even weakened, she was still a great powerful sorceress. Until the attacks of the Draith Wyvern-rider, Parallan as you term our world had produced no challenge to her. By keeping her mind's eye on the waters of the seas of the Magick, she could monitor the plans of the Draith Lord. She has known of your arrival since you breached the gate to our world. She seemed to know Roscoe but did not fear him. Knarra was also recognized at the final moment. A bitter thought of the name "Chalar" was the last thing her consciousness revealed to me."

Deron shouted, "We must leave now. I long for even the strange skies of this world to be over me."

The dwarf winced as his neck ached in spite of the balm applied by Faryn.

Roscoe stood and gripped his staff.

He said matter of factly,"Let us be on with it. Perhaps in addition to losing our greatest asset, we have also destroyed the only means to defeat the enemy we came here to seek."

Eomore and his ten companions started to descend the stairs. When they reached the window which was now visible as such, Banon could not resist the urge to fire an arrow into the guard standing nearest the ballista at the opening gate of Castle Aulgmoor. The arrow passed through the illusion and clanked against the stone. The ballista and its crew vanished, as was typical of the Magick of illusion to disappear when disturbed. The group descended uninterrupted and followed the main hallway to the great entrance to the castle. They simply used the inner portcullis and exited the stronghold of the Deathqueen. They collapsed, exhausted, in the brightening light of the three suns after reaching the edge of the foliage on the other side of the footbridge.

Vannelei gave the new found longsword to Magrian.

Magrian clutched the Draithsbane and studied the runes etched upon it diligently. The runes did not glow brightly when the sword was in his hand. Eomore couldn't help but notice that the old Drelve appeared much younger while holding the blade, maybe only because his spirits were lifted by its discovery.

Roscoe developed a flushing to his face and leveled his staff toward Castle Aulgmoor. He resoundingly brought the end of the staff to the ground; there was clearly great anger in his voice as he cast the Earthquake Spell that created large breaks in the walls and ultimately brought the Castle to ruin with great and small fragments falling into what in effect had been a dry moat.

The circular canyon filled a third way up with debris but the central pinnacle was now bare.

"A place that resulted in such treachery cannot be allowed to stand." The mage uttered after the deafening sounds of the crashing boulders ended.

He dropped to a knee, exhausted by the effort.

Cara compassionatly wiped the profuse sweat from his brow and the archmage of Donothor rested his head upon her blithe shoulders.

All collapsed and fell asleep; trusting the Fates as there was no organized watch. Indeed, the party was too small to cause any concern for passersby. When Eomore awakened they were in the midst of a dark period. Cara had drawn near him and continued to sleep by his side. Magrian continued to study the runes etched upon the weapon. Eomore sensed that the old Drelve looked rather imposing as he clutched the artifact that was so treasured by his race but not to the extent that Vannelei did, or as did Vaylin. The prince of Donothor knew that the great powers of the sword had been activated when held by Drelven hands, and the swordsmanship of the prince wielding a weapon as great as Exeter had barely been a challenge for the frail Vaylin when he had held the Draithsbane. If the weapon were indeed more powerful against the Draiths, the prince felt wondered in his warrior curiosity, what might it do? Why was Vannelei able to activate the runes on the blade?

But the more practical side of his mind intervened to wonder how this small group could hope to accomplish their goal at Castle Ooranth. Eomore was somewhat bothered that the young Vaylin who had been his adversary at Auglmoor had been reluctant to reclaim the blade. If what the old one said were true, any hope of success would depend on the sword. Vaylin had scarcely spoken. The golden mail had crumbled to dust with the leaving of the Deathqueen and the Drelve certainly seemed frail. Others in the party had expressed concern about his holding the blade again as well, fearing the reactivation of some arcane Magick. Exeter, Cara, and Roscoe had reassured that no evil emanated from Vaylin and nothing emanated from the sword itself unless the runes were glowing as they had when it was held by Vaylin, Magrian, or Vannelei. The heat of battle had been furious in the chamber of the Deathqueen but in the aftermath it had been noted that only Vannelei had not been injured by the many swings of the blade by Vaylin. Maybe the dark elf prince was just more dextrous but then Vaykin was moving so rapidly with the enhancing effects of the blade. Cara had not held the weapon but swords had never been her choice of weapon

"Magrian, let us test the blade with the maiden," Eomore asked.

The old one seemed perplexed by the request initially, then turned to Cara and asked,"Do you wish to hold the Draithsbane?"

Cara reached out her small hand and grasped the blade. She was seen to struggle with the weight of the weapon. There was faint glow on the blade. Several small scratches on her smooth skin healed as she held the blade, but she appeared awkward in her efforts to move the blade through the air.

She sighed and commented," I fear we learned of my lineage before."

None had detected Vannelei relaxing the grip on his own shortsword and exhaling with deep relief when it was apparent the the young sorceress was not effected by the blade. Thus, it was Vannelei or Vaylin who would be their champion against the Draith Lord.

It was hard to think of Magrian as a warrior capable of charging into battle against the Draiths, even with this artifact. Yet there was a gleam in the Old One's eyes as he studied the runes and stroked the cold edge of the weapon. He looked far different than when Cara had saved him from the clutches of the Kiennites and Drolls at the Gap Keep. Could the Old One be attempting to learn how to wield the weapon effectively? The runes still did not glow brightly when he held it.

Their bodies still demanded rest. What nourishment they had was taken, again supplanted by some fruits of the forest obtained by the Drelves who knew better than the Drolls and Kiennites where to seek the forest's aide.

Cara lay down by the side of the Prince of Donothor and soon slept. Eomore's mind was racing and sleep did not seem near.

Thinking of the woman sleeping so peacefully at his side, Eomore wondered how deeply she might have been affected by the words of the Deathqueen, claiming bloodline relation to her. Could the claims have any truth? Certainly the girl possessed great forte with regard to Magick – far beyond that of even the evasive dark elves of the Lachinor. Eomore wished for the wisdom of Knarra now as he had turned to her so many times before during the course of the painful adventure. The absence of the priestess left him with a haunting insecurity. How would it affect Roscoe, who had said nothing after uttering the spell that destroyed Aulgmoor? Would the mage be ready for battle?

For the first time, he realized that he had forgotten to place a guard and he felt guilt about not being more vigilant about the matter himself. But Exeter sensed these feelings and began chastising him.

"You are a great warrior, but you are only human, my Lord. Even with the effects of the healing balms applied by Faryn your wounds weakened you greatly. Let us talk no more of failure."

The prince smiled and acknowledged the words silently, when upon arising, he realized that Deron was missing. He rose and, trying not to disturb the others, whispered a query to Magrian as to the location of the dwarf, to which the Drelve nodded and pointed down the path. The prince moved forward to find the little warrior astutely watching the approaches to their rocky hiding place. Eomore placed his hand upon the broad shoulders of the dwarf and ushered him back to the camp area, saying he would watch a while. The usually robust little fighter silently obeyed and the prince watched until he had reached the others and had collapsed upon the ground. Eomore allowed Deron and the others a few hours of rest – well, he though about four, but as usual, he was uncertain about the veracity of his judgments regarding time passage in this foreign place. Returning to the camp, he awakened those still sleeping and they fashioned a meal from the scant rations they had and from berries that the drelves gathered. They were fortunate to still have the knowledge of the forest that Magrian possessed and Vannelei was adapting quickly as well. Vaylin remained little help. The forest sustained them and its denizens gave them hope with the weapon. But the Draiths would be so many and tenacious in guarding their home. Knarra was not with them to counteract the Magick of the Draith Lord and the brief encounter with the raiders back on that dreadful night at

Castle Lyndyn when Trya was taken had revealed to them that the Draiths possessed items or at least means to temper the attacks of Roscoe and Cara. But they had the immense power of Roscoe and two magical weapons. They had strong hearts and willpower. Eomore felt something else continuing to grow deep inside his own heart. Now, there were three women that he longed to return to his home- two of whom he loved; his sister and the dark elven maiden of mystery.

"We must make some plans," the prince said. "We know little of the fight before us. We really aren't sure if the battle still rages."

"Give me some time and I'll return with some answers for you," Roscoe said in an emotionless voice.

"Be careful," Nigel encouraged. "The evil in this wicked place owes us a great debt, and I aim to collect it. We'll need you."

The voice of the thief dripped the words like acid and he said them clutching the hilt of Sweetheart.

"Thief, you can only begin to feel what I do. You cannot know what I have lost. We shall try to exact payment, but the debt will never be paid. I'll soon return," Roscoe answered.

The mage then lifted the staff, rose into the air, and faded from sight. The others sat down for a bit more rest. In a short while, the mage returned to report the rout of the Drolls and Kiennites and the victory of the Draiths. He also told of again seeing the great winged lizard and its rapid departure toward the smallest sun which was the direction of Ooranth. A second smaller party was nearing the approach to Aulgmoor. There was no resistance to the approach of the Draith scouts. They advanced far enough to seen that the castle was collapsed and now have turned to follow the larger force. Any Droll or Kiennite faction, if one exists, escaped my detection. There is great carnage on the field surrounding the river. Scavengers will be feasting long, since none of these opponents seem to honor their dead with pyres.

"It seems that we have aided the Draith King greatly in his struggle. Ironically, we must now try to destroy the victors of the great battle," Magrian mused as he continued to fondle the weapon.

Roscoe then said, "Are you going to share the secret of the Draithsbane with us or are we going to have to keep guessing?"

The impatience in his voice was accentuated by the bitterness he felt.

Roscoe barked, "I'm ready to kill somebody."

Magrian stared at the wizard.

The old Drelve did not project the pleasant expression characterized his kind face much of the time.

Eomore worried to hear such words from the powerful wizard.

Then Nigel said, "Do we have any idea as to the timetable the Draith King will follow now?"

To this Magrian replied, relying upon his extensive knowledge of his old enemies and their ritualistic behavior, "The army will return to a triumphant celebration. The Draiths have never achieved such a great victory. It will take them three amber periods , about one of your days, to make the journey to Castle Ooranth, but the winged lizards will traverse the distance – well, they will already be there. The Draiths will travel by forced march, never resting. So there will be no chance of our arriving there before them unless the magician can transport us there. But they would never leave Castle Ooranth undefended. Its walls are imposing, but the ferocity of the castle guards is known from the defeats of the Droll legions in many wars, even though fecundity always gave the Drolls superior numbers."

Magrian did not know that Calaiz had chosen to march with his scouts back to Ooranth to honor their service.

The old one continued, "Roscoe do you have the power to transport us there with the staff?"

"I would if I could, but I cannot. The fly spell is a function of the staff, and can affect only the bearer of it," Roscoe answered.

Magrian continued, "Then our most direct route will take us back to the Gap, past the Keep, and through the mountain pass then on to the plain of Ooranth by the same route they follow."

Vannelei asked, "Won't the way be guarded?"

"Unlikely," the Old One replied. "The Droll remnants will head back to their homelands on the far side of the Valley Ornash to lick their wounds. They will then go through the time-proven attempt to replenish their numbers, but I'm not sure they will ever again be able to challenge the Draith King. The Draiths have nothing to fear from the peaceful dwellers on this near side of the valley. At least not until now."

He finished again stroking the hilt of the Draithsbane.

"Do you not think that one as powerful as the Draith King will sense the presence of the sword or even that of our Magick?" Roscoe asked flatly.

"That is a possibility, but I know little of Magick," the Drelve replied.

"I can only sense great power, greater now that the witch is destroyed, but there are no powerful emanations from the weapon you hold. Again, I ask for clarification on this," Roscoe said with more inflection in his voice.

"In the time of the creation of the Draithsbane, there were the four major peoples of Parallan; the Draiths, the Drolls, the Kiennites, and the Drelves. The Kiennites were never to be reckoned with before the arrival of the Deathqueen, more of a nuisance with their tricks and never to mount any organized threat. The Drolls warred among their own tribes and were never organized to any extent. The Drelves have always been a peaceful people, but eventually, the Draith Kings became more powerful, as did the race itself and began to rob our people of their freedom to coexist with the forest by coercing them into slavery. "

"There were occasional visitors to our land. From strange places they came and stranger deeds were recorded. The Draithsbane was said created by the great wizards that graced our forests and were of and served our people as a tithe to one of these visitors who posed a great threat to our peoples. A treachery befell the creators of the blade. The great blade was taken afar. "

"On rare occasions, the gray sun reaches close proximity to our land, there is great imbalance upon the land and the waters, and it is said that beasts of the forest briefly develop the powers of Magick. Legend has it that it was during one of these rare times, which occur once in a hundred lifetimes that the Draithsbane was created. "

"By some means the weapon was retrieved and came back into the possession of our people."

"Then there was a period of peace between the peoples, forced upon the Draiths by the presence of the weapon as the bearer of the blade could cut through the great defenses of the Black Castle itself. Then through an act of treachery, the sword was taken from

315

its resting place with our king. The details are long lost regarding this treachery, only that we know a young drelve Ramish, out of jealousy and contempt for the royal family, perpetrated the treachery. I suppose that we'll never learn how the Deathqueen came into possession of the blade. Nor how she knew the significance of it. The runes sing praises to the powers that gave the sword its talents. The weapon enables its bearer to move at twice normal speed and strengthens its user. That is why Vaylin was able to keep you at bay," Magrian recounted.

"Yes, but how do you know that Vaylin was charmed by the Deathqueen and not by the weapon?" Cara interjected.

"He was charmed before the blade was placed in his hand. The sword has no sense of good or evil. Its power represents the gray sun and the forest. It is loyal to its wielder, and tries to enforce neutrality and peace. The full powers are released only in a royal Drelven hand. It was a safety feature installed by our forebears. It doesn't reveal everything to me. For instance, I do not know how it is that your elven prince can activate its power. I don't know whether full battle will continue to bear this out. I do note that the weapon drew no blood from Vannelei and those of our ilk during the fray, whereas Vaylin inflicted wounds upon the noble dwarf as well as all three of the men that opposed it. Maybe the forgers did not quite fully accomplish their goal or maybe they lacked trust in the individuals with whom they were dealing to enhance the blade. I find it interesting that the runes bear references to one Morlecainen, and Knarra's story of the evil twin sisters spoke of the same name. I know not if these are one and the same. Perhaps that is how the Deathqueen found her way to our land. I can only speculate. I do not know what will happen in battle. The runes talk of pointing the blade toward the gray, wandering Andreas, and repeating the phrase, "To you all must come" three times, but the words must be spoken in the native Drelven tongue. The blade then enhances the abilities of its wielder. The runes state that the command also increases the healing abilities of the weapon. The runes insist that the blade will not draw the blood of the forest. I always thought that my people were the only race tied to the forest and having deep love and respect for it. The blade must recognize this in Vannelei. There is also the stated rune of regality. Only royal drelven blood can fully utilize the weapon."

He then said the phrase and Vannelei was quick to pick it up, since mimickry was one of Nigel's traits, he too was able to utter the sounds. Cara was also soon able to say it, but Eomore, Deron and Roscoe and the other men of Donothor were unable to master the rolling musical tones.

All seemed to know that it was time to travel forward and they began retracing their steps to the gap. They knew the path initially and were able to avoid the pitfalls that had been hindrances to them before. All felt relief when they passed the Alluring Falls and the booming voice of Tjol Bergen did not sing this time as they crossed.

A decision was made to send Vaylin back to the forest realm to update them on the situation. The young Drelve would be needed there and he refused to again hold the blade. Cara cast silence and invisibility spells upon him and he was rubbed down with the juices of the leaves of pungent grayberries so that he would be undetected.

Thus they numbered ten as they carried onward. Reaching the gap, they found the keep in rubble and there was the stench of death and battle so strong that they were grateful when they were passed. Reaching the crest was easy along the road, though bodies of Droll and Kiennite littered the way. There were also Draith battle dead but there were few to be found. The Valley of Honor, the Valley of the River Ornash was a site of terrible carnage as Roscoe had stated. The changing of hues of the light magnified this. Also to the north could be seen the dark scars of battle upon the grasses. They marched forward traveling three periods per rest period, mimicking the "day" of Parallan, and had rather uneventful travel, as they moved along the edge of the forests. For the most part, they were silent.

Vannelei was entrusted with the Draithsbane. Magrian had learned all that he could from studying the runes upon the blade. They were as strong as hey were going to be.

Roscoe burned inside.

Calaiz returned to the cheers of his people when they heard of the battle. The elders had been informed upon his return and a great feast was prepared for the returning troops. The Draith King went to the chambers of the maiden as soon as the details of the victory were given to the scribes who laboriously went about the tasks of indelibly making the accounts of scrolls that would be placed in the library of the King.

Trya was beautiful as she stood in a blue flowing gown with a green floral crown upon her head.

Calaiz bowed deeply as he entered and said, "I hope my victory brings you honor, my Queen, as I endeavor to make this land safe for our sons and hopefully daughters. We are rid of a great evil, but there are still forces that I cannot account for, so I requent that you remain within the castle. Have you been treated well?"

Trya found herself admiring the proud features of the man before her – yes, for the first time she saw him as a man. There was a familiarity of the eyes and face that she could now identify as distinctly elven. "I have been treated well by the matrons. I think they have some exciting news for you."

Calaiz had not anticipated this.

One of the older matrons, a human called Brendl, carried in an infant in wrappings.

The Draith Lord surveyed the child and commented, "Beautiful son – a compliment to his parents."

Brendl bowed and said, "But my Lord, the child is a female child."

Calaiz was silent.

The Draith Lord then nodded and excused himself, giving the excuse that his counsel awaited him; Trya saw the smile and the tears streaming down his proud face as he fled to prevent the detection of his joy.

CHAPTER 40
The Battle on the Field of Ooranth

At the end of the ninth amber period after the return of Calaiz, the final war legions returned to Castle Ooranth led by Izitx. They had encountered no organized resistance from the Droll and Kiennite remnants. Izitx had advanced far enough to confirm the destruction of Aulgmoor. There was no evidence of surviving evil. All of Ooranth greeted the returning victorious force. Izitx walked triumphantly at the head of the troops and if the first advisor and chief lieutenant of the king felt any fatigue, he did not show it. Izitx disclaimed any honor for himself and asked audience with the king. He was led to the chambers of Calaiz and was pleased to see that the heavy guard was still present.

On entering, he bowed deeply and said, "We return to serve you further, my Lord. I have confirmed the destruction of the lair of Anectrophinea. I could find no evidence of survivors in the wreckage of Aulgmoor."

Calaiz had been staring into the scrying crystal when the advisor entered.

He raised his eyes and said, "The preparations for my consummation are underway. When the cresent of the great Orphos occurs in seven amber periods, I shall wed the beautiful maiden."

The terms wed and beautiful had not been used before when the Draith men had spoken of consummation with conscripted females. Izitx noted the terms quizzically.

Izitx boomed, "You have attained greatness beyond any of your forebears, my Lord. The honor is wholly that of the human wench."

Calaiz glowered back, "I have accepted a victory that even I cannot account for. The people know only that the Deathqueen is no more. Many assume that she fell at my hand, when in reality I was nearly slain by her minions. I know not the force that slew her and saved me. I only know that it exists still, is moving this way, and jeopardizes everything- my victory, my people, my consummation, and her. My feelings grow stronger by the passing of each amber period. It nears us from the direction of the Keep. But my attempts to ascertain its nature are blocked. Yet, I sense more than Magick. There is an uncertainty, a foreboding – I sensed it as we neared the fortess Aulgmoor and I sense it now. Why is this moment being tarnished for me? Who are these foes? Even my scrying spells are blocked. I can see but not sense the enemy. There is great power of Magick among them. They destroyed that which we could not. I sense the approach of danger and preservation at the same time. I feel stronger as they approach and I don't understand why. The scrying devive and the Magick are only graying my thoughts more. We must rely on what has always protected our people in time of conflict. We must make all preparation for a defense. Yet have you heard that in the nine periods since I have returned, there have been eleven livebirths of a womanchild. Healthy, womenchildren."

Izitx, noting the concern on his master's face, retorted, "The female spawn are the fruit of your great victory. Could not the Deathqueen have been a victim of the failure of one of her own spells? We would have brought her down, my Lord. I feel the land rid of a great pestilence. You have freed our people from great tragedy and hardship. Our race can grow pure and strong again. Soon, I will go from shore to shore and establish our dominance over the entire World of the Three Suns. All will bow before you and pay their tithe to the greatness of our people. I am not familiar with Magick, and I consider that a blessing. I likewise felt a sensation as we approached the stronghold of the witch, but it was a bloodlust and what until now had been an unquenchable thirst for her destruction but that dryness in my throat is now relieved. The Drolls and Kiennites fled before our legions like the vermin they are. We are the Masters of this world and you are Master of the Masters, my lord. Let us make the preparations for your great event. I shall deal with any who threaten you."

"Are you aware of the legend of the curse the Drelves held over our forebears? The time may be at hand," Calaiz answered.

"My Lord, you know that only you studied the scrolls of the teachers more than I. I am aware of the legend of the runed sword, but I also know that there is no Drelve alive that would rise against you. They lack backbone. I have searched their forests at length for any signs of strength and I find nothing but their agrarian artifacts," Izitx answered.

"There is a threat of unknown quantity nearing us. The patrols must be kept up," the King continued.

"My Lord, I shall personally supervise them. Concern yourself with the matters before you. Leave the defenses of Castle Ooranth to her impervious walls of the black stone and to me," Izitx stated and turned to leave.

"Send her to me," he said.

"Yes, my Lord," Izitx said, and then smartly left the royal chamber.

In a moment the door opened and Trya entered. Calaiz motioned her to come to him, and lifted the veil from the scrying device. He uttered an brief incantation and the smoky interior of the glass cleared, revealing the vision of Castle Lyndyn and the surrounding Donothorian countryside. With a few more words, the image focused upon the main chamber of the king and queen.

"You see your father and mother are well. I cannot give them to you, but I can give you images of your land at any time. My life, my power, is yours."

He then motioned with his left hand. The ball developed then a smoky interior, and then revealed the adversaries approaching Ooranth. The faces of Eomore, Roscoe, Deron, Banon, Tjol, Faryn, Nigel, Magrian, Cara, and Vannelei were not discernible to the two gazers in the throne room of Castle Ooranth. Unlike other images Trya had seen in the scrying device, these figures were hazy and vague with faces obscured. Some were slight in frame, while others were large and seemingly heavily armored.

"I cannot see their faces. I cannot sense their intentions. They are shielded by great Magick. They may be minions of my great adversary which I thought had left this world. Two are similar yet darker than the forest people of our land. The dark male projects an aura strangely familiar to me.".

The Draith Lord continued, "Something blocks my efforts. But they approach my castle and my people must be defended. They will have to be destroyed. There is nothing else I can do. Powerful Magick are required to block the Orb of Scrying. "

Trya could see the consternation of the great brow of the Draith Lord. It was clear that Calaiz was not accustomed to uncertainty. Calaiz briefly entertained the thought that Izitx may have been correct to think that the Deathqueen had brought about her own destruction through a misuse of Magick, but quickly he regained the knowledge of the awesome powers of Anectrophinea. There was great power in this seemingly small approaching force. His mind could not escape the thought of a ruse. Perhaps she had feigned her demise at the expense of her servants and Anectrophinea herself approached. No, not even the caster could undo the effects of a Wish. She had wished no living Draith female child as long as she existed. And she had planned on existing forever. It could be a powerful minion that had survived, or, an artifact. Yes. Still. - His racing thoughts were interrupted by the soft voice of the female.

He could not know that the Staff of Roscoe enabled its carrier to partially block the scrying device. Calaiz lacked a frame of reference, for although he had peered into the freehold of Knarra, he had never discovered the home of Roscoe.

"Maybe they are from my world," Trya said trying to obscure her emotions.

Her dim hopes of rescue had never left her.

"Oh, I would have never thought that they would let such a treasure as you go without making every effort to regain you. That could explain some things. The war has made it impossible to maintain our surveillance of the portal. Our scouts posted there have not returned. I have detected no enemies in the area when I have scryed the portal, but there have certainly been greater priorities. The forest dwellers have been disturbed but they usually are when war occurs, even though they are not willing participants. We have not been threatened by the forest dwellers as a rule for many generations. The powers of the Magick left them long ago. Our scouts have concentrated more in areas that our foes concentrate."

He was then silent and turned to her.

She had inserted another variable into the unsolved equations flowing through his mind.

He excused Trya Aivendar to return to her chambers.

Calaiz's mind returned to the battlefield of the River Ornash and his near destruction by the phantom warriors. At that moment he had sensed a great change in the Magick, but he was not sure then, just as he was not sure now, if the change was wholly a boon or an ultimately baneful thing for him. His life had been spared at that moment and the battle tide had turned. The Spawncurse was ended yet uncertainty remained. What power could have ended the reign of terror of Anectrophinea? Was her reign ended or merely passed on to another just as evil or powerful? Was this some well disguised gambit? His scrying was clouded. He sensed power within the small approaching group, but armies of tens of thousands bastioned by the great wizardess had never breached the walls of Castle Ooranth. Castle Ooranth had never held such a powerful master as the Draith Lord Calaiz. He managed a small smile.

Calaiz surveyed his Royal Chamber. He could easily survey the area surrounding the central tower. The castle and city of Ooranth had been constructed with defense in mind. There was no approach to the city that could not be detected by its defenders. In the unlikely event of an attacking force breaching the walls, there was no means of accessing the central tower without being observed. There were hidden defenses, but the greatest defense was the citizenry and the Draith Lord.

The gardens that he had constructed in the city added color to the otherwise drab designs of the walled city. His citizenry had not paid great notice to the gardens, but he had noted that the servants and consummates had enoyed the added beauty of the gardens. The rare smiles he had seen on Trya's face had mostly occurred when the human princess had visited the gardens accompanied by her favorite hand-matron Brendl or the young elf Heather.

"My lord, I see no means of overcoming your power," Calaiz remembered the earlier words of his steadfast servant Izitx.

Calaiz felt reassured. Inexplicably, he felt brief surges of strength. The Draith Lord had never felt stronger physically and even he could not understand why. He allowed himself a deep sigh in the privacy of the throne room which doubled as his living quarters.

As Trya left, the princess again paid careful attention to the mechanism opening the chamber door. She had worked hard to memorize the opening sequence.

Calaiz had noted her pausing as she left the chamber and were it not beneath his stature Calaiz would allow himself a chuckle at her "spying efforts" The maiden did not realize that the Fireglyph could be triggered even if the proper sequence was followed. He had chosen well. She would be a strong queen; she might even rival even his mother.

Trya had finally succeeded in learning the sequence. She did not realize how superfluous her accomplishment was. When she returned to her chambers, she pricked her finger with a thorn from one of her favorite flowering bushes in the garden and etched on her handtowel in her own blood a message, and gave the material to Brendl, urging her to use the information in an emergency. The simple servant woman failed to understand the significance but accepted the note. At least the young woman had not exhausted hope.

Izitx changed to a new battle robe; he went to the wyvern stables and instructed the keeper to ready a steed. Soon the advisor was in the air surveying the countryside. Calaiz had been able to get a general idea of the approach of the invaders, but in the final analysis it took hard foot work and sweat and blood to find and defeat one's enemies. The sergeant of the guard instructed the patrols to increase their surveillance of the surrounding areas. A large force of the elite castle guard was mustered and split to thirds. One group edged out of the city gates to accompany Izitx to more glory and victory. Another third remained mustered at the gate, and the final third was in reserve. Even the Masters of the World of the Three Suns needed rest.

Calaiz continued to study the faces vailed in mist that pushed toward him. The Draith Lord felt an internal feeling of dread. Yet there was something else; an inexplicable sense of warmth and invigoration. The gray wanderer faintly illuminesced above him and sent its grays of haze through the skylight in the great chamber. The warmth of the faint sun replenished him further.

He had imparted a general idea of the approach of the adversaries to Izitx. He trusted the mighty Izitx to find the audacious invaders and in all likelihood his preparations would become superfluous. He used this moment to conjure and cast numerous spells in the chamber. An observer would have noted little effect unless…

They encountered more Draith Patrols after they had traveled four dark periods. They were discovered only once, to the dismay of the Draiths, since the five of them were smited in a moment by Vannelei, who was wielding the Drelvish weapon. The others and the Elven prince marveled at his speed and accuracy as he seemed to mold with the blade.

Vaylin's departure left the elven prince the only choice to wield the blade.

Banon was learning about the devices entrusted to Faryn by Sedoar and Knarra. His greatest skill was with the bow and not the sword or spear and all feared that injuries would mount in the coming fray. He might serve the group and his prince better with knowledge of their remaining meager healing measures. Roscoe had tended the balms and a faint glow briefly appeared in each phial as he spoke in words that only Cara could even partially understand and touched the phials gently with his staff.

"I cannot create Knarra's Magick, but I can perhaps enhance them," the Mage had said with heavy heart.

But Vannelei was utilizing the blade well. After each foray, Vannelei glanced at the gray sun and seemed to give homage.

Eomore twice pointed Exeter subtlely toward the elven prince, but each time the thought appeared as "no enemies".

Still Exeter shared with Eomore a sense of danger from within the group. The threat, if it were real, could not be defined. Maybe there was simply Magick friction between the two enhanced weapons. Maybe it was the foreign world.

Exeter had not been at full capacity since they had arrived in the land they called Parallan.

If the Draithsbane had a consciousness, it did not express it. Certainly the possession of Vaylin had been the work of the sorceress and not the blade. Vannelei had thrice voluntarity released the blade to others of the party, which had reassured all, including the elven prince, that he had the willpower to do it. The blade created of the elven prince "a wrecking machine" in the words of Nigel.

After traveling seven amber periods from the site of the great battle at the River Ornash, they came upon the fringes of the beautiful plain of Ooranth.

Time was still difficult to ascertain in this world, but their internal clocks had adjusted somewhat. Even though the cycles of the bright sun were not exactly constant, it seemed about 8 of their hours corresponded to each of the periods of the ebbing light. They had become accustomed to the ever presence of the great dark sun that did not give light but seemed to exert the greatest forces on this world. But just when they thought themselves familiar with the light cycles they would find themselves completely fooled by the unpredictable cycles of the third grayish sun. This was the sun that the fighting men disliked, but Cara and Roscoe seemed to glow in its faint rays.

They looked upon amber waves of grain, foliage, flowers, and brooks; indeed, a lovely and extremely ordered and manicured place. They stayed in the fringes of the forests, avoiding contact. After two more periods they saw in the distance a black dot that as they neared, became the edifice they had long dreaded. The black walls of Castle Ooranth and its surrounding city reflected the light of the three suns in a beautiful fashion.

The patrols were more frequent. They did not use invisibility because they would have been unable to see each other and coordinate their efforts. Likewise silence would prevent the casting of spells should they be needed. They did use the effect of the grayberries and this created an odor pungent enough even to impart an unpleasant fragrance upon Cara.

Deception and guile had to be their tools as there were thousands of Draiths in the area.

A black wave moved outward from the distant castle. Over the living wave was a dark speck: right away their thoughts returned to the carnage brought upon the Drolls and Kiennites from the skies by the wyvern rider at Ornash. Roscoe's prism investigated the wyvern and its rider. Were they about to be inundated by spells as the unfortunate Drolls and Kiennites had been at Ornash? Roscoe lowered his small prism and frowned. The host was clearly moving in the general direction of Eomore's party.

"The wyvern rider is neither robed nor armored. No force of Magick emanates from him. There are at least two thousand Draiths advancing from the castle," the mage said flatly."Another five thousand, at least, stand in reserve. They are heavily armed. There is powerful Magick force emanating from the central tower of the castle and it focuses exactly where we stand. Cara, do not cast. There have been attempts to scry upon us since we left Aulgmoor. I can only partially shield us."

They were at the fringe of the forest and no more cover would be available to obscure them from non-magical observation.

"They obviously know our position for they are moving directly toward us," Roscoe said firmly.

The Mage removed a phial of liquid from his robe.

He continued,"I have been saving this Haste Spell for a critical situation. There can be none more critical. Please extend your hands."

Roscoe sprinkled a red liquid on each of their hands including his own. He uttered a brief incantation. Each member felt light upon his feet.

"Move your party to the left. Move now as fast as you can, Prince Eomore, and take advantage of your gift of speed. It will be short-lived for I had very limited quantity of the hare's blood needed for the spell. Then try to make your way to the castle. You cannot defeat this foe and legion. Cara, it might be best if you did not cast. The enemy may think that I am the only source of Magick within our group. Leave them to me, but in the miniscule chance that you survive and return to Lyndyn, relate to old Eraitmus the efforts of his servant Roscoe," the Mage concluded.

His steadfastness could not be debated and gave them a sense of great urgency.

Defensive spells would avail them little now. Even invisible creatures would move the thick grasses and had smells and sounds as the magicians had stressed. Spellcasting was not the order of the day. Fleetness of foot was needed now. Cara did not possess the knowledge of a Haste Spell. Even if she had, she lacked the hare's blood required to facilitate the spell.anyway. She did have a little mercury stashed away.

The castle was still a substantial march away, but there was no alternative. They followed Roscoe's instructions even though his plan was not clear to them.

They saw the mage grasp his staff and activate the Fly Spell to move far to the right, landing on a small hillock covered with the now familiar reddish grass of Parallan. They moved with great speed in the opposite direction, creating as much distance between themselves and Roscoe as they could and as he had suggested.

Roscoe appeared as a speck to them as he launched his first spell toward the approaching Draith tide. A wave of green smoke encircled the first three ranks of the Draiths who were marching about 50 abreast. Many fell gasping and choking from the effects of the Poison Spell, but the Magick lacked the lethality that it produced on lesser foes. Still, many were incapacitated.

Eomore hesitated, but was pulled away by Nigel, who said, "He must know what he is doing. Continue to run!"

Roscoe leveled the staff and white hot heat singed the next three ranks of the advancing Draiths.

The wyvern circled in the sky.

After Roscoe had cast the first spell, Izitx had turned toward the mage abandoning its approach to the remaining nine members of Eomore's party.

Eomore and his companions were running as fast as they could in a direction 180 degrees from the mage to maximize their separation.

Roscoe had emphasized to them that this was important and they had not questioned his instructions.

The ground forces began to close on the mage; archers entered the fray, coming perilously close to their target.

Roscoe's Shield Spell would have protected him from most Magick, but he would not have been able to effectively cast outward. The slings and arrows directed at him would have penetrated the Magick shield anyway. A Magick Shield would block the fiery breath of a red dragon, but an accurately thrown rock could penetrate and end a wizard's life.

From the distance it appeared that the Mage had not cast any defensive Magick.

He was purely offensive in his spell casting.

The others pressed onward although the direction of their running was not a direct approach toward the castle.

They had no immediate plan and Roscoe was not with them.

Was this a diversion by the mage?

Roscoe battled brilliantly, slaying great numbers of the enemy.

But in the heat of combat, the mage failed to hear the swishing of the great wings and he did not sense the wyvern until it was upon him. The great beast hovered just above Roscoe and grasped the mage with a great talon. Its rider urged it skyward. Izitx uttered a shout to the beast and it attempted to fly into the air carrying Roscoe in its talons. Roscoe managed to turn and thrust the staff upward and into the underbelly of the beast. The beast roared with pain, and released its quarry, so the fall was only a few feet. The beast, its rider and intended victim were on the ground. Roscoe had fallen from the talons, rolled to the side, avoiding the great dragonlike body and narrowly avoiding an attempted impaling blow by the barbed tail of the beast. If he had the luxury of the time to look, Roscoe could have seen the glistening drops of poison streaming from the barbed tail. Roscoe stood and turned to face the foes.

The wyvern snarled.

Izitx moved toward the mage raising his arms to hold back the multitude of Draith scouts who had neared the intended quarry. The party felt their hopes dive as Izitx approached the fallen Roscoe but the mage again leveled his staff and a bolt of lightning struck the advisor and sent him sprawling, howling from his wound. He leaped to his feet and directed his troops toward the source of the bolt; the party could see Roscoe standing in the middle of the plain upon the hillock as a stick figure that was about to be enveloped by angry ants climbing up their nest. The great Izitx was closest Roscoe and he appeared only as a larger stick man, albeit a thicker and taller stick. The nine had managed a great distance from the wizard.

The Draiths were closing in on him from all directions. The great staff blazed; white-hot blasts of Magick emanated from it and scorched the foes as they approached. Literally hundreds fell before the flames of the staff, but Izitx became bathed by a ray of light which emanated from the donjon, the great tower, in the Draith city which protected him from the powerful Magick cast by Roscoe. He moved toward the mage. Roscoe sent a Thought Spell message to Cara.

"You will be safe for a moment. You are far enough away. Good luck. Knarra awaits me," the message said.

They saw the tiny figure raise the staff above his head in his outstretched arms.

The Draiths surrounded him and bolstered their ranks.

Roscoe rotated the staff furiously above his head with blinding speed. Prismatic flames left it in 360 degrees.

The Draiths climbed over their own dead trying to reach him.

The staff continued to consume them... The mage continued to battle.

Stepping over the carcasses of the fallen, Izitx laughed and approached even though he sustained direct blasts. Great numbers of Draith scouts reinforced from the castle.

The battle turned against the magician.

Eomore realized the enormity of the accomplishment of the wizard when he thought of what a great toll he had taken. What a burden this would have been on a warrior force! Hundreds or thousands of sons of Donothor would have been lost in such an assault.

Deron was impressed.

"Even Boomer would appreciate Roscoe's power," the dwarf conceded.

Suddenly, Roscoe raised the staff over his head and began to utter an incantation.

They were too far away to hear his words or to help him.

Izitx neared his intended prey and motioned to the others to separate.

Izitx wanted to make the kill.

When the huge Draith was five feet away, Roscoe shouted a single word which had no meaning to Izitx- "Lylysis" - and broke the staff.

Instantly, the entire valley filled with total blackness and utter cold which lasted only a moment.

There was a deafening silence.

When the darkness lifted, Eomore stood.

Roscoe, Izitx, and the Draith warriors had disappeared.

All the grass was dead to an area about a hundred yards from the party. No Draiths could be seen upon the plain. The wyvern could not be seen in the sky. The only stench left by the outpourings of the forces of Magick from the staff was that lingering from the grayberries upon them. The prince looked toward the intact castle now standing ominously before them. The ground was scoured to a point about two stadium's length from the castle gates.

True, the minions of the Draith Lord were destroyed, but Roscoe was gone.

They had no way in.

Again, a dark wave formed outside the walls, spilling out of the castle gates.

Vannelei reached for the sword.

There was a faint glow from the sword.

The elven prince pointed the weapon toward the gray sun, uttered the Drelven phrase three times as instructed, and pointed the tip of the blade toward the castle.

A brief flash illuminated the near wall of the edifice.

The blade increased in intensity.

The end of their journey, whatever that end might be, was near.

They could not hear the wails from the tower of Castle Ooranth as Calaiz witnessed the loss of his advisor and loyal warriors. Calaiz had never experience such flux in Magick. The World of the Three Suns had never been in darkness. An absolute darkness had covered the plain in front of the castle.

He could now clearly see the faces of his nine adversaries in the Orb of Scrying.

There were still powerful Magick forces existing in the nine.

"No more of my people are going to die!" the Draith Lord screamed.

He ordered his counselors to order the gates opened and arms lay down.

"Let them come to me. It will be settled." he said defiantly.

CHAPTER 41
Castle Ooranth

Calaiz looked out onto the plain before the walled fortress and surveyed the conflict. The protective spells that he had cast upon his greatest and most loyal servant Izitx had failed. Calaiz had been unable to cast destructive Magick without imperiling his own forces. The battle raged too distant for the Draith Lord to enter into direct physical contact. He summoned the ever present guard at his chamber entrance.

"Bring to me the human female consorted to me and the elf chosen as her matron. They shall remain with me. Place the palace guard off alert and send all the females and children to places of safety. The Elite Guard shall defend them if they are attacked in the areas of sanctuary only. Mark the way to me clearly such that even the dumbest Droll might find me," he instructed his minion.

Calaiz then turned to face the large portrait of his parents and said, "It would seem there is yet another battle to fight. Now I must proceed without Izitx. We have suffered so many losses that I privately ponder the price of victory in my heart. Mother, I have so many feelings that I cannot understand. Yet I feel I must do that which is expected of me. The victory over Anectrophinea was in some way stolen from me, but this battle I will fight myself. Izitx shall be avenged! I have the children to protect. We have a future as a people now. "

In a short while, the guards returned with the women. Both were perplexed by the situation. The throne room was being transformed into an arena of Magick. There were auras of various colors in areas of the room. Clearly the great Calaiz had been busy.

Calaiz turned to Trya and spoke, "Were it in my power, I would have changed the circumstances of our meeting. Perhaps then your feeling toward me would be different. I must face a great challenge and I have brought you here for your protection. I do not know the nature of these invaders, though they may be remnants of the Deathqueen's legions in disguise. Illusion may be at play here. Great carnage has befallen my loyal citizens in their homeplace. I must take certain measures. Do not be afraid. There will be no harm or discomfort from the spell," he said as he conjured.

A peaceful feeling came over them and they sat motionless upon the great ottoman in the side of the huge chamber opposite from the doors leading into the chamber. There was no pain associated with the Hold Spell and their breathing was not labored. Another incantation covered them with a translucent dome. They were able to speak but their voices did not escape the dome. They could see Calaiz laboring in the chamber. The Draith Lord cast many spells. The women did not understand the purpose of Magick, but it was clear that there were nasty surprises in store for the unknown party approaching the city.

Calaiz walked over to the one-way window that was shielded from view from without the tower. He was observing the progress of his quarry.

"Let their Magick try to harm my chosen one now," he confidently thought.

Calaiz turned again to face the plain.

"It will be up to me now," he uttered.

He faced the window; he made ready the materials for several spells.

The Draith Lord went over to the small chest that sat upon his great desk near the scrying orb. He gingerly removed the amulet within and placed it around his neck. A large green stone dominated the necklace. He glanced again at the large portrait. The amulet had adorned the neck of the female in the portrait. The background of the painting revealed that the gray sun almost filled the sky above the woman heavily with child.

Calaiz tenderly kissed the amulet.

"I hope that you would be proud of me mother," he uncharacteristically murmured.

The words could not be ascertained by his two bewildered observers shielded by the Protection Spell.

Nigel uttered, "I never thought I'd be attacking a castle with just nine guys."

Tjol growled, "We will make them know that we were here!"

Banon echoed the sentiment. Suddenly all were buoyed emotionally.

Even the frail Faryn swelled with emotion.

Eomore considered laughing at the comments of the thief but the circumstances of the moment precluded it. They moved rapidly toward the castle. The host of Draith scouts and warriors continued to flow through the great gates, funneling into two columns separated by a few paces.

"Cara, please make ready the most destructive spell in your arsenal. Perhaps we can destroy enough of the enemy from the distance to give Vannekei a chance with the blade to gain access to the castle. The odds are surely insurmountable, but after coming this far we must give our all, "Eomore stated.

Cara nodded but said nothing. She drew a small piece of sulfur from her robe.

Eomore extended his right arm forward with clenched fist. The others circled around him and nine fists touched together in a symbolic reinforcement of their commitment.

Suddenly the situation changed.

The Draiths outside the Castle doors started laying down their arms. Another three thousand red robed warriors had filed out of the castle and formed two ranks separated by about ten arm lengths. The great castle doors creaked open.

"Are they surrendering?" Banon asked perplexed.

"Is the fight gone out of them?" Nigel pondered.

"Did Roscoe's efforts take the fight out of them?" Cara queried.

"I don't think so," Eomore said subtlely.

He noted that a purplish hue appeared a few paces in front of the party and retreated before them toward the open gates.

The purplish hue was intermittent and periodically came from the central tower, as though directing them there.

They continued to approach the growing force of Draith warriors outside the city.

Vannelei broke out in a cold sweat as they walked. The runes on the weapon that he carried glowed intensely. Exeter however was not detecting any threat to Eomore at the moment even though thousands of Draiths were within the range of the weapons detection.

"Perplexing!" Magrian shouted.

This summed up the feelings of the group.

They advanced.

Vannelei was in the center; Eomore and Deron walked four paces to each side as Eomore had instructed; they thought they might give the elf a slightly greater chance of reaching the castle if they flanked him in the event of a sudden attack by the Draith host.

The prince admitted that he did not understand why the Draiths were so passive.

Eomore was on the right.

Nigel was a few paces in front of them though.

Cara walked behind them, armed with her crossbow. She clutched the yellow powder between her thumb and forefinger.

Tjol walked beside Nigel in the front.

Magrian, Banon, and Faryn were in the rear and all were bearing short swords.

There was no time for bow shots and no need to try healing in these close quarters.

As they neared they could see the ranks of Draiths wearing orate capes and armed with long swords. They did not advance toward the small party. Roscoe had certainly improved the odds, but they had never seen Draiths armed so; the Masters of Parallan usually chose to use their speed and dexterity in hand to hand combat.

The Elite Guards were taller and stronger in stature than the usual Draith scouts.

Perhaps the Draiths thought all of them possessed the powers of the mage, but they knew that the scrying from within the castle before had pinpointed them so accurately that they suspected that the Draith Lord knew more about the party than vice versa.

Reluctantly they neared the first of their adversaries' ranks, with both Nigel and Eomore gripping their respective weapons.

The path to the open city gate remained unobstructed.

The most prominent aspect of Ooranth was the donjon, the central tower which rose above the rest of the walled city castle. This was clearly visible to the party as they reached the divided Draiths.

Cautiously, Nigel moved forward, abandoning all his instincts which screamed about the foolhardiness of entering an area where such a large number of enemies flanked both sides and easily blocked retreat or advance.

Calaiz muttered, "Let me give them some more guidance and directions."

He conjured.

The women saw great white hot flames leave the outstretched hands of Calaiz.

Suddenly, a stream of white fire left from the pinnacle of the tower beamed toward them.

Vannelei uttered some archaic phrase and motioned with his left hand for them to falldown while raising the weapon with his right hand.

The flames were drawn to the blade which became a glowing orange and the elf winced from the burns he received, but the force of the Magick fires was abated and none were hurt.

Calaiz frowned.

He had intentionally aimed the spell high intending only to tease his enemies forward.

He was not expecting the move of Vannelei.

Calaiz then smiled.

He felt a surge of strength and confidence.

"Can you do anything about the tower, Cara?" Vannelei asked.

He spoke in the Elven tongue.

Eomore understood the elf, but others looked quizzically.

"No, the distance is too great and I would be unlikely to penetrate the walls of the tower. It seems solid, yet there was an attack upon us," the girl replied.

She replied in the common dialect.

"What was the command you used to protect us?" Eomore asked.

The usually composed Vannelei responded by saying, "I wish I knew myself. The words just appeared in my mind. My burns are healing."

Eomore then sensed the thoughts of Exeter, "The Draithsbane, my Lord, may indeed be a double edged sword. I detect possible harm to you from it. I cannot fathom its nature for certainly there is no risk from the elven prince. Be on your guard. I sense we should enter the fray without the artifact. I cannot shake the fear that you are to be harmed by this weapon, but I detect no threat coming from Vannelei as he grasps the sword. I am confused!"

Eomore returned the thoughts, "Are you sure this isn't to some extent jealousy on your part, my friend. The weapon has served us well to this point and indeed may have just saved us."

There was no reply.

Eomore remained on guard, holding Exeter forward and pointing toward first one side then the other, but they were still not attacked by the armed Draith guards only a short distance on both sides of the party.

The single Heat Spell cast toward them seemed to be a means of getting their attention, but they were already concentrating on the central tower.

"Run toward the castle!" Cara shouted.

They rushed forward and ran through the open castle doors. The aligned Draith guards did not move to oppose them. A corridor led directly to the base of the central tower.

The only attack was that of a small bird which dropped its excretions on the dwarf.

"What a delightful experience," the dwarf uttered.

He continued, "Let's go on up there and kick some butts. I don't want whatever is in the tower taking pot shots at us."

"I have to agree with you, my little friend," Eomore added.

Vannelei agreed.

They were now standing within the well constructed Draith city. The black stone constructing the outer wall was also used in many internal structures. Austere was a lavish word to describe the interior.

Red robed guards stood at intervals before the doors of the structures but they were keeping weapons sheathed and were not showing aggression to the party.

Quiet.

Too quiet.

They were unnerved.

Cara yelled, "Down!"

But there was only a gaggle of the dark birds flying overhead.

The dwarf raised his shield over his head but did not suffer the indignation of another "attack".

Instinctively, they had obeyed Cara's command.

All nerves were certainly on edge.

They entered one of the large gardens of Ooranth. Although the city itself was very plain, the gardens were quite lovely. The gardens had been a new addition to the city created with the ascent to power of Calaiz, but the party could not know this. This had been one of many acts of Calaiz that the Draith citizenry didn't fully understand. Why grow a plant that only flowered and did not provide nourishment?

There were no children to be seen anywhere.

Other than the posted yet immobile guards, only several humanoid servants scurried about; an older woman, a matron, moved from beneath the brushes toward Eomore.

The prince assumed a battle stance suspecting treachery.

He recognized the raiment she carried; the handkerchief belonged to his sister.

The old woman handed the handkerchief to him; the content of the writing upon the handkerchief revealed the crest of the Aivendar family surrounded by the series of codes written in dwarven with the ink of blood.

There was a sequence that read; first, three turns left; second, four turns right; third, four turns right; fourth, five turns right; fifth, only touch; sixth, one turn right; turn all again one turn left. The first is on your left.

Eomore was thankful for his sister's powers of observation, even though he was unsure of the significance of the message.

It certainly confirmed that their quest had taken them to the right destination.

Banon had said nothing for a long while. He and Tjol felt like fifth wheels on a wagon without the sting of battle.

He suggested,"My prince, we are not attacked by these guards. How about a test? A nonlethal wound from my bow might stir a response."

Tjol added,"My Lord, I'm ready for a fight. Knarra and Roscoe have paid the sacrifice and have carried the load. Why don't they attack?"

Eomore did not hesitate to answer,"No, my loyal friends. They far outnumber us. If we should have success in the tower, my concern is how we will deal with their numbers then."

Eomore really didn't have a plan. When the road only offered one course, the decision of the path to take was made easy.

The path to the central tower remained unobstructed. Now a few hundred yards away, they could see its great doors standing widely ajar. Several decoratively robed guards stood motionless at either side of the door. Eomore and his charges inched forward.

No more spells came from the tower.

Vannelei's blade was now luminescent. The darf elf sweated profusely, even though the others were slightly chilled. He scanned his eyes upward toward the gray sun which flickered above, its rays bathing the castle.

Cara slung her crossbow and freed her hands. She briefly touched Eomore's shield hand and this gave him strength. The prince did not see the precious mercury placed upon his shield. Cara had used the precious mercury to strengthen his shield; Eomore noted that his shield now seemed weightless; his load was lessened; the shield was unchanged in appearance.

"Thank you," Eomore said.

He smiled at Cara.

Cara quietly acknowledged the Prince's gratitude. If the others noticed the interchange, none commented.

Eomore realized that they had no choice but to proceed to the tower. Perhaps Tjol was correct that they could at least make a good showing. Their quest had created so many challenges and hardships and this final task remained. What was the plan of the Draith Lord?

Vannelei said, "Follow me. Somehow I think we may as well take the most direct route to the tower."

Nigel inserted "There is no room for stealth. Reason seems to have taken the fight out of our foe. Were it not for the single spell cast against us, I would say that Roscoe's efforts have brought about their submission. Maybe they feel we all wield such power. Maybe they don't know that we lack another Knarra or Roscoe. No offense or disrespect intended, Cara"

Cara answered," None taken. I have no solution for our situation. I cannot discern the motives of the tower. I do not sense evil as omnipresent as it pervaded Aulgmoor. Yet I sense danger, Eomore. What is most disconcerting is that I can't define a source."

Cara briefly stared at Vannelei and the elven prince returned her gaze.

They walked forward, quickening their pace, as a mouse walking into the cat's lair.

At the base of the tower, though, there were many guards.

Yet they did nothing to oppose them.

Nigel audaciously walked over to the nearest one and placed Sweetheart near the throat of the guard.

Yet the Royal Guard stood motionless.

Nigel stopped then and returned to the group shaking his head in disbelief. They passed between the doors and entered a brightly lit foyer.

Deron said, "Be wary!"

The foyer opened into a great chamber. A large table with many chairs dominated the large room. The party could not know that they were staring at the Draith War Room which had never been seen by an enemy of the Masters of Parallan before. There were twenty or so elaborately dressed Draiths, who looked much older than those encountered in the field, seated in the chairs. The room was quiet. None of the Elders looked toward the group.

Eomore stated, "There is no conflict for us in this chamber. We are led to the stairs."

The pesky purplish hue bagain appeared and began to ascend the stairs.

Nigel nodded.

The others agreed.

A great stairwell spiraled upward. There seemed but one choice, so they began an ascent.

"This world sure is fond of spiraling staircases," Deron grumbled."The builders must not have had to wear mail."

"Good luck to us all" Nigel shouted defiantly.

There did not seem any reason to disguise their presence. Perhaps it was only an outlet of frustration and pent-up energies, but the entire group briefly made as much noise as they could. The Draith Elders did not acknowledge the commotion.

The stairwell ascended a great distance.

Eomore, Nigel, and Vannelei took the lead. Magrian, who felt of little worth to them, Faryn, and Cara were in the second rank, and the third tier was Tjol, Banon, and Deron, who was constantly vigilant to their rear.

These steps were hewn or molded from the black stone and were smooth and solid. The only threat warnings from Exeter were mixed and the weapon confided to Eomore that she could not be certain of enemies here. The stairs wound to the next floor. There was an opening that led to a large room with many volumes of books. It was obviously a library or reading room. The party could not realize that this was indeed the archives of the Draith race. A close inspection would have yielded the presence of volumes from their own world and many writings of the Lord Calaiz, but there was no time for inspection of the room. They were drawn upward.

Cara could only sense that great magical power was near. The glowing Draithsbane in the hand of Vannelei illuminated the area around them to the extent that those with sensitive eyes had to squint. The Donothorians had not seen light this bright since their homeland, with the brief notable exceptions of Roscoe, Knarra, and Cara's spells.

Eomore and Vannelei assessed the odds. They had passed at least ten thousand Draiths in getting to the central tower. These guards seemed more conditioned than those they had seen in battle and the guards within the city were armored and with weaponry. Both princes hoped that Nigel might be correct in the possibility of concession. But neither really believed it.

Eomore greatly missed the power and the Priestess and the Archmage. If only their counsel were available. The stairs continued and they passed many floors. The number of guards diminished as they ascended and thay wasted little time investigating the floors they passed, usually only pausing to allow Nigel a peak. The tower rooms were less austere than much of what they had seen outside; but for the occasional portrait on the wall there was little for them to see and even less treasure to be gathered.

Finally they reached the apex of the stairwell.

Eomore, like Deron, felt they had been ascending stairs to face certain doom too many times on this journey. There was a foyer, well lit and again two heavy doors with a complex opening mechanism. There were six circular dials and an ornate doorknob. Cara detected the emanation of fireglyph Magick from each one. Eomore realized now the message of his sister, but just as the prince was trying to remember her sequence, there was a loud clank and the doors opened outward toward them.

The great door swang open and before them was the goal of their quest.

Cara quickly said in a hushed voice,"The Fireglyph is dissipated."

Nigel quickly said,"Let me check!"

The thief gingerly checked the door jams but shook his head.

He added,"I can detect no traps."

Cara extended her hands and briefly uttered arcance phrases.

Before she could finish a voice from within the room boomed, "There are no other glyphs, young wench!

Cara confirmed that she could detect no magic barriers to the room; the party tarried before entering the room. The opening of the doors revealed the chamber to them.

The room was a large circular chamber with many windows. The entry door opened widely enough to allow all of them to enter spontaneously had they desired. The ceiling was many feet above them amd a central translucent area revealed the amber skies of Parallan.

It was disconcerting to the party that the gray sun was seen in the skylight. It seemed to linger there. The furnishings were elaborate but they took little notice of them. On a lush oversized ottoman in the far side of the room were the Princess Trya and the elf Heather. Both appeared to be healthy, in no distress, and at peace. A large translucent doom covered the two females. A large throne sat near the ottoman. It appeared to be carved from the black stone and seemed contiguous with the floor of the room. A huge table sat against the opposite wall and upon it was many arcane artifacts. Much glowed within the chamber. There were many hues and auras. There was so much luminescence that they failed to notice the dimming somewhat of the runes on the Draithsbane. Many portraits hung on the walls. The furnishings certainly seemed out of place in Ooranth, because austere had been replaced by elaborate. Large armoires with many drawers were there.

Calaiz stood in full battle raiment between the Donothorian warriors and their goal.

The massive Draith Lord dominated the room, causing them to scarcely notice the many tools of wizardry within the room.

He was adorned in a finely woven cloak which was held in place by a belt adorned by many glistening and shimmering stones of all colors.

They could see their faces reflecting clearly in the uncovered scrying orb in the far side of the room. A large painting adorned the wall behind the two females of Donothor.

The figures in the portrait were those of an imposing Draith and a beautiful elven woman. She was mature but had lost none of her beauty. She was great with child in the portrait. The gray sun filled the sky over the couple.

Calaiz' voice boomed the challenge, "Take what has become mine if you think you can! Come and meet your doom."

Eomore saw a look of anguish on the face of the dark elven prince Vannelei. A tear betrayed his efforts to hide his pain and grief.

"What is wrong?" the Aivendar heir asked.

The elf replied in an emotional voice, "The painting – the woman is, was, my mother."

Calaiz heard this and shouted, "You would be advised not to claim descendance from the Queen of Ooranth, my matron, my father's mate."

"I... I can't believe that she...her amulet adorns his vile neck!" Vannelei's voice trailed off.

Nigel shouted,"Let's end this now!"

With blinding speed the master thief drew forth his Sweetheart and hurled the throwing dagger toward the Draith Lord. As the blade neared its target the group anticipated the gore that would be evident when the blade sprang open and ripped the throat from the huge warrior.

Calaiz effortlessly raised his huge right hand and snatched the dagger from the air, just inches from his neck. Dark ichor flowed around the blade as he gripped it in his digits.

Calaiz glowered at Nigel.

Banon unleased an arrow, but the Draith deflected the projectile as it neared his chest.

The nine hesitated then channeled into the chamber. Eomore and Vannelei stood in front of the others but Tjol, Banon, and Deron immediately went to the sides of the princes. Nigel moved to the side of Eomore. Standing six abreast they stood to face the great figure that to this point just stood defiantly before them in the far reaches of the room just in front of the dome shielded females. Magrian, Cara, and Faryn stood behind. Cara studied the room and its inhabitant to try to uncover some sign of weakness. There appeared none. There could be seen no other guards or defenders in the room. She tried to conjure but no sounds emanated from her tongue. Belatedly she recognized that she was standing in a silenced area. The warriors did not notice the lack of sounds as they clamored into the room. There was no clamoring.

Vannelei appeared to shout but there was no sound. The dark elven prince remembered Roscoe being debilitated by his own spell on that fateful night in Castle Lyndyn. Cara's spell would have likely been reflected even if successfully cast.

One of the stones adorning the belt of the Draith Lord became a beautiful dark pink. Calaiz growled a few phrases and a ray flashed from the stone toward Cara. Instantly Cara was knocked backward to the stone floor, immobilized by the Stun Spell. Worse yet, Magrian and Faryn, who were standing near Cara, were stunned as well.

A metallic sound resounded as Calaiz dropped the dagger to the floor.

Eomore stood in confusion. He risked a quick glance toward Cara, but saw that her breathing was not labored.

Vannelei held up the sword. All noted now the fading of the intensity of its glow, but the elven prince charged forward. Initially there was only the moving of his lips but as the elf reached a few feet from the Draith Lord his speech became audible again.

"I refuse to believe that evil such as you can be a child of my mother!" the dark elf blurted again.

Eomore had not been able to hold Vannelei back. There was nothing for the others to do but run into the interior of the room. Their steps made noise in some areas but not in others.

Calaiz wore an elaborate amulet around his neck.

He held an ornate scepter in his left hand, but kept his right hand free. Dark fluid still dripped from the hand.

Without giving them the warnings of a conjuration, the Draith Lord raised his right hand.

Tjol, Banon, and Deron were immobilized by the Hold Spell previously cast by Calaiz when the three tried to flank the Draith Lord to his right.

Only Eomore, Nigel, and Vannelei were not taken by the spell which held the others unharmed but unable to act. The odds were down to three to one. Vannelei resisted the spell and and was first to reach the foe.

Eomore did not know all of Exeter's powers and he suspected that the weapon may have protected him. Nigel felt slowed but could move. The thief tried to circle behind Calaiz, who was facing the direct onslaught of the berserk elf. Eomore charged a few feet behind Vannelei.

Vannelei struck at Calaiz, but the Draith was too fast and avoided the first blow. Nigel brought out his scimitar to enter the fray, but the hulking form swatted the thief aside.

This gave Eomore the chance to act, but Exeter crashed against the scepter with no harm done to either opponent. Nigel, Eomore, and Vannelei closed their foe, and in the next round of battle Exeter caused a shallow wound on the right hand which seemed enough to stop the incantation that Calaiz was beginning. Nigel slashed the lower left leg of the Draith Lord with his curved blade and it gave Vannelei the opening that he needed.

Vannelei thrusted the Draithsbane toward its quarry and scored a direct hit to the mighty chest. The weapon entered to its hilt and the force of Calaiz's lurching backward pulled the weapon from Vannelei's hand; the elf fell forward and landed hard on the black stone floor.

Eomore paused thinking the quest complete only to see that the deep wound drew no blood.

Calaiz drew the weapon from his flesh with his right hand.

To Eomore's dismay, the runes began to glow brightly and the weapon radiated the greatest light by far since it had been in their possession.

The Draith Lord stood tall.

He studied the runes on the blade for only a moment.

He had to sidestep to avoid another attack by Nigel and scored a hard kick to the side of the thief, knocking Nigel to the floor several feet away.

Calaiz boomed,"Do you not know that the blood of the forest also flows in my veins. You cannot harm me with this blade. I have long sought it, but I thought to destroy it."

Calaiz cast down his scepter and held up the gleaming weapon. He pointed the blade through the ceiling light toward the gray sun and uttered the Drelvan phrase perfectly three times. The blade erupted in flames.

Calaiz was struck three times by Eomore. The blows from Exeter should have ended the battle, but Eomore gazed in disbelief as the wounds of his opponent healed as quickly as the prince of Donothor could inflict them. Still Eomore valiantly opposed the Draith Lord but Exeter's blows were parried by the glowing sword wielded so eloquently by its intended victim. Finally the prince backed away to see if there was any other options available to him. Exeter parried many blows. Ultimately, Eomore fell exhausted to the floor.

Exeter's thoughts appeared to the Prince,"I have failed you.'

Eomore said aloud,"I have failed."

The Draith Lord marveled at the swordmanship of this opponent. But he had never sensed so much power and felt no fatigue.

Calaiz surveyed his opponents.

Vannelei had righted himself but held no weapon.

The beautiful dark elf had been unable to shake off the effects of the immobilization spell. Nigel had arisen, but the usually blithely moving man was quite hobbled; the others were still held immobile. Eomore was wounded and on the floor on one knee, breathing heavily.

The Draith Lord risked a glance toward the portrait and said,"Victory is not denied me this time, my parents. "

He stopped and briefly stared at the portrait. He stroked the amulet around his massive neck.

The great figure then turned toward Vannelei and their eyes met. Calaiz gaze started as a glower, but changed. Eomore saw something in the huge warrior's eyes. Had he been injured? Something flowed from the eyes.

"The blood of the forest flows through my veins. It has given me great power. It has at times been a baneful thing but I have never felt conflict more than now. I cannot harm you with this weapon because the blood of the forest flows in your veins. I cannot harm you with my Magick powers because you are my brother."

With a deep sigh Calaiz added," There has been enough killing."

Calaiz turned first toward Trya; the Draith Lord then faced the portrait of his mother. Calaiz dropped the Draithsbane to the floor; with a wave of his massive right hand, he dissipated the Magick that he had cast in the room. He then turned and sat on the great throne located near the plush couch from which Trya and Heather had witnessed the conflict.

The room was silent.

Trya and Heather stood as the dome dissipated. The others regained their capacities and all eleven stared at the hulking figure that slumped silently on his throne. Tentatively they stood and pondered their actions. Cara and Trya moved first, both running to Eomore. The elven girl Heather ran to Vannelei.

Eomore's mind was aware of Exeter, "My Lord, I have failed you in more ways than in the battle. Too late I know more of the nature of the artifact and how it threatened you. It cannot spill elven blood, and the Draith Lord is part elven."

The joys of reunion were tempered by lingering uncertainties. A clamor could be heard from the staircase. Deron looked to Eomore for guidance, but before any could speak a young Draith warrior, fully armed, rushed into the room.

Looking to Calaiz, he said, quizzically,"My, Lord?"

Calaiz raised his great right hand and made a simple motion to the young warrior. Although the Draith Lord said nothing his servant knew to stand down. He lowered his sword and glowered at Banon to whom he was closest. By now there were innumerable Draith warriors of the exterior of the room. But no others entered from the great foyer.

An elderly Draith entered from the opposite side of the room. The entrance had been obscured by one of the large armoires which swang into the room to allow the old Draith passage into the room. The elder advisor went over to the silent Calaiz and placed a wrinkled hand on the massive shoulder of the Draith Lord.

The elder said, "My mother was elven as well, my lord. Long have I hidden my feelings and emotions. I lack your powers of Magick but I share your compassion. I never revealed this to you because I feared the retribution of Izitx and the other elders. Many of your people feel as you do."

He gestured and three healers came into the room to check the bewildered eleven for injuries. Initially reluctant, the questers accepted the aid, as well as refreshing beverage brought into the royal chamber. Little was said.

Calaiz stood and said, "Nourish yourselves and take rest knowing that I will guard your sanctuary."

The Draith Lord said no more. Finally the silence was broken by the dwarf.

Deron muttered,"After all this you would think that they could come up with some ale."

A subdued laughter followed, but the drink was refreshing.

The Donothorians were taken from the tower to a nearby eating chamber where they feasted upon the fruits of the Draith orchards. The taste was bland but the fruit was nourishing and appreciated. The dried rations that sustained the rangers on their missions had been rationed greatly in the last few periods. The concept of days seems to have left them.

The beauty of the Draith architecture was largely in its exactness, which reflected the personalities of its builders. Deron was particularly interested in the constructions. After the meal, they retired to some of the more comfortable chambers in the halls of Ooranth. Fatigue continued to overpower suspicion and they welcomed rest. No guard was posted. They had nothing left to gain and seemingly little to fear.

Calaiz had said nothing more while they were in the throne room. He positioned himself with his new found longsword near the entrance to the Donothorians place of rest. His citizenry predictably obeyed the wishes of the King. His keen ears detected a shuffling approach. His keen eyes detected the outline of the quick moving visitor whose comrades had called thief.

Nigel began,"It looks like you are going to need some help. I'm in need of a job."

The Draith quizzically replied,"Don't you yearn to return to your own land?"

Nigel replied, "I served only myself in my past. I earned my freedom by taking this quest. I have no reason to return to my world. Perhaps I can use my skills to serve in this one."

"If that is your wish, I will need assistance in shoring up the defenses of my realm. I have children to protect." Calaiz added.

With that, Nigel retired to the rest chamber.

They arose the next morning rested. True to his promise, Calaiz had stood by the door of their chamber throughout the rest period.

He spoke as they exited, "The Spawncurse is ended. Whether you realize it or not, you, through your sacrifices and losses, have done my people a great service. We can never repay this debt. We can never undo the heartache we caused you in our efforts to sustain our race. I have much work to do to instill in my people the concept of feeling for another. That, not Magick, is the greatest gift of our mother, Vannelei. I never knew her as she was lost at my birth, but I shall honor her greatly in my land with all of my abilities."

The Draith cleared his throat and wiped the green tear that betrayed his feelings.

He continued,"You are all free to go. Any of your people who are here against their will may leave as well. I will secure their safe passage through the gate to your world. I can only ask your forgiveness and I do not fault you for holding me in contempt."

"You will not be troubled by my people as long as I reign," Calaiz continued."But ours is a warring world, and even I do not know the Magick needed to create or destroy the portal between our worlds.

Others may learn to access it. Not all the Kiennites were destroyed. They dabble in Magick and occasionally one develops significant strength. The Drolls will repopulate. They will always be a threat. Even the giants in the north still pose a threat to us and perhaps to your world as well. I will do what I can to protect you from this side, but you would be advised to post from your side as well."

Calaiz did not look at Trya.

He added, "You owe me no favors, but my mind's eye yearns for the means of the destruction of the caster of the Spawncurse. Can you tell me how you accomplished this?"

Eomore simply said,"We lost one as good as she was evil. The high priestess Knarra was her bane."

"How? By what means? Anectrophinea eluded all my efforts and those of my forebears," Calaiz said, stumbling somewhat on the words.

It was the frail Faryn who said,"My keen ears heard the name of the spell. It was called "Lylysis"."

Calaiz managed a smile. "I've scryed much of your world. Lylysis is a place of sanctuary in your priestess' stronghold."

Cara added, "Roscoe communicated to me that Knarra awaited him. I naturally thought that he meant on the other side of life."

Calaiz added, "Maybe your losses won't be as great as they seem. If you are rested I and my personal guard will escort you to the portal. We will have to travel by foot and steed, as your wizard slew the last of my wyverns."

Trya left the side of her brother and went to the side of the Draith Lord dwarfed by his great stature. Again, tears streaming down his face and made him appear far less foreboding.

She said, "Do not make the portal impassable, my Lord. Allow me to return to my people and then perhaps I shall visit you again if you desire, but under a banner of peace and free will. I do not know if love will be able to form a bond between us, but I trust you, and that is a strong beginning."

Eomore remained silent. The words of his sister did not make the prince more talkative.

Eomore was glad to see Cara by his side, and he was aware of the tight grip her small hand placed upon his own.

Vannelei recovered from his wounds and was joyous as he stood by his treasured Heather.

Trya touched the hand of Calaiz and returned to Eomore's side, caressing her brother and perhaps realizing all they had endured.

Finally Nigel appeared, wearing the uniform of a Draith scout. The thief came to Eomore and extended his hand.

He said, "Prince, I suppose I have fulfilled my part of our bargain."

"Indeed, you have," Eomore acknowledged.

"I hope you understand. There is but the life of a thief for me in Donothor. The memory of the priestess Knarra and her words will sustain me from this day forward. It was on this land that I became a changed man, and so here, with the permission of Calaiz, I shall remain," he continued.

"If that is what you desire, then so be it," Eomore added. He looked to Calaiz and saw a silent nod of approval from the Draith Lord.

Nigel then said, "My first duty will be to help escort you to the gate, then I am to deliver letters of peace to the Drelves."

Magrian added,"I shall remain here as emissary for ahhile. I will help the Draith Lord teach the draithlings the ways of the land and the forest."

Calaiz said,"Just address me as Calaiz, son of Mariniel."

Vannelei added, "And address me as Vannelei, brother of Calaiz."

The two half-brothers clutched forearms.

CHAPTER 42
Return to the Portal

Soon were on their way back to the portal that had brought them to Parallan. The light of the three suns seemed warm upon them. They were well supplied and well rested, a far cry from the journey toward Ooranth. True to his word, Calaiz accompanied them with his newly appointed security advisor Nigel. Sprigs of reddish grass were already peaking through the scorched earth created by Roscoe during the conflict that seemed so long ago.

The trip was uneventful.

Large numbers of Drelves greeted the group in the field before the portal. King Drolan welcomed the return of Magrian and the others. Calaiz approached King Drolen.

"Your people do not have to cower within the forest. Magrian has agreed to stay in Ooranth and help me instruct the children in the works of the nature. I invite you to Ooranth. I invite your people to send emissaries to make suggestions as to how we can improve our lands. The Drolls and the Kiennites are not destroyed. I doubt that they will ever be amenable to reason, but together we can possibly make the world safer for our peoples. My scouts will help guard your people. We will share the knowledge of the great sword. I should like to change its moniker to the "Guardian of the Forest". "Draithsbane" is unsettling to me," Calaiz said, managing a smile as he finished.

The Draith Lord extended his huge hand toward the small Drolan.

Initially, the Drelvan King had a quizzical look upon his face, but he accepted the gesture of Calaiz saying, "I feel our alliance can create a better world. We will teach your children the ways of the forest."

Calaiz smiled. He extended the sword to Drolan and allowed the Drelven liege to hold the blade. The runes illuminated the area. The king returned the sword to Calaiz, and the Draith held the sword above his head and uttered the Drelvan phrase three times.

The Dark Lord said, "You have nothing to fear from my people. This blade shall assure that. My progeny will learn first the way of the forest. I owe my life to one known as Knarra. I shall create great places of homage to this woman that I never met. Our lands owe her much that we can never repay. We can learn from our mistakes. May violence never occur again between our peoples. My followers will construct a guard post here at this portal that our peoples can manage together," Calaiz concluded.

With that the Draith and the Drelve clutched forearms.

Eomore and his group excused themselves and approached the portal. Trya approached the Draith Lord and kissed his cheek. She whispered into his ear.

The others could not hear that she had said, "Come to Lyndyn and meet my parents."

Calaiz only smiled.

The group approached the portal and without incident traversed the gate.

Boomer shouted as Eomore descended the steps. Cade ran to embrace his sister. The night air bit into them. Only the campfires illuminated the area.

"What a relief!" Deron shouted as he was surrounded by darkness and cold.

The familiar night was welcomed by the group.

Boomer asked, "What of Nigel?"

Eomore responded. "I shall ask that he be rewarded the Order of the Kingdom by my father."

"What of Knarra and Roscoe?" the dwarf continued.

Eomore shook his head negatively. A hush came over the group.

The prince suggested they proceed to Castle Lyndyn. All were in agreement. Boomer started to instruct several of the rangers to maintain the guard of the portal but Eomore superseded the dwarf's order, saying "The gate will be guarded from the other side. We have nothing to fear from this portal."

"Then we will protect them from our side," the dwarf declared.

Eomore agreed that this would become a ranger outpost. It could serve a double purpose of watching events in the Misty Forest. The Rangers of Donothor would secure more of the domain of the Aivendars to be safe for the populace.

With that the tired group began the return toward Castle Lyndyn. There was an uneventful rest period along the way but they reached the city in two days without event.

There was great celebration within the city with the return of the prince and princess of Donothor. King Eraitmus decreed a three day holiday to conclude with a great feast to celebrate their return. It was a time of great joy.

After three days, the King dispatched the dwarves Boomer and Deron to the Temple of Hiram and Lydia to assess the status there. Tjol Bergin volunteered to accompany the dwarves. Life was just too quiet in Lyndyn.

This was not true for Eomore. The prince had finally acquiesced to his father's wishes and announced his betrothal to the elven maiden Cara. Arrangements were being made for the wedding. Cade was given an invitation to carry to the liege of Ooranth to attend the ceremony.

Calaiz accepted gladly.

Trya was pleased that he did.

Boomer and Deron and their party reached the temple of Hiram and Lydia expecting to find a morose scenario. Instead, they were invited in.

Knarra and Roscoe were enjoying ale in the "Lylysis" sanctuary. The two patriarchs of Donothor invited the dwarves in to join them. Both appeared older in some ways. The tresses of the priestess had lost some of the brilliant hues and had the hint of gray in some areas. The mage looked different without his staff.

The "Word of Recall" had returned Knarra to the place of safety and had destroyed the lifeforce of Theandra. The ancient Magick cast by the evil Chalar upon the old Room of Wizardry in the effort to doom her sister ultimately had done so.

Roscoe's Wish Spell had cost him his staff and much of his vigor but had returned him to Lylysis and made him pure enough to enter.

Boomer told Knarra and Roscoe of the wedding plans.

Both agreed to come to Lyndyn for the ceremony.

They talked of a double ceremony.

The ale never tasted so good.

Printed in the United States
48955LVS00004B/238-258

9 781420 890112